ALAN WARNER has written the novels *Morvern Callar* (which was filmed in 2002), *These Demented Lands*, *The Sopranos* (now filmed as *Our Ladies*), *The Man Who Walks*, *The Worms Can Carry Me To Heaven*, *The Stars In The Bright Sky* (which was longlisted for the Booker Prize), *The Deadman's Pedal* (which won the James Tait Black Prize), *Their Lips Talk Of Mischief*, and the short stories in *Good Listeners*, with Brian Hamill. His new novel, *Kitchenly 434*, will be published in 2021. He is a senior lecturer in Creative Writing at the University of Aberdeen.

IRVINE WELSH comes from Edinburgh, Scotland, and is currently resident in London, England, and Miami, USA. He is the author of several books, film, television and play scripts. His interests include love, life and laughter.

JOHN KING is the author of nine novels – *The Football Factory*, *Headhunters*, *England Away*, *Human Punk*, *White Trash*, *The Prison House*, *Skinheads*, *The Liberal Politics Of Adolf Hitler* and *Slaughterhouse Prayer* – and is working on a tenth, *London Country*. He enjoys drinking beer in public houses and listening to loud music. He lives in London.

THE Seal CLUB

THE Seal CLUB

ALAN
WARNER

IRVINE
WELSH

JOHN
KING

LONDON BOOKS BRITISH FICTION

LONDON BOOKS
39 Lavender Gardens
London SW11 1DJ
www.london-books.co.uk

This collection first published by London Books 2020

A catalogue record for this book
is available from the British Library

ISBN 978-0-9957217-6-0

Printed and bound in Great Britain by
CPI Group (UK) Ltd, Croydon, CR0 4YY

Typeset by Octavo Smith Publishing Services
www.octavosmith.com

CONTENTS

Those Darker Sayings *Alan Warner*   9

The Providers *Irvine Welsh*   107

The Beasts Of Brussels *John King*   181

THOSE
DARKER
SAYINGS

ALAN WARNER

ONE

Autumn: The early 1990s

I HAD HEARD of John Robert Slorach well before we first met. I knew which office he worked in: East Wing, fourth floor, diagonally across from the Central Hotel. A row of five dirty windows high above the railway station's echoing main concourse and up close to the vast glass-and-metal canopy in the heavens. These five sash windows produced some rare natural light inside the British Rail Telephone Enquiries Bureau.

The British Rail Telephone Enquiries Bureau was a long, rectangular room, fluorescently lit even on a July afternoon; at peak shift it held over thirty-five Grade 1 clerical officers who talked constantly on their headsets, a microphone always hovering on a tense wire just before their obedient lips. The clerks' bench desks faced in both directions, and prominent at each end of the long office were two large, lozenge-shaped wall lights. These lights were divided into three coloured segments. Yellow instructed phone operatives the average CWT (call waiting time) was thirty seconds. When the orange light also illuminated it warned operatives the CWT was experiencing two minutes of canned music – Wimpy Bar music, they called it. When the red lit, irate callers were waiting an average of four minutes, being told by an automated Thames Valley voice their call was in a queuing system and would be answered – shortly.

All this just to learn the next train time from Dalmuir to Craigendoran or the price of a cheap-day return from St Austell to Liskeard that coming June. With the red light on, the two senior clerical officers supervising the bureau from their glass office to the side would grab a headset each, hoist the mighty, biblical folders of

11

the *British Rail Passenger Timetable* and join the struggle to extinguish the red light.

It was Slorach himself who – with microphone briefly on mute – could be heard in his whipped-cream voice singing the chorus of 'Roxanne' by The Police, before plunging in to answer another call. 'Good morning. British Rail Enquiries. How may I help you?'

Hear Slorach aground in some unfamiliar pub, with that same voice, pointing out that the three-code light system was 'A permanent crisis, oh yes, sweet lord. No sign of approval can ever be achieved for we poor dismal workers – only this permanent condemnation – the orange of that light is the carrot on the stick, we are led donkeys who never reach our destination. Mind you, neither do many of our customers.'

That's how Slorach spent his shifts and his overtime, like all the clerks: the *British Rail Passenger Timetable* and the *Fare Index* on the desk before them, their palms often placed flat upon the covers, as if divining for small earth tremors; eyes closed, trying to decipher the tortured questions coming down the phones from all over the United Kingdom – the collective psyche of the Great British Public, unleashed upon an institution they had been nurtured to despise and all too soon were to lose: British Rail.

The headset cable connects into the control panel with three black buttons: Next Call, Mute, Log Off. You're permitted thirty minutes Log Off in every shift for food and toilet breaks. The supervisors' recording system logs all calls: time taken on each, average call time, which clerk achieves the least calls in a shift – which the most. Supervisors, unknown to the clerk, can and do listen in silently to any call, God-like; Soviet apparatchiks, ensuring that incorrect information was not being disseminated through ignorance, indifference or deliberate sabotage. Was this clerk giving out weekday times for a Sunday journey? Has that clerk overlooked major engineering work on the East Coast Main Line on a particular day of travel? Are they quoting the cheapest possible fare? Are their readings of the timetable simply incorrect?

Modest prizes are given out for the operator consistently and faultlessly answering the most calls each month. Slorach never won.

I literally heard Slorach before I met him because he was not originally recruited by British Rail to become a low performer at Telephone Enquiries. He was initially trialled as a station announcer. It was that voice – still the voice of a twenty-five-year-old, just taking on the coating of a modest eight-to-ten-a-day Rothmans habit. There was his control over that brimming instrument, those growling pauses, the low gearing as a sentence got into traction. It was a radio actor or a noble defence lawyer's voice – though it was just a soft, curvy Fife intonation behind it all. You heard a word birthed in at the back of his throat – source of the Nile – insect-like clicks of formation in by those tonsils, the rising of it up onto the tongue and out – plosive, through the teeth like a rich thought. And often it was a rich thought. One sentence from him could be a series of innuendos and meaningful, stressed inflections. Until, lo and behold, like recorking a wine bottle, the rim of a pint glass plugged Slorach's garrulous lips.

Up in their booth, that first morning, Slorach's station-announcer trial commenced promisingly and pleasingly; from above the troubled crowns and tactile hairspray of the city commuters, those enriched vocal tones occasionally came smarting down like the urging of Moses, twelve trumpet-shaped loudspeakers were bracketed up there among the canopy girders.

Tech was on the march even then – alas. Public-address info had been partially automated, so that another English-shire female voice would make synchronised announcements in conjunction with the station's enormous Solari board, the split flaps tickering out updates, departure times, platform numbers, the standard set stops of each train. A Euston-bound, stopping at Carlisle, Oxenholme, Penrith, Lancaster, Preston, Wigan, Crewe – the auto-voice would recite all this. But there was still need of a non-automated auxiliary voice which could humanly communicate last-moment changes and up-to-date information to passengers: incidents, lost children, sudden platform changes due to late running, signalling or rolling stock failure, cancellation due to latest weather or mechanical problems. So there was Slorach's calm voice declaiming. His voice was so beautiful it was as if he was sharing it as well as any information it imparted. 'Platform change. The 11.37 to Stranraer Harbour will now leave from Platform 12, not Platform 4. Platform 12 for the 11.37 to Stranraer Harbour, calling at: Paisley Gilmour Street, Irvine, Troon, Prestwick, Maybole, Girvan...'

Beautiful. For his first few days, Slorach had an experienced station announcer riding shotgun up in the CCTV booth; old Duncan Muir, whose station-announcer's voice contained warmth, yet a certain Presbyterian rectitude – the Cathcart Circle was made to seem like a preordained certainty. Duncan had been immediately impressed by Slorach's innate confidence, the authoritative nature of that voice, its tonal control, the lack of shyness and total absence of pauses or hesitation in delivery.

For instance, the empty coaches of a train were being slowly reversed into Platform 7. Duncan, on a swivel chair next to Slorach, was watching the monitors. 'Right, son, this one backing into 7 has no engine at the buffer end. Risky. That's aye a hazard; no noisy engine at the top as she comes in.' He held his finger up to the monitor screen which covered 7. 'Get the news out to them dafties; look, all of them stood along there close to the edge of the platform, impatient to jump on soon as she stops and get their favourite seat. Silly so-and-sos. If one of them goes under the wheels and gets the Mary Queen o' Scots, that's no our fault, but it's essential we give clear warning first. Look at them. Too close to the edge by half and the lot will have their mind on what's for their tea and no notice the train coming in. Tell them punters to stand well back, son. On you go.'

Slorach cleared his throat and hit the mike button. 'Would passengers on Platform 7 stand well back from the platform edge immediately please, as a train is arriving.'

'Well put, son,' Duncan nodded. 'You form logical statements.

A few still close to the edge, though. Get them a bit back if you can.'

'Could all passengers on Platform 7 kindly stand well back from the platform edge, please.'

One man showing on the monitor, halfway up the platform – a business-looking type: long coat, ripe with aspiration and efficiency – continued to linger at the platform edge, gazing down into a leather-covered portfolio, an attaché case secured between his polished leather shoes. This was still the blessed era before computers and mobile telephones filled our hands forever.

'Would passengers on Platform 7 please stand well back from the platform edge. Immediately.' The dark end of the rear coach reversed on inwards.

'Stand back on Platform 7.'

The back of the train rolled slowly on towards the hydraulic buffer stops. The huge station tannoy squeaked in volume to a thousand ears, like a summoning. 'Hoi, you! Platform 7! Aye. You. Pus stuck in yer work. Told you time and again to get your arse away from that platform edge before I come down there and kick it myself. AYE. YOU. Get BACK!'

Duncan Muir stabbed the Mute button hard with a shaking finger. The businessman on 7 was now looking up and around himself helplessly, as though struck by lightning; the train coaches ran in beside him and other passengers chuckled or nodded towards him. He stepped back.

Slorach was immediately taken up to Cheesie Ferguson, the station master, in his office by the clock. Slorach loved to act out that lecture in the pub...

'That's a customer, son. That's a custom-are. No a punter. No a goose. No a member of the great unwashed – a customer. There's gonna be changes coming on this railway, son. When it goes private they'll all be customers.'

'God help us,' Duncan Muir had muttered.

'Never, never in my life have we had a bloody... a dashed idiot swearing at a customer over the fuc... the flipping blower.' He turned and looked at Duncan. 'Threatening assault! Your fellow there is gonna put in a letter to Area for sure,' he sighed. Flustered. Looked around. 'What'll we do with this yin? Use him as track ballast?'

'He's good. Good manner. Up till now. Frustrating business when folk winnie listen.'

Ferguson leaned forward and touched a golfing toy on his desk, a sort of plastic tee attached to a pen holder. 'I was gonna give ye your books, son, but we'll give you a second chance, stick you in the telephone bureau where they'll keep a weather eye on what you're saying to folks. Any karrie-on there, and I'll issue you one and you'll be up that road to the Job Centre faster than the Royal Scot.'

So that's where Slorach was when he first sent for me – slave to the three-aspect light, headphones on, often at 6.30 a.m., like some minor air-traffic controller up a draughty tower, shouting to planes which weren't even there, stacking the British folk up in high circles of expectation when they just wouldn't wisely stay at home.

'Good morning. British Rail Enquiries. How may I help you?'

'Does the Cathcart Circle go all the way round?'

'Well, where are you at the moment?'

'Somewhere on the circle. Front room.'

'Nearest railway station?'

'Well, what one is closest?'

'I don't know where you are.'

'I don't know either. Spontaneous romantic night. Know what I mean, pal?' he whispered. 'Time to go before she wakes up.'

'Do you know that address?'

'Are you joking? I'm no giving you her address. She's awesome. You'll be round here like a shot.'

'How about this? You go out and find a railway station then phone me back from there; we'll be expecting your call.'

'But does it? Go all the way round? The Cathcart Circle?'

'In both directions.'

'Is it quicker going back one way or the other?'

'Depends where you came from. It's a bit like life really.'

'Aye, but. There must be an answer.'

Next Call button violently pressed, and, as is often the case: out of the frying pan, into the fire.

'Good morning. British Rail Enquiries. How may I help you?'

'I'm going from Edinburgh to Stirling, son.'

'Are you? When would you like to travel, please?'

'Sorry?'

'When do you wish to travel from Edinburgh to Stirling?'

'I don't know, son. That's why I'm calling you.'

'Well. Will it be this year or next? Are you travelling today? A weekday? A Sunday? Christmas Day? Because the train times vary on different days, you see.'

'I thought there wernie trains on Christmas Day?'

'There aren't. We can't find enough sleigh bells to hang on them all. Trains from Edinburgh to Stirling, generally, leave the Waverley station at eighteen and forty-eight minutes past every hour.'

'What are you saying there, son? Eighty minutes to what and forty-eight minutes past? Past what?'

'Every half-hour.'

'Past every half-hour?'

'No. Listen now, please. The trains in general go from Edinburgh to Stirling at eighteen and forty-eight minutes past every hour: 2.18 and 2.48, 3.18 then 3.48, 4.18...'

'Just those ones?'

'No. Every hour, twice an hour, throughout the day in general. They differ on a Sunday. To Dunblane, via Stirling.'

'I'm no going to Dunblane. What's via Stirling? An Italian restaurant or something?'

'It's the Dunblane train that stops at Stirling. You need to take the Dunblane train to get to Stirling, and there's one at eighteen minutes past every hour and another at forty-eight minutes past.'

'What? Like at around quarter to and around quarter past?'

'That's it! That's the spirit. That's the way to think of it.'

'Well, why didn't you just say that then, son?'

'The times vary. It's not a twenty-four-hour service. If you turn up at midnight there won't be one. Then you'll be angry with me.'

'Och, why would I be travelling all alone at a time like that at my age, son?'

'I don't know, madam. You might be returning the metal heart of Robert The Bruce to Bannockburn? Generally they go every half-hour.'

'Och, that's even easier to remember then. It's every half-hour.'

'That's what I already told you just now.'

'No you didn't. You said about quarter to and about quarter past.'

'That *is* every half-hour.'

'But not on the hour and half-hour.'

'No. Not on it. A bit before and a bit after. If that helps you.'

'Oh, okay, son. Right you are. Why don't they make all them trains just leave on the hour and the half-hour; everything would be easier then?'

'Well, if every train to everywhere left on the hour and the half-hour they would all crash into each other on the way out of the station, wouldn't they?'

'Just the Stirling ones then?'

'I'll have a word with the minister of transport in the Houses of Parliament, madam, and see what we can do for you.'

Some of Slorach's work colleagues looked towards him, smiling, impressed, but slightly sorrowed.

'Son?'

'Yes?'

'How much is it?'

'Edinburgh to Stirling? Is it a single journey or a return?'

'How do you mean, son?'

'Will you ever again return to Edinburgh? Or is that it?'

'Of course I'll return. Or I hope so. Do you think something might happen to me?'

'A return journey then?'

'Aye, of course. I bide in Edinburgh.'

'Congratulations. Now. Here's a tougher one. Will you be returning? Back to Edinburgh. On the same day?'

'Why?'

'Well, if you did return on the same day you could then avail yourself of one of our Cheap Day Return tickets for off-peak travel.'

'To where? Peak? The Peak District? Hills. I don't want to go away to hills. Been there in 1962. With Janice.'

'No. Not the Peak District. Rush hour. Would you be able to avoid the rush hour? Now before you ask, that's after nine thirty on weekday mornings. In other words, on a weekday, you would need to leave Edinburgh on the 9.48 train or later in the morning. The Dunblane train.'

'Och, for goodness sake, this is all awful complicated.'

'It is, isn't it? Would you like to call back later? After you've thought this epic journey through. It's a big move. You wouldn't want to do anything too hasty.'

'Janice has moved through to Stirling, you see.'

'Has she?'

'Aye. That's the younger sister.'

'Is it?'

'Not the elder sister.'

'Not the elder?'

'No. She's in Carntyne there. The elder sister.'

'Is she?'

'Aye. So say, son, say I stay the night with Janice there in Stirling. If she has the back room ready of course.'

'The back room?'

'Aye. The back room sorted. It's needing sorted, the back room.'

Slorach leaned into his blue plastic swivel chair, raised his palms off the *British Rail Passenger Timetable*, drew his lower arms up and behind his head and neck. He looked around himself in the office, making eye contact with two or even three workmates, his expression somehow simultaneously communicating both joy and frustration. Fellow clerks dealing with their own calls – largely based upon the challenging personality flaws of public members – nodded briefly but sympathetically.

'Well, I do hope the back room will be ready.'

'Aye, but it's her laddie there, isn't it, doing the decorating you

19

see. He's painter and decorator to trade. But you ken? Chips in when he's an hour here and there to spare and that. He's busy on his own work and that, ken?'

'Yes. Yes. So, if the back room gets done, and you stay there overnight at Janice's, it's not going to hugely affect your ticket price. It's five forty for the Cheap Day Return.'

Slorach knew the fare by heart.

'What? I've to take the twenty-to-six train only?'

'No. No. That's not the time of the train, that's the cost of the ticket. Five pound forty.'

'Oh. Five pounds and forty new pence, all told?'

'Yes. All told.'

'Now hold on, son. What if I just went the one way? Say the nephew, my sister's son, has a day off his work there and runs me back through to Edinburgh in the works' van rather than taking the train?'

'The works' van?'

'Aye. What'll the price be then, son?'

'Well, madam, you'll need to take into account the price of petrol on the international oil market, though you will pass Grangemouth Oil Refinery, so maybe you could pull over and negotiate a deal. Or diesel. Fluctuations on the market price of oil per barrel. Maybe your nephew's van is a diesel?'

'Oh, I'm no sure, son. I could ask?'

'So a single journey by the train to Stirling?'

'Aye, son, just one way on your train and no coming back on it.'

'Yes.'

'Coming back, though, mind you! I'm going to be coming back, it just might no be on the train?'

'Yes. Coming back, though. It might be in the works' van.'

'Aye, son.'

'A single to Stirling is four ninety.'

'Eh?'

'Four pounds and ninety. New pence.'

'Four ninety? But, son, you says that it's five pound and forty new pence to go both ways, now you're saying... how can it be that it's near five pound just to go the one way? That's just plain daft.'

'This is a frequent and popular question. Let me say that the way the railways see it, is that we're actually giving you a discount to encourage your commitment in choosing to return by rail as well as to venture forth by rail. After all, those of us who do venture forth, do – like Odysseus himself – return to our own Ithaca, no matter how modest an Ithaca it may be.'

'Eh? Eh! I'm sorry, son, I'm that wee bit hard of hearing these days. Did you just say something about Bill Oddie; scruffy fella off the telly chasing birdies round with his big spy glasses?'

'No, madam, it must have been a crossed line. A row of crows have been reported lined up on the wire somewhere near Larbert.'

'How come then it's near five pound to go just the one way?'

'Much like I told you. You have to reconsider the whole concept and look at it, that it's not you being overcharged for the single journey, oh no, no, no; it's that you're getting your return journey by rail at a bargain price for the honour of using British Rail twice. We always have your interests at heart on our national transport system.'

'Aye, well, it all depends on getting that spare back room sorted at Janice's, doesn't it?'

'You are right. It does. I wish I could sort it for you, so some of the British Rail maintenance crew came round to your sister's. Stop wasting their time working on the railway tracks and help you finish off the back room at Janice's, then we could be clearer about what kind of ticket you might need and when you might actually be going to Stirling.'

'Och, you're joking me now, son. You couldnie sort that out for me. Or could you?'

'No I couldn't. So there we have it. Now you have all the information to hand. When do you think you'll travel? And don't forget, even with a Cheap Day Return, there be will restrictions on when you can return in the late afternoon, between half-four and six basically.'

'Oh gosh, will there? I'm going to huff to have a word with Janice about it all. Eventually.'

'What do you mean: eventually?'

'Well, the thing is, son, me and the sister, we're not talking right now.'

'You're not talking to her?'

'Naw. We've had that wee bit of a falling out.'

'A falling out? Well, what are you planning a visit to Stirling for then?'

'I was, you know, son, toying with given her a wee visit when we sort things out a bit more.'

'Toying.' Slorach took a long sigh. There was a silence on the other end of the phone. Slorach said, 'How about going to visit your other sister instead? The elder one in Carntyne?'

'Naw, son. She's a total cow.'

One October day I was coming through the snowflake-white light of the Ops office, when Lorn the Rooster Clerk rapped a few times on the Perspex window of the payments counter.

Yes. The 'Rooster' Clerk. When Lorn was on his second day in the new promotion, he left an envelope of late payment for a Sunday working, made out to Andy Irving, an old-school driver at the Polmadie depot. Andy grew roses in his back green in Rutherglen – showed me a photo of them once in the photocopied community association newsletter. Andy wasn't slow in displaying this handwritten envelope around the Operations Centre:

For: Andrew Irving
From: Chief Rooster Clerk

'Look at this, would yiz, from the roster clerk. Where are they sending the kids to school these days? Old MacDonald's Farm?'

That was it. Lorn was baptised forever. Many a driver, secondman or guard, pissed off at a bad shift draw or not getting to work a rest day with Christmas coming up, would strut before the

Perspex window of the reception desk, elbows jammed back, and yodel 'Cock-a-doodle-dooooo!' Even the Stones' version of 'Little Red Rooster' was seen to be performed.

The Rooster Clerk spoke through the grille, 'Hoi. University. Lennox. Call for you from someone in accounts over at ICOBS.'

'What?' I frowned. 'What would Onboard Services possibly want with me?'

'You probably spilled a cup of coffee in the buffet car when you were tying on an engine one day and that's them billing you for it, pal.'

'Ha ha,' I responded. But you never knew.

'Left a number. Ye can use this phone,' he slid the inky numbers through the opening on the metallic counter, written on an unused wage slip. This is where I sometimes collected cash payment which was surplus to salary, say for an unexpected mid-month Sunday rostering that you could claim in advance – a practice which was, of course, soon to vanish.

'Candice! Maybe you've got a date, ya lucky bampot.'

Candice Ex 265

'Hello. Intercity Onboard Services? Accounts.'

'Can I speak to Candice please?'

'Speaking.'

'Peter Lennox in Operations. Had a message to call you.'

'Oh, Peter. Hi there. Thanks for calling. Yeah, someone at Telephone Enquiries was trying to reach you, but he couldn't make an outgoing call, which is sort of ironic as he is on the phone for twelve hours on the trot.'

'Telephone Enquiries? About what? Like. What about?'

'There's someone there wanting to speak with you.' She lowered her voice considerably. 'Not entirely a railway matter.'

'Oh. What is it then?'

'Thing is we were hoping you would meet us. For a pint or four.'

'Us?'

'Yes. Best you talk with the others, but basically it's about, well, let's say, a pub quiz.'

'Oh! A pub quiz,' my voice sounded lighter already.

'A pub-quiz team?'

'Oh, nice. Yeah well, but sorry, nah I just. I hate all that sort of thing. Bunch of folk in a pub competing and all. I hate live music in pubs too. I mean, I love being in the pub for a few jars but. Competition. I have no interest in competition because I have no interest in winning. I have no interest in pub quizzes. Unless the question is how to stay in them even longer.'

She chuckled. 'Well, we might be able to answer that question. We aren't really an ordinary pub-quiz team, and we heard – well, I heard – there was a driver guy in Ops nicknamed University.'

I laughed. 'Aye. I went to uni. Like the railway, I spent most of that time in the pub too. I don't know much. That's one thing I learned.'

'You know, our quiz team comes with benefits? It's not really a competition either.'

'Oh.' She had a nice, slow voice, somehow serious. 'Like?'

'Money.'

'You make money? Out of pub quizzes? How many a week do you do?'

'Meet us. Name a day. Ocean's Eleven, Sauchiehall Street, next to The Venue. If shifts allow, we'll all be there. We're all on the railway too.'

'Ocean's Eleven? I don't think I've ever been in.'

'We go to some odd pubs. Meet us when suits and we'll explain. John is not back shift, so anytime this week is fine.'

'Why me? How come you even know about me? Who's John?'

'John Slorach in Telephone Enquiries.'

I laughed. 'The guy who was station announcing?'

'He's the one.'

I laughed again. 'A bit of a hero, from what I heard. Well, if you're paying I'll have a few pints, sure, but I'm telling you, I'm not a team player and that's that. Darts, doms. Forget it. I hate the limelight. Any carry on. Know what I mean? Just let me stew in my pint with a decent book.'

'You sound ideal. Hear us out and there will be money.'

'Yous aren't anything to do with drugs, are you? I'm not into all that hassle.'

She chuckled. 'That's a new one. No. Nothing like that. Just heard you had been to uni. Heard you were a reader, castaway on the railway like us, but you're on Operations. We've never had anyone from Operations. You lot keep to yourselves. The A-Team, eh? Just so... exotic.'

'Ah, it isn't exotic I can tell you.' But I was weirdly flattered her soft voice made some sort of dreary fame dwindle out before me. I said, 'I'm back shift from Thursday, so how about tomorrow? Three-ish.'

'John will be there; we all will.'

There were four of them in Ocean's Eleven, sat up on a raised mezzanine area over my right shoulder. None of them talked. Like a murder of crows, each slowly hauled their head round on their necks, looked down and carefully considered me. My old British Rail uniform had immediately given me away: the short, zip-fronted collarless secondman's jacket, the silver (not gold) BR double-arrow insignia, the non-issue thick black cotton trousers and the heavy brogues; a mush of Ops bulletins and some carriage movement sheets were still stuffed in that left breast pocket, the tops of the paper grey with rain. So far Ops had been unable to order me one of the new uniforms to fit my height. I felt they didn't believe I was worth the investment. Anyway, I liked the old togs. To me, the straight black lines on them had something of the religious cleric about them, a slight nineteenth-century effect: Church of Scotland, or better, a touch of the Jesuit. I enjoyed pointing this out to the more fervent Rangers supporters among my drivers. In fact – *all* my drivers were Rangers supporters – and those of them who owned cars had them in blue.

I noticed three of the mezzanine group wore no railway uniform at all. And one the red piping shirt of the Travel Centre.

The voice of John Robert Slorach vibrated down at me – it was like that hapless passenger being spoken to by the public-address system. Also the manner in which he sat, elevated up there on the balcony of the mezzanine, added to the impression. Call to prayer. It was like hearing the voice of a popular actor or radio presenter behind you – and only recognising them from the voice.

'So. A reader,' the voice pronounced in a thoughtful, absent way.

I said, 'Hi.'

'Come on up then. We're all here awaiting you, like Romeo or Juliet, or whatever one stood on the balcony? That's the sort of stuff you're here to do for us. Gillan? Plunder the kitty to provide him with beer.'

There were no real introductions in the very Scottish way. I had come up past a blinking, flashing fruit machine of some kind, round a pretentious staircase that must have caused havoc with girls' stilettos on a Saturday night, till I had reached them. I nodded and I said, 'The disparate cognoscenti.'

Slorach spat out a laugh, looking from left to right admiringly.

The one called Gillan gave me an eye which I understood and I replied, 'Guinness.' Gillan wore US sports gear, a Boston Red Sox baseball cap, training shoes of elaborate provenance, bagged trackie bottoms.

I nodded at Candice. Candice Fossenkemper. Fossenkemper was a young woman, flat-footed, very heavily on the stout side – emphasised by a blue-and-white padded anorak which she always wore, as if she was forever about to race for a specific city bus. I was to come to like her a great deal. I found something soothing in her size, which she always seemed comfortable with – her rolling, laughing pelican chins, her odd energy which came in flustering bursts and those lively, super-smart eyes. There were surprising details regarding her past which would emerge – dux of her Kilmarnock state school, grew up in a council house, turned down an acceptance to the University of Oxford. I sensed some kind of nervous breakdown and a lost year, after the fury of seven Highers at A grade. A collapse which scuppered Oxford. Spoke fluent Italian, despite never having set foot on the soil of Italy – German too, from her mum. Jewish. Was once in a band called Good Times

For The Vain. Keyboards. Started languages with physics (!) at Stirling University but dropped out somehow in third year. She drank pints, many and quickly, with a concentrated aggressive stare directed at their surfaces.

Slorach was already gathering that weight across his stomach and around his jowls which would become so conspicuous in a few short years. He had lovely skin – clear, childlike, slightly rose-tinted on his cheeks but with a salubrious, bucolic tarnish; nervously busy lashes on chestnut eyes. He had an unusually fine, long jaw for a short guy, but I cannot ever recall witnessing him clean shaven. He grew beardy, curly adolescent sproutings which would turn into patchy stubble; but he never had a real beard, yet was never clean shaven. I couldn't work it out.

Lorimer was clearly much older than all of us. Bald with two scallops of buzz-cut chocolate hair above each ear. Busy eyes which settled upon you and remained. That baldness made it tough to decide his true age: high end of his thirties or beyond? He worked the station ticket counter, hence the Travel Centre white shirt with pink piping – oddly, he was drinking from a can of Red Stripe lager, so it matched his shirt. He had some sort of shoulder-strap documents bag up on the seat against his leg. He had been on the railway decades, ever since dropping out a maths post-grad degree at Strathclyde back in... some undisclosed era. Despite the air of abstraction and mathematical exactness, he took intense interest in the gossip of the great station and in railway lore in general, so long as it pertained to his uncomfortable mental archives regarding: sackings, sectarian nepotism, child molesters, office adultery, till pilfering, contraction of venereal diseases, dismissal settlements and unnatural deaths.

I was then of a hopelessly good-natured disposition, which might even have been partly fake, and mainly just came from having had a spoiled upbringing. My altruism had never been truly tested and if I had finally been crushed beneath one of those trains, they might have said of me in the pub after the funeral, 'Lennox always had a good word for everybody.' Wasn't really true. For instance, I immediately disliked Lorimer – which was rare for me.

Christ, his mind was quick, though. I have witnessed him total up a column of seven or eight numbers just by glancing at it, before I had even read the first three at the top. About Lorimer there was always a touch of the community-centre amateur magician who is dreaming of that contract aboard a cruise ship; but I was to learn a lot of my suppositions about him were wrong.

Gillan came slowly back up the stairs then handed me my pint, not spilling any. Extra Cold and too quickly poured, but I wasn't going to moan – catastrophic though this was. I said thanks. Gillan was, I thought, obvious enough: the reversed baseball cap, the loose movements, hand and finger gestures for streetwise emphasis. Straight Outta Drumchapel! Bampots With Attitude. Round, thick specs took off the edge he thought he had. One rave too many in his twitch, he had turned to rap for respite.

'So you're...' and Slorach paused across the table to get a run of about seven syllables into the word '... *Operations?*' His lips were parted and the mouth sounded wet.

Lorimer was off the blocks. 'Aye, he's Operations but no really Operations: mainline *or* suburban, more like he's just station, he's just a starving, end-of-platform shunter chucking couplings.'

'What's a shunter?' Fossenkemper's eyebrows were up.

Lorimer grinned, which caused a multiple band of rubbery wrinkles to rise up his bare forehead towards his naked crown. 'He'll be telling folk all over that he's a train driver, eh?' He looked at me.

I sat down. 'I don't tell anyone anything. I'm a happy shunter. Are you looking for a driver? Planning the great train robbery?' I glanced about, feigning discretion.

Slorach yelped. A laugh.

Fossenkemper was staring. 'I thought you *were* an Inverness train driver?'

'Was. I'm *on* the engines but I'm generally down on the track spitting into my palms, coupling and uncoupling the bloody things.'

'Glad we never shook hands.'

'Drive the coaches back over the bridge to the carriage-cleaning depot; or the rostered driver'll let me take a big 87 from the depot back into a platform to top her on. That's fun. But I'm just a shunter. Don't have perfect eyesight any more; quit the railway once before.'

Slorach quipped, 'You had the good foresight to do that.'

I shrugged. 'They're never letting me drive out on the main lines again, or they'd have had me on the signalling course by now. Haven't even got me a new uniform.'

Fossenkemper sounded sad. 'What's a shunter? I thought that was something to do with pornographic films?'

Slorach whispered, 'Candice.' Gillan snorted. Lorimer laughed, 'That's a fluffer.' Lorimer locked his eye onto the young woman and jagged out a finger at me. It was as if he thought she fancied me or something. 'All he does is go back and forth all day with a driver on the station pilot – knackered 20 or a 25, or just a wee 08, eh? Is that about the size of it?'

I shrugged, 'Aye.'

'Shunters take engines and rolling stock that's come in, back out, release the locos trapped against the buffers, eh? Return them back to depot, or put them on top of another train needing an engine; but they never drive a train out the station to bloody anywhere.'

I said, 'Lorimer, is it? You could write me a good reference.'

Slorach slapped his own thigh and yelped again. 'I had imagined you throttling over the dales to Penrith at ninety miles per hour, driving the Royal Scot.'

I said, 'All I throttle are pints.'

Lorimer shook his head. He was adamant, 'He doesn't drive anywhere.'

I ignored him and addressed Slorach, 'More like twenty miles an hour to Polmadie depot. Sometimes drivers let me drive for the whole shift and they watch the signals. *If* their hangover is bad enough.'

Slorach nodded solemnly, 'Then you fulfil a vital function.'

'Complex signalling on those gantries,' I told him.

'Aye, but you don't drive the real trains.'

I had had enough, so I gave Lorimer my attention, meeting his eyes, and I said, quietly, 'Down boy. I'm sorry if you have a wee train set at home and are disappointed.'

Instead of that sudden, taught, pre-violence tension, at last Lorimer had got what he was waiting for. A reaction. His face burst into a smile – a really genuine one. 'Just winding you up, son. It's a wind-up.'

The others chuckled.

'So, am I to understand, Mr Lennox, that, in many ways the shunter, the shunter's job doesn't fulfil your full potential what with, what with you being a… *reader*?'

I shrugged and told the truth, 'Me? Potential? I don't have potential. Reading's nothing to do with it. It's okay graft. Bit weather-dependent getting down between the trains. I wouldn't like to be doing it when I'm sixty.' I glanced round this odd circle, and they were all looking at me.

Slorach went on, 'You see, our little project which we have met to discuss.'

'Pub quizzes?' I twisted my lip a bit cruelly.

Slorach said, 'Well. That's not really the whole story.'

'How do you mean?'

'Isn't quite pub quizzes. Well, it is. But it isn't.'

'Oh-oh. Enigmatic.' I smiled and tipped back a good chug of beer.

Gillan chuckled.

'Mr Lennox…'

'Pete. Peter. Call me Peter. Or Pete. For Pete's sake. You make it sound like I'm at the police station.'

Slorach spoke even more slowly, 'Well, you brought it up, not me. Pete. May I ask – before I talk much more and officially request your confidence – do you have any close friends, relatives, loved ones, sisters, brothers, father, who are members of Strathclyde's finest? The police force?'

'Me? No. I have nothing to do with the police. No record and I don't like hassle. Sniffs make me nervous. Where is this leading?'

'Well. We aren't actually doing anything illegal. And on that topic. The topic of the great institutions of our country. Do you have any connection with that august body, the Inland Revenue? Any pals or relatives work for the taxman?'

'No. They take their chip from my pay slip every month and that's that. George Harrison was always right.'

Fossenkemper laughed. '"Taxman" by The Beatles.'

Slorach didn't get the reference, but he nodded. 'Peter. I'd like you to do something for me please. Go to the top of the stairs please, and take a look down and tell me what you see.'

'What? The top of the stairs?'

'Look down and what do you see?'

I turned round and I looked down. Frankly I was starting to feel uneasy among this unthreatening gang of goddam freaks.

'You need to go to the top.'

I stood up, stepped over then looked down. 'I see the stairs.'

'And?'

'The puggy machine and the end of the bar.'

'The puggy machine.'

'Aye, the fruit machine.'

'Never take a punt on fruit machines then?' Gillan had butted in.

I looked at him. 'No. Waste of money. The bank always wins.'

He looked around at the others.

Slorach said, 'It isn't a fruit machine.'

'What is it then?'

'It's a quiz machine. Its brand name is *Thirst For Knowledge*. Fifty pee a shot.'

I turned round and I chuckled. 'Yous play quiz machines in pubs?' And I laughed. 'How much are you making?'

'A hundred general knowledge questions. The jackpot is fifty pounds. A fiver for thirty questions right, a tenner for eighty, then thirty-five for the jackpot. One question wrong and you need to start another game.'

I sat down again and looked around them.

'One hundred questions.'

I said, 'Not bad. Hardly Monte Carlo, but not bad. Okay,

Magnus Magnusson. Okay I'm with you, but. Well, fifty quid five ways – it's a few pints. Just don't tell the taxman. Who does? That's just a wee bit gambling income, nothing they need to know about. I wouldn't worry about it. So your idea is, we are the A-Team, ex-university students who take a shot at grabbing fifty quid on a few pub-quiz machines round town?'

Gillan made it quite clear, 'I didnie go to nae uni, man. Nae my style.'

Slorach coughed, 'Mr Gillan is a colleague of mine from the British Rail Telephone Enquiries Bureau. He is our... sports man.'

'Aye,' Gillan made an abstruse gesture with three fingers towards me. Some kind of gang sign perhaps – but in LA, not Sauchiehall Street. 'No *a* sportsman but *thee* sports man, if you get ma meanin.' He giggled and snorted.

Fossenkemper told me, 'Gillan has an amazing recall for football league stats.'

'And US baseball. And basketball,' Lorimer added, with an uncharacteristic air of reverence, which surprised me.

Slorach went on, 'And obscure sports. Gillan had satellite TV with lots of sport channels, shall we say – from a very early age – and a passion for obscure sports, pastimes and their statistics. And a good memory for players.'

'And scores.'

'And scores.'

Gillan shifted from side to side, touched his wrong-way-round hat, said, 'Makin a killin with the Gillan.'

I nodded. 'I get it. I'm the book man, you're the sports man, you're... what are you?'

Fossenkemper said, 'Well, I'm not a man-anything,' she did a throaty laugh. 'Sciences and languages tend to be my thing.'

'History, economics and politics at your service,' Slorach said. 'University of St Andrews. Some general knowledge. I must say I wouldn't quite put it as a book man, we were more hoping for? Arts & Entertainment? And Mr Lorimer is our numbers man, he did postgrad maths in his time and he keeps *our* unique books.'

'Books? For divvying up the odd fifty?'

'Yes. Well. Peter. Here. Take this. Go downstairs and have a go.' He held out a fifty-pence piece.

'Oh, come on! No. Is this an audition? Now you've just made me nervous. And shy.' I turned to Fossenkemper, 'A bloody audition. See that's exactly what I said to you on the phone. I hate quizzes, competitions; I hate show-offs, and I get the vibe here. I see what yous are all up to. I'm smarter than you and I'm smarter than you and whoopee-doo I'm smartest of all. Quiz-machine thrills. I'm sorry. Shit, guys. Folks,' I looked quickly at Fossenkemper again – 'I know yous are all smarter than me – I have not a second's doubt about it.'

Slorach said, 'No show-offs in our endeavours. Quite the opposite.'

I went on, 'I have no interest in University Challenge. Help yourselves to the glory. I don't doubt it for a moment. I'm thick. Fucked up my life; rent a shitty room in a shitty flat off Woodlands Road and my girlfriend chucked me cos she thought I'm a loser. So I crouch between the fucking trains and it's all diesel-oil puddles down there, I can tell you, and when it's no that, don't forget where it goes when you flush the lavvy pan on a train; that's why the sign says don't flush it in the fucking station, but you can't get that into the thick heads of the British people. Sorry. I've nothing to prove to myself or nobody else. Don't waste your fifty pence. I won't get through four questions before I'll be stumped.'

They all looked across at Slorach, after my outburst. I try to be honest in life, or your compromises just heap up and up and overwhelm.

Slorach spoke as if to a kitten in that beautiful voice, 'It's not an audition. None of us could get more than a few questions in first time we took a shot on *Thirst For Knowledge*.'

'What's the point then? What's it prove?'

'Nothing to prove about you. Have a go. See what happens. We aren't even going to watch. We're going to stay here and finish our drinks, aren't we?'

I protested, 'Aye. Then the first question is gonna be a sport one. I'm one of them guys that doesn't know why St Johnstone isn't just called Perth. I get the Gunners and Spurs mixed up. I don't follow the Jags and I know fuck all about the football. And I'll need you, Gillan, if sport comes up, and you, if science does. Can I shout up the stair?'

Others laughed and Gillan too. 'Aye. You shout up the stair. It's multiple choice so take a guess, no bad odds.'

They all laughed. Bastards. So between forefinger and thumb I lifted that gleaming new fifty-pence coin from Slorach's palm, sighed and stood up.

'Don't be a pessimist and take your pint,' Lorimer gently told me. 'They stand nicely on the flat top of the machine.'

I lifted my half-done pint.

'I'd down it, mate.' Gillan looked away towards the window.

Fossenkemper called at my back in a slightly high-pitched voice, 'There's a timer on it that speeds up. You got to answer quick.' They all laughed. Bastards.

I went down the stairs towards the machine, turned and stood before it. I sighed then hoisted my pint up and placed it on the flat top, in that familiar motion of the veteran puggy plugger. *Thirst For Knowledge*, the swirling caption on the restless screen told me. *Test Your Brain Against The Race Of Time. General Knowledge Sport History And Entertainment*. Blah blah.

I dropped the fifty pence into the slot. The screen organised itself with a sudden, money-grabbing seriousness, and I looked down at the chunky buttons: Start/Commence, A, B, C, D.

I hit Start.

Which Shakespeare play features Iago?

My lips moved immediately to mouth a silent, 'Wow! It saw me coming.' I deftly punched D, for *Othello*.

CORRECT!

Who is the boxer who won three Olympic gold medals between 1956 and 1985?

A – László Papp
B – Henry Tillman
C – Teófilo Stevenson
D – Barry McGuigan

'Excuse me.'

I was staring hard at the screen and jerked my head irritably to the right – just for an instant, wired into the game already.

'Can you not use the machine please?'

I frowned then glanced quickly back at the screen. 'I'm sorry. What?'

'You can't use the machine.'

'What do you mean I can't? What's wrong with it?'

'We've told you before. You can come in here, but you can't use the machine.'

'What do you mean?'

It was a small barman stood next to me – he seemed younger than me. He was standing beside me and nervously wringing a dish towel in his hands.

'I'm trying to play, mate, what are you on about?'

'You're with your...' and he pointed up the stairs. 'You're with your party, and none of you are allowed to play this machine in here. You know that.'

'What? Why?'

TEN

'You know fine why.'

NINE

Sure enough. As warned, *Thirst for Knowledge* had begun its countdown on me since I had not entered an answer. I needed Gillan's advice on this one as well.

EIGHT

'I've got to answer this question,' I told him. I shouted, 'Gillan! Boxing.'

SEVEN

'I'm not with that party, mate. I mean I vaguely know one of them from my workplace. Gillan! We're on the railway. Just met

35

them, and now, I'm playing this. I've put fifty pee in, and I need to answer this, so, would you fuck off actually, please.'

SIX

The guy leaned smartly down, reached out his arm and just switched off the machine at the plug in the wall, so the screen died in front of me.

I raised my voice in surprise, 'Hoi. Ya fucking mug, ya. I just put fifty pence in that; what the fuck is your problem?'

'Your party has been told time and again not to play on the machine.'

I took a step towards the wee guy. You need to watch wee guys, they can unpack a powerful punch to your sternum when you don't expect it. I knew fuck all about Olympic boxing medals, but I know you keep close up to a cunt when there's going to be aggro, so they can't take a proper swing with any power. But the wee guy was no fighter, cause he leaped back as if I'd lovingly touched his arse.

'Come along, Pete, and finish up your pint of beer.'

It was that voice. Again it came from On High, like a holy command. I had to turn aside and look up, to see that at the top of the stairway, Slorach stood, smiling and beatific, and he came slowly down, hands held out like the pontiff. Peace on earth. 'No need for any worries. We're just leaving now, thank you very much, I'd forgotten to mention to our vague work acquaintance here not to use the machine. I'm so very sorry.'

'Aye. Well, yous all know the score in here.'

'Yes we do.'

Lorimer was following behind with his satchel thing hooked on his shoulder. 'Finish your pint, mate,' he nodded. I shook my head, reached up and swallied the remaining. I considered launching the empty glass across the bar, there were no other clientele at this lower level – but that was a younger me, and I thought of Slorach's mention of the police. I didn't want to bring it on him, so I held out the pint glass – on the inside of it were the slightly yellow froth smearings; the wee guy took it and said, 'Thanks.' I gave him a horrible smile.

Off our procession went. John Robert Slorach leading us, followed by Fossenkemper, Gillan and Lorimer; I slotted in at the end and followed them to the cross-hatched, art deco door of Ocean's Eleven – then out onto the wide boulevard of Sauchiehall Street.

They formed a horseshoe about me, and I looked at them.

'You can see the problem?' Slorach quietly asked.

I shook my head. 'Jings. You smart devils have cleaned out that machine there so often they just aren't having it?'

'That's it. You've got the concept.'

'You need a new face, don't you?'

Slorach winked at me. 'Come on and let's walk a while and then have another pint or two in Nico's.'

'Och, that's a poseurs' joint,' I said.

'Peter.' Slorach put an arm out and touched my shoulder. 'I think you better get used to going into all kinds of pubs you don't aesthetically see eye-to-eye with. Come and walk with us. We can't talk openly in a pub. Ironically.'

Gillan said, 'Fight The Power, big man; thought ye were gonna fucking blooter the wee fellow there, get him in his dome zone.' He laughed.

I shook my head. 'How much money have you actually won in there to get barred? I mean, hold on, I mean legally can they fucking do that? I mean just cos yous are smart enough to win the jackpot, what right have they to?'

We walked along Elmbank Street towards The Griffin pub, then went right on Bath Street and down past The King's Theatre. Slorach on one side of me, Gillan the other, with Lorimer and Fossenkemper following behind. Fossenkemper had a flat-footed, dragging walk – you could hear the sole of her shoe scraping the pavement, and it was impossible not to glance round; she had her hands, as a matter of fact most of her lower arms, thrust into the deep pockets of her blue-and-white rain jacket. She looked from side to side across Bath Street, mysteriously, I thought.

'Let us talk,' Slorach repeated as if he had forgotten he'd said it before. He was quite a dreamy personality.

But we carried on for a brief spell – the five of us – without speaking, like peripatetic Athenian philosophers, our postulations thoroughly focused upon this earth.

'I get it.' I then said, 'You need a new face. All the pubs round the city centre know you, so yous need a new face to go round them again, but how long is it going to take you to – no pun intended – train me up, to learn all them answers to all those machines' questions?'

'Training you up is not the problem; we have every answer already written down.'

'What?'

He shrugged and looked meek. 'Well, of course we do. That's how we do it.'

'Every answer? But there must be literally infinite numbers of possible questions that come up?'

Slorach said, 'Now you would think that, wouldn't you? I was amazed myself. We all were, when we first discovered *Thirst For Knowledge* in a couple of pubs and started messing around on it.'

Lorimer quietly added, 'You first discovered it, Robert.'

Slorach nodded, 'Yes, yes, initially I just started plugging away on it in a couple of pubs – The Ranelagh mainly – but it was only when I gathered our little crack team here that we made real progress, and that certainly didn't happen overnight. We worked to get where we are today. To achieve this position on the spectrum. Back then we pumped a good few hundred quid into *Thirst For Knowledge*. Our start-up investment package. It gives you a fiver for sixty consecutively correct answers. It gives you a tenner for eighty. One hundred consecutively correct answers in a row – and the fifty quid is yours. Just imagine – every day, the pubs of Britain are checking that there is at least fifty quid in fifty-pee pieces inside every machine,' he laughed, quite harshly. 'That used to get me out of bed in the morning. But we were amazed how little variation in the questions existed. At first I thought the machine was faulty, and I certainly did not believe that every single machine had the same series of questions. I was stunned.' He turned to Lorimer. 'How many questions is it on the count?'

Lorimer's voice spoke immediately from behind me, 'We make it seven hundred and twelve questions including the rogues.'

'Rogues?'

'Seven new rogue questions we identified have been randomly generated on rare occasions, but that only ever happens once you're beyond the ten-pound jackpot with twenty questions left, and it only ever happened on a few machines.'

Fossenkemper said, 'We've all been stumped by a rogue in our time.'

'Now we get the funky confessions,' Gillan giggled.

'You're shocked when a question like that comes up, but you just commit it to memory and take the fall. After a guess!' she laughed. 'Learn the answer and add it to the Archives.'

'The Archives?'

'We'll provide you with a copy of the seven hundred answers,' Slorach smiled, 'if you agree to our terms.'

'Terms. Archives. I'm getting jumpy again.'

'You don't need to. It's simple. We've been splitting every fifty quid we win four ways. If you join us we'll split it five.'

I looked back immediately at Lorimer. I felt resistance would come from this quarter, but he said nothing. 'Seems a bit generous,' I said. 'You have worked up all this. You built the Archive not me. I benefit from it.'

'We need another body. Doesn't mean we won't ask you to make sacrifices.' It was Gillan who said it. I laughed, but I didn't know what he meant.

'A few bob is a few bob, though. Eh? Shunt that,' Lorimer just laughed, and he seemed genuine. He went on, 'We'll get you the Archives and that's yer bedtime reading for the year – ye can fuck off with your books. She prints the answers out, courtesy of the photocopier in the ICOBS accounts office.' He frowned, running those wrinkles up his forehead. 'You see, if you think about it, the makers of *Thirst For Knowledge*, the programmers or whatever, they have to strike a very delicate bloody balance with the good people of Great Britain.'

Slorach said, 'So do I. Every damn day.'

'The makers of *Thirst For Knowledge* have to gamble too. They want to milk our money. That's the plan. You conceive and develop a machine that can't be beaten, but the same machine has to make us *think* we can beat it. If pure knowledge is the challenge, they have to base it on and aim it at the intellect of the British people. Well. They also have to make the punters think they *can* get far enough into the questions by remembering some answers. The questions vary in running order each time, so some become familiar to a hopeful punter and that leads them on. They never thought anyone would be daft enough to lose a few hundred quid straight off and just learn the questions. And it helps we bring a wide range of knowledge to start with. It seems too costly, but we made that investment. So the punters will keep trying, putting in more fifty pences, thinking they can remember some of the questions and answers, leading them on to the five-pound jackpot but only letting a small percentage ever get to the ten-pound jackpot. But the moment those first coins are pumped back out. That's it. The difficulty level of the questions, the tricksy stuff just vaults.'

Gillan chipped in, 'But no the variety of the questions; their place in the order changes. You know there are four or five possible variations gonna come up at ye, but no more than that. But if there's enough of yous – if teamwork is used, if you stay sober and write down the questions and answers, like any good sports team, if you devote time, an excess of time, you can beat it. It's just the same questions, man! We just learned them – so many each at first. That's the amazing thing. It's way past cool. I couldn't believe when I come in on the team the questions were aw the same on every machine. What were they thinking?'

'You had to be in on the team, Gillan.' Slorach nodded. 'Those top-end sports questions were impossible. We're not very sporty. We needed you and we will need you.'

'Aye, mate. They were impossible for anyone. It's no problem, but I am still fucking baffled that while the difficulty goes up beyond the five- and ten-pound payouts, the quantity of questions doesn't.'

Fossenkemper said, 'Obviously, though, getting beyond that ten-pound jackpot was a frustrating time for us.'

'Aye. Many a pint was tipped back between the tenner and the full fifty quid. Remember, eh?'

Lorimer said, 'Those pesky rogue questions; just when you thought you'd got to the summit of Everest.'

They all laughed; I smiled.

'That was The Ranelagh pub,' Slorach reminded them all again, with an odd nostalgia. He looked at me. 'Typical publicans, though. You see, Peter, the way it works is that the pub does a deal with Providence, the manufacturers of *Thirst For Knowledge*. They split the takings seventy/thirty to Providence, but the contract is that the pub always pays out any jackpot winning from its tills. So we were welcome regulars.'

'When you were learning the questions and pumping in the fifty-pence pieces,' I said.

'Aye. A few congrats on the fivers, less so on the tenners, they were amused by our first fifty-pound jackpot. Then we did it again. And again. That's when our friendly landlords got the pus on. The Ranelagh was our haime from haime no more. Word started to get out and around that a crew had cracked the route to the jackpot.'

Gillan drawled, 'The Empire Strikes Back.'

'And we were so clearly a wee team. Four of us clustered round that machine for hours. That's when we realised – appearance, image and stealth were everything.'

'We needed a method.'

'So. We assembled the answers together.'

'And we learned them by heart. Like back at school.'

'Then we all went solo. A single punter – a new face can go into a new pub. Hit the machine and be out before they know it.'

'Two ways of approaching it.'

'We usually fake it. If you get your pint of whatever first. Look at your watch a lot as if you're waiting to meet someone, so that's why you're no a kent face in there. Stroll over, pop your pint on the top of the machine as if it's the first time ye tried it.'

'Look. It's one hundred Qs, ten seconds a question max, but when you answer, you skip ahead, plus the two jackies at five pounds and ten pounds you can milk fifty pounds in…'

'Eight to nine minutes if you're really quick and don't pick the coins out the deposit tray at that point.'

'Aye, well, in the early days we used to race each other with a stopwatch just for the crack.'

'You can pull it down to seven minutes if – for cultural reasons – you might be wanting in and out of that particular hostelry quick. It was certain Glasgow pubs taught us that.'

Gillan said, 'I was fucking stunned there *was* a *Thirst For Knowledge* in some of thae places. It wasnie knowledge they were thirsty for in The Red Rabbit, I tell you that. They strippers were all professors already. But I tell you. You stand out like a yellow plook on the nose if you rush at a machine in a pub. Yer at the five-pound jackie in five minutes and the tenner two minutes after that and then the heads start turning towards ye.'

'Aye. All heads turn to watch as the hunt goes by, and they look at you when the machine starts pumping the coin.'

'A good tip, Peter. Stick in two fifty pences. Fake it for two. Burn up some time. Get up to Q22 or something and get it wrong.'

'Luxuriate in that raspberry sound.'

'Aye. Then the nosey heads turn away.'

'They've nae interest in you.'

'Like a pool shark deliberately fluffing shots to lure you in.'

'Is that not something in a porn movie?' Fossenkemper spoke from behind me. I laughed. I thought that was funny.

'Lose a couple of times.'

'Folk are no interested in losers.'

'The old yins go back to their paper.'

'The young neds go back staring at Page 3.'

'Nae one cares.'

Lorimer said, 'Then stick in another equilateral curved heptagon.'

Fossenkemper added, 'A *polígono de Reuleaux*.'

'This time, type into the five-pound jackpot. You will get some attention. Then deliberately wipe out and get a question wrong. Let out a groan.'

'You'll get a few winks of sympathy.'

'But no one will look at you again. You're marked off as just lucky.'

'Say shit, out loud.'

'Drain yer pint.'

'And go for it.'

'But still go for it slow at first,' Fossenkemper said. She had moved up close to my shoulder when she said it, her hood of dark hair behind her earnest, pale face. 'Take the full eight or nine seconds on many of the countdowns, as if you don't know the answers.'

'No showing off. Ever.'

'Once you get the five-pound jackpot, collect slowly and hit the Commence button.'

'Then race for it, son. Race for the tenner and just keep going on beyond.'

'Once you go past the tenner, some nosey regular might even come up behind you and watch your screen. They have no manners some of them. Just don't let them see if you have to refer to your notes. Just sometimes I have had to.'

'Fuck them.' I was a bit shocked to hear Fossenkemper swear so vehemently; and she went on, 'A, B, C, D them. Go right through those last twenty questions. Have your rogues memorised just in case one comes up. When the machine kicks off on the jackpot, just ignore it and start shovelling.'

Gillan said, 'It'll flash every light and it'll shake like a washing machine with a pair of old wellie boots in it on the fast-spin setting.'

'We'll issue you with these wee canvas bags we use. Candice gets them all at The Body Shop.'

'We found plastic bags tended to burst with the weight. What a scene that makes.'

'Grab those one hundred fifty-pence pieces. Chuck handfuls into your bag.'

'There is going to be a commotion, cause almost no one will have seen a jackpot won before, but just fill your bag, be polite and nod and agree, turn tail and get out of there.'

'Hanging around leads to trouble.'

'It's the golden rule.'

'Never fails.'

'If you've played your cards right, nobody will have taken much interest in you, though.'

'It'll all happen too quick and before behind-the-bar even know what's up, the person fucking round for a half-hour on the quiz machine has hit jackpot and you're out of there.'

'And that means another of us can go in a week later. Then another of us, then another. We work relays in every pub, round and round and round, a new face each time, till we drain jackpots off all of them.'

Our party had come to that great automotive gulch at the bottom of Bath Street. Like the face of some mighty cataract on a vast, wide river, the M8 hissed and plunged with massive reverb before us. This manic gulch lay sixty feet beneath us and had been carved through the old city like a tunnel which was never roofed – its precipitous intrusion exaggerated by the climb of Garnethill on its promontory up above. The motorway carried traffic in both directions. Across the bizarre sightlines of sudden air, stood the Mitchell Library and the similarly unchanging frontage of the Koh-i-Nor Indian restaurant. Above the dome of the library, a balloon of starlings turned their black lens and elongated, like a cloud of propelled smoke blown from God's own mouth.

We struck out north ourselves – up Newton Street, below the curious prefabricated plastic buildings which had been laid along the top of a one-time motorway-slip-road planning folly, which had led nowhere. We had to raise our voices to counter the hysterical slither of the traffic, the heedless, impossible need of private motor vehicles.

'Then came another complication,' Slorach called out. 'The arrival of the man from Ashby de la Zouch.'

I frowned. 'Is that not a firm of accountants?'

Fossenkemper laughed. 'That's Deloitte & Touche.'

'Ashby has no railway station so none of us know it. It's near Leicester, and the HQ of Providence, and *Thirst For Knowledge* pub-quiz machines.'

Slorach said, 'See, when a machine in a pub gives the fifty-quid jackpot ten times, it gets flagged, and the technician and the pub know it. They send up a programmer from Ashby.'

'They reprogramme the machine.'

'This is what has started to happen.'

'There's a second generation of *Thirst For Knowledge*, and we're gonna have to learn it.'

'At least you know not to drain a machine more than ten times.'

Slorach looked at me. 'From the manufacturer's point of view, what is the fundamental, logical weakness with this game, to your mind?'

'Well, I dunno. That the questions are all the same?'

Slorach kept looking at me as we walked on. 'That's too obvious. Think about it. It's not that the questions are all the same. If there were only one machine in the world, it would be interesting to us, but just amusing to plug fifty quid out of now and again. What changes the game?'

'It's that the machines are all the same.'

'Exactly. So?'

I looked at him. I turned my head and I looked at the others.

'What's the obvious thing to do, Peter?'

'Eh. The best thing you can do is... the best thing you can do is what you are doing. Get access to as many machines as possible. Before they start changing them all to the new gen.'

'Exactly,' Lorimer nodded.

'So?' Slorach threw his arms up.

'So what?' Then it hit me. I stopped walking. They all stopped as well – as if they were coaches I was controlling on an air brake. The blundering swoosh of the M8 had been left behind and we were back up Sauchiehall Street. I said, 'Shit. You bunch are not just hitting the machines round the town centre.' I shared a smile out over them all. I felt a weird sort of thrill and admiration for them.

Slorach said, 'What job do we all do?'

I actually opened my mouth, then I semi-shouted, 'You're using the trains to move around! We work on the railways. You're using our free-travel passes to go to find other pubs where the bloody machines are!'

'Ta-rah.' Gillan laughed. 'Tie goes to the runner – to the runner – to the runner.'

'Holy shit,' I pushed some hair back off my face; I'd grown it quite long that year – I'd stopped bothering with it because nobody loved me. 'Edinburgh. Dundee. Aberdeen.'

'Mr Lennox. You are thinking too small.'

Lorimer smiled. 'East Coast Main Line. Newcastle, Durham, Darlo, Donny, York, Peterborough. The Big Smoke. Down on an early, back on a late.'

Slorach spoke, and of course it sounded like a mighty station announcement, 'Aberdeen, Dundee, Newcastle, Leeds, Wakefield, Sheffield, Derby, Birmingham, Cheltenham, Bristol, Taunton, Exeter, Newton Abbot, Totnes, Plymouth. We can get off and on wheresoever we please with our passes, which no one bothers to punch up, as we know, unless you meet a fussy inspector, and he can only punch one.'

Fossenkemper said, 'West Coast Main Line.'

'Manchester.'

'Liverpool.'

'Overnights.'

Gillan said, 'This is the age of the train, someone once told us.'

'Change at Crewe.'

'Chester and Holyhead.'

'Rhyl and Prestatyn. Plenty pubs.'

'Blackpool.'

'Coventry and Rugby.'

'Think about the Aberdeen-to-Penzance train. Machines placed all along the spine of the country, like a strip of Sellotape we're ripping up.'

'*Thirst For Knowledge* is in a lotta pubs.'

We had resumed walking back up Sauchiehall Street. We were

circumventing city blocks which served no purpose to us. Walking out a rectangle, like that great old Tolstoy story about the greedy man who wanted too much land and kept walking the rectangle to mark it out, chasing the sunset till it killed him. I said, 'I can see a problem, though.' I frowned. Lifting a finger as if to criticise them.

'Shoot.'

'You must waste hours trekking from pub to pub arriving in a new town, finding what ones have machines and what ones don't – and the temptations of a pint in each.'

Slorach and Lorimer shook their heads sadly.

Gillan spoke, 'Let me tell you a story. No last year but towards the end of the year before, a certain mega-cool guy appeared in Ashby de la Zouch. Taxi from Burton-on-Trent railway station. The locals didnie know what had hit them, man. This slick, dick dog, OG, met with an employee of a certain local company in a pub. The pub had nae *Thirst For Knowledge* machine, which was ironic. An exchange took place; a small cash payment in an envelope.'

'Not that small.'

'I was off haime with a certain document. Bust the cap on the Moët, sister.' He high-fived Fossenkemper, who grudgingly slid an arm out her jacket and raised her palm. Then Gillan circled about the pavement, doing a strident dance move. He was quite a fud, but I liked him.

Fossenkemper took the German view. 'I've told you. It's pronounced Mo-ett, Gillan. He was Austrian, not French like Chandon.'

'Tech nine to your dome-zone baby.'

Lorimer told me, 'That was a shipping document collated up for an annual sales meeting, and it listed every pub in the UK with a *Thirst For Knowledge* machine – or with a confirmed order for one.'

'We just used the main lines to start. Hit the towns with stations first, obviously; then we started using the branch lines. York and Scarborough, all in a day. What a crop. But we are starting to spread our wings and venture out beyond the railway now and again. Use a bus. We even hired a car one day for a change, cos Lorimer here can drive. Candice has it all mapped out. We have accurate records: what pubs, what takings, how many jackpots.'

I looked at him and I shook my head. 'You guys have worked out a way to print fucking money.'

'Well. To mint coins.'

We were passing The Griffin once again. Thoughtfully, Slorach said, 'Peter. Another thing. We did a little enquiring of another kind. Spoke with Lorn the Rooster Clerk. Persuaded him. It seems that you still have accumulated three weeks' annual leave and nine days in lieu.'

'Not a great holidaymaker then?' Lorimer drawled.

I looked as them. 'That's confidential info, guys.' I laughed and shook my head. 'I don't care, but it's true.'

'Mmmm,' Slorach nodded. 'It's just, this is another reason we elected to make contact with you specifically. It's hard to underestimate the value of your annual leave and days in lieu. I mean, literally hard to estimate the value of it. Can I also ask? Your sick record? The Rooster Clerk drew the line at revealing that.'

'What about it?'

'How is it?'

'I've not had a sickie in a year and a half. I've had hangovers, but I've learned to deal. That's what sickies are, isn't it? Hangover days.'

'Oh yes!' Lorimer clapped his hands.

'It might be profitable for you to develop flu symptoms and take a week or so off, quite soon,' Slorach said. 'These are some of the demands we would have to place on you. To blot your sick record. To use up every holiday and day off. We have pretty much exhausted our sick-day toleration levels from management. Obviously we take days off work, eh... in order to do our real work. We would ask that you work hard in relation to licensing hours. Even after or before work at the railway we will want you in a pub.'

'The dream job at last.'

Slorach replied in a low, confidential voice, which was perhaps as if to reveal he and Fossenkemper had a connection, 'Candice and I had two weeks' annual leave about three months ago. Took ourselves on quite a few long journeys on our little travel passes through this green and pleasant land.'

'Two weeks and a day,' she reminded him, as if something significant occurred on that extra day. A missed anniversary or overlooked birthday perhaps?

'We worked every day.' Slorach leaned slightly forward to catch Lorimer's eye. 'What did it come to?'

Lorimer carried that strange, flat, imitation-leather satchel with him, and he flipped over its covering flap and removed a large jotter.

'Well, I mean just a round figure.'

Lorimer bit his lip. 'I like to get things spot on. In your fifteen days between the two of yous, you were averaging seven machines a day and sometimes more; that is, so eh... eh, one, zero, eight, five zero.

I looked from Lorimer to Slorach. 'What?'

Lorimer repeated, 'One, zero, eight, five, zero. Seven machines *each* of course. Seven each.'

'You managed almost two grand in your holidays?' I said. 'Fuck me! That would pay for your ice-cream cones.'

Lorimer frowned at me that way, with the wrinkles on the forehead. 'Two grand?' He smiled and looked between me and Slorach.

Lorimer clarified, 'In the fifteen days of their annual leave, Candice and John's combined earnings from *Thirst For Knowledge*, amounted to ten thousand, eight hundred and fifty pounds. £10,850. Which was split four ways. Gave us two thousand, seven hundred and twelve pounds each. And fifty pence. That's was a helluva lot of fifty pences in our backpacks.'

'Tax-free, old boy, tax free,' Slorach added, quoting Orson Welles in a perfect imitation.

I found myself leaning back against a wall on Bath Street.

TWO

Moon & Sixpence, Chester... The Wagon & Hare, Blackburn... Finnegan's, Chippenham... The Wellington, Yeovil... Pultney's, Newport... The Hairy Farmer, Ledbury... Mick's, East Retford... The Lone Bugler, Lincoln...

We lived on Lucozade and Burger King. Beer too of course. I see the pub names, written in Lorimer's careful handwriting, but I remember nothing of the hostelries. Nothing. And some of these I believe I visited twice. I don't remember them. No stale-beer smell, no cheese rolls tightly wrapped in cellophane, no pretty barmaid.

I have picked them randomly from the ledger of accounts and earnings for that autumn, winter and spring which we so faithfully assembled.

Have you ever thought about fifty-pence pieces and how much one hundred of them weigh? Why would you? Less than a kilo for the 1990s coins. The '70s coins were each a little heavier – the alloy was different. In general, a little over two pounds in weight. So seven jackpots in a day for each of us (if we achieved that), when you couldn't get to a bank in between, amounts to nearly seven kilos – or pushing eighteen pounds. It weighs you down. And banks can be resistant.

We looked a bit like dedicated fell ramblers, strangely unfit hill-walkers, mature students returning to university, with our hiking and camping backpacks. It wasn't a good look for certain pubs and occasionally we had to deposit our backpacks in left-luggage lockers and Travelodge hotel rooms.

Sometimes in the early days I think they just used me as a porter, made presumptions about me effortlessly lifting loose train couplings, throwing buckeyes, lifting off screw couplings – but couplings just have to be briefly lifted; you don't need particular strength, more a knack.

I found *Thirst For Knowledge* life harder going than the shunting. A lot of travelling (though I liked travelling on trains, reading at night and looking out the window by daylight). The pressure of remembering the correct answer, of reaching the third jackpot without attracting attention. The fuss from locals when you won, and the sudden stage-left exit. And the peer-group expectation to get seven jackpots if you had a full day. Then the work shifts to get back to in time. I often wore my uniform away, as I never reached the room in my flat. I'd come off a train at Central from somewhere – Girvan or Halifax – then go straight into Operations to clock on, often with a backpack of coin I'd stash in my locker.

For those trips Fossenkemper and Slorach would have worked out and photocopied a fantastically accurate and detailed itinerary for you. She and Slorach used the *British Rail Passenger Timetable*, plotted the trajectory of our routes, with maps and directions to the pub address, which they gleaned from that year's *Good Pub Guide*; they marked how many times the machine had been hit (if it had) and by whom, ensuring it wasn't the same one of us returning again or too soon. For particular pubs, Slorach even added a few real-ale recommendations to try while we milked the machine: '*A particularly interesting and strident pint is the Wagon-wheeler ale. If it's still on tap.*'

Gillan, through some murky network, had found out that we could do 'no questions asked' deals at amusement arcades on the seafronts of various Scottish coastal towns and in some of the games arcades in Edinburgh, which were still going strong in those days, before home marathons on PlayStation and X-Box completely took over. In general we didn't like to exchange the coins at too many places closer to home base. Arcades would skim a little charge off the top – two or sometimes three percent – to convert the fifty pences into fifty-pound notes. Mostly we exchanged the money in little batches so we appeared small-time enough: five hundred pounds here, six hundred and fifty pounds there, every couple of months using differing places, so as not to particularly interest them. They wanted our coins. Lorimer was angered by all of this, as he insisted we should in fact charge *them* a percentage to part with the coins. The reason they wanted the coins, Lorimer alleged, was that these places had long-established means of efficient money laundering, and large amounts of coin currency was manna to them and their methods.

Gillan argued that it wasn't wise to insist on terms or dig deeper with these dudes – he had even told some of the arcade guys the truth of how we were coming by the coins, and they were wryly impressed, but just thought of us as quaint. Which, looking back now, I suppose we were.

Some have fabricated and some have invented, but I do know established facts about John Robert Slorach, and I even once visited his family home where he grew up.

He and I alone had come over the Forth railway bridge, early one spring day, on a Dundee stopper. We hit a few machines in Kirkcaldy, changed some coins into notes at an arcade then took a Perth train north to a *Thirst For Knowledge*-listed pub none of us had ever been to before – including Slorach – in a small town called Ladybank.

I can remember the quietness of the pub, out in the flatlands of meadow that weekday afternoon – the metronomic plonk of a dripping cistern came from the gents. The middle-aged barmaid who had pulled our pints was sweeping the paving stones out in the beer garden with a bristly brush that she dipped in an aluminium bucket of bleach water. It was almost a restful sound, like low waves on beach pebbles. The pub was virtually empty in what seemed like a middle-class area. An incredibly low threat level, so I stood at Slorach's side. I had never seen him do a seven-minute run before. It was pretty impressive. The fingers, like those of Vladimir Horowitz, hovered above the buttons – the fingertips were not used, just sudden, invisible compressions, only an instant hesitation on the A, B, C, D buttons – which my reactions almost didn't sense – to ensure he didn't screw up any answer with his speed. Every answer was still lodged in his vice-like mind. It was as if he was typing a manic confession on a typewriter but with no paper in it. When the five-pound jackpot pumped out, he didn't even pause but kept moving beyond as I kneeled by his shoes and plucked out the first ten coins; then the tenner was following and finally the thirty-five-pound jackpot spat the fifties like a Gatling gun.

The brushing outside stopped and the barmaid came in through the beer-garden door to see what was happening. 'Oh, my goodness.'

Slorach looked across at her and said, 'My-oh-my. I've gone and won on the thing.'

'Goodness!' the lady repeated. 'You lads know a thing or two.'

'Guesses!' Slorach sort of chortled and shouted at the same time. 'It's all guesses, this life.'

'You guess helluva well.'

Slorach's cheeks were up. I had noticed it, the way his nostrils had pulled in, the childlike hairs along his jaw, the cool way his untended fringe hopped around on his pale forehead. It was something beyond his calm acceptance of things, his intelligence and what I always felt around him – that slight pain. What was it? I wondered that spring afternoon.

'No one's ever won a bean on that thing before. Except Mr Ebdale the teacher got something out it once. Down from the university are we, boys?'

'That's right. Just guesses. Just lucky guesses. Would you happen to know if there is a bank in town?

There was a quiet branch of the Royal Bank of Scotland where the teller seemed as excited as Slorach was pretending to be. He was glancing at me continuously. 'Gosh-and-crikey,' (he actually said to the teller in that voice!) 'I don't think you will believe me, or can help me, but I got lucky on a quiz machine when we were having our lovely pub lunch. It was delicious too. A battered haddock I had. I know this probably isn't possible, but you couldn't change all this into notes? Could you at all?'

'Well,' said the elderly lady, 'isn't it your lucky day! What notes would suit you?'

'Oh no. What notes would suit you today?' Slorach leaned an arm along the counter top, craned towards her, and I could see she approved of him – pure maternal instincts he somehow ignited. He crashed the avalanche of coins into the metallic dip.

When we got outside he did that Oliver Hardy thing of pulling the money notes taut then flicking the ends of them with the top side of your fingers. 'Mmmm-hmmmmm.' He held the two twenties and ten note up to the bright sky. He told me, 'And that was the lady in the bank in Ladybank.'

Then suddenly phoning from a red telephone box close to the station, he insisted on taking me back to 'the acres which spawned me', and we were collected in a very short time by his mother – a busy, able, but slightly frantic woman, driving a silver Opel Kadett. It was an unusual vehicle they had chosen for the family, as neither Mrs Slorach – who was surprisingly tall and rangy – John or even me fitted comfortably within. They had insisted – it's a sort of conspiracy against taller people – that I must sit in the front seat beside the driver (who is always a stranger to you).

Mrs Slorach talked in high, bounding tones, her voice soaring nervously from one topic to another, as we speedily carved over the Fife farmland. It was strange to be in a car after so many, many months on trains – daily – for me both in coaches and on engines. Mrs Slorach seemed amused by my status as a minor train functionary. But each time she looked across at me, and in a high, melodious voice repeatedly told me, 'You couple them up, you couple them up, fancy!' I saw a little line of pain or angst just back, right there, from the corner of the eye; the same eye which shot continually to the rear-view mirror, checking for her son, making sure he was still there and had not also slipped down from the middle class, too far to get back up that social scale again.

They lived in the village of Dairsiemuir, beyond Cupar, Fife. Rather than saying it was on the outskirts, their family home was on a descending road, and it was literally the final dwelling in the village. A modern, low and large place, with a happy garden on the lower slope, on a plot at least the same size as the house itself. Then there were the wide rapeseed fields of the farms round Dairsiemuir. This meant the open view over to the east was all out there before the Slorachs – the shallow, broad valley through which the river Eden flowed down to the North Sea, beyond Balmullo, at Guardbridge.

Rather than get trapped in the house, Slorach immediately took me on a walk – I quickly sensed it was a walk which dated from his childhood and youth, a cherished routeing – and sure enough, before we came to Dairsiemuir Castle, about a mile and a half down from the village outskirts, we crossed the main railway lines there on a road bridge. Slorach paused and looked down on the double-track railway lines beneath us. He had not stopped while crossing the bridge itself, for the walls on either side made it difficult for a person of his height to see over the capstones. He stood instead at the end of the wall where it curved down into the ground and from where you could look across a thin wire fence and see the brown tracks below.

'Used to come here when I was little. I always wanted to see the Deltics. You know what Deltics were?'

'Sure, big diesel express engines; English Electrics. None left on the railway, withdrawn in the early '80s or something. There's a framed photo of one in Ops.'

'Oh. You never drove any?'

'Course not. They tended to be more WCML. West Coast Main Line; express engines between Aberdeen, Edinburgh, London. Or London and the Midlands. I was just twelve or thirteen when they disappeared.'

He nodded silently. 'I used to love Deltics. I thought they had big sad faces like my own.'

I laughed. 'Funny, isn't it? The childhood need to anthropomorphise things. I used to do it with cars and lorries. Do they have sad or happy faces?'

'They are mostly sad. Or you remember the sad ones. Face recognition. It's an instinct from infancy – to communicate with the mother's eyes.'

I thought of his own mother – her worried disposition towards him.

We walked on. I learned Slorach Senior made good money in one of those many, many jobs where I don't understand how people turn a profit. He 'provided security systems to private business and factories'.

What did that even mean? Did it mean he wired up bells on burglar alarms and fitted surveillance cameras, or did he infiltrate the potential for industrial espionage which employees may display? People with job titles like that often live in pleasing houses. I was quietly proud of the manner in which our official occupations, at least, could be crisply summed up. Slorach Junior gave out the train times, and I hooked the engines onto them. Of course our unofficial and more lucrative earnings could also be easily defined. In a morally grey way, we obtained cash from a morally dubious machine which was intent on taking cash from us all.

'It's so strange I ended up giving out train times,' Slorach whispered numbly. The breeze moved some curled, brown leaves which still lay in a sprouting flax field beside the wire fence. Their dry tumbling almost obliterated his words.

'You haven't ended anywhere, Slorach. You're a visionary. It's a strange wee life we lead. We all know it's not going to last but it's not a dull one.'

He raised his voice. 'Well, you're okay. You don't have to sit in that moronic room, dealing with a lost people. I wish I had your job, up riding on the engines.' He turned to me. 'And you do night shifts. Real night shifts till six in the morning and stuff. How still the station must be at that time. Mail trains and parcels, eh? That's pretty exotic.'

I laughed. 'Put in for a transfer on the vacancies sheet.'

'Why? Thinking of quitting?' His sudden eyes held mischief.

This sinister undercurrent had started to emerge since Christmas. *Thirst For Knowledge: New Generation* was taking up all of

Slorach, Lorimer and Fossenkemper's spare time. Gillan and I were not permitted to work on it. Gillan was consulted about new sports questions, but I noticed I was consulted on nothing.

Gillan and I were sent out to continue milking the existing first-generation machines, to try and extract as much cash as possible from them before they too were updated. Our lifestyle was facing obsolescence, like coal miners. I was starting to feel like a donkey as I often found myself carrying backpacks of coins to Fossenkemper's flat in Dennistoun. I was not even allowed through the main door and up the stairs. Fossenkemper came down to the street door and carried the backpack on the stairs herself, rather than let me up to the flat. 'The girls are a bit weird like that,' she said. I wanted to ask, like what?

We had been sitting in The Horseshoe Bar, and tinsel was hanging on the gantries. We were not playing the machines – just drinking. The five of us. Slorach had cleared his throat, announced, 'It wouldn't be such rotten news if one of us got the heave.'

Lorimer said, 'What do you mean? Threw up?'

'From the railway. Well, it's coming with privatisation, isn't it? I mean really, think about it. We'll all be on bloody different contracts – they'll take overtime and double-time payments first, Sunday working, then they'll chip away at allowances and holidays, then the wages will freeze.'

'The wage has been fucking froze since World War II,' Lorimer added. 'I cannie take the heave. I've got to keep going till the pension. I've paid in a bomb. Or what will be left of it? And there's the wean.'

To my surprise it had turned out Lorimer was divorced – and he had a fourteen-year-old daughter. That's where his share went. Daddy showing off to Mummy in a tug of love. Paris Disneyland two years back. He still went on about the look on the lassie's face. He'd be better stashing it and get her off to uni or college. I'd told him so, but he took the hump.

'What about you, Mr Gillan? Last in first out.'

'Cool it, man. Dinae do a drive-by on me. I was here about two week after your heels, mate. I like the green, I like the green, but then whit? You don't want the dole sniffin at your crotch about how you're living, man. It's like Too Short says, there's money in the ghetto, but the days when lads would turn up to sign on with paint on their overalls and a fucking works van outside are long gone.'

'What about you? Brave engineer of the Old 97? Told us you didn't want to be doing your job when you were sixty.'

'I've a bit to go yet.' I could feel he was singling me out.

'Yes, but think about it.' He looked around the pub, leaned forward and lowered his voice. 'If she and I can clear ten grand in a busy fortnight, you could bring in what, full time? Three years' wage in two months.'

'Oh, come on. You know I wouldn't raise that. That's blue-sky thinking.'

'We could. If Fossenkemper,' (he used her surname, though they were sleeping together and she was sat right there), 'if Fossen-kemper went at a national plan for two of you. Say, for you and Gillan. You two quit this bloody railway and work full time. Go professional. Think of the possibilities? You'd have enough to start yourselves up in something else and be free of the great domed roof forever.'

'But we'd only get a fifth. It would be a way over a year's wage in total but no individually.'

'Eh?'

Gillan repeated, in a sudden formal diction for him, 'We'd be quitting our secure income to devote ourselves to generating a totally insecure one with four-fifths of it going to someone else.'

'This is sedition!' Slorach laughed.

'Oh, come on,' said Lorimer. 'Dinnie start dividing up the royalties. That's what bands fall out over, splits up all the good bands.'

'If that's the case, Slorach,' I said, 'by logic we should all quit and all just burn ourselves out, trying to empty every machine that's left in Britain, ten times.'

'Why not?' He shouted it, and we all looked at him; a guy at the standing bench behind him, who he didn't see, shifted and stared at Slorach, then turned away.

'Come on. This has always been a laugh – a great laugh – and the money helps, but basing our lives totally around it?' I shrugged.

'We do. She and I do base our whole lives on it, to support you. We slave out those bloody plans for you, yet at the same time we have to try and break the code on this new bastard. And this fucking job, talking to these morons on the phone it...' he huddled up his body '... it holds little interest.'

'You'll get there on the *New Gen*.'

'But all the time we're losing money. If we had some full-time members... The possibilities are infinite. We could start pooling our profit, buy property and...'

There was an awkward silence.

Surprisingly, the voice of moderation, Fossenkemper, said, 'John. We start buying property and that and we come above surface. It gets serious. The tax'll be on us asking questions. This way it's perfect. It's just enough and not too much among five.'

Slorach sighed and said, 'You're right. It's a bad idea. I'm just, I'm just ambitious. I resent that cash slipping away.'

'It's like going fishing, John.' Lorimer stood up. 'My round. You don't come home from fishing, pissed off you didn't reel in every single fish in the sea. Keep perspective.'

'Don't tell me what to do.'

Now we all really were silent.

He twisted himself round on his bar stool and crossed his legs. 'We're not the only ones at this game. I know fine there is another gang operating out of Liverpool doing the same as us.'

Lorimer said, 'What? Railway?'

'No way. More like they use cars. Fuck knows who they are – or what – but our hits are getting garbled when there isn't a fucking MENSA conference in town.'

'It's true; like those two the other week,' I said.

'Exactly.'

On my rest day, I had made a jaunt to Pontefract to find that two machines we had never touched had been tenned-up and already converted to *New Gen.* I was helpless. For fun, I tried *New Gen* and didn't get beyond the first question, which was about Scandinavian bridge projects. I'd had to phone Slorach in the British Rail Telephone Enquiries Bureau to be put on hold as I was transferred to the Scottish section, then about a quarter of an hour later I was eventually put through to his voice. Calling in always caused a fuss, and there was a danger his supervisors were listening.

'I'm in Pontefract and they've both been done.'

'What; tenned or changed?'

'Well, why else would they change to *New Gen*? I'm not gonna ask the bar staff. They are gone, man. Do you have anything else for me down here?'

'I don't have the lists. I'd need to go see Candice on my break, and I don't think she has anything with her. They are at home.'

'What should I do?'

I could hear him rustling the pages of the *British Rail Passenger Timetable.* Bless him, he was trying to launch me out on another trajectory. A counterattack. 'Oh, fuck it. Go to Leeds or York. Go to Hull and snoop about, we don't do Hull much. Scout around. What a waste of time. You're only gonna get three or something sat on trains. Do we have to spell everything out for you, for fuck's sake?'

'Okay. I'll try Hull, cause York and Newcastle is cleaned out, is it not? Slorach? Slorach?' He'd hung up.

That day in The Horseshoe he had looked across the pub with The Waitresses singing 'Christmas Wrapping' in the background. He said, 'I'm going to have to take another sickie and I'm at my limit. My limit.'

From Dairsiemuir Castle that day, Slorach walked me onto the far ridge, and we went up, round towards Kemback where we could see all the way down the vale of the river Eden.

Something odd happened when we came by the auld kirk of Kemback. In the grounds there was a short pillar; I couldn't work out, was it a font? Do they have exterior fonts outside a kirk? I was brought up Catholic. Perhaps it was a birdbath? It had rainwater gathered in it and some seeds floated on the surface. From out of his jacket he took a foil of pills, he forced one out with his finger, carefully cradling it in his palm, so it didn't fall to the ground; he then placed the pill on his tongue. Suddenly he scooped handful after handful of water out of the font, slurped from his hand and knocked his head back. He ignored me staring, so I said, 'Lumbago?'

He smiled. 'Amitriptyline. It's an anti-anxiety med.'

'You've had a few pints.'

'Four. Hours ago.'

I later learned it was the medication young Nick Drake was using when the world lost him.

We crossed back, this time under the railway, then returned to the village by a new route. Slorach started to talk very openly about his time at university in St Andrews. He had spent the entire first year in pubs and in poker societies, often with a few student high rollers, so that he was immediately out of his financial league. Playing cards until late into the night was the norm. He was living at home, so he felt he was saving a great deal of money, but increasingly he never came home to his mum's dinners each evening and spent more and more time on sofas. When he went to sit his first-year exams, he had started studying for them around noon the day before. He came third in his year. The following year, his lifestyle was profoundly unchanged: pubs, poker machines in pubs, pool games and, in the evening, card games and regular trips to the bookie's for horse racing. He sort of hinted at gaming casinos and possibly prostitutes in Aberdeen as well. I am innocent of such worlds.

It had been right in front of me but I hadn't noticed. By exams in his second year he followed the same approach – he defined it as 'independent study'. He turned the exam paper over and couldn't answer a single question. Failed the year. The university tried to support him, but by this time he was under pressure from fellow students for the repayment of gambling debts. These chaps were not heavies. They were from good families down south. They were polite, even pleasant, and still stood him pints. But they had a different type of connection. Registered London lawyers' letters – quoting the existence of 'outstanding private cash loans' for sums of £1,700, £900, £1,645.89 – began to arrive at the home address in Dairsiemuir, and his mum or dad opened them.

His father bailed him out and paid the debts. The penalty was not another course in history, but starting as an undergrad again. International Business & Commerce at Glasgow University. He had blown what state grant he got. His parents set him up privately in a small solo flat in Hillhead, and they paid him another monthly stipend. What were they thinking? He had the place sublet in a month and began sofa-hopping with casino-fly mates – quite a lot of them seemed to be young Chinese men.

We didn't really acknowledge many things back in my early adulthood. Male mental health, depression, even the idea that you could be addicted to things other than drugs. I had never in my life met anyone who had been in therapy before. Therapy was something which was mentioned in American movies; it was associated with Woody Allen, Los Angeles, the Betty Ford Clinic. Jimmy Stewart in *Harvey*. You didn't actually ever meet anybody in therapy, and of course you would never need it yourself. But, at the age of twenty-one, Slorach had been undergoing treatment for gambling addiction. The parents paid for it all. Then to try and sober him, they cut him off. He ended up homeless for a week in Glasgow, a few nights in hostels, dawn soup kitchens. He talked of it, amused and even happy. But he came back to his childhood bedroom in Dairsiemuir defeated. A compromise was struck. A small stipend to set himself up again. He would be allowed to live in Glasgow – a city he liked – but he simply had to find a steady job and the stipend ceased. Any job, but a job to learn about 'the real world'. Personally, I believe he understood more about the real world than his parents did, but you know how it goes. He took the first thing he was offered: station announcer at the Central.

*

Money is a strange thing. Very strange. Almost mystical. When you have never had money, as we learned in our days of *Thirst For Knowledge*, there is no real difference between ten pounds, a hundred and a thousand. We have all walked with those amounts in our pockets, and it just didn't influence our youth or our attitude. I had a cousin who back then was an international airline captain. Not just an airline pilot – he is ten years older than me; he had started on the airline when he was eighteen and became a senior training captain, involved in management at the carrier – it was a major carrier. I would meet him at family weddings, and he amusingly referred to both of us as 'the mass-transport division of the family'. I know back then he was earning over one hundred thousand pounds per year. It was a fantastic sum of money then. Still is. Yet, as we leaned together at those weddings, our chairs pushed back, away from the tables and close to the wall, as we watched his two pretty daughters dancing with other family members – all he did was moan about money. The two girls were at a private school. There was the London house, there were the three expensive cars, his wife's pottery and clothes, and then there was the house in the south of France. And as his earnings increased, somehow he flew less and less – which was what he loved to do. Expensive holidays. Yeah, you fly there for free, but you don't put the family up in a Travelodge and dine nightly at Burger King. Salary-wise, I had earned in a year what he earned in just over a month. But I had no costs. He said it himself. The pound in my hand was worth so much more than his – even though he had ten more of them. Because I cherished what it bought me. Or was he just romanticising the humble worker's lot?

It was true. In fact I sort of horrified myself. Since Teresa dumped me, I needed virtually nothing. Twenty Penguin Classics a year and a ten-pint night out every month. I was appalled at the frugality of my own needs and the cerebral nature of my ambitions – a sort of physical lack of interest in the world around me. I was mentally interested but was committed to nothing. That's what I found so restful about chucking the couplings at work. I didn't go anywhere. There was a Zen power to setting those trains up and going nowhere.

Locke, the Communist Party rep in the union, came to me one day and lectured me about joining the party and the need to crush the bourgeoisie. He begged me to help the working classes of the world. I remember the look on his face when I said I couldn't even help myself, and I looked down onto the pages of *Madame Bovary* once again. I knew the way I was living was my justification. All the communists and even staunch Labour voters I knew were like the middle class – they had mortgages and wanted bigger houses, they had cars and possessions. I had nothing. I was free – without being self-congratulatory, I was the solution they thought we all needed. When Locke came at me again and told me I was a decadent individualist, I told him to fuck off back to his mortgage and his wife's dinner set. He really had both, since one day, early in my spell on the railways, I had ended up back at his place late at night. He was the hypocrite not me. He was actually a bourgeois and I was the working man. It was the truth. When he walked away, I regretted the real hurt I saw in his face.

You only get a few brief spells in your life when you really are living in truth – authentically. You need courage and courage comes easier when you are young and stronger. I have no virtue now and I lost my courage, but I believe I did possess some then, in those days of freedom.

I think Slorach was like that too. That's why I started on about money. If you think Slorach was driven by money, you are crazy. Money, literally, was the counters in his game. Money wasn't the game in itself. It was the playing that made him feel alive and whole. It's the same for an artist I have now realised. All those great writers I read which I could never become, all those great painters – we all think it's about an end product. The book, the canvas. Just counters in the game. The end product is there, but those writers were most alive when they were writing – not when they had finished and sighed and slumped back in their chairs. Picasso never stopped – I would bet it wasn't the finished painting, it was those rare moments before it was finished that he lived for.

Slorach had a sort of virtue about him which I admired. And at that point I began to clearly understand something about him. It started with the way he smoked his Rothmans. I used to observe and take note. He smoked them at the oddest of times. Always exactly ten a day but in no order. He simply took himself aside and smoked one, but not at set moments and not in obvious situations – with coffee – with a pint – after eating – after completing a seven-jackpot day or when he was stressed. No way. It was more like a spiritual rhythm which controlled him. He smoked in the still, empty moments of true peace. You could be walking down a street, actually going to the pub, and he would suddenly stop in the middle of a pavement, forcing pedestrians to step around him, glancing at him; he would stand and begin to smoke a single cigarette in the rain, blinking, drops even darkening the white filter in his mouth. And these were the days when you could smoke inside pubs. Then, I would note, late on some evenings he might take out his pack of twenty, open it and peer into it. He was counting. Standing in the middle of the lit station concourse off a late shift, talking strategically about pubs in Britain and how we should do another sweep down the WCML, paying attention to Penrith, Carlisle and Lancaster. Talking in his low, beautiful voice he would suddenly smoke three cigarettes in rapid succession after all the restraint of the day. It was because he had fulfilled his quota and was going home to sleep. For a man so addicted in other ways, this showed a strange, stalwart discipline. Like me, I realised he actually led a Spartan life. His mysterious relationship with Fossenkemper aside (a silver bracelet – very beautiful – one day appeared on her wrist and I noted it – she was puffed with a touching pride), he was not an indulgent man. He didn't even drink very much. In a strange way, our ordered lives which revolved completely around licensed pubic houses, resulted in all five of us probably consuming less alcohol that we ever had in our previously chaotic lives. That was when I realised: Slorach was saving all his money. He was saving it to pay back his parents for all the hurt he had caused and the expense he had imposed on them. That's what drove him at that time. But something went wrong. He lost sight of those cigarette moments of nothingness.

We walked back through the village into the garden of his family home. There was a sort of exterior balcony or platform which you ascended to up a staircase from the garden – the platform spread out in front of the panoramic French windows of their front living room. It gave forth the view across the vale of the Eden. A cosy glen. It struck me then what a devastatingly beautiful place it was, what a sublime view. With the railway hidden down in the dip, nothing had changed before our eyes, apart from maybe a modern barn, in five hundred years. Take a look at that place some day, if you can. I realised I had been seeing a great deal of our country from trains, a country which in those days was still bound together by an odd network of institutions – British Rail, the Post Office, Royal Mail, British Telecom, British Gas – institutions which were to fragment in the decades that followed. The view across the shallow declivity which the ancient river had carved was universal. It was the opposite of the M8 fissure. This could almost have been anywhere in the United Kingdom. It could have been Suffolk, it could have been the Welsh borders. Only a brittle, plumed fresh-ness to the air told my face and lips this was old Scotland, as Slorach and I looked across this earthly Eden to the old Kirk of Kemback high on the opposite ridge where we had been.

'This is a beautiful place to grow up,' I said.

He nodded. 'You get it, eh?'

His kind mother gave us another lift to Leuchars railway station where we got an Aberdeen up to Dundee. Hit a machine out of duty and took a southbound down to the Queen Street station.

THREE

'Good morning. British Rail Enquiries. How may I help you?'

'Aye fit like. That was some wait, whit? I could o got the stirks done in that time rather than sat here on a telephone line waiting for you to pick up the receiver with good daylight oot.'

'And how can I help you?'

'Is that the railways, finally? I had this lassie going on and on at me, but she wouldn't talk back, like she wasn't really there it was like. You ken? She had been recorded doon, like on a radio station when they repeat the show. Like Robbie Shepherd or that?'

'Yes.'

'So that's Aaa-bear-deen railway station?'

'No. We're not at the station.'

'Whit? Who are you then, loon?'

'We're an enquiries number. You've come through to another office.'

'Another office, is it?'

'Yes.'

'But I need the Aaa-bear-deen station. Whit? Are ye no even in Aaa-bear-deen!?'

'Well, what does it concern? Perhaps I can help you in some way?'

'Oh, I don't know if you could. I need them in Aaa-bear-deen. It's a fair complicated question. I need the Aaa-bear-deen station.'

'Go on. Give us a clue.'

'Weel, loon. I'm needing to be sending something away on the train. Regular postman is no gonna do at all.'

'Something? Away on the train?'

'Aye. Well. It's the wife's doing.'

'I see. You want to send your wife away on the train?'

There was a silence then the caller burst out laughing. 'No a bad idea, loon, but nay, it's something else we're sending.'

'Something. A parcel, is it?'

'Aye. Well. I dunno now if I'd be calling it a parcel. It's. Weel. I dunno if I should be telling you. It's a surprise and that.'

'Well, I don't know if I can help you if you don't explain.'

'Well. Don't tell her. The sister-in-law. But it's a cake.'

'A cake?'

'Aye. The wife's a great one for the baking.'

'Is she?'

'Oh aye. There's nae stopping her with that oven. Never should have got it put in; the old range wis grand. So she's sending this one to her sister as a wee surprise, like.'

'And where do you want to send the cake to?'

'From Aaa-bear-deen.'

'Yes and where to?'

'Birmingham in England there. Now it's the New Street station. I've been telt that often enough.'

'Aberdeen to Birmingham New Street.'

'Aye. It's doon in England there. Right doon. Way doon.'

'Yes. Way doon. South of Portlethen at least.'

'Oh aye now. Well sooth.'

'What you need to do is take it to the Red Star Parcels office in Aberdeen, and they'll sort it all out for you.'

'Whit? Who?'

'Red Star Parcels at the station.'

'Whit? I'd need to take the cake there?'

'Yes.'

'And who-oo would that work oot then?'

'Well, they would weigh and measure it for you and quote you a price.'

'And whit would that come oot as?'

'Well, that depends on the size and weight.'

'Who-oo are they going to measure? It's aww covered in icing sugar.'

'You'll need to put it in a box then. Or the sparrows and seagulls will be at it, won't they?'

'Aww I ken that now, loon. I'll put the biddy thing in a box and string and broon paper, but there again that's goan add on fair to the price, eh?'

'You have to put it in a box. We can't just hand it over to the buffet car attendant to take down to Birmingham, can we? Or he'll be selling it at forty-five pence a slice.'

With a grave tone the farmer said, 'A slice is worth way more than that. So they wid weigh it up, wid they? And they'd put it straight onto the train that would go to Birmingham where the sister-in-law lives? It's amazing whit happens nooadays. Here now, though. Wud you no have an idea what it would cost a body?'

'Well, I'd need a rough idea of the size and weight. I mean, I do have a sheet here which would give you a rough idea.'

'Well, it's aboot this by this here. I'm looking at the thing the noo.'

'Yes. But. I can't see you. You'll need to tell me the measurements.'

'Well, it's a cake. So I'd say it's like a foot across and. Whit? Ten inches up and doon.'

'Okay then and what about weight?'

'Och I'll need to be away and ask the wife, and she's down at the gates the noo. There was a fair amount of them almond nuts went in I can tell ye. I mean, I dinnie have the recipe on me. Whit would a body like me be wantin with yon recipes? The weights'll be in there. I'd need to get out the weights and measures and all that. A pound o sugar and everything.'

'Well. What do you think it weighs now that it is baked? Roughly?'

'It's like a severed sheep's heid, mon.'

As was his routine now, Slorach leaned back in his chair in the office of the British Rail Telephone Enquiries Bureau and he made eye contact with Gillan, who was working across from him; he also made eye contact with other clerical officers around him, talking on their own calls, and for their benefit he repeated out aloud, 'I see. The cake is about the weight of a severed sheep's head, is it?' He shook his own head mournfully. 'Let's say about six pounds in weight depending on how clever the sheep was.' Slorach opened his Red Star Parcels folder – a slim document – and he said, 'Do you think this sheep's head has horns on or not?'

'A cheviot, mon?' The voice then chuckled. It was hard to gauge if he was in on the humour or not. 'It would be grand would it not if six poond wis the price as well as the weight?' he added.

'Okay. Red Star Parcels six pounds of weight, let's say twelve inches by ten inches. Now this is just a rough guide, you understand. Just to give you an idea. You can't go into the office saying that you were quoted this on the phone. This is just to give you an idea, okay?'

'Aye, mon, just a bitty idea o the siller to go.'

'Aberdeen to Birmingham New Street, six pounds by those dimensions and you are looking at around sixteen pounds and eighty pence, and that would be station-to-station.'

There was a long, deeply absorbent silence at the other end. So long, Slorach said, 'Hello?'

'Near seventeen poond?'

'Yes.'

'Seventeen poond? Station-to-station?'

'That is correct.'

'But, mon, you really must be joking me now.'

'No. That's the rough price, as I say. If you take it to the office it will be around that price if the weight and dimensions you have given me conform, but obviously you haven't been able to give me exact figures so it's going to be a little different. But roughly seventeen pounds station-to-station.'

'Station-to-station?'

'Yes. It'll go straight from Aberdeen to Birmingham.'

'Station. To station? Seventeen poond?'

'That is correct.'

'But, mon. You must be joking me? That's a ridiculous price.'

'Sixteen to seventeen pounds? I think that's a reasonable price. I mean look what we do on the railway. We take your parcels on the train. It's not like the post office, where your cake would take days to get to Birmingham and it would be getting chucked from one end of a sorting office to another with no guarantees when it could arrive at your sister-in-law's. Okay. You might get it delivered to your door with the post office, but there's a good chance your cake will already be in slices by then. And stale. With the railway you're getting it straight through on the train that same day. That's why so many concerns moving perishable items use the railway parcels service.'

'But the price, mon, ye must be joking me. Near seventeen poond. Station-to-station. I might no get away from the Loch of Skene much, but am no daft. I ken fine there's more than a few stations between Aaa-bear-deen and Birmingham.'

'Pardon me?'

'I'm no a daftie. Seventeen poond. I ken fine there's mair stations than you could think of between Aaa-bear-deen and Birmingham.'

'What do you mean?'

'Mon. Yous says seventeen poond station-to-station. There's hunreds and hunreds o stations atween here and bloody Birmingham. THOOOSANDS! Seventeen poond station-to-station and every bloody station the parcel passes it rings up another seventeen poond. You must be daft. It'll be HUNREDS. It'll be HUNREDS of poonds before that cake is near bloody Birmingham. Just think of it, mon. Station-to-station. Portlethen is first, as you say, seventeen poond... then Stonehaven, seventeen poond, then... then, is there still a station at Skateraw and at Muchalls these days? That's another... whit theeerty-four poond. Och, man, it's robbery... and we're no even at Laurencekirk yet!'

'No, no, no, no. That's not what station-to-station means.'

'Whit? Yous says seventeen pound station-to-station and there's thooosands of stations between here and England.'

'Station-to-station is a phrase we use on the railway, to tell you that it's a direct route. Station-to-station means you don't have to change trains to get to your destination. You don't have to get off one train and back onto another to get where you are going.

Station-to-station means direct. You go straight there, your parcel wouldn't have to be taken off one train and put onto another. It doesn't mean you get charged seventeen pounds every time the train passes a station.'

'Whit? But that's what you says.'

'It would be seventeen pounds flat fare. To get your cake to Birmingham.'

'Awwww. You wouldn't be charged that each time the cake passed a railway station?'

'No. You wouldn't be charged that each time the cake passed a station.'

'Oh, that's relief, man. You had ma heart pounding here. Seventeen poond flat, eh? That's no a bad deal then. I'll see whit the post office charge. I'm away to do the stirks; thank ye now and I bid ye good day.'

He hung up.

Slorach and Fossenkemper had cracked *Thirst For Knowledge: New Generation* by late that May. Slorach had taken a full week off with 'flu symptoms', a designation which he felt covered all possible angles. But he was now on a final warning with regard to his absenteeism. He had worked obsessively on the machines.

It was a time-consuming chore, cracking the questions. They had been working in Newcastle, mainly. Remember this was that age before the internet. No Google. No Wikipedia. General knowledge was still a slow science and it still mattered what you knew and depended upon the resources of the individual. The universe was not at beck and call on our mobile phones. Slorach and Fossenkemper travelled with two compact encyclopaedias. They had *Cummell's Giant Science Quiz Book* – a fat American publication which was carried in backpacks. On many occasions they visited the public library in Newcastle to consult matters.

Fossenkemper and Slorach moved into a Travelodge hotel for four nights. He would work in pubs from eleven in the morning until midnight. The costs were considerable. Gillan and I were never fully informed about the 'investment costs', but I had the feeling it might have run into the thousands-of-pounds range. There was a sudden slump in the need to process fifty-pence coins. I got the feeling Slorach was not actually keeping accurate records of how many coins he was feeding in as he tried, again and again, to reach the jackpot on *New Gen*.

Gillan was telephoned at his desk in the Enquiries Bureau on several sporting issues. Newcastle was a good place to break the questions in the new machines. It is a fairly compact city, an up-and-down place with many public houses which had always housed *Thirst For Knowledge* machines. Just far enough away, and it allowed them to travel quickly from one pub to another.

There were problems, though. The question repertoire had expanded vastly. It was now a vocabulary of around two thousand possible questions. Fossenkemper worked for weeks, assembling the New Gen Archive. They both looked shattered when they returned from Newcastle, but the working Archive was given to Lorimer, Gillan and I. We kept working on the old machines, but began familiarising ourselves with the new questions.

In June a very curious trip took place. York was available again as the pubs there were now exclusively populated by *New Gen* machines. It was felt Gillan and myself should begin our work on the machines there. Fossenkemper, Gillan and myself juggled lieu days and rest days, departed at six in the morning, reached the huge, elegant canopy of York station and checked into a Travelodge hotel near the Jorvik Viking Centre in the middle of town. That way we could plug away in the pubs until late, then we could rise early and have a full day in the pubs once again, before catching the latest possible train back to Edinburgh for a final connection home. Gillan wanted to visit the Jorvik Centre for an hour, which I found surprising and out of character. He got into a really nasty argument with Fossenkemper about it. He was forbidden, because it was then opening time and there was not an hour to waste when we could be chasing jackpots.

We worked separately among the pubs in those old English lanes and streets. A great, beautiful place really, but we were there to work. That work was slow. I did terribly. By the late afternoon I had managed only two ten-pound jackpots and I kept wiping out on the timer with questions in the final run to jackpot. The New Gen Archives were handwritten, photocopied sheets in a thick ring-bound folder. It filled my backpack, and it was impossible to try to consult it while running the risk of getting spotted reading the answers off sheets of paper.

Then, in a pub called The Robinson Crusoe Of York, a shocking thing occurred. It started well. I made it beyond the ten-pound jackpot and suddenly I began to be familiar with the final run of twenty questions rolling out before me. I'd had a fantastic feeling the moment I entered that pub. I liked the name, I allowed myself a pint of good IPA and, though the tourist season had begun, it wasn't heaving, yet the amount of people in there seemed to shield me more from the bar staff. It was a good-natured lunchtime crowd. I had confidence I was going to crack this one and suddenly, in a run of luck, I could recall every single answer to every question. I raced to the ninety-ninth, and then finally the hundredth question came up. I frowned for only a second.

The Elegy Of Madonna Fiammetta is a work by which author?

A – Dante
B – Boccaccio
C – Teresa of Ávila
D – Petrarch

Immediately, I gently compressed B, in the elegant style of Slorach, and the *Thirst For Knowledge* machine began to thunder and to flash in a biblical way, its siren rang and it began to feed out. Some tourists who had been standing behind me supping pints watched and began to make cooing noises and to say things to one another in Dutch, as the seventy fifty-pence coins began to pump out. I leaned down instinctively and began loading the coins quickly into the small Body Shop canvas bag.

When I calmly rose up from my knees, I looked at the screen and I saw:

Jackpot! Jackpot! Jackpot!
Next Player. Question Change.

A strange, cold feeling came over me. I had never seen that announcement before. Was this a *New Gen* anomaly? And another point. Obviously I had a tendency to recognise book, film and literary questions; to be confident I could answer them. I was absolutely convinced I had not seen that Boccaccio question in Fossenkemper's New Gen Archive. I would have remembered it. *The Elegy* is a beautiful but not well-known book. I preferred it to *The Decameron* – in fact I believed it was a greater work than Dante's *Inferno*. I would have remembered that there was a question on it in *New Gen*. Yet Fossenkemper and Slorach had once again assured us there were only seven rogue questions which sometimes showed up in the final twenty, and they had listed them. I supposed it was one they had not yet encountered.

But what was this 'Questions Change' statement. Was it a bluff?

I then did something I had never done before. I looked around me, gauging that my jackpot win hadn't brought too much attention on me, and I placed another fifty pence in the slot.

Which of the following is not an isotope of hydrogen?
A – Tritium
B – Deuterium
C – Protium
D – Yttrium

I didn't recognise that question! I didn't fucking recognise it.
TEN... NINE... EIGHT...

I hit B, because it reminded me of the book in the bible. The machine made the sad, descending raspberry of an incorrect answer. I picked up my Adidas backpack, turned to my right, nodded politely at the Dutch people, then walked out of The Robinson Crusoe Of York.

I started searching the pubs which I knew housed *Thirst For Knowledge* machines. Neither Gillan nor Fossenkemper were in The Old White Swan, but I didn't even consider hitting the machine. I was heading for The Minster Inn, but dropped off in Slim Jim's, a rubbish, open-plan modern pub, but one with a machine. The blue-and-white jacket loomed over in the corner.

'Aye,' I nodded as I halted beside her. Then I said 'jackpot' and winked.

'Good show,' she said. 'Bully for you. But I'm not done here.'

'We need to talk.'

She looked around briefly and punched in a B. 'Pete. You know the rules. Don't show we are together.'

'I think we have a problem.'

She hit an A. 'With Gillan?'

'No. Meet me when you're done. Where are you going next?'

'I'll see you at the hotel tonight. Keep working please. You're wasting time. I'm pleased you got a jackpot.'

I left Slim Jim's.

Gillan was in The Banks Of The Ouse, a modern place, catering more for a night-time crowd; it was almost empty. He wasn't working, though. He was sat in his latest stupid Italian sports jacket – the ones with a badge on the arm that football casuals wore. He was addicted to their purchase and they cost four or five hundred a pop.

He was against the wall, drinking a pint. As I walked to him, he looked up at me with a stricken expression and squinted. He'd taken off his glasses and placed them on the table in front of him, you could note how the weight of their heavy lenses marked his nose. He was a good-looking kid without the specs, but his hair seemed not to have been washed in weeks and he'd grown it long. I dunno why he didn't get contacts instead of daft jackets. He said,

'Homie. The fucking thing in here just changed the questions on me. It's quiet, so I was like, fuck you and yer rules, Fossenkemper, I'm just milking it twice, and I dunno. It's no the same questions that are here in their New Archives. I never seen these questions before.'

'Fuck. You too? I've just jacked one for fifty in The Robinson Crusoe and it did the same on me. I'm sure of it. Like. Completely new questions have come up on it.'

We both stared hard at each other.

'Fuck,' he whispered. He shook his head very slowly, staring at me. Those poor-sighted eyes were vague. We both knew the implications of that shake of the head. I sat down next to him on the banquette.

'What are the programmers doing?'

'They're fucking changing, man. When you jackpot them, the questions change. Why didn't Pinky and Perky suss that?'

'I dunno. It didn't seem to be doing it to them in Newcastle.'

'Unless they just got so excited when they topped the first one they didnie even see it? Just leaped into bed the-gether and thought that was that? Shit, man. These machines could have fifty or a hundred thousand questions in them now. Each time the jackpot, a new programme. We're fucked. They've just wasted weeks of work. Slorach is going to have a fucking meltdown, man.' He mumbled some rap lyrics and held his hand in a gun-shape to his temple and made the sound of the firearm going off. I didn't get his references half the time. 'I'll get you a pint,' he said.

I was actually too stunned to move. Sad. And I felt awful for Slorach. I just sat there with a sick feeling as wee Gillan went up to the bar and then he came back with a Guinness. Extra Cold. Too quickly poured.

We sat for an hour or so just drinking, not even thinking of going to a machine. Then we moved to another pub round from the Travelodge we were staying at. That pub didn't even have a quiz machine which seemed bizarre to us. Then it felt good. Stress-free. Normal. Just two blokes drinking – the pressure that the expectation of constant money-making placed upon us was gone for the first time since Gillan and I met.

We had never really had a proper conversation which ranged beyond his vast sporting knowledge and the culture of *Thirst For Knowledge*. He talked a little about growing up in the Drum Estate. He frowned a lot and described difficulties with his parents. To my surprise they were fanatical Evangelical Christian members and he had been brought up in the strict brethren – which was deeply important to his parents. He hinted at personal issues from adolescence which caused his parents wild distress and how his Maw & Paw tried to control him. He had lived for long periods with an uncle who let him watch satellite sports channels non-stop. I assumed he meant pills and parties were his problem. He asked me about being a 'pape'. If there were parallels. I explained, No. That my mum was a Prod and my Catholic father had made me go through communion 'Just in case they are right, son.' I hadn't been to Mass in seven years. I still read the Bible – a mix of the beautiful and the terrifying, that crazy book. I still felt that a mystery lurked at the heart of our world, though. I just wasn't interested in proving it.

He found that amusing. Then he changed the subject, said, 'Just think. She's still out there. We're sat here chillin, bro – and she's still out there plugging and plugging. It's Slorach does it to her. She's a nice girl. She's great, she's fucking laid-back, man, but he puts the heat on her. Treats her like his bitch.'

I was shocked. I said that I didn't think that was really true. That they seemed deeply fixed to each other.

He chuckled, he called me a dreamer who saw what I wanted, and I noted his head fell forward a little with the chuckles. I don't think he normally drank that much. He said, 'I thought you were Ice Cube when I met you, man. You stepped up to that gadge in Ocean's Eleven, man, but you're okay. You dinnie like sports, which is weird. But. You just stepped up to that punk-ass. You just stepped up to that grimy MF, man. You don't fear who you step up to.'

'Gillan, I'm nothing like that. I'm a wimp with a temper, not a fighter.'

'Aye. You're gentle. That's what I see now. You're a gentle guy.

You're sweet really. And you're not.' Then he stopped and, as was his habit, changed the subject again. He said, 'LA, New York. Well, I was gonna go there, but I want to save money, though I'd like to see them for myself.'

I said, 'Watch yourself romanticising places. I respect you're from the Drum, but often you get somewhere and it's not as great as you think.' But then I thought of all the feelings the vale of the river Eden at Dairsiemuir had given me, that day with Slorach. 'If you are worried about the money drying up, Slorach will work something out. He's a fucking genius. There must be an answer.'

'Naw. I'm no even sure I need to go to LA. Look. I've been like a semi-quaver raver. I was like rattling with the pills in me. Now rap is my wee thing, but if I had a bit more to put in my money clip, so's I get some honey drip, I was thinking of getting myself some tarny lush wheels next, no quite a Cadillac. I was thinking of changing style and becoming a boy racer.'

I laughed out loud at him. 'Why not? If that's your thing.'

He shook his head, his myopic eyes looking ahead. 'They're on to it, man. They're on to us and anyone else who's bum-rushing the system, down in Ashby de la fucking Zouch. What kinda name is that for a toon, eh? That crew arenie daft. They know it was too easy. We just learn the questions and we tidy up. I mean, if you're a puggy saddo, going to the same pub every fucking day of yer life – which is what we've fucking become – you're gonna get roond it, aren't you? You might have sunk a hundred quid but you'll bust it and get fifty back. But they always win and they saw we had sussed it. The computers, Lennox. The computers are getting smarter, mate. That's where the future is if you want to make money. Soon they'll be in everything, man. They'll be able to have a computer that talks to another computer and just draws the questions down. There'll be nae quiz machines worth shit. It's dyin oot. Everything's dyin oot. Railway timetables too, man. They'll all be on one computer soon, in a machine, standing in the station that talks to ye like a cop, and they won't need a gadge like me or mental Slorach reading them train times out down the phone to losers, mate. It's coming soon. Ah fuck it, man. I just wanna get dusted like Schoolly D and forget about it all. I thought there'd be more money, but easy come, easy go.' He turned and looked at me. I didn't know if there wasn't a tear in his unfocused eye. Then to my utter shock he leaned at me and kissed me on the mouth.

His small young mouth was cold on mine for that instant, and I was actually indifferent, but I had to lean slightly backwards and turn aside in a gentle way, then, disappointed in myself, I couldn't help looking across the pub to see if anyone had noticed his clumsy move. There was a couple of old folk, over beyond a serving station stacked with sauces and cutlery, but no one had seen anything. He was still looking at me, trying to read me, I smiled and said, 'Gillan, you're very good at suddenly changing the subject, and right now, when you really could do with it, you're saying nothing.'

He chuckled. 'I'm sorry, man,' he said.

'No, you don't need to say that. It's okay.'

'I'm into everything, man.'

'Just high on life itself, eh?'

Then he smiled at me. 'You're odd. Are ye ever into it with a guy or not?'

I shrugged, 'I just refuse to judge you, Gillan. That's all it is, but nah. I'm hung up on a beautiful girl called Teresa. C'mon, mate, you're pissed. We'd better find Candice and talk through this problem we have.'

'Och, she'll be pumping that alphabet till fucking midnight.'

'Stay here then. I'll go find her. Don't lose your glasses.'

She was in the The Old White Swan. She wasn't at the machine. She was sat alone on a stool at a bench along the wall – so people couldn't see what she was reading – and her face was angrily buried in her own ring-bound Archives folder. As I approached she looked up straight at me and said, 'Something's wrong.' She came back with me to the pub Gillan was in. She started guzzling pints in her old style, her bad posture hunched over the glass. She must have been worked up because she suddenly leaned back and slid that jacket off her arms then kicked it in under the table. She had bare arms, strong and heavy, but with beautiful creamy skin.

Gillan still hadn't put his glasses back on and was a bit all over the place. I sat on a chair and Candice got in next to wee Gillan. But he still nodded at what she said. Her news was even worse. She had taken three jackpots and moved from machine to machine, no problem. She had come to The Old White Swan to find a player before her already on *Thirst For Knowledge*. She witnessed this player take the first five-pound jackpot, but then he wiped out and left the machine. She waited a polite few moments then stepped to the machine herself. She put in fifty pence. The questions she saw were totally unfamiliar to her.

She cursed over the top of her pint and told us, 'They've sussed. They've put in a geographical variation. A machine in York isn't on the same programme as Newcastle. That means they will be different in London, in Birmingham, in Brighton. And the machines are now drawing up new banks of questions, sometimes as soon as after the first jackpot has been hit. We are royally screwed. Basically, if no jackpot has ever been won, including the five-pound, it is conforming to the factory-set questions in Newcastle. If even the five-pound is won it is gonna be reprogramming itself before the next player. We only got straight runs through on these new machines today because nobody has ever won the jackpot on them before in any way. No one had even got to a fiver. That's what we did wrong in Newcastle. We didn't play the same machine twice because we thought that didn't matter. We just moved on to a fresh machine. The moment it gives out money now, it changes all the time.'

Gillan looked her in the eye. I noticed he'd had his glasses off so long the mark on his nose had evaporated. 'Candice. We're fucked. It's all over.'

She sighed. 'It doesn't look good. We need an inside person at the factory or something, to tell us where specific machines are going or... I dunno.' She carried on drinking. We all did. Somehow subjects drifted. She told a funny story about the band she used to play in, how they had performed at a small-town festival in a farmer's field near Mauchline. It was raining and a mist descended which was so thick the band couldn't see the audience and the audience couldn't see the band. They carried on playing their full twelve-song set – which included a cover version of Mister Mister's 'Broken Wings' – then, just before their triumphantly performed set finished, the mist lifted. The field was empty of a single person. Literally empty, except that the farmer had let the cows back in to graze and even they weren't interested.

I went to the toilet. When I came back round the side of that food station, Fossenkemper and Gillan pulled away from a snog too slowly for me not to notice it.

Thank God one of our luxuries when we elected to stay at hotels on jackpot sweeps was single rooms. To hell with twin beds and sharing. It would have complicated that cursed trip. My room was next to Gillan's, which makes you wonder why Gillan and Fossenkemper chose to use his room rather than her own, which would at least have placed the dead air of an empty room between us.

There were thumps and there was laughter, something was knocked over and there were cries. I didn't even try to resist, so to get it over with I stood on my bed and I put my ear hard against the wall. With dreadful timing, I clearly heard Fossenkemper's lager-heavy, educated voice against their bedhead command, 'Put your tongue right up my asshole and twist my nipple.' I listened no more and pulled the spare pillow over my head.

There was no point staying in York the next day with the machines barred to us. The train journey north was a tense one of ill health. First class was quiet, so the three of us sat in it at a table – as travelling railway staff on free passes often used to do. Our passes might be checked by the guard, but it was the unspoken culture that our fourteen free journeys a year were never stamped, thus our passes were never going to be used up unless you came across a really snotty inspector or were dumb enough to get in an argument about seats with a paying punter, then you would get one clipped.

There was virtually no conversation. Fossenkemper put her worthless Archive ring binder on the table but she didn't even open it. She went up to the buffet car to get bags of McCoy's crisps. She was only gone through the far carriage door a moment when Gillan said, 'Work out the rights and wrongs of this one. If ye'd come back with me then I woudnie have done that with yer pal's girl.'

'Fuck off, Gillan, you're a dickhead,' I softly replied. Yet he had a point – work out the morality of that.

I don't know what Slorach knew or sensed about the York Disaster, but of course he realised all his work had been in vain. Lorimer had taken over as torchbearer of our team, and he went to work, calculating which few old-generation machines remained in which pubs and how many jackpots might still be available. Travelling too far from Scotland now didn't seem worth the profit. Like Napoleon's, our empire was fast shrinking. We did hit a few old-generation machines now and again, but something had changed. The full enthusiasm of the early days was gone. The illicit gains didn't seem so illicit. Since all this had started the previous autumn, I had accumulated nearly four grand in a savings account, so I was willing to let things go.

About two weeks after York, I was working a back shift till ten in the evening. That whole week, my driver had been a guy I often worked with, a guy called Jackson Huxley, who has probably retired now, but I still shouldn't really name him. Yet I thought it was a remarkably cool name – and guess what? He was an incredibly cool guy. That name to me, it sounded as if he should have had his own amateur jazz-swing band or even his own radio chat show. It sounded to me like one of those names that an actor makes up because he shares his real name with another actor. You select two pleasing-sounding names and you fit them together. Jackson Huxley. It was such a great bloody name.

And much more than this, the guy was simply very, very good looking. He was so handsome. Probably in those days with all those males around (when we didn't have a single lassie train driver in our depot) – you were thought to be gay if you did so – but nobody ever commented on Jackson's good looks. He was like a bloody matinee film idol. David Bowie and James Dean mixed in there. The fine jawline peppered with stubble and the delicate, small, well-proportioned face. He had brilliant, cool hair – long, but not hippy-long, a mix of black and silver, so at least he didn't dye it – and you could see it was carefully cut so it swept back over his small ears. He was always touching it away from himself and his lantern jawline. Then his discriminating, drilling brown eyes (twenty-twenty vision: I asked), his trim, neat figure. This guy did not look like a train driver, more a Formula One racing driver, or a New York fashion photographer or a horse jockey. Fuck's sake, man, even his uniform looked good on him, as if it had been perfectly cut to fit only him. As if he took it to the tailor's to get it adjusted.

And he was a really nice guy; mellow. He never put me down for being a coupling chucker, he let me drive the engine if I asked, and he didn't have that acerbic, bitter edge that so many older, grumpy drivers had. I probably made myself suspicious in Ops by asking other drivers too many questions. Like, 'See Jackson. What does his dad do in life?'

'Whit?'

'Jackson. Do you know what his father did?'

'His faither?'

'Aye. Was he on the railway or the boatyards or what?'

'His faither? I don't have a fucking clue what his faither did. Why are you asking me?'

'I'm just curious how he got that name. It's a cool name.'

'He got the name cause his dad's surname is Huxley and his mither named him Jackson, detective. Any more questions?'

'He must be conducting a survey for that university he once went to,' old Tam Bruce said through his nasty beard.

I tried other approaches.

'Have you known Jackson long?'

'You what?'

'Have you known Jackson Huxley long?'

'Jackson? Aye, I've known him years. We was at the traction school together for the blue trains in 1974, when we were nineteen.'

'Where did he go to school, like where did he grow up in town?'

'Jackson? Old Python Lee Jackson? He's from Govan originally, is he no?'

'No. He's no. Jackson's frae Mosspark,' someone chipped in from behind a newspaper.

'Is he? Is Jackson from Mosspark? I never knew that. There you go. He's from Mosspark.'

Or I would try, 'What does Jackson do with himself outside the railway?'

'Jackson? Goes to the fitba.'

'Aye I know that. But other than a keen interest in the league, you know?'

'Other than fitba? What do you mean?'

'Has he got kids and that?'

'Fuck sake, University, are you thinking of proposing to him?'

'Does Jackson play five-a-side or anything?' I once asked some drivers.

'You putting a team together? Shunters versus nosey cunters?'

'You wouldnie know what team to play for there.'

Nobody seemed to know anything about Jackson of any noteworthiness whatsoever. Nor have any interest in him. Nor be willing to say any single negative or positive thing about him. He was an enigma. What worried me was: maybe he was just fucking boring? Hard to explain my immediate fascination with the man. And he had this sort of intense, forceful presence where – he just did exactly what he wanted, in a cool way. He always seemed to be reading was one thing. Not books, there was no point getting my hopes up there. He was just always looking downwards at the back sport pages of the *Record* or the *Evening Times*. But ALL the time. I mean literally all the time. He must have had bets on games running, because it was almost obsessive. And of course if he wasn't looking down, with the cool hair falling forward, into the sports pages of the papers, then he was peering down into the *Wee Red Book*. More football knowledge. Slorach maybe shoulda got this gadge on the team rather than fucking Gillan. Jackson either seemed to be looking ahead, at the signals on over the bridge, or his head was out the engine window, looking backwards as he reversed in, the hair hanging and held on the perma-designer-stubble of his jaw, or he was looking down, reading only those three sports features. The *Daily Record*, the *Evening Times*, the *Wee Red Book*. He constantly chewed gum as well of course.

In summertime, when the cabs were so hoaching hot on diesels (electrics were cooler), he would stand out on the platform by the open door of the cab, but with the head canted down, reading. And he had this way of folding the *Record* and the *Evening Times*. He folded them over tight, four times, almost as if he had ironed them on an ironing board, so just a small square of the paper was displayed. You sometimes see people who like crosswords do that to a newspaper, so they can quickly access it and work on it. I had actually seen Slorach do it, since he liked crosswords. But Jackson never touched a crossword, yet he folded the sports sections into these tight, wee squares. I know the practicality of why he did it. So he could slip the paper quickly into his driver's jacket pocket. Any time, the minute the engine was resting, it was out of his pooch with the square of paper and peering at it, onto the platform, it was only seconds till he reached into the side jacket pocket and out came the square of paper, and he was stood there, head down, not making eye contact. Like it was a devout prayer book.

Here's where it gets unhealthy, I started to develop a gruesome fascination with Jackson Huxley's wife. Terrible. Sometimes I would find myself thinking about her – imagining her perfections.

I could see her in my mind – I could hear her soft voice – the local accent. He was so cool, I concluded his wife must be a remarkably attractive lady. He did have a wife, cause he had mentioned she worked in Marks & Sparks. I had gone so far as to casually ask him which Marks & Sparks branch, and I then wandered round that branch on a day after Christmas in the middle of the bloody sales, trying to guess which assistant might be Jackson Huxley's fair wife. There were a lot of attractive sales assistants in their late thirties. In fact I did that twice in the shop after Christmas. Creepy. I had a strong hunch she worked in the hosiery and ladies' under-swear department, so every morning with no clothes on, in their well-appointed house, she would have a constant supply of the best stuff, wearing only the most delicately patterned, matching M&S underwear, standing with a steam iron at the ironing board, flattening off Jackson's newspapers into perfect squares. Though this was not possible, as how could she get that day's *Evening Times* to him?

Then one day in the spring – I remember we were tying off a train on Platform 3 – he quietly mentioned the inconvenience of next week's shift on the Carlisle run, as he couldn't drop the wife off in the car at her new branch. A bit too quickly I blurted out, 'New branch?' and maybe just for a second a frown came on his usually expressionless face. He said, 'Aye, did I no tell you they moved her to another branch just before Christmas there?'

I was so angry I could have got up and kicked the door of the cab shut and started shouting at him, 'Fuck's sake, Jackson, I demand you tell me more about yourself and especially your wife. Any photos of her on that holiday in Tenerife last year?'

Sometimes I worry about myself. One mild day in May, we were waiting long minutes on the signal. Jackson removed his jacket, took out the square of the newspaper and placed the jacket onto the secondman's console. It was a Class 47 we were going to take up off 7 and put over on top of some stock on 11. He was wearing a pale-blue shirt under the jacket, and I noticed how neatly the sleeves on that shirt were rolled up past his elbows. He had brown, tanned arms. How? Had his wife lovingly folded up those cuffs of his sleeves with her manicured fingers that morning before he left their house? Did they share trips to a solarium lying naked side by side? I was in love with her. No doubt about it. Was it possible to be in love with your sometime-workmate's wife, when you had not only never met her, but didn't even know her name? Nor anything about her? And in a way I knew nothing about him.

He stood up, said, 'Warm, eh? Watch when that signal's off, will you?' and jumped out the cab, leaving me on the engine. I stood up and peeked out the open cab door. He was standing a distance up the platform in the shade, towards the direction of the station. His face was down on the paper and he had his back to me. I crossed to his jacket. I knew he kept his wallet in the inside pocket. Polished brown leather. What if there was a photo of his wife in it? I almost reached for the jacket then I realised what I was doing, how it would look if he caught me, and I shuddered. I slumped down in the driver's seat and sighed. Then the single orange aspect on SZ5676 came on and the red went. I leaned out the window and I barked loudly, 'Jackson!' He was still faced away and couldn't hear, so I nudged a short blow on the horn. He didn't even look up from the paper square, just wheeled on his pointed leather shoes and strolled back, stepped up into the cab. 'Aye. You take her then, Pete, and stop her at the shunt.'

That night after the York Disaster, me and Jackson Huxley had a Class 40 engine up on Platform 10, waiting for release, and we were both stood out on the platform. Some trainspotters had come up the platform, written down the engine number and left again. Jackson and I looked at each other pitifully, then he stuffed his face back in his paper square. We were just going to put the 40 on the coaches right beside us there, on 11.

I didn't like the 40s after I started working on them. I was a bit scared of the brutes to be honest. They were powerful, long and heavy – the visibility was never the best. Jackson was telling me that there used to be a wee incline on 11 and that up till a few years back, if you took the air brake off a 40, with its weight it might slowly roll back just on its tonnage and it was quite nice for gently squeezing a coupling up, on its weight alone, but a few years ago heavy rain had got down onto that track and somehow the incline had vanished, or he couldn't find it anymore. The ballast could shift over the years, he was explaining.

Who should come up the platform then but Andy Irving, the Rutherglen rose-grower, the driver who inadvertently had christened the Rooster Clerk. He was going out on the train we were tying off.

All three of us stood outside by the flank of the engine, but clear of the fan vents and their talk fell to some of the legendary drivers of old out of the Central: James Callaghan and Paul Piden were Jackson's era, but Andy talked of older steam drivers like Teddy 'The Monk' Monkton, Nat Curran, John Penalty, drunken Matt Dolan – there was even a shunter mentioned, one John McRae, who'd taken a Britannia Class on his own down to the shed one night, through a galaxy of signal lights he just didn't understand. A tale which made any footplate people take a breath.

While they were talking, Andy suddenly nodded across to Platform 9 and said, 'What kinda trainspotter do we have here then?' I looked across and to my amazement saw John Robert Slorach. He was standing alone at the end of 9 by the final signals, before the gathering dusk began. He was talking, quite animatedly. But he was alone. Hand gestures and facial expressions came and then went. This was before our era of headsets and hands-free phones. Slorach was in full communication, but there was no phone involved. As the three of us stood staring across, horribly, I felt myself reddening. Slorach didn't appear to have seen me, and I was glad but felt ashamed at this relief. He was meant to be my friend.

Some of his monologue involved more joyous considerations and his face looked happy or full of gladness; but then he would slightly shift his standing position and his mood seemed to become more subdued, in fact it seemed frantic – a darker look came on his face. His lips moved urgently, pushing out words, but because of the engine on the Class 40 hammering away beside us we could not hear that beautiful voice nor the portent of those darker sayings.

I finally spoke. 'That is John Slorach. He was the guy who was station announcer for a couple of days and then started swearing at a punter over the tannoy who wouldn't stand back from the platform edge.'

For the first time ever, Jackson Huxley laughed easily and smiled. 'I heard about that guy, aye.' He chuckled again. 'That's the way to treat them.'

'He works the telephone enquiries now. They bolted him up there.'

Andy said, 'Aye, looks like he has a few fucking urgent calls he's dealing with right now.'

'Aye,' said Jackson. 'Train times on Mars.'

'Fuck's sake,' said Andy. 'That's no right, is it?'

Jackson shook his head, and for the first time I felt he was just a bit too slick and perfect.

'Aye he's got all his best mates there with him tonight,' Andy added.

Slorach had thrown an arm up towards the sky, as if he was worshipping the invisible moon; he muttered a few more things then turned and headed off back down the platform.

The signal went, but rather than pointlessly ride on the engine, after Jackson had taken her up and out of sight from under the canopy, towards the shunt signal, I just jumped down off the platform and crossed to the top of the coaches to wait. Andy Irving walked ahead down the ramp on 10, crossed the track at the easy bit, watching his footing on his old legs, then walked back up the ramp onto 11. I stood on the actual track of 10 so I could wave Jackson in, but my head was kind of numb and I felt awful about Slorach. I wanted to get off the shift and find out what was happening with him. Andy had walked down the platform a bit more, out of sight, to talk to some of the platform guys who were unloading a metal brute around the door of the first coach – a BG parcels van. I stepped over and ducked a bit just to check the bags on the coach.

How did Slorach get like that? Was that Fossenkemper's doings in York or was it the long shifts and implosion of his grand schemes? I would need to go see him and soon. I thought of those pills he was on, the pressure he was getting to keep working. He had to keep working to pacify his troubled and supportive parents. There were threats of a disciplinary or even dismissal on his sick record. And the way he had tried to crack the *New Gen*. How much was I responsible for what had happened in York? If an independent assessment was made – how? I turned aside, and the 40 was there. Looking back on it I have no idea how it got so close, nor why I was in the middle of the track, nor why I hadn't heard it. An 'uh' sound came out my mouth – a scared, child-like sound – and I tried to do a huge step backwards so I could throw myself clear, but my heel slid on a sleeper so I stumbled and it was just too late. I tried to fall to the ground at that point as we had been taught – against all instinct – to do. If you lie flat in mid-track a train will clear you unless you have a backpack on; but I was terrified and couldn't remember what side the low-hanging apparatus was on, on a 40. Then I was just struck. I felt insulted it happened so quick, and I recall I held out a ridiculous arm, as if I could just push the loco away from me. I was just struck so hard on my right arm I couldn't believe the force. I went down so smartly my cheek slapped into an oily puddle – the deafening noise of the traction motor was above me, and I screamed.

FOUR

'GOOD MORNING. BRITISH Rail Enquiries. How may I help you?'

'It's evening.'

'So it is. Sorry. Long day. How can I help you?'

'Yes, the evenings are drawing in.'

'No. They're lengthening actually. It's summer. How can I help you please?'

'How I can help *you*, darling?'

'Well, you can't. I'm here to help you.'

'No, darling, I am here to help you in whichever way you please.'

'I'm sorry?'

'Now you don't need to be shy.'

'I'm not.'

'Oooh. Exciting for us here. My girlfriends and I.'

'I'm sorry? Look. Where are you going, or when or why do you want to travel. Well, actually I don't really care why you want to travel, to be frank. I've had enough of that. I just need to know when you intend to travel.'

'Where do you want to go?'

'Home. This has been a twelve-hour shift.'

'Poor boy. Me too, love, a twelve-hour shift on the phone. But I could take you to heaven and back.'

'Look, are you sure you have the right number here?'

'Are you?'

'I didn't phone you.'

'Yes you did. Naughty boy. You know fine it's a premium-rate line, but none of you care. It's worth it to get you where you want to be.'

'No. I didn't phone you.'

'Yes. You did.'

'This is British Rail Enquiries.'

'Well, this is enquiries too. Enquiry into your soul. I want to tell you a story, a true story.'

'I don't have time for that, sorry. I'm way behind on my calls, and my supervisor will be on to me.'

'Your supervisor! Madam Pain. Tonight I'm your supervisor, and I'm going to tell you a story.'

'Where do you wish to travel to please?'

'What's the matter, not like the sound of my voice? You have a lovely voice. So look. Like you I have the calls coming in all night.'

'Like me?'

'And you can imagine. You know the score, don't you, the things you men want, all the things you seem to need to imagine? Petty in some ways, deadly in others.'

'Sorry, do I know you?'

'The things you want me to do for you and with you and with my girlfriends.'

'I think you'd better hang up. Or I will.'

'I don't think you will. Not till we're finished, so just you relax and keep the cap on the baby oil.'

Slorach looked around himself in the British Rail Telephone Enquiries Bureau. The same brittle fluorescent light, a lard-like cast bestowed. Fifty voices going.

Her voice went on, 'So I'm there and the next voice comes through and I answer. "Hello, it's Trixie here and what can I do for you tonight?" I just had a fantastic time – absolutely fantastic time with Malcolm. Not just Malcolm – his wife was listening in on the call too. Malcolm and lovely Jane. I shouldn't say, but exclusive to you, Slorach. From Croy. Oh, Croy, what are they doing out there with one another? I am just ashamed to think! Just. The three of us. Oh, it was an interesting call. We really should make tapes, but you punters wouldn't like that for obvious reasons.'

'Look here.'

'Listen now. I had a usual call and then came another, that voice. I frowned. I say, "Hi, I'm Trixie." So I listen to what he wants and it's as disgusting as usual. Not disgusting sexually – I don't have any squeamishness there. Slorach. Slorach, are you listening?'

'Hey. How do you know my name? Who transferred you?'

'I was transferred by fate. It's the usual power games. Having power over a woman. He wants to put his fingers into my hair and he wants to direct my head and you know where he wants to direct it and what I must do with my mouth when it gets there and he's going to push my head back a little and then push it in, then back, and that's when I recognise the voice. It's my father. It's my own father who I haven't seen in four years and he doesn't know I do this and I don't know he does this. What he's doing, what he's describing to me and what I'm describing to him and he cries out. He doesn't recognise the voice I put on, and a good few years of cigarettes, I suppose.'

There was a silence on the line. Slorach nodded. 'Go on please, caller.'

The voice continued, 'I hung up when I realised. Of course I did, but just for a second in that realisation who it was. I did not feel proud. I cried. I had to cry.'

'Okay. That is pretty rough, I admit,' Slorach said. 'That is pretty rough.'

'So that's when it happened. The next call, Slorach.'

'The next call?'

'Yes. The next one. It's the call above all calls. I have been waiting on it all my life. After I've made my own father imagine he's... the next call comes through. So you're just like me, Slorach. The calls keep coming in, but admit it. There's a special call you're waiting on, and it's not me. You can get me anytime on a premium-rate number, like my dad did. They say computers are coming and soon we'll be gone from the phone and you too – all our wee voices and all the things we said – all forgotten.'

Slorach said, 'Probably for the better. They aren't radio waves. They are lost forever – they don't travel on through space like vacuous DJs will.'

'John?'

'Hello?'

'Who's that, Slorach?'

'John? Who are you talking to on this call, please?'

'Is someone listening in? Are they getting a thrill listening in, like Jane from Croy, hearing her husband tell me what he wants?'

'John. Can you answer a call please? You are sitting on a dead line.'

'I am on a vital call.'

'John, you're talking but there's no one else there. Are you having problems with your headset?'

'Oh, to fuck with my headset.'

'Who is this, Slorach?'

'It's MacDowall, my supervisor. Spying on me as usual. Trying to get some tips on cultivating a personality.'

'Dirty voyeur.'

'He is a dirty voyeur. Fuck off, MacDowall.'

'So do you want to hear about the next call, Slorach?'

'I do.'

'That's when it happened. The minute I opened the line for the next sex call I felt it. There was music, and it was music like I'd never heard before, really, like bells in a celestial church and I don't know. I will never hear such music again – like long icicles chiming together, and then there was His voice, and His voice was a bit like yours in fact, but more – you know, that voice contained knowing, if you get what I mean, profound universal understanding, and He spoke to me, Slorach. He didn't want to know what my mouth was going to do. He spoke, Slorach. He said, "Trixie. I know your true name, I know your true self. Trixie is not your name; put aside these things of the common earth."'

Slorach said, 'Uh, uh.'

'"Not Trixie. Truth. Truth. I know the true person Trixie, and I know this bad life you find yourself in. I see every sparrow that falls. I saw every little bored sin you committed, Trixie, but now I have phoned you, I have come to save you, I have come to take your heart to a new place." It was God, Slorach. Or it was Jesus. They called me on a premium-rate sex line, Slorach, and he is going to call you too. You'll take the call soon.'

Slorach turned aside.

'Terminate the call,' MacDowall said.

'What?'

'Come and have a word in the office, John, I think you might need to go home.'

'What?'

'Come and have a word.'

'I'm on a call.'

'There's no one on the line. There's no one else on the line.'

'Yes there fucking is. God's on the line. It's the best call I've had in here.'

'The line is dead, Slorach. You're no doing your job. You haven't taken a single call since you started the shift. You're just talking to dead air.'

I was taken to the Victoria Infirmary in an ambulance, though I wanted to go home. Then I wanted Jackson Huxley to come with me to the Infirmary as well; he looked so shocked. For the first time I had got a reaction out of him.

The parcels boys and Jackson had pulled me out from under the engine onto Platform 10's running track, and I could actually sit up okay, but I couldn't move my arms. Andy Irving had his wits about him. He started shouting, 'If he's still breathing and even if he isnie, get a viz jacket on him, for Christ's sake, or Jackson and him are sunk at this time of night when the traffic inspector gets here.'

It was a wise point. No way at that time, even on a summer's night, should I have been working without a high-visibility vest on. I hadn't even been using a bloody signal torch. When you worked summer nights, just on the lip of the station canopy, the overhead lights seemed adequate. It was a bad habit that you could drift into.

Jackson was standing beside me, he kept repeating, 'Thought you were on the platform side, I thought you were on the platform side, just, ye ken, letting me come in onto it like we were just talking about on the incline. Fuck, I'm sorry, I didn't think. I, I just looked out the windae too late. I am so, so sorry. I thought you were on the platform.'

I knew what would happen if this didn't come out right. Jackson would be suspended pending an inquiry. 'Jackson,' I said, looking up at him, 'Jackson. Listen to us. I *was* on the platform. One hundred percent, this was my fault. My fuck up. I fell. I just fell. I was standing on the platform side. Lost my footing and fell like a stupid foal. I'm not going to let them pin a thing on you. It was my fault, and it was a fall. It wasn't a regulation malfeasance, I just fell off the platform in front of the loco, was unable to move, and that's what I'm putting on my statement, right?' No way was I mentioning that the loco hit me.

Andy Irving gave me a tight look then glanced away. He knew fine I wasn't up on the platform. Cause 10 was free, I was on the track to get in easy for the coupling. If there had been traffic on 10 then there was no way I would – or should – have been stood there. It was against regs, but I wasn't going to stop lying. I said to the lads, 'Aye, for fuck's sake get a viz jacket on me and give us a torch. Or chuck one down on the track there where I fell. I didn't even have a fucking torch on me.'

Getting a viz jacket onto a guy with a broken right arm and a severely strained left one is a bit on the painful side. They helped me to my unsteady feet and I could stand, though I was shaking with shock. A guy kneeled behind me at my arse holding a spare viz vest. I grimaced and forced my arms backwards a bit, and as gently as possible he slipped the armholes up both my arms till it was humped over my shoulders. I yelped a few times and saw Jackson wince.

'What happened?' Paddy Collins, a Celtic-supporting guard on Irving's working, had appeared up on 10.

I said loudly so they all heard, 'I'm an arsehole. This is not Jackson's fault. I was on 11 there and I tripped and I fell off the bloody platform right onto the track in front of the engine. There was nothing he could have done.'

'You been in the pub?' Collins asked.

'Nut. Not a drop in me.'

'They'll test ye up the hospital or here.'

'Not a drop.'

That guard was right, they took a blood sample at the hospital. I was lying in the empty men's ward, and the station's night-duty inspector actually turned up by my bedside at fucking midnight. Since I couldn't write or even use my arms, he had to transcribe my statement. I gave it. I fell off the platform.

He said to me, 'Shunter Lennox. I couldn't help but notice there was no traffic standing on Platform 10 at the time of the incident. It's not possible, is it, son, yer heid's got a bit of knock there and that ye were actually stood on running tracks to save you time coupling her up, and, I dunno, attention wandered a wee bit, maybe? There can be a lot of noise under the canopy, and maybe Driver Huxley wasn't looking back on that side as he fully and rightly expected you to be safe on the platform side of the curve there – as you should have been according to movement regulations.'

I looked at him gravely. 'That didn't happen, Inspector Wright. I was on the platform, and at the worst possible moment I took a step forward and lost my footing. I knew I was falling, so I tried to throw myself to the centre of the track to clear the wheels, get my head down, and that was the impact that done in my arm.'

'Aye, well, son, you shouldn't have been that close to the edge, but if you're saying this was just a fall, when there was no ice or rain, then it was a fall. Just goes to show, the closed-circuit television we have lower down the platforms is getting fitted up the top end there in a month or so. Shame we didn't have it the night. So. What you've said complies with what Driver Irving – as a witness – reported as well.'

He wrote it all down and asked me to read it. Since I couldn't hold the clipboard he had to hold it under my chin while I read through. There were two spelling mistakes he had made, and I most definitely did not point them out to him. I couldn't sign it either, so he wrote my name on the line in capitals.

They started giving me painkillers immediately after the inspector's departure, and I realised that had been deliberate, they were keeping me compos mentis for the interrogation – a bit harsh as I'd begun to hurt everywhere. Then I started to feel great, thoughtful, and to be honest, I got the best night's kip in a long, long time.

Guess who my first hospital visitor was the next day? By this time my arm was ringing like a brass band all on its own, so they had upped my dosage. It was bloody Lorimer! He had even beat my mother to the bedside.

'Aye, aye,' he smiled with the wrinkles going up the baldy head. 'So the shunting's going well for you.'

I laughed. 'How's Slorach doing? I saw him last night and he wasn't looking too hot.'

'Did you not hear? He's jacked in the railway. Let loose verbally on his supervisor and went up the road. He's losing his marbles, man. Apparently for a crack he had called OUT from the Enquiries Bureau to one of those premium-call jerk-off lines a few times, rapping with the lassies! Gillan was on the shift with him last night and, seemingly, Slorach lost the plot on the phone. The full works. Claimed he had God on the end of the line.'

I said, 'I bet God still wanted the Cheap Day Return.'

'Aye. Look. Slorach has got you presents.'

'What, have you been with him?'

'Course I have, we've just been hammering a few last machines in the South Side. Look what he's got ye.'

They were two brown-paper bags. In one were peanuts in their shells and in the other... hard-boiled eggs. I laughed. 'Oh, that's brilliant. It's a Laurel and Hardy joke. We're fans.' I was touched Slorach would respond so quick. How did he even hard-boil the eggs? Fossenkemper I guessed.

'Laurel and Hardy?'

'You never see the Laurel and Hardy, where Ollie is in hospital, all trussed up with every limb broken and Stan just brings him nuts and eggs? That's the joke. He can't eat them. It's such a thoughtless present.'

'Oh. He got you this as well.' He opened a paper bag from the newsagent and there was a disturbingly thick copy of *Playboy* in it.

'Fuck's sake Lorimer, my arms are buggered. One's bust. I'd have to turn the pages with ma fucking nose.'

'Aye, and what'll you do with the centrefold? Well, it's like the nuts and the eggs – that's the joke.'

'My mum's going to be visiting. You can't leave it here; take it away. For now. I want it back, mind. And say thanks?' From out of the newsagent's bag he then pulled another magazine. It was one I had sometimes seen he and Slorach consulting. *The Publican* trade magazine.

'Check this out. It's all Slorach can talk about.' He leaned a bit closer and held open the pages for me. It was a full-page advertisement.

Providence Hostelry Entertainment Presents
The Providence Box
From the makers of Britain's most successful arcade quiz game
Thirst For Knowledge

'What is it?'

'It's a new quiz machine for the pubs. Get this. Five pound a punt. FIVE-hundred-pound jackpot.'

'You're joking me. He can't be serious?'

'Aye, he's on to his next project. Him and Fossenkemper are making contacts with computer-science folk they knew at uni. You can see they have a new crusade.'

'Fuck's sake, Lorimer.' I smiled at him. 'You always were the only one of us with your head screwed on.' I frowned. 'Why did John not come and visit me too. I'd like to see him.'

'Are you for real? Those happy pills he takes, man, and then forgets to take, he won't set foot in a hospital, he thinks one look at him and they'll be making up a bed for him in the psych ward.'

'Aye, he might have a point.'

'How long are you in for then?'

'About a week they reckon. It's about the bruising more than the break, and this arm is sprained but should come back.'

'Lucky bam, off the work on the sick pay. Just as well your arms are broken or Slorach would have you round the pubs tomorrow plugging the multiple choice.'

They seemed to up my painkillers. After Mum left to get the train back up to Inverness, I was feeling quite ethereal by evening visiting. This nurse – a really nice lady from Ghana called Mary – held a wee carton of orange juice under my chin so I could drink it out a straw, told me I had a lot of very bad bruising on my back that I wasn't seeing. She peeled an egg for me.

What seemed to be hours were passing. Later a figure appeared at my side. He was already sat down. 'Jackson,' I said. My head immediately swivelled to his right and I stared at the space where his wife should have been.

'How are you doing, man?' he said in that soft, cool voice.

'Where's your wife?'

'Eh, I never asked her along.'

'Och, Jackson. You should have.'

'Oh, okay. If you don't mind?'

'Don't mind. Jackson. It's been a privilege to have been run over by the most handsome train driver in Scotland. I've got to tell your wife that myself.'

He burst out laughing. 'Aye, they told me you were on quite a few painkillers.'

'Fucking right, man, they should give them out on the railway when we clock on.'

He laughed again, 'Aye.' Then his voice went sober. 'Especially if you're working with fucking me. They were saying yer right arm's broke but it's clean. You're gonna be okay, eh?'

'I'll be fine, man.'

'Look, Pete. I feel awful, and I've got to get it aff my chest. Hope you'll forgive us.'

'What? You haven't left your wife, have you?'

'Eh, no. What's the wife to do with it? Look. I kenned fine you were waiting for me down on the track on 9. I'd of done the same myself, and I was coming in. Thing is. I was reversing in and… I was scoping the form on the football scores. Ken? I fill out my coupon a lot? I don't know if you've noticed but I fill out my coupon – you know? – and I take a wee interest in the football scores.'

'Do you? I hadn't noticed,' I said.

'Aye, I like to check the scores on all the divisions. England too. So I was coming back in, and I'd the scores there down on the console by the fault lights which were bright on that one, so I could read them and was just having a wee ding at the scores, and next thing I know I'm in past the platform signal, and I fucking rammed the air brake on, man. I didnie ever look back. I didn't look back once, son. I'm so sorry, and I seen what you told the inspector. I mean, I'm back on shift nae questions asked, but I feel, I feel that's no the whole story and you went covering for me.' He sounded close to tears.

'Jackson. It was my fault, man, it was my fault.'

'Are you sure? I feel awful.'

'Jackson Huxley?'

'What?'

'Keep up with the scores. It's good to have an interest.'

Was it the next day? I'm not too sure. I opened my eyes, and there she was. I said out loud, 'Mrs Huxley. You've come, Mrs Huxley.' She was fucking beautiful. Stood at the side of the bed looking down at me. Pools of emotion on her face. 'I want to say. It was an honour to be run over by the most handsome train driver in Scotland.'

'Peter? Look at you. What have you gone and done to yourself this time?' She seemed so upset. It was amazing. While my feelings for Mrs Huxley were growing, she too must have had similar passions for me building up in the house, as she lay in her underwear on the John Lewis duvet, as Jackson told her all about his fantastic days working the pilot with wonderful me at the Central. 'Peter,' she said again, and her manicured fingers came out and touched my face. It was Teresa. It was beautiful Terri, my ex. The beautiful bisexual dabbler with the lovely tattoo on her shoulder who still went to Mass every couple of months.

'Terri,' I whispered and I began to cry at how gentle her face always was.

Things changed. Not just with me and Terri – with the world. The big old ball is always turning. I took the sick as long as I could – six weeks – milked some money back off the railway. Gillan would have called it 'payback time'.

Once I had my left arm working and the right in a sling, I went back and lived in Terri's flat. The girls there were a bit put out, though, so Terri and I moved into a flat together – with my *Thirst For Knowledge* takings we could get a decent place.

The railway started to give me gyp and made it clear they weren't letting me back on the engines but were very happy to provide me with other positions. Well. One. In the British Rail Telephone Enquiries Bureau. So that was the end to that song. I was out of there.

Me and Slorach were gone from the railway and Fossenkemper wasn't far behind. She and Slorach ended up living together in London for a while – an uneasy move. Gillan found a boyfriend – I heard through Lorimer – and ended up in Spain with him running a bar.

All the varieties of diesel and electric engines started to vanish from the railways, and they split the network into different private companies so the timetables were a welter of confusion and the fares framework made no sense. The chief engineer of the railway, who used to live in a decent detached house, now owned a grouse estate in the Highlands. Then suddenly home computers arrived and things called modems and phones you could carry around and never escape from. I probably just sound like an old stick-in-the-mud, but I mention it for a reason.

If you have a gambling addiction, like Slorach or like Jackson Huxley, in the past it was a sort of physical addiction. It was attached to locations: to the bookies, late-night casinos, gambling nights, pub machines.

When gambling went online it was not a fair wind that blew for John Robert Slorach. You could bet anytime, anyplace. Apparently his attack on *The Providence Box* bore some fruit for a while, but as the possibilities widened out on the internet, new ways of gambling appealed twenty-four hours a day. Slorach saw it as more opportunities for winning, but that meant he spread his money more thinly and lost more. Fossenkemper moved on. Slorach somehow owned an apartment in Southend, but that got sold off to be pumped online. By early 2003 he was back in Dairsiemuir.

I still saw Lorimer every now and again. It was nice, for old times' sake, to meet him in the pubs near the old Central. He was holding onto his seniority at the ticket office. There had been no Friends Reunited for our group, and it was Lorimer who broke the news to me in The Horseshoe Bar that it had been a sudden private funeral, so that's why he never tracked me down.

Because he was railway, Lorimer had somehow got hold of all the details. Horribly, he had even seen a copy of the post mortem, and from that he let slip a detail I have never been able to forget. Money gone, the taxman on him big time, parents selling equity on that lovely house, electronic addictions raging, his medications reducing in effectiveness, Slorach had taken himself one night on that walk I shared with him all those years before down into the beautiful vale of Eden. He had sat in the middle of the up line, right by that bridge we crossed, where he used to wait in hope of the big Deltics as a kid. I don't know how long he had to wait on that line that night, but the train which came, came from behind him as he sat. He was facing away from it by chance or by design. That's what hurts me most, and I don't know why. It angers me too that a driver had to be involved. It was as if – even though Slorach was only railway for a short time – he was exerting some sort of regressive revenge upon all those train journeys he once took, all those timings he once gave out across the telephones, until only that final night schedule was left for him.

THE
PROVIDERS

IRVINE WELSH

ELSPETH RUTHERFORD, IN tight, long, off-the-shoulder black cocktail dress, heavily made up and a little lit up, distractedly loads the dirty Christmas dinner plates and pots into the dishwasher. On the island worktop, the carcass of a turkey congeals and other leftovers sweat in dishes. She would have binned the lot straight away. Disinclined to refrigerate old food, Elspeth particularly finds turkey seconds and thirds unbearable. One day of that rubbish was more than enough for her, she thinks, then contemplating her reflection in the glass patio doors. Sucks in her stomach. Festive bloat is digging in. No question. At New Year she will fast and get back to the gym and yoga. It is her age, she grimly considers; easier to put it on, harder to shed it. Thinks about just throwing the turkey in the bin now.

No, give it time.

Play the game.

Greg always insists that it's a crime to waste good food. Scanning across the kitchen area and its island, granite worktops and insert appliances, to the spacious lounge area where she can see her husband engrossed in his iPad. With the light shining up in his face, four years her senior at forty-two, Greg, in a white shirt and fawn slacks, is suddenly looking old. The light shows an intact hairline, but now so thin in contrast with the bushy brows. The lines are deeper and the bags heavier under the wrecking uplit glow. A moment of frozen fear strikes Elspeth in the chest. Then Greg looks up and over at her and smiles. To her relief, he is somewhat restored; she can envision not just the young man she'd fallen for, but the boy she's only known from photographs or sees in their sons, particularly Thomas.

The Christmas tree already looks shabby – Chairman Miaow, their imperious Siamese cat, has never learned, or become inclined, not to attack it – augmenting the precipitous air of decline Elspeth detects in her environment. Even the pampered feline has jumped ship, wandering around outside somewhere, in spite of the cold, or, more likely, having located a neighbour's warm front room. Cats aren't pets. They came and went, a bit like teenagers. Elspeth thinks of her two boys, George and Thomas, dozing contentedly upstairs. Dreads the onslaught of their puberty. Glancing at the cat flap in accusation, Elspeth then pushes her nose against the large French windows. All she can see is blackness, obscuring the patio garden, where she shamefully wishes to go to smoke one of the cigarettes in the pack she'd bought yesterday. Well, it was a stressful Christmas Day with her mum, and much worse was yet to come.

Apart from the tree, the lounge portion of the large room is dominated by a roaring log-and-coal fire and a large flat-screen TV, switched off, and a big, mounted Van Gogh print. Two large, plush sofas curve in luxuriant L-shape, augmented by a solitary armchair positioned by the fireplace. An oxygen tank and mask stand beside it. The furnishings include a sideboard and bookcase and a big, rectangular glass-topped coffee table. At his iPad, Greg enjoys stretching out on this luxury couch, looking at his screen. It's something he never gets to do enough, a rare break from his stress-filled middle-management job.

– Forty-five people dead in an earthquake in Iran. On Christmas Day, he shakes his head. – You'd think they'd just let up for one day. Aye... the game isn't straight.

Elspeth tops up her glass of wine from a bottle sitting on the worktop. She moves over towards the French windows. Turns to Greg. – It sounds horrible, but I don't want them here!

– Show some compassion, Elspeth, Greg looks at her in pain. – They'll be refugees, fleeing a humanitarian crisis, and they'll have to go somewhere. We Scots have a proud and noble record...

– I'm no talking about refugees, Greg, Elspeth steps over into the lounge area, – I'm meaning Frank and Joe! I don't want them in the house, even for a drink. I've lost count ay the number ay Christmases they've ruined. And it's been such a nice day...

Greg rises and lowers his iPad to the settee. – It's Christmas! They're family! Your own brothers! Besides, you invited them.

– And what a bloody mistake that was, Elspeth laughs sardonically. – It was only because Mum kept on at me. The next time I do something like that because it's a special occasion and I get a wee bit sentimental, do me a favour and stop me!

– You aren't that easy to stop when you set your mind on something! Greg notices a red stain on his white shirt. Maybe it was the wine.

Elspeth smiles and gratefully drops herself on Greg's lap. She wriggles her buttocks, grinding his groin. A stirring insinuates, and he raises his eyebrows flirtatiously. But quickly distracted, she suddenly springs up. – Fuck! I just wish we'd left it at us and Mum and the boys!

Greg rises to go in for a comforting embrace and kiss, but groaning, creaking sounds begin to emanate from the lobby. They pull apart like disturbed teens and look over to the door. Elspeth skips across to open it. Her mother Val, billeted in the downstairs bedroom, is trying to use a small toilet, which is packed implausibly with a shower and sink under narrow stairs. – Alright, Mum?

A faint, croaky voice, – Aye... fine... it's awfay cramped, but ah'll manage... be through in a minute.

Elspeth closes the door, moving back over to the kitchen area, waving a vodka bottle at Greg, who shakes his head in the negative. He picks up his tablet. – I suppose we just have to suck it up... his voice drops to a whisper and he looks to the hall, – for your mum's sake.

– Shouldnae mix vino and voddy... fuck it, it's Christmas, dry January ahead... Elspeth says to herself, filling her glass and moving over to stand close to Greg, who has sat himself down on the settee. Suddenly overwhelmed, she chokes up. – I know... it could be her last Christmas... That's why I dinnae want them ruining it. All her life she's had nothing but hassle fae the men in her family; my dad, God rest him, even my bloody granddad.

– And now Frank and Joe.

– And now Frank and Joe, Elspeth confirms, in a wide-eyed stare.

– Well, Frank's doing well since he left prison. It seems like this art thing is paying off for him, Greg contends, evidently impressed. – Every time I google him there's more on him! It's a pretty incredible success story, for such a violent man to find salvation in art.

– But it's total pish, though, Greg! He'll never change, and Elspeth shakes her head in disdain. – His art stuff's a joke, he's just conned a few bleeding hearts that like to hear sob stories. He'll be back in the jail soon: he's nae self-control. Neither has Joe.

– Joe's an alcoholic, and Greg grabs his glasses case from a small table by the side of the couch. He starts wiping his lenses. – It's a disease. This is a bad time for him, Christmas.

– Aye, because everybody else's pished tae and he cannae get the attention he feels he deserves.

Greg laughs bleakly, though there is something in what Elspeth says. The marginal in society were not exempt from the crippling disease of narcissism that now polluted all aspects of our culture and politics. How could they possibly be? – No, I meant because the temptation to overindulge is all around him. And Frank, well, at least he'll have his new girlfriend along to keep him in order!

– You always see the best in people, Elspeth says, looking at her husband in tender, if slightly sad, appreciation. – I sometimes wish I could be more like you. But then again you never grew up in my family… and she starts to sob softly.

– C'mon, sweet love of mine… Greg pats the space on the couch next to him.

Elspeth doesn't respond. Instead of joining him, she moves behind the large Christmas tree, peering out at Greg with a smile, playing hide and seek. But he is back into his iPad tablet, so Elspeth turns and strides back over to the kitchen, silently opening the patio doors and stepping outside. The front-porch light trips on. Hunching against the cold, slightly enjoying its bitter assault as evidenced by the goose bumps on her arms, she sparks up a cigarette.

Greg shivers as a sweep of ozone invades the room. Returns briefly to his tablet before going into a shuddering spasm. – It's freezing!

But she doesn't hear him.

Greg rises puffing out his cheeks as he steps towards the doors, watching, courtesy of the deck-mounted floodlight, Elspeth's cheeks buckle inwards as she takes a drag, then another. She's oblivious to him, looking at the cigarette in her hand, then, in a fit of rage, angrily stubbing it into submission against the wall. Coming inside, Elspeth closes the doors.

– That's better, Greg trumpets as he heads back to the lounge area and his couch.

In the kitchen, Elspeth runs the cigarette under the tap, then puts it into the rubbish bin. Returning to the lounge she sees Greg look at her in faint accusation. – I know, I know, I've started again… Frank and Joe have got me a fuckin bag ay nerves already!

Greg registers her swearing with a disdainful frown, knotting his thick brows together, looking to the ceiling in mild reprimand.

Elspeth knows he doesn't like the boys to hear her swear. She doesn't either. She's about to apologise, but then there's a rustling sound at the door, followed by laboured breathing. The handle keeps turning but the door doesn't open.

Elspeth heads out to assist. She affords entry to Val – frail, stick-thin, hunched-shouldered with her chemo wig slightly askew. Her mother, wearing a quilted dressing gown, nightdress and slippers, is breathing heavily. – Some door that… like trying tae get intae Fort Knox, bichrist…

– Aye… so you managed alright, Ma?

Val moves over to the fire, wrapping her skinny mole-blotched arms around herself. – Aye, fine. Just thought ah'd be mair comfy like this. It's got awfay cauld in here!

Greg looks to Elspeth in an 'I-told-you-so' manner.

– I just stepped out for a minute. It'll warm up again. C'mon,

Elspeth assists her mother, easing her down into the armchair. Val sits down but is exhausted by the effort. Elspeth holds up the mask.
– Ye want some ay this?

– Aye...

Elspeth helps Val put the mask to her face. Watches her mother slowly take in some oxygen. – There ye go, Elspeth coos, suddenly aware she's talking to her mother as if she's a child and uncomfortable at this. – It's like one ay they things ye used to get at the big raves. Mind, Greg, that one they had Ingliston, back in the day, where ye could get the oxygen... or helium...

– Rezerection.

Val lowers the mask. – Well ah'm no at any bloody rave!

– Naebody's sayin that, Ma.

– No, raving wouldnae be your thing, Val, Greg offers. – Would it be rock n roll or the hippy era? What was your time then, Val? Beatlemania?

Val looks at him, face pinching in offence. Says nothing.

– She liked Elvis, Elspeth contends. – Ay, Ma? Elvis Presley.

– Wisnae bad. Till eh goat fat.

– That was the drugs, but, Ma.

– Drugs, Val croaks, looks to her daughter in impatience, – what drugs make people fat?

– Some can, though, Val. Cortisone, Greg explains. – My dad ballooned when they gave him that. There are drugs that slow down the metabolism. You get fluid retention.

– Well thuv gied me enough drugs, but ah've no got fat, Val raises her spindly arms in the air. – Look! Wasting away tae nowt here!

Greg goes back to his iPad. – 'Suspicious Minds'. Did you like that one, Val?

– Wis awright.

– What was your favourite? We can put it on here. Wired for sound, you see, he looks to each side of the fireplace and an in-built set of speakers. – Can do it all from here. Spotify. From my iPad. What's your favourite Elvis number?

– Ah'm no wantin tae pit yis tae any trouble.

– Not at all, Val, Greg upturns his palms, – it's absolutely no bother whatsoever. Spotify. That's the beauty of it. It's the polar opposite of trouble! Just one click: this is the internet age!

– My ma doesnae ken about aw that stuff, Greg, Elspeth downs her vodka. It burns and tastes bland after the wine. That's the one: she'll open another bottle when she finishes that spirit.

– Doesnae ken about what, Val protests. – Ah ken aw about that internet. They put us on a course. For senior citizens! Up at the library!

– Did they, Elspeth says, at the worktop, opening a bottle she's taken from the fridge, – Leith library?

– Aye… Val says, then changes her mind. – Naw. MacDonald Road.

– You never telt me that.

– Well they did. N ah like that internet, but just doon the library, like. MacDonald Road. Ah widnae have it in the hoose, but, she scowls.

Greg winks at her. – Surfin the net, Val!

Elspeth points at her mother in accusation. – Ah hope it's no that online bingo you're at!

– Naw. Ah've tried it, Val says. – It's no the same when ye cannae be there.

– A bit like football, Val, Greg says.

A silence follows.

– So what's it be, Val, Greg holds up his iPad. – I've every single one of Elvis's hits right here!

Val looks grudgingly thoughtful. – 'Hound Dog'. Or mibee 'Jailhouse Rock'. Ah dinnae ken.

– Shall I play 'Jailhouse Rock'?

– If ye like.

Greg taps into his iPad. 'Jailhouse Rock' plays. – *Voilà!* He sings along to the opening lines.

Val seems massively underwhelmed. – The wee felly's asleep?

– Aye, Elspeth explains, – they wanted to stay up and see their Uncle Joe and their Uncle Frank, but like that's gaunny happen now… She looks at the clock.

– Well, Christmas. Ye never can tell, Val contends. – They've their ain families tae see.

– Aw aye, Frank and Joe, the great family men!

Val looks like she's going to take exception to her daughter's comment. Then the doorbell rings, and she sits up, straight-backed, in vindication.

Elspeth rises and heads through the alcove hallway to the front door. She yanks it open to see her brother Frank standing before her. He's clad in a brown designer leather jacket, and has a dark blue scarf and gloves. Her first thought is that he looks well. He unzips the jacket and removes the scarf, indicating he's lost a burgeoning paunch and seems taut and muscular. Yet even the smile round his mouth can't conceal he's as flinty-eyed as ever. But what really grabs Elspeth's attention is the youthful, elegant-looking blonde woman by his side. Dressed in a long, black coat and scarf, her magnesium hair beams under the lamp on the doorstep.

– Frank. You're looking well, come in.

Her brother steps inside, looking her up and down, and at first it seems as if he's going to reciprocate the compliment, but then appears to decide against it. Elspeth notes this as he settles for, – Aye, merry Christmas, Elspeth, as he looks to his companion. – This is Melanie.

– Merry Christmas! Melanie speaks in a generic American accent, stepping inside and removing her coat to reveal a light-blue designer T-shirt and some stretch jeans.

Elspeth regards them, taking the coats and pegging them up on the vestibule hooks. – Right... so you're the famous Melanie, then.

– Yes. Well, I dunno about famous, but I'm certainly Melanie, she says as Frank closes the door. – Pleased to meet you.

– You too, Elspeth says as Frank hands her a bottle of wine. – Very nice, she says, leading the couple through to the lounge. 'Jailhouse Rock' is still playing. Greg rises to greet them. – Frank! Merry Christmas!

– Aye, you n aw, Frank looks to the speakers. – Trying to make me feel at home?

– No! It was for Val, Greg laughs nervously. – I'll turn it down.

As Greg lowers the volume, Frank looks at his mother, bending down to hug her.

– Let ays get a cuddle ay ye. Yir still ma bairn, Val screeches as she fastens arthritic, hooked fingers tightly around the back of her second-born son.

– Still got a grip on ye, Ma, Frank says.

Melanie smiles at them, then looks to Greg. – I guess you must be Greg, right?

– The one and only!

Val is now blinking from Frank to Melanie, like a client in a social security office who can't see the numbered digital display and has to ascertain if it's her turn.

– Ma. This is Melanie, Frank introduces them. – Mel, this is my ma.

– Hi, Mrs Begbie, pleased to meet you!

Val starts to speak but it disintegrates in a rasping croak, like a student band tuning up for their first gig with no sound engineer in the house. – Call… me… Val…

– I beg your pardon?

– Call me… Val…

– I'm sorry… I can't make out… Melanie moves closer and squats down.

All eyes fall nervously on Val, who screams, – CALL ME VAL!

– Great! Val! Melanie straightens up.

Greg is skittish, almost dancing around, as he points to the kitchen area. – Drinks! Melanie?

– Just water for me thanks.

– Are you sure?

– Yes.

– Oh… right. Still or fizzy?

– Tap water is fine.

– Oh, I think we can do better than that, Greg's face puckers. – There's some Highland Spring here…

Melanie dispenses an X-ray smile. – I really like the Edinboro tap water.

– I thought being a health-conscious Californian you'd prefer filtered, bottled water. It's from a natural spring!

– Honestly, tap water is good, Melanie shakes her head, lifting her palm up.

Val turns to Frank. – Aye, you've goat her well trained!

Frank squeezes Melanie's hand. – Other way around.

Greg looks to his brother in law. – So, Frank, what's your poison?

– Water's fine by me tae n aw. Tap water... naw... tell ye what, I'll take some ay that Highland Spring.

Elspeth gapes at him in disbelief. – What?

– Sacked the peeve a while back.

– You? You've stopped drinking? Elspeth laughs loudly, slapping her own thigh. – Tell ays this is a joke, right?

– Naw. I don't drink alcohol these days, Frank smiles to a brow-raised Elspeth then at an open-mouthed Val, who clutches her mask as if it might be torn from her skeletal hand. – Been a few years now.

– Well, it's Christmas, Elspeth declares, – so ye have tae have one. A wee yin.

– I don't drink alcohol. Water's fine.

– It's supposed to be Christmas! You'll have a wee yin, Elspeth insists. – Wi muh ma! We've no seen ye for years!

Her brother stands like a slab of marble. – Never touch the stuff these days.

– What dae ye mean, Elspeth asks. – Are you telling me you're an alcoholic? Do you go to AA?

– Never bothered with any of that. Just got fed up with it and stopped, and Frank looks at his sister with a cold smile. – Just like that, and he snaps his fingers.

Elspeth keeps her gaze on him, in silent standoff. A nervous Greg intervenes. – Water it is!

– Ah'll take some of that Highland Spring off ye, Frank offers as Greg heads over to the kitchen area.

– Mum'll have a wee gin with me, Elspeth looks at Val, then challengingly at Frank. – Christmas spirit!

– Ah darenae, Val purses her dry lips. – It makes me sick, wi aw the medication ah'm on.

– Seeing as it's Christmas, but! C'mon, Mum!

Val looks skewered. Her creased face turns to Elspeth. – Maybe a wee yin then.

– Dinnae take one if ye dinnae want one, Frank contends, turning to her. His mother, he decides, is rotting not only from the inside, but externally too. It's as if cancer and gravity are slugging it out in a prizefight in which neither is prepared to concede defeat. – Nae law says you have to drink.

– Of course she wants yin, Frank, Elspeth pushes it, nodding her head vigorously. – It's Christmas, ay, Mum.

– A wee gin tae sip might be nice, Val says, her eyes haunted as her mouth buckles inwards, crater-like. – Jist tae sip, mind.

– See? Elspeth glares at her brother and heads to the kitchen area, where she helps Greg prepare the drinks, making sure to pour herself one. Yes, white wine was a better bet than the vodka. She refills her wine glass, takes a sip. Then Elspeth pours some Gordon's, trilling in saccharin ecstasy, – A gin and tonic for my ma at Christmas!

As they settle down on the settee with their libations, an uncomfortable silence lodges. On the hour the clock chimes with disconcerting loudness. To Elspeth's chagrin, Greg goes over to the kitchen worktop and puts the remains of the turkey dinner into the fridge. – Waste not, want not, he says, before he looks to Frank. – So where did you guys have your Christmas dinner?

Frank looks to Melanie, urging her to explain. – Some artist friends in the New Town have a big apartment, a beautiful big Georgian home. We were there.

– Aye, heard that they are awfay drafty those auld places, cause they cannae pit in double-glazed windaes due tae the conservation, and she points to her big windows and patio doors.

– No, Melanie insists, – this place was so warm. Very well sealed. No drafts at all. It was great, huh, Frank?

– Terrific spread, Frank says, patting his stomach. – They cooked a chicken, pit it in a duck, cooked the duck, pit it in a turkey, cooked the turkey, pit it in a goose, cooked the goose.

– Aw separate, Elspeth muses. – That would take yonks!

– Naw, aw the gither, Frank says.

– Well the wey you sais it, it made it oot tae be separate.

– Then I humbly apologise for giving the wrong impression, Frank says formally, smiling at Melanie, who fights to keep a straight face.

As Val looks intrigued, Elspeth's face screws up. – That's maybe a wee bit excessive!

– Just a little, Greg smiles.

– All the rage these days, Frank states. – Besides, Christmas, ay. Went doon a treat, and he slaps his flat abdomen again.

He's showing off that he's no got a gut any mare. Elspeth is driven to look at Greg's expanding waistline. It was sitting at a desk all day, eating rubbish doughy rolls that they called Italian names like *panini* and *ciabatta*, to give an illusion of Mediterranean wholesome health, when they were just cheap flour and fat, gloopy cheese cremated under hotplates. And her Greg was too exhausted when he got in from proper work to be able to exercise. Not like Frank with this art nonsense. He could please himself. Get up when he wanted, work when he liked, train in an empty gym during the day, eat proper food. A man like that, who had spent his life brutalising others. It was beyond unfair. She looks at her husband, experiencing him as both a valuable servant and pitiful victim of society.

– I expect it would be an American thing, Greg is offering, as he looks at Melanie. – We tend to import all our ideas from you guys!

– I'd never heard of this practice till I came to Edinboro, Melanie confesses. – And goose is the traditional Christmas bird from these islands. It's the turkey that's native to America.

Val, who has placed her mask under her chin, making it appear in the crumpling light like a blistering display on a scavenging vulture, looks at Melanie. – What?

– The turkey is a bird that's native to America.

– So we bring aw they Christmas turkeys ower fae America!

– No, Val, they are farmed over here, I expect, Greg ventures. – Remember Bernard Matthews from Norfolk turkey farms. Bootiful!

– Was that no the boy that blew his brains oot, Frank asks.

– No, that was Ted Moult. Everest double glazing. Crackers.

– Must have been bloody crackers tae dae that, Elspeth gasps.

– No, honey, Greg shakes his head, – he advertised crackers. And he was a farmer; they traditionally struggle with depression.

– Of course, ah cannae eat much, Val says, – no these days. I used tae eat like a hoarse, though.

– She means a horse, Frank whispers in Melanie's ear.

– I kind of figured that, she smiles back at him. Picks a piece of lint from his shirt.

Elspeth has been observing the exchange. – So, where did you two lovebirds meet then, she asks, shuffling to edge of her seat. – Gie us aw the gory details!

The rasping tone of his wife, her tight facial expression, at odds with the loose body language she displays as Elspeth flops backwards into the couch, draping her arms over its back, disturbs Greg. – Honey, don't, he protests.

– It's just a simple question, Greg!

Melanie gazes deeply at Frank, whose uncharacteristic coyness both fascinates and repels the watching Elspeth. She looks intently from one to the other, as Val picks up her oxygen mask. – That's okay, Melanie says. – I was an art therapist and I also curated the show where we first exhibited Frank's paintings.

– Yes, I read the piece about you in the *Scotsman*, Greg says. – Well done, Frank!

Val holds her mask off her face. – He was ey good at drawing. As a bairn, likes.

The eyes of the room's occupants fall on Frank. – Wisnae that good, he shrugs.

– Ah mind ay that painting ye did ay the man ootside the pub. That yin wis good!

– Was awright, Frank laughs. – Wonder where I got the inspiration for that?

Val's face crumples. She seems to be going to speak, then decides against it.

– I liked Frank's work, Melanie explains, – and I got a collector friend interested. He purchased a couple of the pieces. Obviously, they wanted to meet the artist and… she looks to Frank.

– Melanie met me in prison, he says bluntly.

Elspeth rolls her eyes, and rises to recharge her wine glass. – Aw aye, here we go!

Greg shoots Elspeth a look of dismay.

– Then I got out, Frank shrugs, – intae the halfway house.

Val loudly purses her parched, pleated lips. – Thought ah'd see mair ay ye, that's aw ah'm sayin.

– I'm afraid that's my fault, Mrs Beg… Val, Melanie explains. – Frank's been spending a lot of time with me. We've been renting a flat in Islington.

– Oot by the airport, Val says. – The Royal Highland Show. Ah widnae fancy bein stuck oot thaire, but each tae their ain. Ah suppose it's easy for you tae get ower tae America.

– That's Ingliston, Ma, Frank raises his voice. – Islington's in London.

Val looks a bit soured at this revelation, as Frank and Melanie slowly entwine their fingers. – Look, it's cairds on the table time, Frank sighs, raising his eyes in a spirit of tired divulgence. – We're getting married and we're moving tae California. Mel's visa for here runs out soon, and I've had my artist visa application for the States in for a while. This will speed things up, he says, delivering this news more to Elspeth than anyone else.

She meets his self-satisfied grin with an expression Frank reads as hard-won indifference; a tightening of the mouth followed by a cagey raise of the brows. She takes a sip of wine.

– California… it's awfay far, Val curls down her bottom lip.

Elspeth, suddenly exploding in laughter, spits out her drink. Looking at Frank, she's aware for the first time he seems really angry, and turns to Melanie. – Sorry… ye just don't seem his type!

– Well congratulations to you both, Greg sings. – We should open some champers!

Greg is ignored as Melanie meets Elspeth's gaze evenly. – Please be so kind as to tell me: are you Greg's type?

Elspeth is taken aback. Then she finds her voice. – Excuse me?

– Are you Greg's type?

As Elspeth is about to react, Greg cuts in, – Well, we're two kids and a killer mortgage on this place into the relationship, so I certainly hope so!

– Beautiful bairns, Val muses as Frank breathes in heavily, as if barely repressing his rage. Melanie's face has pinched in annoyance too, but then she whispers something in his ear. Frank squeezes her hand and breaks out in a big smile, which she reciprocates.

Elspeth watches them in agitation, her face pinched as she sips nervously at her drink. The empowering rush of alcohol hits her brain, and she enjoys the reckless edge it confers. Settling back, she throws a haughty glance around the room, sweeping her hand through her hair.

Melanie, perceiving the shift in the social temperature, adopts a conciliatory tone. – So, Elspeth, Frank was saying that you work in a lab. That must be like two full-time jobs, with the kids, right?

– Aye, tell ays aboot it! I'm a lab technician at a secondary school... a high school, she adds for Melanie's benefit. Then she suddenly realises that we now designated schools here the very same way. When had this happened, and, more importantly, why? Who authorised this? What was so special about fucking America? Why no press outcry when we had their stuff foisted on us, yet there was this constant obsession with Europe and Brussels controlling our lives?

– I'll bet that's interesting.

– It can be, Elspeth says, the subtext in her defensive tone being: *what fucking business is it of yours?*

– Right...

More silence. Then a dry hack from Val. It gains traction, developing into a wheezing, urgent bark, then a full-scale coughing fit. She bends over like a penknife being closed.

– Are you okay, Val? Greg asks. – Sip of water? He runs to the sink to fill a small glass.

Elspeth is at her mother's side, comforting her. – Well done, she briefly whips to Frank in accusation. – Easy, Mum... the swift movement and surge of alcohol uncoordinates her, and stumbling, she knocks over her mother's oxygen cylinder, which crashes to the hardwood floor.

– Watch... Greg shouts, moving over to help.

Frank also stands up to assist. He asks Elspeth, – Well done what?

– Fuck! Elspeth gets the mask on Val, who double secures it with a wizened arm, as she heaves gulps of air into her thin chest. – Easy, Ma, Elspeth coos. As Val's breathing starts to settle, Elspeth again attends to Frank. – Well done telling a terminally ill woman that her son's going over tae the other side ay the world! Timing!

Frank looks at her in disdain, as he pulls the oxygen cylinder back up, before casting his eyes on her drink on the coffee table, then back to Elspeth in reprimand. – Aye, like you've fair got things under control!

– I'll have you know...

Val removes her mask. – Enough... she croaks, – the pair ay youse... enough!

Frank and Elspeth regard each other, their glances contracting an uneasy truce.

– Cat and dug they two... Val wearily explains to Melanie and Greg, – ... eywis wir. No when she was the wee baby sister, though... him and Joe doted on her at first...

Frank and Elspeth avoid each other's eyes in mutual embarrassment at the revelation of this former intimacy, as Greg, in strained cheer, gestures her to step away. Elspeth sits back down with him on the couch.

Another awkward silence hangs in the room.

The only sound is the rustling of the cat flap. Chairman Miaow seems in two minds whether or not to enter, one leg, head and shoulder coming through, cagily scanning the room. Decides against it and reverses back out.

It's Elspeth who feels moved to break the edgy quietude. – Nae word on Joe? Naebody phone him?

– Ah tried, Frank says. – He's no picking up.

Elspeth suddenly starts crying; her tear ducts open and rivulets run down her face. There seems no change in her otherwise: it's as if a switch has been turned on. Lowering her drink to the glass coffee table, she wipes her eyes on her sleeve.

– What's wrong, honey? Greg asks, putting his arm round her shoulders.

Elspeth does not succumb to his embrace. She looks at Val, and her bottom lip trembles as she turns to Frank. – Look at her, Frank. The state ay her. My wee ma.

Frank bends forward in his seat and scrutinises Val. – Ye okay, Ma?

– Aye, son… it's a sair fecht. Ah just thought that ah would have my family aroond ays at this time ay life… that's all ah'm sayin…

– It's not like we aren't gonna be around, Melanie explains. – We'll be back and forward all the time. Frank has business here.

Elspeth turns a dagger scrutiny on Frank. – So ye just got oot eftir aw they years in prison, and now ye just swan off, away tae California.

– Pretty much, aye, he concedes, with minimal shoulder shrug. – So?

Elspeth thumbs at Val, breathing in slow rhythm under her plastic veneer. – So, timing really isnae yir strong point, is it?

Frank considers this, retaining a calm that bewilders Elspeth, who bites on her bottom lip. – It's improving, and he smiles at Melanie.

– Aw is it now, is all Elspeth can manage.

– Aye. It is.

– Come on, Greg urges, clenching a fist and waving triumphantly in front of him. – Let's try to enjoy a family Christmas together! We're lucky we're all here! I mean, he brandishes his iPad, – this Iranian thing, Frank, did you hear about it?

– Nup.

– Forty-five dead. Some of them just kids.

– Aw aye, I did, Frank corrects himself in recollection. – It was on the news earlier. An earthquake, they said, wis it no?

– Yes, and we get them in California, Melanie digs him. – You sure you wanna come?

– Aye.

Melanie smiles at Frank, but then sees that Val is talking to herself under her breath in soft distracted murmurs. *Poor woman.*
– How long have you had that oxygen mask, Val?

– Ah'm no movin ootay ma hoose, Val responds to her in some animation, still in the chair, but shuffling laterally in small vibrating movements, like a boxer who anticipates they'll soon have to slip a punch. – Ah telt them, you'll just have tae bring in respite care. Ah'm no movin.

– Do they try to keep you at home, Melanie enquires. – Are the resources they provide any good?

– They've killed the NHS. Killed it stone dead, Val looks into the fire. Then she turns back to Melanie. – The Tories. N Labour's just as bad. That Blair, he was just a Tory. You can tell by the mooth.

– Mooth? Melanie looks around.

– She means mouth, don't you, Mum, Elspeth says, more formally.

– Ah mean mooth, Val snaps. – It's a guid Scots word. That Blair, he hud the mooth ay a hoor! A cocksucker's mooth!

– Ma! Elspeth chides, but laughs, then exhales a long breath and rolls her eyes. Frank giggles too, while Melanie smiles tightly and Greg stays studiedly neutral.

– Do you think things would be better if there was an independent Scotland, Melanie asks Val.

Greg rolls his eyes.

– Couldnae be worse… Val tuts.

– Dinnae kid yirself, Elspeth pitches in. – That Salmond, that's another yin ah widnae trust as far as ah could throw.

– Less thin that Cameron, Val asks.

– That's a right oily bastard, Elspeth concedes. – Pardon my French, she smiles tightly at Melanie. – You must think we're aw radge.

– Sorry?

Frank whispers in her ear. Melanie nods, then proclaims, – Oh yes, I know what radge means. No, I don't think that at all.

Elspeth knocks back some more drink, appears not to hear Melanie. – Thir all the same, they politicians. Aw bloody crooks.

– So, how's the probation coming along, Frank, Greg chips in.

– Probation officer not... he clears his throat, winks at Melanie, before speaking in bad New York 'wise guy' tones, – bustin your balls? Or parole officer, as they say in the movies!

Frank looks fixedly at him. – What you on aboot?

– Sorry, I've been watching too much *Sopranos*. Going through it all over again on Netflix. Genius. Have you seen it? I still rate *The Wire* as better, though. Do you ever watch *Ray Donovan*? Boston Irish family transplanted to LA...

– Nup, dinnae watch telly, ay.

– You've never seen *Breaking Bad*?

– Nup.

– Of course, I forget you've been in prison! You have to see *Breaking Bad*. You are seriously missing out, Frank, Greg shakes his head, searching on his iPad for an episode.

The doorbell rings, with Elspeth rising to answer it. As she heads down the hallway, she prays it's not Joe. But the curved malevolence of the form in the dimpled glass tells its own story. She draws a breath and pulls the door open. Her eldest brother stands before her. He looks unkempt in a tatty old fleece, holey jeans and wrecked trainers. Greying hair curls in greasy tendrils down his forehead from under a red-and-white Santa hat. His face is lumpy and scratched, chin pitted with protruding tufts of hair, indicating he's scrape-shaved with an ancient razor. His eyes dart slyly in reptile mode. This was one habitual setting for Joe's gaze, Elspeth considers, the other being a goat-like bemused belligerence. – Ho ho ho... he says in a mirthless department store Father Christmas imitation.

She notes he comes bearing no gifts. – Joe.

– Sounds like Scapa Flow, she hears Frank's voice insinuate from the front room. The snide fake bonhomie drips from his tones. *I cannot stand being in the same room as the two of them.*

– Aye-aye, Joe says, remaining rooted to the spot as if he needs a formal invitation to enter.

– So ye made it then. Come on in, Elspeth urges, shivering in the inrushing cold air.

– Merry Christmas n aw that shite, ay, Joe says as he steps inside and closes the door.

– Aye, you n aw. C'mon through. You no got a coat?

– S'no that cauld, Joe says, shivering in his fleece. His hands are so red it's like the skin has been peeled from them. His face throbs in the heated home as he follows Elspeth into the lounge, his bleary eyes taking in the room and its occupants. He speaks in sneering, challenging tones. – This is cosy...

– Merry Christmas, Joe! Greg offers.

– Aye... aye... Merry Christmas... n aw that shite... Joe repeats his greeting as his eyes scan the kitchen, settling on the worktop, where the drinks are situated. Greg takes the hint and rises to the fridge, producing a can of Stella.

Joe's eyes, now in caprine mode, settle on Melanie. Frank is about to make introductions when Val's claw rises to tug on his brother's sleeve. She looks up at Joe. – Merry Christmas, son.

Joe grabs the back of her chair and leans over her for a kiss on her wig. – How's ma wee ma? How's that chemo been gaun?

Val hauls in a long breath. – It takes an awfay loat oot ay ye...

– Yir a fighter, but, Ma, he rubbernecks back in the direction of Melanie.

Greg pushes a can of Stella into his hand. – Remembered you were lager!

– What? Joe snaps belligerently, but opens the can.

Greg looks like he's ready to explain, before opting to let it slide. – How was your Christmas, Joe?

– Shite.

– Sorry to hear it, Greg says. – Could be worse, though, yes?

– Aw aye? How's that then, Joe responds with a truculent, square-go face.

Greg points to the TV. – Well, you could be in Iran. Forty-five dead in an earthquake.

– Fuckin brilliant!

Greg looks at him in shock, his hand literally rising to his chest.
– Sorry?

– Who gies a fuck aboot they cunts!

– A lot of children were killed!

– Aye, cut that oot, Elspeth rounds on Joe, – at Christmas!

Joe lets out a sharp exhalation of breath. – You might call them bairns, but ah call them fuckin terrorists ay the future, and he collapses onto the couch. The beer bubbles up, and he slurps at the foaming spill. – Git thum fuckin fried now before they come ower here... come ower here n blaw every other cunt tae fuckin shreds wi thir suicide bombs! If thir gaunny dae it anywey, take the cunts oot first, ah say. He looks around for support. None seems forthcoming. – Ayatollah? Aye, a fuckin tollie. That's what ah call them. She'll tell ye! He points to Melanie.

Frank sits up.

– American! Joe points at Elspeth. – That's what you said she wis!

– So, Elspeth questions.

Joe keeps his eyes on Melanie. – Youse hate they cunts even mair than us, he shouts. – Twin towers!

– Keep yir voice doon, Elspeth hisses, – the bairns are asleep.

– That was Al-Qaeda, Melanie says to Joe.

– Ayatollah, Al-Qaeda, El Cordobés: aw the fuckin same, Joe flicks his wrist in disdain. As the others fight their varying degrees of anger and confusion, he looks to Frank. – Mind they posters that Auntie Ina brought ye back fae Spain? PLAZA DE TORRES. EL CORDOBÉS. FRANCIS BEGBIE. They pit yir name printed oan it like ye were a bullfighter?

Frank looks steadily at his brother. – Aye, you burnt mine wi a lighter.

– Ah mind ay that, Joe grimly chuckles. – Ye got tae have a laugh at some ay the things we used tae get up tae!

Frank isn't laughing.

Joe seems to register this through his alcoholic fug, raising his can in a mock toast. – Auntie Ina, she wis a case, ay. Ina, Ina, show us yir vagina! Mind we used tae sing that, Frank?

Val bristles in her chair, takes a hit on her mask.

– *You* used tae sing it, Frank says.

– Aw is that right, Joe scoffs, then looks at the glass of water in Frank's hand in bitter accusation. – What's that... he points to the clear liquid... – Ye no huvin a peeve?

– Just rehydrating, Frank raises his glass in toast. – Merry Christmas.

– Re-hy-fuckin... is this what we're gittin now then, ay?

Frank is about to react, when Melanie, who has been studying Joe with fascinated intent, cuts in, – Are the pope and queen both the same?

– What?

– Well, they're both Christian, right?

Joe looks from her to Frank and back again. – America. Youse are meant tae hate Pakis even mare than we do!

Greg shudders as Elspeth raises her eyebrows. Frank remains poker-faced.

– I don't think you're grasping what I mean, Melanie contends. – Saying all Muslim groups and leaders are the same is like saying all Christian ones are the same.

– They are tae me, Joe snorts, taking a slug of his Stella. – Thir aw fuckin poofs as well.

– What?

– Christians. That Jesus cunt: twelve fuckin disciples, aw ay them other fuckin gadges? Tell ays that cunt wisnae a fuckin bentshot, Joe takes another sip of beer. – Aw aboot poppy wi they cunts. That World Trade Centre, that wis a fuckin insurance job, if ah ever saw yin.

– What?

Elspeth looks at Greg, and twirls her finger against her head. – Hijacked planes, aw they people deid, just for insurance money, she taunts Joe. – You're nuts!

– Ah'm tellin ye, it's a cert it wis the fuckin insurance, Joe throws himself back in the couch, slurps some more on the Stella. – Mind ay Granddad Jock, Frank? Aw the insurance jobs he'd dae! Hud us torchin warehooses for um as bairns! Aw insurance!

Val looks up, takes a heavy toke on her oxygen in agitation.

– Ah never torched any warehooses for him, Frank says. – Done enough crimes ay my ain. No taking the rap for yours!

– No? You werenae there? Joe asks, seeming to struggle in recollection. – Surprised at that! You wir ey his favourite.

Elspeth looks to Frank. – The gangster. How does that no surprise me?

– You were Dad's favourite, Frank contends. – The alcoholic.

Elspeth recoils at that, lowers her drink. – My dad was a good man, before the peeve got tae him…

– If you say so, Frank smiles firmly, as Melanie looks around nonplussed, struggling to follow the conversation.

– Aw aye, he was good tae you, his wee angel, Val tears the mask from her face, – but only when he was oot ay the jail. He was never a provider, Jimmy Begbie. No like his faither. Jock was a provider.

Frank, Joe and Elspeth, all disconcerted by Val's strident defence of Granddad Jock, exchange glances.

– Aye, well ah dinnae call daein insurance scams n stealing stuff fae Leith docks providing, Elspeth says.

– Eywis aboot insurance, Joe insists.

– Well that World Trade Centre wisnae, Elspeth barks.

– Out of all the outlandish theories I've listened to, Greg nods, – I've never come across that one!

– Aye, but notice how they never mentioned how much the insurance money wis, Joe waves Greg's contention away. – Notice that, but, ay? Goat tae be a fuckin insurance job, yon! Guaranteed!

A jagged sound as Greg ostentatiously clears his throat. The others look to him in tired indulgence. – Well the people who died in the World Trade Centre would be another example of folk less fortunate than ourselves.

Frank turns to Melanie with a grin. – You could be right.

Joe lets his mouth hang open as he scans the lounge. – Well ah dinnae see anybody less fortunate than me. No in this fuckin room, anywey. He looks at Val, who pulls the mask to her face. – Mibbe you, Ma, but you've hud a decent fuckin kick at the baw. But leavin you oot ay it, likes, thir's naebody worse oaf thin me in this fuckin place. Tell yis that fir nowt!

Frank shoots him a flinty look. Joe falls silent. Melanie diverts Frank's gaze by holding her phone up to him. It is a swirling image of white blotches on a black background. He smiles, as Val turns to her firstborn. – What's wrong, son? Did you no get tae see the bairns the day?

– Did ah fuck. Nae chance. No wi her, Joe's eyes narrow as his teeth push his lips apart. – Fuckin evil slag.

– She'll no let ye see yir ain bairns! Sandra!? Val replaces the mask and sucks.

Joe doesn't make eye contact with anybody. His head suddenly hangs heavy as he mumbles in dismay. – Will she fuck.

Val is horrified. Her eyes bulge above the mask. She lifts it to snap, – At Christmas!

Suddenly animated again, Joe's face flushes as his eyes quickly dart over the room's occupants. – That's her, but, ay. Fill ay spite. Usin the bairns as weapons against ays. Ah telt her. Poisonin thum. Fuckin hoor!

– Keep yir voice doon, Elspeth hisses. – *Ma* bairns are asleep.

Something sparks in Joe's eyes, a calculating light. He turns to Elspeth and Greg, conciliatory in his manner. – Listen… ah need a wee favour. He pulls an A4 envelope out of his pocket. It contains several sheets of paper, which look like quasi-legal documentation. He stands up and waves it in front of Elspeth, who rises, takes it from him, places it on the worktop and reads.

– What is it, Greg asks.

– Just a wee bit ay faimlay stuff, Joe smiles.

Greg moves over to Elspeth who stands bolt upright. – Honey?

Elspeth is scanning the document with a blazing intensity that seems to burn her into sobriety. – Aye, right, she scoffs.

– What does it say, Greg requests.

– Sumthin or nuthin, Joe mumbles.

– It's fae social services, Elspeth turns, waving the paper in the air. – It says that if him or Sandra cannae look after Connor and Anthony they have tae come and live here, her jaw juts out. – That'll be right!

– Means nowt. Just a precaution, Joe shrugs.

– What are ye asking ays tae sign it for if it means nowt? Elspeth's eyes bulge as she stares at Joe.

– Paperwork... lawyer's stuff... ye ken what they cunts are like... means nowt...

– Is anything wrong wi Sandra?

– We should aw be sae lucky, Joe sneers. – Just had some tests done, that's aw. Ye ken what she's like, fuckin hypo... what's it they call they cunts whae think thir's something wrong wi thum but there isnae?

Melanie comes to his aid. – Hypochondriac?

– That's it. Hyper fuckin condriac, he toasts Melanie and nods to Frank. – Did awright thair Frank, brains as well as beauty. That was whaire ah fucked up, ending up wi the wrong kind ay bird, and he looks at Melanie. – No goat any sisters huv ye, hen?

– No.

– Too bad, Joe leers, oblivious to Frank's burning gaze on him.

Elspeth lowers her hands to her hips. – Aye, n it's too bad for you that ah'll no be signing this, and she throws the paper back down on the worktop. – Ah'm no looking after your bairns!

– It's jist the two youngest yins, but, Joe flips his palms. – The other pair look eftir themselves.

– Aye, well young Joseph's in the jail and Carly's got a bairn, when she's just yin herself! That's them lookin after thirsels, is it?

– Ah telt her tae keep away fae that wee radge, Joe snarls, lifting his beer and guzzling some back. – Telt her that the Sutherlands were rubbish!

– Got that right, Frank says. – Didnae ken it was one of them that had knocked her up. Sair yin.

– Her ma's fuckin influence... Joe muses, necking another hit of Stella.

– Well your youngest two arenae staying here, Elspeth shakes her head.

– It's no aboot that, Joe contends, holding the can of beer to his chest. He burps and his eyes water as he forces down acid reflux, before hauling in some breaths and continuing, – It's just aboot helping me oot wi me bein homeless n that, but, ay. Soas they

133

dinnae get taken intae care, in case that dozy fat cow Sandra faws under a bus or something.

– Fat, Val repeats under her breath.

– Well, that's no our responsibility, Elspeth shakes her head. She goes and pulls another bottle of white wine from the fridge, unscrewing it and refilling her glass.

– Honey, have a heart, Greg says, sitting down with the letter in his hand, reading it carefully. – It helps Joe out, and doesn't inconvenience us.

– That's right, Joe jumps back in, – it's jist a formality, they sais. Keeps ma access tae the bairns.

– Aye, right, Elspeth sneers, taking a sip of the fresh wine. She snatches the letter out of Greg's hand and puts it back on the worktop.

– Aye, its awright for some, but, ay, Joe looks at Frank, as he nods to the ceiling. – Some bairns get tae sleep soundly in their beds. No a care in the world. Aye, awright for some, right enough.

– Yes it is, Elspeth forcibly agrees, her voice rising, – because Greg and I have made it alright for them, and she looks to her husband with some gratitude. Greg smiles thinly back at her.

– Mibbe, Joe shuffles before settling back onto the couch.

– There's nae mibbe aboot it, Elspeth says. – What the fuck's that meant tae mean, Joe?

– Nowt, Joe mumbles. He takes a long slug out of the can.

– Better no mean nowt, Elspeth snaps. – Mind whaes hoose yir in, and whaes bevvy you're sitting drinking!

Joe looks at her with one eye shut. – Aye, what bevvy is that then, he shakes the now empty can.

Greg rolls his eyes in exasperation, and looks around the company. – Oh-kay… anybody need their drinks refreshed?

A grin splits Joe's face in two. – And maybe a wee Christmas nip n aw, as a chaser, ay, he grins, then turns to Elspeth. – Think about what ah sais, likes.

Elspeth is pointedly silent as a semi-apologetic Greg rises to the kitchen area and starts fixing the drinks. She turns to Frank. –

What about you? Have you seen Sean or Michael? Or that other laddie, what's his name?

– River.

Joe laughs, a low wheezing sound. – River!

– His ma's idea. No mine. Frank shrugs, looking around the room, before sharing another whispered joke with Melanie.

– River! What kind ay name is that? Joe pushes.

– Like I sais, his mother's idea.

– River... ye hear that, Elspeth! River? River Begbie! Ignored by his sister, Joe laughs loudly on his own. – River Begbie...

Frank looks at Melanie in apology. She smiles and squeezes his wrist.

Greg returns with a can of beer and a whisky for Joe. He's aware of Frank looking at him as he passes the drinks over. He gives a defeated shrug.

Joe opens the can and toasts them. – Ho ho ho! Merry Christmas everybody! Look to the future now, it's only just begun!

The toast is met by a collective response that is both grudged and embarrassed. – Merry Christmas...

A loud grating snore under the billowing mask signals that Val has gone to sleep.

– Best fuckin Christmas song ever! Slade! Joe turns to Frank. – Am ah right, Frank?

Frank nods in a neutral manner.

– Mind ay they Slade socks every cunt wore at school?

– Aye, ah mind, Frank says with some fondness.

Melanie curls her bottom lip down. – Slade socks?

– Aye, they were hooped socks, Frank explains. – Usually fluorescent orange or green and black.

– 'Fairytale Ay New York', Elspeth says.

– Nae chance! Slade! Joe barks.

– Ah like 'Fairytale Ay New York'.

– It's a great song, Melanie agrees. – That guy is one hell of a songwriter. It's like a Cole Porter number crossed with an Irish folk song and some punk rock thrown in for good measure!

Elspeth turns to Joe in vindication. – See?

– Slade was aroond before 'Fairy Tale Ay New York' was even thought ay! Slade wis early seventies, 'Fairy Tale Ay New York' no till the eighties. Dae the math, as youse Americans say, and Joe looks at Melanie. – Ah'm a right, or am ah fuckin well spot on?

– So just because Slade's aulder it's better, Elspeth's face sets. – That makes a lot ay sense. *No.*

Joe adopts the bronchitis laughter again. – The aulder the fiddle the better the tune, ay, Frank?

Melanie and Frank exchange a lingering smile. Elspeth notes this tender moment between them and is visibly soured. She looks away and picks up her drink. Her eyes go to Greg, who appears preoccupied with his iPad, then Val, who is still in a fitful doze, her eyelids rippling.

Joe is talking to himself, in repetition on the jakey loop, Frank observes. – Aye, the aulder the fiddle, the better the tune...

Elspeth notes Frank is kissing Melanie lightly on the lips. Then they giggle like teens at some whispered joke or observation. – Ye never answered ma question, she challenges. – So ye seen them then, your bairns?

Frank looks round slowly at her. He takes his time before answering. – Nup.

– Ye gaunny go n see them? You've been oot for months now.

Val has jumped back into some kind of wakefulness. – Ye should, son, ye should go and see yir ain bairns. At Christmas!

Frank remains silent, raising his brows, as Melanie again squeezes his hand.

– Wish ah could see mine! Joe bleats.

Melanie turns to Val. – I've told him he should go and see them, but I respect his reasons why he doesn't want to.

– Aw aye, what are they well, Elspeth looks pointedly at Frank.

– Thir's no much good ah kin dae them now.

– It's your bairns, bichrist!

– Ah sais ah wish ah could see mine! Joe whines, sounding to Frank like a dog that has been run over.

Frank addresses Elspeth, ignoring Joe. – If I could dae them any good, I would. But I cannae. I wasnae around for them when they were growing up. That was when they needed me. That ship has sailed.

– That ship has sailed? Is that aw ye kin say? Ah dinnae get you at all Frank, ah really dinnae.

Frank shrugs, settles back into the couch.

Joe looks at Elspeth. He points to the document on the worktop. – Tell yis what, youse would be daein me a big favour by signing yon letter. Seriously… if anything was tae happen tae Sandra, it would mean ah'd be able tae keep them ootay care…

Greg looks at Elspeth, in plea. – C'mon, honey, it means nothing. It's just a legal formality, helping out family. It's Christmas, and his gaze strays to the letter on the counter.

– Do you think I want his bairns living here? Bringing a couple ay wee neds intae this hoose, when we've got two wee boys upstairs!

– Thir good bairns! Joe protests.

– Aye, they're no in jail or playground parents yet, but gie them time!

– What's that meant tae mean, Joe twists around in his seat.

Elspeth is totally unfazed, taking a step towards him, her hands on her hips. – It's meant tae mean that ah doubt you and Sandra's parenting skills have improved since the first two!

– Oof, says Frank.

– And dinnae *you* even start, she rounds on Frank. – At least he's trying tae see his bairns!

Frank remains silent. Melanie takes his hand, watches him slowly draw in a long breath of air. Another squeeze and he smiles.

– Aw aye… is that it, then? Joe looks genuinely wounded, and Elspeth inhales deeply, as if in acknowledgement she's gone too far.

– Look, it's only window dressing, Greg says. – There is absolutely no way that Joe's kids are coming to stay here. It just helps him out with the social services and potential rehousing.

– Windae dressing… Joe mumbles, as it seems another debilitating unit of alcohol has seeped into his brain. – Listen tae the words ay wisdom, he raises his can at Greg while refraining from looking him in the eye. – Windae dressing, he repeats.

Elspeth raises her eyes and blows hard in exasperation. – God! Alright! Where is it! She heads across to the worktop and signs the document, looking at Joe and Greg threateningly. – See if any ay this goes wrong...

– It's good tae see family help each other oot, Val says. – It's Christmas.

– I think that's a really great thing you just done, Melanie's remark is meant to be supportive, but Elspeth winces as she heads across to Joe with the document.

He takes it and sticks it in the pocket of his fleece, then slumps back into his seat. – Ta... anyway, he holds up the whisky, – might as well enjoy a scoop while ah kin!

– Aye? Frank nods.

– Aw change eftir New Year for me. Daein dry January... getting it the gither, and he looks at Frank in accusation. – Notice you're no drinkin.

– No much gets past you, bro.

– Anti-social at Christmas, but, and Joe looks over to Elspeth. – Ay that's right, kid sis!

Elspeth does not respond, rising and heading to Val and adjusting the tartan blanket on her legs. – Warm enough, Ma?

– Aw aye, roastin now... she tugs Elspeth's hand with her bony claw. – That wis a good thing ye done, muh darlin. If a faimlay cannae stick the gither at Christmas...

– Truer words never spoken, Frank agrees. As Elspeth is about to react, he points at two reindeer ornaments on the mantelpiece. – I like these boys.

– John Lewis, Elspeth informs the room.

Joe is mumbling to himself. – Fuckin Christmas... too commercialised... a fuckin con... n that fat bitch... aw full ay spite... ah love they bairns...

Greg nervously intervenes to detract. – So, what about the art, Frank, is it still going well?

– Aye, no bad.

Melanie laughs gently. – He has a major exhibition at a top

gallery in London next month, she explains. – It's going a little better than *no bad*. You Scots sure like to understate things!

Joe shoots to alertness at this. – An exhibition! Is this what we're getting now? An exhibition?

– It's what ah dae, Frank nods. – Make art. Exhibit it. Hopefully people buy it.

– Aye, making an exhibition ay yirsel, Elspeth says, – ye were always good at that!

– What's that supposed to mean?

– You ken. Even they so-called works ay art you dae now, Elspeth scoffs, necking more from her glass, – getting the heads ay celebrities and mutilating them. Ah dinnae call that art!

As Greg looks on and nervously picks up his iPad, Frank smiles tightly, but Melanie is more defensive. – Plenty of people do. And they pay good money. His work is in demand.

– Making a model ay somebody's heid then slashing it, Elspeth jeers, where's the art in that?

– Well isn't that what celebrity culture is? Melanie argues. – Building people up and then destroying them? That's what Frank, very successfully, has tapped into.

As Elspeth snorts in disdain, Frank shrugs off the exchange, retaining the grin on his face.

Greg keeps his head in his iPad.

– Better choppin bits ay clay than choppin a boy's hand off, ay, Frank? Joe says, looking at Melanie for her reaction. She winces slightly. – Did eh no tell ye eh chopped a boy's hand off?

– He tells me everything, Melanie glances at Frank.

– Slight exaggeration, Frank shrugs, – that ah chopped a boy's hand off, he turns to Melanie. – Not that I don't tell you everything. Cause I do, he looks to the others. – It was just two ay his fingers I chopped off. People are prone tae hyperbole.

– Prone tae hyper-fuckin-what, Joe gapes into space.

– Oh, a nice gangster tale from Uncle Frank at Christmas, Elspeth says. – Get the bairns doon, shall I?

– Ah dinnae want tae hear this! Val spits. – Had this bloody nonsense aw ma life!

Greg looks up from his device, staring at Frank, in morbid fascination. – Why did you do that, Frank?

– Boy sharing a cell with me kept playing with his iPad, and it got on my nerves.

Greg looks at Frank in horror, his iPad sliding onto his thigh. Then sees a faint smile on his brother-in-law's face. – Ahhh!!!! They both laugh at once, Greg in a relived liberation.

Joe has been witnessing the exchange, nursing his wrath, his features scrunching to the middle of his face. – Wisnae an exaggeration when ye battered ma heid in wi a brick. Or that Christmas when we were playin Monopoly n ye burst a boatil ay whisky ower it!

– Enough! It's Christmas! Elspeth says. – We've got guests! No wantin tae hear aw that!

– Couldnae dae a thing wi they laddies, Val laments.

– Aye, some ay the things we got up tae back then, ay! Frank winks, smiling at Joe. – The brick was when we were just young laddies. Ye deserved it, cause ay yir constant bullying. Left ays naewhere tae go. That's never wise. Sorry aboot the second. That's why ah dinnae drink these days, he holds up the clear glass of water. – But ye did cheat tae get Park Lane!

Some strained laughter is followed by overwrought hush as Joe sits nursing his wrath.

Elspeth turns to Joe. – You've missed aw oor Frank's news.

Frank regards Joe with a slightly exasperated, impatient air. – Yes, I didnae formally introduce youse. Melanie's an artist, fae California. We're getting married, n gaun ower thaire tae live, Frank looks at Melanie, then round the faces of his family.

Joe is struggling to process this. – Aye… live in America…

Val looks fretful. – It's awfay far.

– But there's mair… Frank says. – Thir's a bairn oan the way, ay.

Elspeth regards Melanie in wide-eyed horror and gasps, – Jesus Christ, ah've heard it aw now!

Melanie ignores her, compressing Frank's hand.

Joe closes one eye, fixing Frank in the other. – New bairns… California… paintins… is this whit wir gittin now then, ay?

– Aye.

– Well seein as we were talkin aboot parentin, you might want tae check oot his track record, Joe looks at Melanie, pointing at her stomach.

– Pot-kettle, Elspeth says, as Melanie rolls her eyes.

– Be the first tae admit it isnae great, Frank's laughter is low and sardonic, – but ah'm starting fae scratch, turning over a new leaf, looking forward tae it, in a way I never was before, he looks over at Joe. – What aboot you?

– Different when you've goat money, Joe says. – It's aw sorted oot then. The nanny. The posh school.

– Well ah'll never get tae see any new bairns, Val moans. – No in California. No in ma state!

Frank raises a solitary brow.

– Oh, I'm sure you will, Val, Melanie rises, then kneels by her, taking her hand. – We'll bring the baby over!

Val tilts her head to the side, retaining a doubtful expression. The world was changing so quickly. New faces bursting into it, coming into her life, and she barely understood why, what they expected of her. Frank and Joe's first kids, and even Elspeth's two up the stairs, she got that, felt it on a deep emotional level; they were proper family. But Frank's other one she had barely seen, and then when his youngest boy from June brought a new bairn home… and after that Joe's lassie with her one… it was all too much. They were nothing to do with her! And now Frank and this lassie, why did there have to be new bairns again? She looks deeply into the pale-blue eyes of the blonde American. Still slim and beautiful in her mid-twenties, in the way women of her class never got to be. Either they ran to fat eating cheap chemicals packaged as food, or poverty and struggle hardened their features. Not this lassie, she would in some ways retain a kind of splendour until she got to where Val was. Life would catch her eventually, that was the destination of all, but it would show her abundant grace on the way. She possesses, and would be offered, Val realises, a gorgeousness she herself had rarely been afforded more than a glimpse of. Now Val is eaten up with a resentment as embedded and devastating as her cancer; not towards this woman, but at the crushing limitations of the life choices proffered on the menu of her own existence. – You're a good lassie, hen. I can see that, she takes the woman's hand in her own. – Live well, she almost threatens.

Joe observes this scene in a burgeoning rancour, and swings around to point at Elspeth. – Ah notice we're no good enough tae sit doon tae a meal wi ye, me n Frank, n this California lassie... but ye huv us roond fir drinks once the bairns are aw tucked up in bed...

– It's too much for muh ma!

– Whae's sais? Ah dinnae hear hur sayin nowt, Joe points at Val, who starts to sob, as Melanie comforts her. She nods to Frank to join them.

Frank gets up and tries to soothe his mother. – Hi, hi, hi... what's aw this? We'll bring the bairn over tae see ye, Ma!

– Ah jist wanted it tae be a nice Christmas...

Elspeth meets Joe's belligerent expression and counters with a paint-stripping glare. – You should just go now. You're only upsetting my ma.

– What ye talkin aboot?

– He's just a bit pished, Frank says. – Ah'm gaunny take him up the street, get him intae a cab.

– Best suggestion I've heard yet! Elspeth agrees.

– Ah'm awright... Joe mumbles, – just let ays lie doon a minute... He settles back into the couch, puts his head on the armrest and almost immediately falls into a drunken slumber.

– Peace at last, Elspeth announces.

– Well, he can't lie there all night, Greg says.

– Best place for him, Elspeth's chin juts out. – Let him dae what he kens best: couch surfin!

– Leave him alaine, Val's anger is genuine and monumental.

– Naw ah'll no leave him alaine, Elspeth stands her ground. – Aw my life it's been Frank and Joe this, Frank and Joe that! Well I'm done, Ma, I really am.

Val curses the cruel biology that, down the years, has compelled her to apologise for the excesses of her sons. That primordial urge to storm to their defence, even as the weightiest, most damningly irrefutable evidence was deployed against them, how it tormented her, even now.

– Leave me out of this, Frank says.

– C'mon, babe, Greg begs his wife, – Val doesn't need to hear this...

– Laddies are different, Val declares, skeletal hand twitching over the oxygen mask like a gunfighter's over a holstered Colt 45. – They're lovely until they get intae their teens and start hanging oot on the streets wi their mates, then it's goodnight Vienna. You've lost them.

Elspeth points at the ceiling, scowling at her mother. – Aye, well ah've got two laddies. Upstairs asleep. They arenae like those two!

– Just wait till they git intae their teens, Val warns.

– Hormones, Greg adds helpfully. – And frontal lobe development. The risk-assessment function isn't fully formed in men until we hit our mid-to-late twenties.

Elspeth contemplates Frank and Joe. One brother has a tight expression, giving away nothing, the other dozes in an open-mouthed, slack-jawed stupor. – Teens nothing, she shakes her head slowly at her mother, – it's the wey they've been brought up.

– So ah'm a bad mother, Val snaps at her daughter. – Just come oot and say it!

– It isnae aboot being a bad mother, it's aboot being a daft woman, Elspeth bites back. – Daft women marry useless men! She gasps in sudden recognition that she's gone too far and doesn't even need the mortified reactions of the others to determine this. – I didnae mean it like that, Mum. Ah loved ma dad. He was always kind tae me.

Val turns away, pulling on the mask. She looks into the fire, seemingly contemplating something in its licking flames.

Greg sidles up to Elspeth. Speaks in a low hiss. – Can't you just stop this?

– What?

– All this nonsense, this arg...

He is interrupted by a voice, which, although not loud, is pitched at a certain frequency and carries a level of threat that compels attention. – Tae you ma faither was a good man, aye, Frank says firmly to Elspeth. – Tae me he was just a weak drunkard.

Just when it seems all the oxygen has left the heated air in the stare-down between brother and sister, a loud snore erupts from the couch. In a spontaneous moment, Elspeth and Frank both look at the comatose Joe. They meet each other's eyes and burst into a cathartic laughter. It shocks them both. Elspeth looks at Frank. *When have I ever laughed like that with him?*

– Ah'll say one thing aboot him, he never lifted his hands to me, Val recollects, – even when he was on the bottle.

– He was in prison for housebreaking when I was born, you said, Elspeth laughs. – Aye, he had his problems, but he was always good tae me, though, my auld dad.

Val bristles in the chair, her near-corpse fighting into some ghoulish animation. She appears ready to say something, but instead again hauls her oxygen mask over her mouth. Elspeth watches her eyes over the top of her visor, how they burn like the coals in the fire.

– You were just a wee lassie, but, Frank asserts. – He was a fucking shitehoose tae us. Snidey, wi a nasty drunkard's mooth on him.

Joe's eyes flicker, before springing open. His mouth follows, augmenting the look of alarmed shock.

– Aw aye, no like big bad Granddad Jock, your pal! Elspeth says, trying to make out she's laughing at the memory of Frank and Jock, not Joe's bemused face as he tries to work out his surroundings.

– You'll no mind ay auld Jock, but aye, he was a bad bastard, Frank agrees, repressing a snigger. – And he wisnae my pal.

Joe suddenly springs up from the couch, pointing at Frank. – An evil auld bastard! It wis him that telt you tae batter ma face in wi that brick! When ah wis asleep!

Frank remains composed. – The only useful advice ah ever got fae him. Like ah sais, you were a bully, Joe.

Melanie reads Joe as very drunk, almost as if he'd ingested more alcohol during his nap. She notes how he looks threateningly at Frank, who is unfazed, breathing in a steady, controlled way. *Frank is wise to them. He knows not to let them get under his skin now.*

– Enough! Sit doon, you! Elspeth commands her eldest brother.

Joe doesn't move. Stays focused on Frank. – Think you're a wideo still? He juts his chin out. – You've loast it! Franco Begbie? Yir poncey art...

As Frank remains immobile, bar a faint smile playing in the corners of his lips, Melanie intervenes, sitting forward in the couch. – What point are you trying to get across, Joe? Can you please make it without being threatening?

Joe looks pugnaciously at Melanie, then again at Frank, – ... n yir fancy California bird... cannae even stand up for yirsel... and he stumbles, staggering sideways, toppling and falling through the coffee table with an almighty crash. The metal legs buckle and glass shoots everywhere.

– THE FUCK, Elspeth roars, and immediately there are cries from upstairs.

Melanie gasps, – Oh my God... the children...

– That coffee table was a wedding present fae Jeanette and Harry, Elspeth is horrified.

As Joe rolls on his back, like an overturned tortoise, the Santa hat shed, Greg is on his knees. – Watch out for the broken glass...

Val bursts into tears. – It's eywis the same! Every time! Ma last Chrust... ma last Chrust... she explodes into a gasping fit.

Frank and Greg attend to Joe, trying to pull him to his feet, as Elspeth comforts Val.

Melanie looks at the ceiling. The crying is still evident. – Shall I go up and calm them down?

– I'll go! Elspeth sings.

Suddenly a foul smell assails them.

Frank waves a hand in front of his face as he gets a hold of Joe's arm. – Which cunt's shat, Joe, ya dirty...

– Oh God, it's muh ma... Elspeth looks at Val.

– Just a wee accident... nothing to worry about... Greg helps

Frank pull Joe up, and sit him on the edge of the couch. The table's shattered, and shredded glass has inflicted what looks like a not-too-deep wound, as claret drips from Joe's hand onto the floorboards. Frank and Greg try to ascertain whether he's cut elsewhere, then the latter heads to the kitchen to get a first-aid box. Over the gasps of Val and the groans of Elspeth, as the foul, fecund, chemical stench of death rises, the cries from upstairs continue. Greg looks to Melanie, as he digs out plasters and bandages. – Would you mind going up and seeing to them?

– I'm on it, Melanie says. And she heads outside and up the stairs.

Elspeth, who had been in two minds whether or not to leave Val and go herself, flashes Greg a look, but then sees that he is returning quickly with towels, kitchen roll and a basin of hot water, as well as the plaster and bandages.

They stop the bleeding in Joe's hand and bandage it, Frank binding it tight. – Might need stitches, Greg says. Frank and Joe both look at him as if he is insane.

Joe then tries to stand up, but needs Frank and Greg to help him to his feet. – Right. Ah'm getting you oot ay here and up the street, Frank tells him.

– Ah'm awright…

Greg puts the basin and towels by Elspeth, who is trying to get Val to stand up. He points upstairs. – I'll see to the lads, and gratefully departs.

– Ah'll gie ye a hand, Frank says to Joe.

His brother petulantly shakes his hand off. – Ah sais ah'm awright!

Elspeth turns to Joe. – Are you fuck awright! You're wrecking our hoose and my kids have been woken up! What the fuck is Melanie gaunny think ay us, and she turns to Val. – It's awright, Ma… c'mon… She helps her mother to her feet. Val weighs nothing, but looks bemused. On her chair and the top of her legs, a black, malodorous chemical slime which is beyond excrement. Elspeth has the chilling sense that her mother is trying to expel her disease. – I'll take her tae the downstairs toilet.

– She met Frank in the tin pail… Joe slurs. – She kens… she kens what we're like… ay, Joe looks at Frank.

– Thir is no *we*, Joe, Elspeth says, wrinkled nose in the air as she takes a shaky, shell-shocked Val into the hallway.

As her daughter steers her into the under-stair toilet, Val moans, – What happened… ah dinnae ken what happened…

– Like Greg sais, Ma, a wee accident.

Frank, the Santa hat in his hand, and Joe stand in the hall doorway, supervising their departure, transfixed by the dark mess clinging to their mother. The door of the downstairs bathroom closes behind them and Elspeth says, – Dae the best ye can, Ma.

– Still spoiled, snooty wee Elspeth, Joe shouts down the hall. – You got everything! N yir daft wee doonstairs toilet, he turns to Frank. – We hud it tough, ay, Frank…

– C'mon, Joe, let's go… Frank says.

The door of the WC opens, and Elspeth's head pops out like a jack-in-the-box. – AYE! FUCKIN GO!

– Money wis tighter when ah hud the boys… Val's apologetic voice.

Elspeth emerges from the WC, slamming the door shut. Facing her retreating brothers, she shouts, – AYE, GANG UP OAN ME, AS USUAL!

Greg is coming downstairs. – I don't think that's what Val means…

– Hud it aw ma life, Greg! Dinnae defend them!

– From who? What are you talking about?

– Them aw… Elspeth waves an arm in the air, but then seems to step down a level of inebriation. – How's ma boys?

– They're fine. Melanie's great with them. She's got them showing her their presents. I think they're quite smitten.

Elspeth darts past the WC, shouting in to Val, – Dae the best ye kin, before charging up the stairs.

Frank is manoeuvring Joe towards the door, grabbing him by the shoulders. – Right Scapa Flow, let's have ye, bro… Greg comes over to assist. – Aye, Mel's a big feminist, Frank informs him, – but ah think she's looking forward to motherhood!

– Feminists aren't opposed to having children, Frank...

– Ah'll take him outside, Frank nods to Greg, looking at Joe, whose eyes now loll around in his head. – Get him some air, then intae a taxi.

– I'll help.

– Naw, ah'll manage, Frank insists, getting into his coat, looking disdainfully at Joe's threadbare fleece. – And you're right about feminists and kids. That was a wee bit of a caveman statement on my part... He turns to Joe. – C'moan you!

– Do you believe her, Frank, Joe's mouth hangs open in fly-catching pose. – That cow Sandra? Sais ah battered the bairns! Dae ye, he lets his rage reanimate him.

Frank remains silent.

It's Greg who speaks up. – Of course not, Joe! Right, Frank?

Frank looks to Joe. – You ken what happened.

– Wha-what's that meant tae mean?

– Means you ken and ah dinnae, Frank says, keeping a hold of his brother by one shoulder.

– Fuckin right ah ken...

– So, what the fuck ye askin me for?

Elspeth returns with clean underwear for Val. She looks at Joe. – You still here? Go, she shouts, as she disappears into the toilet.

Greg takes that as his cue to open the front door. The icy wind blasts in. – I've got him, Frank says as he half escorts, half jostles Joe outside.

This time it's Val's head that pops out the toilet. – Where will ye take him!?

– Just outside and up the street, ay, Frank says, looking back in, pulling his collar up. – Get him in a taxi.

– But it's Christmas Day, you'll no get a taxi, Val says, before Elspeth emerges and then pushes the door shut behind her.

– Thi'll be plenty, Frank says. – A lot ay people these days prefer tae work than have a family Christmas. Funny that, ay?

Val pops her head back out and looks at him in distaste, then, at Elspeth's glacial expression, closes the door. – Aye, okay, she tells her daughter.

– Ah'm joking. Be back in a bit, Frank says to Greg as he keeps an extended arm gripping Joe as they move out through the front door. – Right, you, c'mon!

– That Sandra, Frank, Joe steadies himself against the door frame, feels the burning cold, – that wis whaire ah went wrong... you hud her sussed...

– Are you sure I can't help? Greg offers.

– Naw, we're fine. Just needs some air, walk off the peeve, Frank says.

On exiting, Joe then turns with a parting shot, – Dinnae talk aboot me behind ma back... if youse huv goat anything tae say, say it tae ma face...

Elspeth tears out after them. Stands in the doorway, watching Joe, supported by Frank, lurch down the path towards the front gate. – YA FUCKIN USELESS JAKEY CUNT! FUCK OFF! THAIRE! SATISFIED?!

Greg pulls Elspeth away and slams the door. – The kids are awake upstairs, with Melanie! Get a grip of yourself, for God's sake!

Frank and Joe lurch out into the night. Greg gratefully shuts the door behind them.

Elspeth starts to cry. – I'm sorry... it's thaime... it's always thaime... it's always the same... and she beats his chest softly with her fists. –They drive me fucking insane, Greg...

– It's okay, honey, they've gone. It's over... he coos, holding her tightly.

Val exits from the toilet, compelling Greg and Elspeth to break their embrace and help her into the lounge. – Sorry, hen... it's the medication. Ah git loose. Either that or nowt'll come.

– It's awright, we git the picture, Elspeth assists her mother back into the lounge. Elspeth removes the foul seat cushion, and takes it outside into the refuse. Greg gets some replacements from the couch and resettles Val, placing the mask on her lap. – Ah'm mortified, Greg...

– One of those things, Val, Greg says breezily, as Elspeth returns.

As they get settled, footsteps on the stairs indicate the impending presence of Melanie, who returns with a big smile on her face. – They're such great little guys! She looks around. – Where did Frank go?

– He's just going tae get Joe intae a taxi, Elspeth says. – Thanks for calming the boys down.

– Not a problem! How are you, Val?

– Mortified, hen.

– It's just an accident. It'll be your medication.

– That's what I told her, Greg says, – no big deal.

– Aye… Val says, raising the mask to her face and looking to the fire.

– So did you get a wee chat with the boys, Elspeth asks Melanie.

– I told them I was gonna be their aunt, Melanie smiles, – that I was getting married to their Uncle Frank. That their Uncle Joe had an accident and fell over, but he's gonna be okay. Then I asked them to show me what they got for Christmas. Such cool little kids, really sweet.

– Well thank you, Greg says.

Elspeth's mouth is turned down. In sudden awareness of this she forces her features into neutral. – Appreciate it.

– They're rare bairns, Val says wistfully, before her eyes narrow as she looks at her daughter. – Wish ah'd hud laddies like your two, she accuses. – That's what ye want me tae say, is it no?

As Greg pretends not to hear, Elspeth says under her breath, – I'll bet ye do.

Melanie has found a dustpan and brush from under the kitchen sink. She helps Elspeth tidy up the glass. – Watch ye dinnae cut yourself, Elspeth says, kneeling close to her. Catches the scent of the perfume on the Californian girl. Looks at her face, it's flawless, not even the beginning of laughter lines. But Americans never laugh, do they?

Looking up, Melanie catches her stare. – I'm good.

– Right, thanks, Elspeth says, anxious to get away. She rises and heads upstairs.

Melanie assists Greg in comforting Val, readjusting her pillows. – Was it an expensive table?

– Not really, Greg concedes, – though I suppose there's a senti-mental element to it. It was a wedding present from two friends who subsequently emigrated to Australia.

They move back over to the couch, leaving Val gently vibrating in her chair. She knows it is warm. The act of shivering itself, from some faulty mechanism in her nervous system, is generating this bone-shaking cold. It's more than age and the thinning of the blood, it's that sensation of dread she knows of old. Those triggers that freeze her; police sirens blaring on a hot summer's night, the knock of those state representatives on the door in the small hours, the shudder of the midnight or early-morning phone call. All those intrusive dramas visited on her by the Begbie men circumstance had compromised her enough to care about. And now, as she lay in the grisly final phase of her life, there it was, still present. Still eviscerating her. All she could do was to dismally serve its grim, self-pitying demands, as it vied with the cancer to snuff out the last of her. – He's living rough now, our Joe. No oan the streets, but on folk's couches, she whines in plaintiff appeal. – Like a vagabond, bichrist.

Greg looks at the shattered pieces of the glass table, then casts his gaze to the decorated tree and the stone fireplace, as if trying to reassure himself that life isn't completely disintegrating around him. There's a rattle on the cat flap, as Chairman Miaow slides in and heads for the empty bowl. He sniffs at it, then looks up at them with a perturbed mew.

Just then, Elspeth returns, making for the kitchen, pouring herself a big drink. – Peace at last, she says, before she feels the head of the purring cat batter her legs. – Oh, awright, pal, deigned tae join us have we, she acknowledges, heading to the cupboard and scooping some food into the bowl. – Greedy wee bastard, Elspeth says affectionately, watching the animal destroy its offerings.

– Is that a Siamese? Melanie asks.

– Aye, Elspeth says.

– Chairman Miaow, Greg says. – Although the breed is from Thailand, or Siam, as it was originally called, and not China obviously. He switches on the TV with the sound muted, and watches the news update on the bars. – Death toll up to fifty-six, he says gravely, before picking up his glass of wine. – Honest to God.

Melanie turns to Elspeth, who sits down with a big glass of white. – So what does being a lab technician at a school here involve?

– Helping the teachers and kids set up the experiments, looking after the equipment, the chemicals, the animals, aw that sort ay stuff.

– She's hiding her light under a bushel, Greg says, turning from the TV. – She's Chief Technician. Worked her way up from lab assistant!

– That Skarrish gift of understatement again, Melanie says, as Elspeth, in spite of herself, feels flattery's subversive glow ignite in corners of her face. – Did you need to study for qualifications?

– I did day release at Stevenson, then Napier.

– These are colleges, right?

– Aye. Napier's a university now, but, Elspeth's shoulders shake involuntarily in square-go bristle. – We didnae need the money, cause Greg's got a good job, and I was part-time for a bit before the kids were at school, but it's good tae have something tae get you out the house, Elspeth explains, taking a long sip of her wine. There was something about this white wine; the swamping, almost narcotic drunkenness it conferred. – Are you going to keep working when the bairn comes?

– I reckon so. Might cut back on my hours, though.

Val shifts in her chair and cranes to Elspeth. – You were eywis a hard worker, and she looks to Melanie. – Since she was a wee lassie. A paper round, stacking shelves at the Co-op, working nights in that chippie.

– Well, I always like tae keep busy. But I work in a lab now, so you're in good hands, Ma, I'll make sure that oxygen tank doesnae blow up!

Elspeth, Val and Melanie share a laugh as Greg is arrested by an image on the TV and grabs the handset to turn up the sound. – Shhh!!

The newsreader's grim voice, – ...bringing the death toll to over sixty. With rescue crews having barely scratched the surface of the debris, this seems set to rise further. Brian Kerr, BBC News, Tehran.

– So, I'm no allowed to speak in my own house now, Elspeth snipes.

Greg turns down the volume, looks to his wife. – Sorry, honey, I just get so absorbed in these things. Those poor families... it makes you think. One minute we're here, the next... it's all so arbitrary.

– I went to Tehran several years ago, Melanie sits forward. – With the VSO, as a student volunteer.

– Wow! That must have been some experience, Greg says and turns to Elspeth. – Hear that, honey, Melanie was actually in Iran!

– Good for her, Elspeth says softly, picking up her drink.

– I still get a lot of hassle from Homeland Security for having that stamp in my passport. I get stopped more than Frank!

Elspeth raises one eyebrow. – Will they let him intae the USA?

– Why wouldn't they?

– Eh, because: *Frank*? Elspeth laughs, before looking at her incredulously. – Because of his criminal record. You do recall where you two met?

Melanie settles back on the couch, unfazed as Greg's bug-eyed stare darts between her and Elspeth. – He'll be married to a US citizen, and he has no drug felonies.

Elspeth and Melanie lock stares at each other and both are about to speak when Greg gets in first, trying desperate deflection tactics. – You don't think Joe could have hit Connor or Anthony, no? Frank didn't seem to be too convinced of his innocence...

– No. My dad was a drunk, Elspeth says loudly, – but he never, ever hit me.

– I'm not talking about your dad, honey, but on that subject, did he ever hit Joe or Frank, though?

Elspeth shrugs and looks to Val, who tuts loudly. – Laddies... different times.

Melanie leans forward, lowers her voice, hoping she's out of Val's earshot. – In my experience of working in prisons, when people are angry and intoxicated, they can do just about anything.

Elspeth looks at Melanie in barely repressed scorn.

– Can we no just forget aboot hitting, Val asks, – at Christmas, bichrist!

– Sorry, Val, my bad, Greg whips to Melanie, – as you Americans say! I just keep thinking of man's inhumanity to man, he shakes his head and points sadly at the soundless TV. Picks up his iPad.

– Well ah dinnae like tae think aboot it, Val snaps.

– And quite right too, Val, Greg agrees, lowering his device to the couch, – it is Christmas, after all!

– Time some folks started acting like it, Val grumbles, pulling the blanket closer to her. It's suddenly almost unbearably hot and she now uses it to shield herself from the fire.

Elspeth picks up on this. – Too warm, Mum?

– Just fine, says Val, a little starchily.

Her mother, Elspeth evaluates, with her rapacious vanity, has always deeply resented ageing. Now that she is dying, Val is more aggrieved than ever about being on the cigarette butt of her timeline. Elspeth thinks about Val as a younger woman; strong and vital, able to withstand the force of being married into the Begbies for decades. She ponders on how short life is, looking at Greg, already deteriorating visibly, the nine-to-five stress eating away at him. His shoulders stooping, the worry lines etching deeper all the time, more pronounced by miles than the deep scarring on the face of her brother Frank that she thought would never fade. She looks upstairs, and shudders as she thinks of George and Thomas being levelled by life in that same way.

It eats away at her how Frank seems so fit, tanned and carefree. It's like he is already living in California! He's made so many people's lives miserable, and now that he's supposedly rehabilitated, we're meant to just draw a line in the sand and forget it! His two eldest laddies, by all accounts running amok in Leith, and this other one, this River, that nobody's even seen? And this daft lassie, her who reckons that because she has an education she's exempted from thinking with what's in her knickers...

Melanie looks at the clock. She'd thought Frank was exaggerating about his family. It isn't the case. Joe is a psychopath and an alcoholic. Whatever he'd done, however he'd been, she just can't see Frank in that way. He is well away from here. His mother... well... she is sick and running out of real estate for sure, but she's not found any grace in her life to make her impending demise palatable. The brother-in-law is a well-meaning doormat, but the sister... what a goddam bitch. Elspeth seems invested in some kind of regression from Frank, not in his rehabilitation. Melanie fervently wishes for the return of her partner. – I wonder where Frank is?

– Maybe Joe's got him to take a wee drink, Elspeth says in malicious cheer, raising her own glass, – wi it being Christmas. Aye, they'll have run into some radge fae the auld days!

Melanie shakes her head. – I don't think so.

Elspeth raises an eyebrow. – Huh! You've got a lot tae learn aboot the Begbie men, hen! Notice how peaceful it is here now? Notice that?

– Frank has told me all about the men in his family, Melanie heads to the kitchen, refills the glass with tap water, then holds up the wine bottle. – May I?

– Be my guest, Elspeth says in revelry. – I thought you didnae drink! In your condition, n aw, she points at Melanie's stomach.

– No, Frank doesn't drink. I just didn't want one. One small glass of wine won't do the baby any harm.

Greg raises his brows, is about to say something, but stops himself.

Elspeth shoots a Forth Estuary-wide grin. – Aye, when the cat's away...

– Well, I've always been able to take or leave it, Melanie declares, then after a thoughtful pause, – Frank's very strong-willed and genuinely doesn't seem to care about it but I don't like encouraging him, Melanie fills a glass and sits down. – Yes, he told me about them all: Joe, their dad and their granddad.

Val bristles in the chair. – Like he kens everything, she mumbles.

– Aw aye, such as, Elspeth probes.

– Well... Melanie turns to Val who has slouched towards her and struck up a semi-indignant pose. – I'm sorry, Val, but I'm only repeating what Frank said...

– Like he kens the half ay it, Val snaps, reaching for her mask.

– That his father was an alcoholic, Melanie is undeterred, – and his grandfather a violent thug who ran thieving rackets on the docks, pilfering goods. But his dad couldn't hold a job down there. He was always drinking and stealing and ending up in prison.

Val is silently seething as Elspeth nods in sarcastic appreciation. – Honest Frank! Well, a broken clock is right twice a day!

– So, this is what he's sayin, Val heaves on her mask as punctuation for her outbursts, – tae everybody! Is that what you're telling ays?

– Look, please don't distress yourself, Melanie pleads. – He doesn't, he wouldn't... he wouldn't say this to anyone outside this room. It's just that Frank and I don't believe in having secrets from each other.

– Aye, ah kin tell yis aw aboot secrets, Val mumbles, – that's aw ah'm sayin...

– C'mon, let's leave all this nonsense right here, Greg interjects, – leave it all in the past where it belongs! Like you said, Val, it's Christmas!

– I don't think it's healthy to have taboos in families, Melanie rubs her finger around the rim of her wine glass. – People ought to be able to talk about things, even difficult things, to get them out into the light.

– Well ah dinnae like airing ma dirty washing in public, Val snarls.

– All family life has a dark side, Val, and Melanie reaches over and grabs her frail hand. – It's nothing to be ashamed of. My parent's families came to America from Ireland and Norway. They were criminals on both sides.

– Norway, aye? Elspeth scoffs.

– Yes, what's so strange about that?

– What did they dae, shag reindeers? She points to the ornaments on the mantelpiece.

– I'm sorry?

– Well it's no exactly known for high crime rates and multiple deprivation, Scandinavia, now is it?

– That's probably where the lovely blonde hair comes fae, Scandinavia, Val looks at Melanie, who smiles indulgently at her. – But that might be a Californian thing.

Greg addresses Elspeth. – Actually, the Scandinavians are way ahead of the game in crime fiction. They've completely revitalised the genre.

– Aye, Elspeth sips more wine, – that's fiction, but, Greg. That's no fact. That's no true crime.

– Authors draw from the real world, though, Elspeth. It must have some basis in fact.

– Aye, like artists. The ones that paint pictures and mutilate coupons, she smiles at Melanie. – But ah'm no huvin a dig, cause it's true what ye say aboot families aw having a dark side, she smiles. – It's the light side in our yin that ah'm struggling tae find!

– As I say, I got all this from Frank, Melanie insists. – We don't keep any secrets from each other.

– No? Well see if he tells ye where he's been the night, Elspeth laughs. – Where he is now!

Melanie tries to look disdainful, but then finds herself checking her phone.

– Ah ha! Elspeth points a 'gotcha' finger at her. All Melanie can do to is point back at her and laugh. Elspeth rises, a little unsteady, takes the wine bottle, and crashes down beside Melanie. Tops her up. – Have I been too radge, she asks her, through one eye.

– No, it's just the Scottish sense of humour that I sometimes find strange.

– It's the peeve, Elspeth contends, sweeping a hand through her hair. – And that's just cause ay Frank and Joe… nae offence… Frank and Joe being here. But you're awright.

Greg has taken the iPad over to Val, and he crouches down beside her to show her some pictures of the boys. – Our Skye jaunt in the summer here, Val…

– Lovely… barry scenery…

– Aye, they knock Scotland, but see when you do get the weather? It's pretty much unbeatable.

– Whaire's that?

– Skye, Val.

– Skye... scenery...

Greg notes that Elspeth has thrown her head back. She's softly singing Herman's Hermits' 'I'm Into Something Good'. Melanie ignores this, her brow furrowed as she whips through her phone. – I should imagine they've found it difficult to get a cab.

– Naw... they aw work now at Christmas, Val says. – Money mad. Was never heard ay before, working on Christmas Day, no matter how hard up ye were. Family eywis came first. No now.

– Curse of modern life, Val, Greg groans. – I'll be back to the grind after Boxing Day, I'm afraid.

Elspeth sits forward, scrutinises Melanie's profile, who then turns to catch her. It compels Elspeth to raise her brows. – So nothing fae Frank then.

– No. I left a message. He'll get back soon.

They lock eyes. There's an awkward moment between them, which Elspeth feels compelled to break by raising her glass and settling back in the couch. – So, California, Melanie. Ye know a lot ay movie stars? That George Clooney, ah shouldnae be saying this in front of you, Greg, but yabadabadoo!

– He couldn't steal you from me, Greg says, looking round from the iPad on Val's lap.

Elspeth ignores him and addresses Melanie. – You must see a lot of stars there, ay?

– It's not really my world, Melanie curls up in the lotus position with an ease that makes Elspeth think she really needs to go back to yoga. – Though I did once sit next to Elliott Gould in a movie theatre in Santa Monica.

– Elliott Gould! Hear that, Ma! You'll mind ay Elliott Gould!

– Elliott Gould. *M*A*S*H*, Val says, as she pushes Greg's iPad away, to the extent he has to retrieve it to stop it from falling to the floor.

– Watch, Val...

– That was Alan Alda! That oxygen's gaun tae your heid, Ma, Elspeth then puts her hand over her mouth. – I'm right enough, but, ay.

– I think that was the TV version, Greg says, relieved to get the device in a solid grip in his hands. His knees crack as he stands up. – There was a film version too, and he strides across the room, looking it up in his iPad. – Yes… Val's right! Elliott Gould was in the film version.

– Aye. Elliott Gould, Val says.

Elspeth starts singing, a high nasal sound, – Suicide is painless doo-doo… it brings on many chan-chis… Then she looks at Val in some guilt. – But that's an awfay depressing song! Mind you, it was in the charts, and she turns to Melanie. – Youse dinnae have that in the States, the charts.

– Like the music listings charts?

– Yes, honey… Greg says, – they have Billboard in the good ole US of A! Am I right, Melanie?

– Yes, the record-sales listings.

– No the real charts, but, no like *Top Ay The Pops*, Elspeth says. – Mind you, we've no got that now. Except at Christmas, that's the only time they show it. But they had tae stop showing it normally because everybody on that show was a fuckin sex offender if you'll pardon ma French, she rolls her eyes, lifting her glass.

– Maybe an exaggeration, Greg says, concerned at his wife's mood.

– They were bloody nonces, Greg, every one ay them!

– Yes, that was absolutely terrible, Greg concedes. – All those sex offenders at the BBC and in the British establishment.

– Should be fuckin hung, Elspeth says, looking to Melanie to contradict her.

– And then Cameron passes a law, making them immune from investigation under the Official Secrets Act, Greg shudders. – It's absolutely sick.

Val is uncomfortable at this, looking into the flames of the fire licking the log as Elspeth turns to Melanie. – So, what sort of music do you listen tae?

– Pretty much anything.

– Do you like dance music? Like, house? Do you ever go clubbing?

– Sometimes. Not much. Frank isn't a big clubber, and I'm not that keen myself.

– Ah like Calvin Harris, but that's pretty much the only dance music ah listen tae now. Well, wi huvin the bairns, ay.

– Changes everything, Greg mournfully grins.

– Tell me, Melanie, Elspeth says, and Greg winces at the devilish fix in her eye, – no being wide or nowt like that, but how is it you Americans never laugh?

– What do you mean?

– Example: my mate Christina married an American guy, Ralph, right? Nice felly, but never laughs. Sumbday tells a joke and he goes 'that's funny'. Ah say tae him, 'if it's funny, just laugh'. Dinnae say 'that's funny'. Ken?

– I laugh a lot, Melanie laughs, her face creasing, – but there is something right about that. A lot of American's can be quite stiff-assed.

– So what do you and Frank listen to together? Music wise, likesay?

– I dunno... everything I guess.

– Frank... he was ey mair intae Rod Stewart, Elspeth says. – Does he still listen tae Rod?

– Not really. I only hear him listen to music in his studio, when he's working, and it's usually classical. Like Bach and Mahler.

– Oh, of course, this is the new-model Frank, Elspeth fingers her nose, – the hoity-toity, arty-farty version!

Melanie battles down the impulse to react to Elspeth's sarcasm. No wonder Frank wants to move to California. To be away from people who only seem invested in his past, rather than his future.

Elspeth refills her glass. – Matt Dillon. He's another yin ah ey liked fae that Hollywood set. Dinnae see him in that much these days, ay-no.

– No.

– Hunky, but, Melanie.

– I suppose so, if you like that type.

Elspeth gives Melanie a sly look. – Listen, ah'm no being funny, and he's my brother, but what do you see in Frank? Ah mean, you're a beautiful young lassie and...

– He's terrific in bed. Your brother: Frank.

Greg coughs nervously, and heads over to the kitchen. – I think that's what they call too much information!

Elspeth rolls her eyes in disdain. – Aw aye.

– Well you asked, and that's one of the things I see in him. Want me to go on?

– I really don't think that's necessary, Greg swallows his drink and takes a new bottle of white wine from the fridge.

Elspeth points at her. – Watch him. He's my brother, but watch him.

– Ah did the best ah could wi him and Joe, Val trembles, holding onto her glass of gin but making no attempt to drink it, – but thir wis nae tellin either ay them, that's aw ah'm sayin.

– Aye, ye did, Ma, Elspeth consoles, almost cooing over at her mother. – Fair do's. Take a wee sip ay that gin!

– Never any tellin a Begbie man, Val ignores her daughter as she lets ghosts of police raids past jolt through her consciousness. – They dae what they like, she says ruefully as she contemplates a bitter and futile legacy in the service of violent, alcoholic males. Men who thought they were hard, but were saplings to be locked away by the state for the best years of their lives, because they fundamentally lacked something. Intelligence? Self-control? And Frank, her boy, he really was changing. Elspeth couldn't see it, but Val could. It was the way he was allowing this lassie in, in a way he never had with anyone in the past. And he seems happy. Francis had never been a happy boy. Always troubled. Always trouble. But she had failed him. This lassie, with her education, money and contacts: she had come through for Frank. Bile rose in Val. Her life now seemed useless: a brutal lie. She wishes she could believe in God, heaven, the afterlife, a second chance, but no. You live and you die and that's it. If only she had been told it was so quick and there was no time to recover from the really big mistakes. And now this American lassie is here, framing her failure. She takes a sip of her gin.

– I'm sure you guys think you know Frank, Melanie is saying, stretching cat-like, then snapping back into position, – but you don't know what he's like now. The work he's put into his rehabilitation. The journey he's been on. He really has changed.

– Aye, right, Elspeth mocks.

Melanie smiles at her. – When was the last time you saw him?

Elspeth considers this. It was a few years. Frank discouraged visits in the later phase of his sentence. When they did drop by he was sullen and uncommunicative, so they tailed off... Now she sees that he was preparing for a new life, as an artist, with this woman, and he'd only seen Val when he learned she was sick. Even then, his family was not considered part of this masterplan. But it is different with this Melanie. Who is she? What does she have? For the first time a deep and sneaking respect for this young American insinuates in Elspeth. – Look, ye got him off the peeve. Well done on that yin. Never thought I'd see the day, but...

– The what? I got him off the what?

– The drink. You got him to stop drinking.

– I didn't do anything, Melanie shakes her head. – It was all his idea.

Val has been sitting squeezing the glass. She suddenly blurts out, – Ma Joe never touched his bairns...

– Naebody here sais eh did, Elspeth tells her.

– That Sandra! Bitter! Like Joe says, Val swipes a bony hand in the air. Lays down the gin, feels her mask for reassurance. – Bitter cause she ran tae fat. Oh aye, ah telt him tae stay clear right fae the start. Said tae him, that yin'll run tae fat. Look at her ma. And a man can never trust a lassie that runs tae fat. They're aw jovial on the ootside but their bitter aboot it in here, and she taps her own thin chest. – And she'll blame you, Joe, see if she doesnae, ah telt him!

Elspeth has been half listening, her head nodding along. – Joe might be a lot ay things, Ma, but eh never touched up nae bairns. Especially no his ain!

Val looks at her daughter for a couple of heartbeats in incomprehension, before fury ignites in her eyes and she tears the mask from her face. – SHE NIVIR SAIS THAT, Val roars. – Sandra! She never sais he touched them *up*, like a bloody nonce! She sais he only battered them!

– Oh, and that's perfectly acceptable, Greg snaps.

– That's where kids learn violence, Melanie says to him, shaking her head, – the home.

– He wouldnae dae that either, Ma, Elspeth contends. – I didnae mean it like that. I meant *never touched them*, no *never touched them up*, and she lets out a hollow laugh. – I'm pished... then she whips back to Val. – No tae his ain bairns!

– Well that wis what ye sais!

– A slip ay the tongue, but, Ma, Elspeth giggles. – It's the wine! Ah'm pished!

– Aye well, Val shudders and inches closer to the fire. – He was never a provider, though, oor Joe: just like his faither that wey. That always causes problems, when a man cannae provide. That's aw ah'm sayin.

– I think that's a very antiquated way of looking at things, Val, Melanie shakes her head. – It's not medieval times or even the industrial era. Women today shouldn't be reliant on men.

– Oor Frank wisnae much ay a provider, Val looks to Melanie, shaking her head. – No wi that June or that other yin, that River's ma. A jailbird never is. But he's changed awright, selling aw this art stuff!

– He's doing incredibly well, Val, Melanie smiles at her as Elspeth rolls her eyes and Greg nods. – You should be so proud of him. There's a big collector in LA, a plastic surgeon, who...

– But you wouldnae have had any interest in him then, hen, Val shakes her head, – no the wey he was before. No a lovely, intelligent young lassie like you!

Melanie tries to respond but is tongue-tied. – Well... I'm not sure how... I mean, I did meet Frank in prison, although I suppose he was... well, on the road to rehabilitation...

Elspeth sits enjoying her discomfort. Greg is about to speak when the landline phone, situated on a small table by the couch, rings out loudly. Elspeth picks it up. – Yes? Yes, it is. Yes. Yes. I'm his sister...

Greg, Val and Melanie in anxious attendance. – What's is it? Is Frank okay, Melanie squeals.

Elspeth waves her into silence. – Joseph Steven Begbie. Oh God!

– What's gaun oan! Val gasps. – What's wrong wi oor Joe?

Elspeth puts her finger over her lips to shush Val. – Okay. Right. Yes, I'll be in tomorrow. Thanks, and she hangs up.

– What's up, honey, Greg asks. – What's up with Joe? Where's Frank?

– Well this is fuckin good, Elspeth says, hands on hips, drinking their anxiety for a beat. – Joe's in the hospital. Found in the street: bad concussion and a broken jaw.

– Christ... a broken jaw... Val moans. – What happened?

– Where's Frank, Melanie is on her feet.

– They didnae say, Elspeth shrugs. – Joe was picked up alone. Found in the street, they sais.

A text pops into Melanie's phone. – It's from Frank. She reads it. – 'Got Joe in a cab, ran into an old mate and went to Starbucks for a coffee. Back in a bit.'

– My laddie...Val whimpers, – my wee Joey...

– He'll be feelin nae pain, no the state he wis in, Elspeth says. – No till the morn, anyway!

Val rambles to herself, – ... nae malice in him, no as a wee bairn... got bitter... that's what does it, when they get bitter...

Melanie is furiously texting. – Obviously he got into some kind of trouble after Frank left him...

– Aye, well... maybe, Elspeth says.

– No maybes, she snaps, charging to the kitchen as she texts, filling up her glass.

– Poor Joe! At Christmas too! What a nightmare, Greg says.

– Aye, well. Ah sais ah'd go up the morn n see him, Elspeth rises and moves over to Melanie. – Bet you never had any ay this sort ay stuff with your family? The Vikings, she half laughs, then checks herself, – like growing up?

– Thankfully, no, Melanie sends the text off. – But I've worked in enough prisons here and in California to know how common it is. But yes, I'm well aware that my own family circumstances were very fortunate.

– So… what does your family dae?

– My mom's a designer and my father's an attorney.

– A lawyer, Elspeth can't refrain from a hearty guffaw as she creases over, – a lawyer!

– Elspeth, please, Greg begs, as Melanie takes a sip of wine.

– He isnae a *criminal* lawyer, is he?

– No, Melanie leans against the worktop, – he specialises in contract law, mainly property.

– Aye, but a lawyer, still, Elspeth slaps her knee. – What dae they think ay oor Frank, your folks?

– They've met a couple of times. They get on well with him and they respect my choices.

– It wid be the Viking thing, they'd understand aboot aw the raping and pillaging!

– What? Melanie looks at her.

– Elspeth! Greg roars.

Elspeth puts her hands in front of her mouth. – Sorry! Didnae mean that! Frank would be pillaging only! As far as I know he's never raped anybody! That wis just Joe!

Val tears the mask from her face. – What are ye talkin aboot now!?

– Kathleen Cargill, you mind ay Kathleen Cargill?

– That never went tae coort, Val gasps. – That wee hing oot, she wis jist eftir money fae oor Joe.

– Aye like he's fucking John Paul Getty. John Paul Ghetto mare like!

– Oor Joe wis workin oan the rigs then! He wis flush! That Sandra… at least she stood by him. She kent it wis nonsense!

Greg hauls in a breath, stands up, head bowed, and hands over the documents. – Let's change the subject! Please!

A text pops back in on Melanie's phone. – It's Frank. He's on his way back, Mum. He doesn't know anything about Joe.

– Good tae see you're standing by your man, Elspeth laughs.

– What are you talking about? Melanie wrinkles her nose.

– I'm talking about the *rehabilitated Frank,* of course, Elspeth surges in mock formality, – the one who would never hurt Joe.

– He wouldnae have, Val declares. – Surely no!

– Elspeth, Melanie asks, – why are you so pathologically driven to believe the very worst about Frank?

– Oh, ah dunno, Elspeth sings chirpily, – maybe call it experience. You need tae open your eyes, hen.

– My eyes are wide open, Elspeth. Maybe *you* need to tell me exactly what you are talking about?

Greg shakes his head. – C'mon ladies...

– Where did you meet him again, Elspeth torments.

– We told you where.

– Those lassies that meet men in prison. The prison romance; there's something weird about that, Elspeth takes the bottle of wine and refills her own glass. – Something lacking.

Melanie seethes in rage, unable to speak. Her teeth grind together.

– That's very unfair, Elspeth, Greg says. – Melanie is an artist herself. She was drawn to Frank's work. She's not one of those unfortunate needy women who meet violent offenders...

– I can speak for myself, Melanie pushes her hands down on the worktop. – Frank and I were aware from the onset that we would encounter those prejudices.

– Well maybe you can explain the difference tae me, Elspeth says, desperate to go outside for a cigarette. – That yin between one dopey cow fae a scheme that gets off on meeting a radge in the nick because they believe that they can change them, and the other, she looks Melanie up and down, – more educated one, from somewhere posher?

– I don't think I can change Frank... Melanie is flustered, – Frank is changing Frank, not me, you don't...

The buzzer goes.

– Saved by the bell, Elspeth smirks, heading for the door.

Melanie turns to Val and Greg, flipping up her palms in appeal.

– I'm sorry, Greg says, – I'm afraid she's had a wee bit too much to drink...

– She's making very big assumptions, Greg. She doesn't know me. I don't see any respect of boundaries!

– Unfortunately that's something you have to get used to in this family.

– Don't tar them all with the same brush, Greg!

– *With the same brush*, Greg says incredulously. – You are aware of Frank's past? As far as I know my Elspeth has never murdered anyone. So no. I won't be tarring them all with the same brush, thank you very much!

Melanie is about to respond, but Frank enters with Elspeth, and she runs to embrace him. – Honey, are you okay?

– Aye, of course I am. What's up?

Frank looks around them.

– What did ye dae tae oor Joseph, Val asks.

– What? I left him at Haymarket. Ah dinnae ken what's going on with him!

– Aye, right, Elspeth says.

– I know nothing other than what Mel's texted about hospitals, Frank rejoins in a pompous bourgeois tone his sister hasn't heard from him before, – so maybe just tell me, instead of casting all this silly innuendo?

Elspeth looks witheringly at him. – We got a call fae the hospital; they told us they've got Joe, wi a broken jaw and concussion. Found him in the street. So, you dinnae ken nowt aboot that!?

Frank seems not to have heard her last sentence. – Fucking clown.

– What happened, Greg asks in hushed tones.

Frank shakes his head, drawing in a deep breath, fighting his exasperation back, as they all look to him. – I got him outside and we walked up tae Haymarket. The air seemed tae revive him; sober him up a bit. He was still going on and on about Sandra and the bairns, but he was making mare sense, so I thought I'd just let him talk. Get it all out his system. After a bit he seemed better, so I got him intae a taxi and slipped him twenty bar. With the benefit of hindsight, it probably wisnae the wisest move tae gie an alky money at Christmas. Then ah wis on my way back, and I ran into Ronnie Pennals, and he looks at Elspeth, raising his hands. – Aye, he's a mate fae the jail, but he's also a teetotaller now. So, we went for a coffee and a wee catch-up.

Elspeth rolls her eyes and sighs doubtfully.

– Well Joe was found badly beaten up in the street, Greg says.

Frank shakes his head in dismissive scorn. – Why am I not surprised? He'd be straight oot the cab as soon as I was out ay sight, right intae the first boozer, guzzling mare peeve and causing bother. Fucking jakey nutcase. He's made a cunt ay himself and some fucker's banjoed him. Ah'll lay ye even money.

– Aye, n ah wonder whae, ay, Elspeth cuts in.

Val looks at Frank in a searching plea. – But you… you didnae hurt yir brother, did ye, Frank? No at Christmas, son! No at yir mother's last Christmas!

– Dinnae be daft, Ma, Frank scoffs. – Ah shouldnae have left him in that cab. Like ah sais, he'd have just got oot. He's an alky. Some liberty taker would have set aboot him.

Elspeth, wine glass and bottle in her hands, has never taken her eyes off her brother. – Aye, that's a racing cert, she laughs.

– What are you trying to say here, Elspeth? Melanie counters.

– Aye, what are ye saying? Frank challenges his sister. – Come out wi it, instead ay just casting aspersions.

Elspeth meets his harsh stare with her own malevolent gaze. – You're telling us that you never battered him?

– Why would ah dae that? He's ma brother!

– Because you're you? Because it's what you've always done, Elspeth derides. – A brick in his puss when you were twelve? A bottle ay Grouse over his heid, at a festive family game ay Monopoly? Another Christmas ruined!

Frank sighs in exasperation.

– Ex-convicts get stigmatised enough by society, Melanie says. – Frank's been on a long, difficult journey to control his anger and anxiety issues…

– Anxiety issues! Elspeth laughs out loud and looks at Frank.

– Elspeth, please... Greg begs.

Elspeth turns to Greg. – I'm sorry, but ah cannae believe this shite! Anxiety issues! She points at Frank. – He's nae anxiety issues! He *gies other people* anxiety issues!

Melanie carries on, – ... and I think he might deserve some support from his own family!

Elspeth turns on Melanie. – I'm sorry, but I dinnae think you ken anything aboot what he deserves fae this family!

– Elspeth, come on now, this is getting ridiculous, Greg appeals, moving across to her.

The phone rings again, driving them back into silence. This time it's Greg who picks it up. – Who's calling? Yes. No. I'm her husband. Yes, Greg.

– Who is it? Elspeth moans.

Greg puts his hand over the phone. – Social services. He gets back on the call. – Right... I see...

– Social... what the fuck... Elspeth feels an ominous sensation cutting through the drink, a leaden weight, crystallising inside her chest.

Greg continues to talk on the phone. – No, we didn't know about Sandra. Is it serious? Oh my God! Yes, we heard about Joe, just a few minutes ago as it happens. Of course, we'll take the kids. Thanks...

– WHAT!! Elspeth roars, forcing Greg to put his hand over the receiver. – No fuckin way! Ah telt ye! What did ah fuckin say tae you!?

– Thank you. Yes, bring them here. Thanks. Goodbye, Greg hangs up and looks sheepish.

– Thir no fuckin well comin here, Greg! No tae this hoose! That Sandra...

Val pipes in, – Those perr bairns...

– What else could I say? Greg begs. – They literally have nowhere else to go!

– FUCKIN SANDRA, Elspeth roars.

– Where is she, Val begs, – what's wrong wi Sandra!

Greg cuts in, – It seems Joe neglected to mention that Sandra's in the hospital, getting her damn leg amputated! She has type-two diabetes and her foot had apparently gone gangrenous.

– Pit oan an awfay lot ay weight since her hysterectomy, Val says.

– Loast a fuckin leg, Elspeth exclaims. – He fuckin set this up… her face contorts in rage… – that fuckin vermin Joe… Elspeth stamps her feet. – THOSE FUCKING MINGING LITTLE TRAMPS ARE NOT SETTING FIT IN THIS HOOSE!

Greg looks up to the ceiling. – SSSH!! For God sake!

– No way, Greg. No fucking way.

– It'll only be till Joe gets back on his feet, Greg implores, outstretching his arms. – They'll be here in about an hour. They can sleep in the spare room. The emergency social worker is bringing them! It's Christmas, for God sake!

– He'll never get on his feet! He set this up, Elspeth hisses. Frank smiles, evidently enjoying proceedings, then straightening his face, but the look is caught by her. – What are you fuckin smirkin at!

Frank raises his hands in the 'don't shoot' position, as Melanie jumps in, – With all due respect, he wouldn't have set himself up to be beaten and hospitalised!

Elspeth focuses on Melanie. – With all due respect, you keep yir fuckin neb oot!

– With pleasure!

Frank looks at Elspeth. – That's no very nice.

– No, it isn't, Greg agrees. – You can't talk to guests like that.

– Look at him! Elspeth invites, pointing at Frank. – You did this tae Joe! You, she denounces her brother, her finger jabbing the air. – Now I've his fuckin bairns dumped oan ays and you swan off tae fuckin California!

– You're no making any sense, I never touched Joe, Frank pleads. – Unreal!

– Yes, Elspeth, Greg shakes his head. – This is not helping!

Ignoring Frank and Greg, Elspeth turns to Melanie. – Dinnae get me wrong. I like you. My kids like you. You're a good person.

So that's why I'm telling you, Elspeth glares at Frank, – him sitting thaire, smirking away...

– Whae's smirking? It's bloody tragic! Frank says. – But it is kind ay perversely amusing, though!

Greg looks pointedly at Elspeth, but his wife remains focused on Melanie, – ... you do not know what you are getting yourself into!

– C'mon, Elspeth, you're drunk, Frank shakes his head tightly, – and you're really makin a fool ay yirsel.

– So, what are you gaunny dae? Break ma fuckin jaw as well?

– That is completely out of order, Elspeth, Greg says, as Melanie nods vigorously in accord.

Frank's composure is chilling to his sister. His paternal more-sad-than-angry expression scares her deep inside, even in a way his crazed rages never did.

– And yes, it is completely out of order, and thank you for that, Greg, Frank whips to the husband before going back to the wife. – I tried to help Joe. That is the basic fact of the matter, his strange, clipped annunciations are like blows to Elspeth, before he reverts to a more familiar voice. – So for fuck sake, goan sort yourself oot!

Elspeth feels her mouth hang open. – What?

– Look at ye. Yir in the same state as them, Frank declares, then adds, – Joe. My faither. Wise up.

Elspeth erupts into apoplexy. – You! You tellin other people tae sort themselves oot! That's a... ah've heard it aw now! Ah dinnae notice you volunteering tae clean up my ma's shite! Or tae take Joe's bairns! You n Miss California thaire, she nods at Melanie.

– Dinnae be crazy, Frank shakes his head, filling up his glass with Highland Spring. – We're in London, heading for America. It widnae be practical.

– Please try and respect other people's choices, Elspeth, Melanie says.

Briefly shooting her a paint-stripping look, Elspeth refocuses on Frank. – How *practical* was it for your bairns, growing up, when you were in jail then? Eh?

Frank glances from a nervy Greg to her. – These days are gone now, and in the past they must remain, and he rises, looking to Melanie.

– What you tryin tae say? That yuv changed? You've no changed! You'll never change!

Closing his eyes, Frank shakes his head, then emits a low chuckle. – And that's the way you want it, ay, he opens his lids and grins starkly at her. – That would suit you, if ah wis tae cause a scene n start kickin off, he starts to pace the floor like a defence prosecutor.

Greg grips the worktop.

– Aw aye, Frank continues, sucking air through his nose into his expanding chest, – that would affirm the cosy wee natural order ay things: jakey Joe, bad-boy Frank and golden-girl Elspeth. Well, you'll no get that satisfaction fae me, he tilts his head to the side and his eyes expand. – Ah've done that maist ay ma life, n it husnae worked, cause ah've spent maist ay ma life in jail. So now ah'm daein something different, like avoiding negativity. It's all yours. Enjoy, he winks at her.

Melanie rises to stand alongside him. – Yes, I think we should go.

Greg bounds over and shakes Elspeth by the shoulders to avert her rapacious gaze from Frank and Melanie. – You really have to stop this, honey!

– Take ma part for once, will ye, and she aggressively pushes his arm from her.

– It's not about sides, Greg hisses through his teeth, lowering his voice to whisper, – why does it always have to be about fucking conflict with the fucking Begbies... and he rubbernecks to ensure nobody else has heard him.

Val is focused on Frank and Melanie, as she pushes herself slowly with great effort, up in the chair.

– Easy, Ma... Frank says.

– This might be the last time ah see ye, Val croaks, her voice wavering, as she struggles to her feet. – Ah wanted tae say so much... but it was aw just the same stuff, arguments, like always!

– Cannae pin that yin on me this time roond, Frank says,

embracing her. It is like holding a small animal. There is nothing but skin, bone and organs. No fat, no muscle.

– Ah ken that, son, but...

– And where's aw this 'last time ah'll see ye' nonsense coming fae? We were gaun tae come roond on Tuesday, Frank laughs. – Think ye'll be able tae hud on forty-eight hours or can you no fit us intae your busy schedule?

– Dinnae be cheeky! You're no too big tae git a skelp fae me yet, pal, so dinnae think it!

– There she is!

– Ma laddie, ma laddie, ma laddie, Val contends in a resigned tone, pitched between elation and sorrow. She breaks off the hug and turns to Melanie. – You look after him!

– You bet I will, Val.

Val touches Melanie's hair. – Lovely... She kisses the American woman. Looks at Frank. – Aye, ye got a good yin.

– Too right.

– Better late than never, Val gasps, but the effort of saying goodbye has visibly exhausted her. As Greg and Elspeth are in a snake-like recriminative conversation by the French windows, it's incumbent on Frank and Melanie to lower her back into the chair. Frank notes that Chairman Miaow also seems to have had enough and rattles through the cat flap.

– Right, see youse, Frank says. – A good New Year and aw that when it comes.

– You too, Greg nods from across the worktop.

– Right then, Elspeth folds her arms and turns away.

Frank and Melanie head to the hallway. Greg and Val look at Elspeth.

– So ah'm the bad one now, she blows out some air and helps herself to another glass of wine.

– God, nobody is saying that, Elspeth. But take it easy on the wine. Remember what drink did to your father!

Elspeth looks at him, grabs her bag with her cigarettes and storms outside.

Out in the street, the fangs of winter snap at Frank and Melanie as they walk huddled together in conference. He wants to get back to the New Town flat of their artist friends, with its roaring fireplace, in which witty, intelligent people with *something to say* chucked golden liqueur around teasingly in big brandy snifters, even if he just watched and listened, sipping his Perrier. The respect, both fawning and wary, that violence had once given him now felt so false, transitory and unsatisfying compared to this balm. That soothing bath of relaxed wealth; not just light years from the scheme and the tenements of Leith, but also so far removed from this stiff showroom petty-bourgeois Murrayfield shit. It astounds him now that he once saw a pebble-dashed bunga-low as constituting the good life. Melanie suddenly stops, com-pelling him to do the same.

He looks at the static, immaculate golden hair curled under into his chest under his chin. Hears that clear and precise American accent, so pure compared to the squashed, guttural vowels of his own family. – Frank, we said we were never going to have secrets from each other, and, ripping her head from his chest, she looks at him. – Did you hurt Joe?

– No. Like ah sais, he's my brother! Dinnae let them upset ye with their nonsense. He holds Melanie close, but she shivers in his arms. – Tell ye what, ah'll be glad tae get tae California, too cauld here, ay. Let's get back, he urges, and they set off again, his neck craning for the taxi that will take them out of this place.

As they walk the frozen streets towards Haymarket, Frank allows himself a grin of satisfaction in contemplation of how well everything had gone. Joe was literally, rather than metaphorically, asking for it this time. – Dae me, Frank, hospitalise ays, he'd begged, standing in the street, his eyes welling up. – It's the only wey ah'll get the bairns looked eftir at Elspeth's and kept oot ay care. Ah'll get off the peeve, he'd pleaded. It was his brother's pitiable and beaten eyes that got him. The fact that even in abject defeat, the spark of calculating snide didn't quite leave them. They were not the eyes of his alcoholic father, but his scheming thief of a grandfather, who had inducted him into his life of violent crime. He'd said thanks to that old bastard in his own way. But Joe...

Franco had shaken his head and turned away, before deploying the venomous rage welling up inside him, to pivot and smash a right hook into Joe's face. He fancied that one was the jawbreaker. As he slammed that open, air-gulping mouth, he'd heard the snap and felt something give. But it might have been the strong brogues licking the face of his prone brother that cracked the jaw as well as did the concussive damage.

New rationalisations float through Frank's mind. The old ones of it being a dog-eat-dog scenario didn't cover this new, unfamiliar territory. He had broken a pact with Melanie, a non-violence concordat, but it was for the greater good. Crucially, the kids will be spared care. Less important, Joe is happy; he gets what he'd asked for. And could you blame him? He did what any father would do. He broke the rules, yes, but it was about providing childcare for his children. He looks at Melanie, her still-flat stomach, thinks of the new life in there. – I don't mean to cause an argument, and I know that it's no business of mine what you choose to do, he says to her, – but we did agree that drinking early on in the pregnancy wasn't a good idea.

Melanie looks at him with a hangdog expression.

She is a genuinely good person, Frank thinks, she'll make a terrific mother. This child will grow up strong and free, uncontaminated by the street poison that infected both him and his previous kids.

– I know. I feel terrible about it, she confesses, – I really screwed up. There was a lot of pressure and tension in the air, and I should have left with you rather than let Elspeth get to me. I'm sorry, honey.

Frank pulls her closer to him and kisses her. – No worries, babe. It is a stressful environment.

Elspeth? Not a bad result for her, really. Well, she can play the martyr and Greg gets to *do the right thing*. And for Frank himself, the highly satisfying release of violence that only being in his studio, lost in his work, can quell the need for. But most of all, his poor old ma is allowed to spend more time with some of her grandchildren. That is so important, Frank considers, as the yellow

FOR HIRE sign on a black cab shoots into his line of vision. At a volume that makes Melanie, lost in thought, suddenly jump, he roars, – TAXI!!

They gratefully climb into the cab, feeling the heat relax them. Yes, the kids are important. Not his older ones, lost to the streets, but the new blood, a child he was now ready for, growing in a woman he genuinely loved. One he could give a proper life to, away from this cold and brutal place.

Back in the house, Elspeth has returned from a cigarette on the patio, daring Greg, who stands in the kitchen, looking at his iPad, to say something. Val seems settled, her mask over her face, her thin chest rising and falling. The silence does not agree with Elspeth, who breaks it, wrapping her arms around herself as she closes the door. – Joe's fuckin bairns... no way, she says to the room, then focuses on Greg. – That Connor, he wrist-burned George when they were last over. The wee felly wisnae gaunny say nowt!

Greg refuses to take the bait. He leans on the worktop, not looking up from the screen of his device.

Val is distressed, sucking on her mask.

Greg raises his head. – Maybe everything happens for a reason.

– Dinnae gies that pish, Elspeth mocks. – It's what every cunt says when they cannae think ay anything else tae say. Fuckin nonsense...

– No, you fucking listen here, Elspeth, Greg jumps up, points at her, his teeth exposed, as Elspeth gasps in shock. He seldom loses his temper. – Maybe those kids need us, he slams his fist on the worktop. – They're young and they just don't have anybody else!

A sob detonates in Elspeth as tears, sentimental and penitent, trickle down her cheeks and her lip curls. – Ah'm a good person, right? Ah'm a good mother, ay, she asks him in a fractured plea.

– You're the best, Greg steps over to her, pulling her shoulders and hugging her to his chest. She surrenders, her head grinding into his breastplate, as if she's trying to burrow into it. – And that's why those kids need you, he says in steely whisper. – It's not what we wanted, but somebody has to do what the hell they can.

– Ah never said ye werenae, Val erupts in protest. – You're a bloody good mother. Better than ah ever was.

– C'mon, Val, Greg looks over, – different strokes...

– Ah was trying tae say...

Greg steps away from Elspeth and crouches over his mother-in-law. He takes her skeletal fingers in his hands. – Your Jimmy, you said he was an alcoholic, he whispers sadly. – That's not your fault.

– Jimmy's no her faither, Val emphatically shakes her head.

Elspeth freezes. Her hands grip the worktop, her knuckles white. She looks at her mother. – What? What did you just say?

– Honey, your mum's stressed, it's the drugs talking... Greg is on his feet. – It was a mistake to give her that gin...

– NUP, Elspeth roars in her husband's face, pointing at her mother. – WHAT DID YOU JUST FUCKIN WELL SAY!! Elspeth has a manic focus trained on Val. It reminds Greg of the time when a bird, a magpie, flew into the house and Chairman Meow was transformed from sweet, laid-back domestic pet, into focused terminator, never taking his demented eyes from it.

– He was never oot ay the jail long enough, Val says, matter-of-factly. – Well, whae provided for me and the boys? His faither. Auld Jock. He was a gangster, but he always showed up wi money.

Greg looks from her to Elspeth in a broken loathing. Wonders, as he does most Christmases, who this strange family is, why is he working so hard to host them, to herd this group of hissing, psychotic feral cats into his basket? – Why can't people just get on! My father was a good man! My mother was a good woman! Why can't that be enough! All this discord over...

He halts his tirade as he realises that Elspeth is hyperventilating and about to go for Val. – That fuckin auld grandfaither... YA FUCKIN DURTY HOOR, she springs forward and grabs her mother by the hair. The chemo wig comes away in her hand. – YA DURTY FUCKIN AULD... YE LIT THAT MINGING AULD BASTARD INTAE YIR SHITEY AULD DRAWERS!

– ELSPETH! Greg pulls her off, but she lays into Val, fists flailing, connecting with brittle old bone. – STOP!

– SHE'S EYWIS BEEN A FAAAHKIN HOOR, Elspeth twists and snarls like a desperate wild animal in Greg's grip, as she points at Val. – Used tae embarrass me as a fuckin wee lassie, chatting tae men in the Walk... Elspeth suddenly relaxes, as in demonic inspiration she seems to realise that at Val's time of life well-chosen words will inflict greater pain than physical blows. – Nae wonder ma poor fai... nae wonder Jimmy Begbie drank!

Greg releases Elspeth to retrieve Val's wig. He lifts it off the floor and hands it to her.

Val quickly puts it back on, unawares or uncaring that it's skewed at a ridiculous angle. – You wirnae thaire... you wirnae... she gasps, – you didnae ken Jimmy Begbie, and she tries to push herself up but can only manage to shuffle forward in the chair. – His alkie cock wis aw soft wi me but no wi everybody else! He slept wi hoors, Val spits in agitated venom, struggling for breath.

Elspeth, with Greg still holding her lightly, looms over her mother in denunciation. – HE SLEPT WI ONE HOOR ANYWAY! WHEN HE COULD PULL HIS AIN FUCKIN FAITHER OAF HER!

Val makes a gurgling sound, and bends double, before jack-knifing upwards, then falling out the chair. She hits the floor with a thump.

– Ma... ah'm sorry! Ma! Elspeth stops and springs to her aid. She screams at Greg, – Phone a fuckin ambulance!

Greg runs to the phone and calls 999.

Elspeth supports Val's head. – Oh, Ma, what are we daein? What did ye have tae say that for, she sobs.

Val looks up at her. – He wisnae a strong man... Jimmy... no like his faither... Jock wis a provider...

– Enough... enough... ah'm sorry, Ma, ah didnae mean what ah said, ah love ye, Ma, Elspeth holds her broken mother.

– Sokay, hen... mind... mind... Val wheezes lightly, – this is important...

Greg is on his iPhone. – Ambulance. I need an ambulance! He

sits back down on the couch, but lands on his iPad. 'Jailhouse Rock' blasts out as he tries to give instructions. – Fuck, I...

Elspeth cannot hear what Val is saying. – Turn that fuckin doon!

Greg grabs the iPad but the music won't stop. – I can't... it won't...

Elspeth gets up and throws the iPad against the wall. It shatters, and the music stops.

Greg winces but returns to the call. – Get me an ambulance! 24 Balmakeith Drive, Murrayfield! My mother-in-law is having a bad seizure.

– Ma! Val is in Elspeth's arms.

Her voice is faint and yet rasping. – I love you, hen... you're the best ay them aw... you're a provider...

Then her mother is limp in her arms and Elspeth can see the light leaving her eyes, as her lips turn blue. The heat is already departing from her body. Elspeth looks up to the ceiling. – Aw naw... it wisnae meant tae end like this... naw... she turns to Greg, her face ravaged in angst.

Greg puts his fingers to Val's wrist and then her neck. There is no pulse. He holds Elspeth. – She's gone, honey. Your mum's away now.

Elspeth pushes him off and stands up, letting Val's head fall heavily to the floor. She walks to the fridge and calmly opens a bottle of wine. Pours a huge glass.

Greg pulls the blanket over Val's head and body. Only her legs stick out. He looks at his wife with the drink. – Honey, is that going to help?

– Aye. And I'm no an alcoholic's daughter, she looks at the corpse with a sneer, – so there's fuck all to worry about.

THE BEASTS
OF BRUSSELS

JOHN KING

ROBERT MARSH BLUSHED as the cocktail connected, its schnapps-cognac mix stirring his emotions, crushed ice and freshly squeezed lemon cooling outright passion. The Spaak Salutation boosted his mood and a ball of righteousness formed as he watched events unfold in the street outside. He knew he couldn't become too involved in the violence, instead closed his eyes and tried to lose himself in 'Ode To Joy', which was playing softly in the hotel bar and lobby. His skin tingled. Power was definitely an aphrodisiac.

He had been living in Brussels for three years, and while he enjoyed the trips to Strasbourg and Luxembourg, this was his favourite of the three governmental cities. From the drink in his hand to the choice of composer to the grand ambition that elevated the city above its inconsequential past, the European Union was always on his mind. He was proud of the part he was playing in the move towards a single state, felt that unification couldn't happen without him, yet he was a humble man, fully aware that he was but one individual in a long line of visionaries. The same high ideals had linked emperors, kings, politicians, priests, philosophers, merchants and artists across the centuries, but now the dream was under threat. Just as importantly, so was his career.

It had been an incredibly stressful morning and Robert was in dire need of this drink and the chance to sit on his own and regroup. His meeting with Clive Simmons may have been conducted in a spirit of solidarity, but the brutal truth was that if Brexit went ahead he would be looking for a job. Robert had plans to start his own agency, it was true, but that was a long-term project. It was far too soon, needed a healthy contract in place, and there was also the small matter of the political goodwill involved. Leaving the EU would be a disaster, yet Simmons was determined to remain optimistic, and so must he. It was time to think of himself and enjoy some downtime.

As a massive footie fan, Robert was looking forward to the Belgium–England game. There was a drawback in that England brought a heavy-drinking following in their wake, and among this number were many violent thugs, but he refused to stay at home and let the hooligans win. Despite the fixture selling out he had managed to secure tickets, purchasing six of the best seats in the house from the legendary fixer Kraken. Robert and his pals would be sitting well away from the English and he envisaged plenty of friendly banter with the Belgians. The tickets weren't cheap, but would go through on his expenses. There was no way he could have let his friends and colleagues down.

Robert loved the way business and pleasure merged so smoothly at the heart of the EU. This was civilisation at its best – centralised, liberal, keen to reward its friends. For those who embraced the system it was the perfect life. While his work was rewarding, the city's restaurants, bars and nightclubs were a joy. For those on the inside salaries were high, taxes low, expenses generous, the rules flexible. Brussels attracted the finest talent from across Europe, and hearing different accents and seeing beautiful faces was a thrill in itself. Young hopefuls flocked here to further their careers in a genuinely progressive environment, actively encouraged and in certain cases mentored by the more experienced politicians and bureaucrats. It was a community at peace with itself and he hoped the English would behave, but feared the worst.

There had been reports of rioting in Germany, where England had just played, and in the age of New Football it was a disgrace that hooliganism was allowed to tarnish the brand. The Premiership was popular across the globe and worth many millions of euros in screening rights and shirt sales, while the Champions League was the greatest tournament on the planet, more important now than the World Cup, all of which made such outbreaks of disorder far worse than in the past. He had no personal knowledge of the dark days of the 1970s and '80s, when the game was run by amateurs and the terraces ruled by fascists, but he did know that the injection of huge sums of money and the subsequent regeneration had transformed the sport, and yet clearly the job wasn't complete. The hooligan element had to be eliminated once and for all.

These people had been such an embarrassment over the years that he often felt ashamed to be English. His UK-born colleagues, who had carved out successful careers for themselves here on the Continent, felt exactly the same. Last night he had paused outside a rough-looking bar and stared at the screen inside, seen footage of the hooligans trading blows with their German equivalents, glasses and bottles flying through clouds of tear gas. The short hair, pasty skin and crude tattoos had made him so angry he'd started to shake. It had suddenly felt as though every passerby was glaring at him, as if he was being accused of complicity. These pictures represented everything he hated about England and the English, and why he was so glad to be living in Brussels, why ever since he was a teenager he'd wished he had been born French.

The Spaak was circulating and Robert again tried to lose himself in the EU anthem. It was important to be detached as well as optimistic, but he was struggling, refocused on the Englishman outside. A gang of locals had surrounded and punched him several times, and he had fallen to the ground where the young men – who he guessed were of Turkish origin (although he didn't mean this in a racist way) – were kicking his head and body. Robert winced, raised his glass to his lips and had another sip of his cocktail, rolling the liquid around his mouth and noting the tang of spirit, the sweetness of juice. He tried not to leer, but couldn't stop himself, a twitching upper lip matched by a stiffening in his groin.

The thug had short ginger hair and wore a red polo shirt and black jacket, a dirty pair of trainers with what appeared to be a Union Jack sewn into the fabric, Robert disgusted at the sight of this fascist symbol. The man was pure gammon, a bully who preyed on the weak and defenceless, one of the racists who had voted for Brexit and put Robert's career at risk. Even if he had wanted to, there was nothing he could do to stop the attack. In any case, it would be wrong to intervene. He was watching a wildlife documentary of sorts, but one without the David Attenborough narration. This was a case of rough justice, but justice nonetheless. Nature had to be allowed to take its course. A different, more progressive narrative was required.

His scrotum tightened as a youth jumped on the fascist's back, while another gang member strolled over with what looked like an iron bar and swung it at the head. Robert had read about these street fights, seen interesting clips on YouTube, but this was his first real-life exposure to the English Disease. He was appalled, yet thrilled. No sound penetrated the window as mouths moved in odd shapes and angry faces contorted. Robert's erection was hardening, pushing at the front of his boxers as the beating continued, and he became whimsical, the idea of a Crusader being punished by an oppressed ethnic minority intensifying the sort of arousal a former colleague had once described as 'radical sadism'. He thought about the publication he had left to come to Brussels, how he had lost touch with some fantastic friends. An idea sparked. He left it to simmer.

Robert detested the fascist who had provoked this assault. He objected to his crass beer culture and lack of respect for educated professionals such as himself, recoiled at the ginger hair and thumping music with its too-loud bass and crude lyrics, never mind the tacky high-street clothes and crude Anglo-Saxon language and sordid promiscuity of the women and the gammon's arrogance in thinking he could march around Brussels as if he owned the place. Those responsible for rejecting unity and creating division had to expect some sort of payback. They could not have their cake and eat it. Actions had consequences. If only more people would recognise this truth.

He found it ironic that he was sitting in the luxurious surroundings of the Charlemagne as this grubby encounter played out, in a hotel named in honour of the father of Europe who had forcibly converted the Saxons to Christianity, because wasn't this ginger pig an unreconstructed throwback to that pagan tribe, while Robert was in the tradition of the Frank, and yet despite his disgust he was becoming a little worried. There were still no police on the scene, and while he knew they had better things to do than protecting English tourists, they really should come and stop this before someone was killed. Robert didn't want to witness a death. He didn't like the man or what he represented, but nobody could accuse him of lacking empathy.

For the first time he noticed a crowd watching from the opposite pavement. Most of these onlookers had remained seated at tables arranged outside a large café, like spectators at a sporting event – or the theatre. He liked this latter comparison. The fight was indeed a spectacle. An elderly couple tried to intervene, but were pushed away. The woman started to shout and the man held up a frail fist and shook it in the face of one of the youths. Robert wished they would mind their own business. It was none of their concern. He wondered if the gammon really would die, or perhaps spend the rest of his life in a wheelchair, but dismissed these ideas as fanciful. He was used to violence and would be fine. In any case, Robert had more pressing concerns.

There was a very real danger that he was going to ejaculate. He had to leave the bar, but how was he meant to do this with an erection? The confrontation outside was addictive and the cause of his problem, and he closed his eyes and gave up on 'Ode To Joy', instead tried to imagine a mountain pool packed with ice; his last skiing trip to Switzerland and the way he had fallen and rolled in the snow; a freezing shower full of pasty-skinned, ginger-haired pensioners; the dull predictability of those British war films that used to be repeated over and over on the television and had led to the current crisis.

It was no use. His mind drifted to a hot-tub full of naked translators craving sex and drugs and his rock-n-roll buddy Plastic Bertrand; a holidaying banker in nothing but her leather G-string; eager young hands turning the shower tap to hot; a night in with Fellini, Antonioni, Zeffirelli and a good bottle of Italian wine; champagne sessions at his favourite love hotel and the money to pay for whatever he wanted. He opened his eyes and looked through the window once more.

The English had arrived. These gatecrashers raised their hands and gestured and shouted obscenities as they swarmed down the street. His erection withered. The locals turned to face the mob, but didn't seem as confident as before. Robert feared for their safety. Faced with the brutality of the English they stood little chance. These were the mindless thugs he had been so worried about. He pitied the young Turks, felt sick as a fist connected and a man went flying, but he wasn't going to stay here and see these people abused. He detested violence. Only stopping at the counter to pay his bill, he left the bar and crossed the lobby, exited the Charlemagne by a side entrance and hurried away from the boulevard, eager to find a taxi and return to the sanctuary of his apartment.

Matt was one of the first on the boulevard and seeing a disturbance he moved towards it with the rest of the lads, and realising it was Pat on the ground hurried him up, his right fist connecting with the chin of the cunt who'd just kicked his friend in the head. It was the perfect punch, knocked him clean off his feet. A proper Tyson Fury moment. The rest of the Turks forgot about Pat and turned to confront the English, a knife pulled and flashed, stopping Matt dead, his hands out and palms up, stomach churning as he remembered Barcelona. Darren pushed past him and launched the Jupiler bottle he'd been drinking from, hitting bullseye through a trail of Belgian lager, thumping the dizzy knifeman in the face as he stumbled, kicking him one, two, three times as he hit the floor, the blade spinning away across the street.

The rest of the English spread out as the two sides clashed, and while the Turks had the numbers they were mainly in their twenties and up against an older, more dedicated England. Matt and Stan stood with Darren, fists raised as the Turks shifted towards the pavement where a squad of coffee addicts and fruit-juicers were sitting dummy-still, suddenly coming alive and scurrying inside the nearest café as the trouble spilled their way. Matt could see the Turks were nervous, that the English were in charge, but that flick-knife meant he was holding back. These wankers had no standards. Look what they'd done to Pat, a lone sightseer going about his business, a gentle giant who didn't have a bad bone in his body, and he thought of the Leeds supporters murdered in Istanbul and was as angry as he was scared.

Darren wasn't hanging around, and Matt followed him with the rest of the England, half the Turks quickly on their toes, the English sending the braver ones on their way soon enough. The knifeman was back on his feet and swaying as he lifted a plastic chair above his head and nearly toppled over, and Matt had to smile as he'd never worked out why anyone would think it was a good idea to grab a piece of lightweight furniture in the middle of a tear-up and throw it, why they suddenly wanted to get into the removals game. Stan thumped the bloke in the face, and this time he'd had enough, stumbling off and taking a few kicks as he went.

Peace returned to the street, and Matt went over to help Stan, who was kneeling down next to Pat. Darren stood over them while the rest of the English milled around. After a couple of minutes Pat's eyes were open, and although he was semi-conscious they were able to get him sitting up and talking rubbish. Sirens blared in the distance. Typical Eurocops. Never too bothered about nicking the locals, they couldn't wait to steam into the English, no matter the rights and wrongs of what had gone before. Matt had seen it countless times with Chelsea and England. It had been the same for every generation.

A bottle smashed on the ground and the calm was broken, the Turks back but keeping their distance, jumping up and down and shouting and making cut-throat gestures, armed with a crate of empties they'd found somewhere. What at first looked like a boomerang sailed through the air, humming as it got nearer, turning to chopper blades that were going to cut someone's head off. *Mad Max* or jihadi-style, it didn't matter, but there was time to get out of the way and watch an iron bar hit the road with a clank and bounce several times before stopping. Darren picked it up and tried to get the rest of the boys to follow him, but they had more sense and would wait until the crate was empty.

When the ammo ran out the English started moving, but the Turks were off and not coming back this time, the sirens louder as the riot squad approached. Matt and Stan returned to Pat and tried to get him on his feet, Darren delivering updates as he watched the flashing lights down where the air seemed foggy around a junction, the boulevard splitting off and the stone blocks fading into a grey horizon, a stroke of luck that the road there was clogged and delaying the police.

Pat was upright, Matt taking one side and Stan the other, draping his arms around their shoulders and telling him to hang on, but it was taking him too long to get his legs working properly and his grip wasn't firm enough. The others were on the move. They'd meet up later at O'Driscoll's. Pat almost fell, and Matt and Stan changed their approach, gripping him under his arms instead, Darren losing what patience he had and telling Pat he needed to sort himself out and use his fucking legs or they'd end up in the cells, that he was too big to carry like a baby, and even though Pat was still dazed and confused he must have taken this in, as he straightened up and found his balance.

Heading into the nearest side street they may have been out of sight, but there was bound to be at least one informer who'd point the police in the right direction. Tucked down here they were sitting targets, and the robocops would do them for fun. Pat decided he could walk on his own and they speeded up, coming out in a pedestrianised area busy with shoppers oblivious to what had just happened. With its chain stores and fast-food outlets and crowds, it was a good place in which to lose themselves. When Pat nearly fell again they sat on a bench so that he could clear his head.

– We need to get out of here, Darren said as the sirens returned. When you're ready...

They continued until they were beyond the shops and on a main road, Darren sticking his hand out as soon as he saw a taxi. This pulled over, and the driver lowered his window.

– He's hurt, the man said, in perfect English. We are going to the hospital?

– No thanks, mate, just back to this hotel, Matt answered, as Pat leaned over with a card that showed the address.

A packed police van was racing down the other side of the road.

– Get in quick, the driver urged, clearly knowing the score.

Cardboard boxes with nappy logos filled the front seat, so they piled into the back, Pat in the middle and Stan spread out across the others' laps.

– Put your heads down, the driver ordered.

They did as they were told.

– Here they come, he boomed.

As soon as he was sitting, Pat's body stiffened and his vision narrowed, bruises swelling into tennis balls and his brain rocking as he peered inside the police van as it flashed past, shocked to see a row of giant ants each with an identical steel head and a single laptop eye. In his muddle the sight worried him a lot more than it should have done, while the warped wail these ants seemed to be making only added to his horror.

– You can look up, the driver announced, watching the van in his rear-view mirror. Sit as straight as you can please.

He swivelled in his seat and looked at Pat, then seeing his confusion turned to Matt.

– We should take him to a doctor. We must go to the hospital.

Pat heard this and forgot about the insect police and shook his head. He tried to speak, but his thoughts wouldn't transfer.

– He'll be fine, Darren decided. Just get us out of here and back to the hotel.

– Okay, the driver said, holding the card up so he could see the address properly, tugging the steering wheel and burning rubber with his other hand, doing an instant U-turn, another car hitting its brakes, the one behind not fast enough. There was a loud bang.

– Fucking hell, Pat shouted.

– That woke you up, Darren said with a grin.

– Bloody French drivers, the driver roared.

Bloody? Matt laughed.

– Better than ECT, Darren continued.

– If there weren't so many signs there would be less accidents, the driver said. How can drivers concentrate when we are looking at these new orders all the time? Fewer rules make life a lot easier to live. The government carried out an experiment in Holland, removed every sign and road mark, and do you know what happened?

Nobody had a clue.

– The accidents stopped. People concentrated fully on their driving, what was in front of them on the road. They were more alert. The Dutch are clever. The French and Germans not so much.

The driver might have had a point about the signs, but he didn't seem too interested in using his brakes, and as he picked up speed he began thumping the horn, and as they raced through the streets Matt thought about Barcelona again and saw how the shops and restaurants and offices turned to blurs of stone and glass dotted with logos, the taxi veering in and out of the slowest cars, the cabbie frustrated by a bus, opening his window and pulling along-side, leaning across the nappies and shouting at the bus driver in Flemish, words exchanged as the two vehicles moved in tandem, the taxi driver shaking his head and accelerating through a red light and narrowly missing another car.

– Slow down, will you? Pat pleaded. I'm going to die of fright back here.

The driver hit the brake and everyone jolted forward, Stan rolling off their laps and landing in the footwells behind the front seats.

– I am sorry, the Belgian said, looking around at Pat. I hope this is better.

The car was moving very slowly, and he could have been taking the piss, didn't like his driving criticised, but the expression on his face was one of genuine concern.

– Thank you, Pat replied.

Matt wondered if the driver was trying his own sort of therapy, and fair play to him, he'd probably revived Pat faster than a doctor could have done.

– You really should have a medical examination, the man said, trying again.

– No, I'm fine. I'll have a rest when I get to the hotel.

– You *should* go to hospital, Stan said from his place wedged on the floor. Seriously, Pat. Why take a chance?

– I hate hospitals. I'm not going.

Pat was firm, his tone surprising the others, although it seemed lost on the driver, who kept turning his head, forgetting and remembering and forgetting the road.

– Help me up, will you? Stan said to Matt and Darren. Come on, I'm stuck down here.

The others didn't move. The Belgian sighed.

– You must lose weight, my friend. Exercise is important. Running, swimming, martial arts. Beer is nice, but not too much, and no more pizzas. Do you like karate? You can train. Prepare for the class. But no more pizzas and no more *frites*.

Matt was pissing himself. The look on Stan's face... They would leave him there until they got to the hotel.

– You are okay moving at this speed? the driver asked.

– We can go a bit faster if you like, Pat replied.

The cabbie adjusted his mirror so his eyes were focused on Matt.

– Do you think England can win tomorrow? he asked.

– We've got a chance.

– The Belgium side is strong. Eden Hazard...

– World class, Matt agreed. We see him every week at Chelsea.

– Chelsea made a couple of big mistakes with Lukaku and De Bruyne, Pat said. How could you let those two go?

– England need the Irish granny-shagger back, the Belgian announced.

Even Pat had to laugh. He was feeling better. They were travelling at a sensible speed with both the driver's hands firmly on the wheel, eyes fixed on the road as if he was taking his test, and he started whistling but lost track of his tune, reached down and turned the CD player on and treated his passengers to some Led Zeppelin as the rain started to fall and Pat felt water in his eyes, saw windscreen wipers shuffling left-right left-right – you're just walking along – Pat felt sick – you're just walking along minding your own business – the wipers were squeaking and the glass was steaming up and it was hard to see the road and the pavement – you're just walking along minding your own business like the ginger cunt you are – and the driver rubbed at the glass with a rag and hunched forward so he could peer through the hole he'd created like it was a tunnel into the land ahead or the sky above or maybe the earth down below.

– Belgium will beat England, the driver decided, after he had lowered the volume at the end of a John Bonham solo. I am betting big on Belgium. It will be 2-1. Final score.

The taxi stopped at the end of the street they wanted. It was single lane and narrow, a delivery van parked outside the hotel blocking their way. The Belgian turned to Pat.

– Last chance. You are sure you will not let me take you to the hospital? Free of charge. I think it is important that you talk to a doctor.

– I'm fine, honest. I just need to rest for a while and sleep it off. But thank you.

– Good luck then, but not tomorrow. Belgium... 2-1.

It took a while for Stan to clamber out, but once everyone was in the street and the fare had been paid the driver saluted and accelerated as he turned the wheel in another mental U-turn, halting a motorbike before disappearing into the traffic. The rain had stopped as quickly as it had started.

– Nutter, Matt remarked.

– Cheeky cunt, Stan added.

– Fucking lucky he came along when he did, Darren noted.

Pat trailed after the others, his heartbeat hitting the top of his head and the bottom of his feet, and as he trudged along the reality of the attack hit him and he felt as if he weighed fifty stone. These three didn't mind a fight, took things in their stride, which made them a lot different to him, but he was thankful they were like that, didn't know what would have happened if they hadn't come along when they did. He could be dead right now.

He was soon in his room and glad to lock the door and be on his own. He went to the window to pull the curtains so the people across the street couldn't see in, and looking down he watched

Matt, Stan and Darren walking away. There was some sort of textile factory opposite where middle-aged women moved in and out of view, measuring and cutting what looked like cloth or paper. There were blinds and bamboo curtains behind their dusty windows, but inside it seemed bright, as if sunlight was coming in from above, although he couldn't see how that was possible, seeing as they were on one of the middle floors.

Pat's hotel was basic but clean, the staff were friendly, and it was cheap for the location. He took off his jacket and put it on a hanger, emptied his pockets and removed his trainers, socks and jeans, went into the bathroom and rinsed his face, surprised by his swollen left eye and split lips. He took off his shirt and saw the black marks covering his body, felt like shit but told himself it could have been worse. He brushed his teeth and went back into the room, put on the oversized Morgellons T-shirt he slept in, arranged the pillows in a hospital V and got through the pain of lying down and finding the most comfortable position, the hurt slowly fading as he started to doze.

Chris Bradley stepped out of the doorway in which he had been standing as two police vans skidded to a halt. The back doors swung open and officers in riot gear jumped out, Chris aiming his camera and taking a series of shots, his lens zooming in on the tools of their trade – truncheons, handcuffs and revolvers on belts that also carried a spray he assumed was a disabling type of pepper. The English had left the scene, and these were routine pictures he would probably dump, but it didn't matter, he had caught the fighting and could hardly believe his luck. He would have to go through the photos properly once he was in his hotel, but he had a good feeling about the images and the days ahead.

The Belgian police took a firm stance when it came to public order and would have shown the scum no mercy, an approach that was at odds with the softly-softly methods practised by their British counterparts. They didn't piss about on the Continent, and Chris agreed with their hardline methods. He believed in discipline, and European policing was years ahead of the innocent-until-proven-guilty nonsense that had brought Britain to its knees. A zero-tolerance policy worked wonders, and he despised the liberal do-gooders and trendy lefties and that whole woolly headed culture of excuse-making that had arrived with Tony Blair and continued under David Cameron. The police needed to target the child dropping litter as well as the youth staggering around drunk on a Saturday night, as this led to more serious crime. If young offenders were punished early, most would mend their ways. It was the same with drugs.

Stick a smoker in prison for six months and it would soon end the use of Class As. Murderers and drug dealers deserved to be executed. The death penalty was the best deterrent going, while it had the bonus of giving the victims of crime, their families and the broader community the satisfaction of seeing the worst criminals hanged or electrocuted. Lethal injections were a cop-out. Revenge should be harsh and served while the recipient was fully conscious. As far as football hooligans were concerned, the riot squad needed to be free to go in as hard as they wanted, with no fear of reprimand in the case of injury or death. The likes of the Belgians, French, Spanish, Italians and Germans took no prisoners. If you got in the way of the European police you paid the price, and rightly so.

A third van arrived, the police inside as pumped up as the first lot, but there was little they could do except stand with the others and wait. They were clearly frustrated they'd missed the English, and Chris shared their disappointment. One officer was busy on his phone while another had stepped away and was talking to an elderly couple. More people emerged from a café, and waiters started picking up and arranging tables and chairs, sweeping away broken glass and scattered food. Chris took a few more pictures, but knew he was going through the motions, and it was hard to ignore his feelings of excitement and relief. He put his Nikon away.

He had been in Berlin and heard rumours of a big meet between the English and Germans. Organised well away from the city centre, there was no way he could have been there without endangering himself, but those involved would be on a high and keen to make their mark in Brussels. These things always escalated. Generally speaking, the media could only operate on the margins, but few if any of the editors and publishers he had worked for over the years cared more for the truth than some easy sales and addictive clickbait. Images of a smaller outbreak of trouble in Berlin had been relayed across the world and would have whetted their appetites. The door was wide open, and Chris needed a result.

Crossing the road, he noticed an object on the ground. He stopped and crouched down to pick up a knife, and clicking it shut slipped it into his pocket, entered the Charlemagne. He glanced in the bar before continuing to reception and booking in, again appreciating his good fortune, his delayed flight and the traffic from the airport huge strokes of luck. He had a nose for these things and sensed he was on a roll. To arrive straight from the airport and be working minutes after telling that idiot of a taxi driver what he thought of him was more than good luck, though. Job done, he was able to stroll across the boulevard and reward himself with some five-star accommodation.

Bach played softly in a minimalist lobby that boasted an impressive walnut floor, the natural smiles on the faces of all those in uniform perhaps a condition of employment. Declining the services of a cheerful porter, Chris was quickly in and out of the elevator, walking along a carpeted corridor and entering his room with a swipe of the keycard and placing his bags on the bed. He didn't like to waste too much time when he was in possession of images such as the ones he had just taken, even if he was sure he had been the only professional present. The world was full of amateurs, so the correct contacts and speed of delivery were vital, but he had to be in control and measured and do things properly.

It was important to pause, focus, proceed. Taking a cold Heineken from the minibar, he removed the cap with the supplied opener and eased the itch in his throat. Crossing to the window, he opened the half-closed curtains to let more light into the room. The areas around these city-centre hotels were much the same across Europe and increasingly the world, but he loved the interiors of the best establishments for their ambience, cleanliness and levels of service. He liked his comforts and needed a good base when he was on a mission overseas. Leaving the view outside, he removed his laptop from its case and established a wi-fi connection, turned his DSLR on and began the transfer of images.

He was immediately into work mode, calm and serious and a lot different to the fun character his friends and colleagues knew and loved. This was his other world, and he was good at what he did. Moving through the transferred files on his laptop he couldn't have been happier. These were sharp, dramatic shots. The first batch showed a simple story – a lone Englishman surrounded and battered by a frenzied mob of slimy-looking Arabs, the sort of Muslim scum Mad Merkel had been shipping into Germany, but while Chris was no friend of Islam he knew the tale the media demanded. A brutal attack on a common-or-garden pleb was never going to appeal to the editor who would be paying his bills, so the arrival of the English had been a godsend. These were the photos that would sell, but they needed work before he sent them off.

Chris sipped his Heineken and took a moment to reflect on his life. He was a maverick who knew the score. These were the good times. It didn't matter if it was a broadsheet or a tabloid, the fact that so many toffs were in positions of power meant the mentality was the same whatever their politics, and he took full advantage. Football hooligans were good earners for publishers and journalists alike. Without an officer class to point out sanctioned targets, and lacking a financial motive, they were regarded as rabble, while the public were simultaneously disgusted and excited. The media had money to burn, that was the crux, and he wanted his share.

He was decisive in his decision-making and immediately dismissed the pictures of the loner being beaten. If anyone deserved to be tasered, pepper-sprayed, hit with batons it was his attackers, but there was no cash to be had there, and anyway, Chris didn't give a fuck about the man. Like the publication that had sent him to Berlin and Brussels, he wanted the stereotypes, shocking headlines, cutting standfirsts. Chris was loving his own genius. He had been on the ball, blending skill and experience and holding his nerve in a tense situation. This sort of photojournalism required courage. He was a brave man.

Working fast, he soon had a series of photos that through careful cropping showed a small group of locals being attacked by a much larger English mob. Individuals were isolated and given the same treatment. The fear in one face was stark, while those of his opponents showed a raging fury. An Englishman stood out, his fist connecting with a jaw that seemed to dent from the blow. Chris neatly removed the ginger idiot unconscious on the ground to the right in the original. This other man was going to be the star. He fitted the brief perfectly. The quality and angle of the shot was incredible, the features crystal clear. He kept working on this and several other pictures he had selected, the editing process as interesting as the taking of photos, but he knew when to stop. This was visual storytelling, and clarity was key.

With his images ready, Chris knocked out some snappy content, his words more or less the same as those written by his predecessors thirty and forty years before, but nobody important remembered or cared. The publication that had paid his expenses, a healthy retainer, image/content fees, would love these pictures and decide what to do with the text. He knew the key phrases sub-editors would apply – 'mindless thugs', 'hooligan shame', 'a disgrace to the nation' and his own favourite, which echoed the wisdom of the Duke of Wellington, 'scum of the earth'. He wondered if his suggested headline might be used. These hooligans were animals. He pressed Send, and his first Brussels dispatch was on its way to London.

Chris finished his Heineken and went to the fridge for a replacement, returned to his Mac and tidied up the desktop. He looked at an image of the unconscious man again, wondered if he was in hospital at this moment, considered the idea of finding him and taking some photos, but what was the point? He could die and who would care apart from his parents? He clicked on another picture, zoomed in on three faces, wondered if they knew the hooligan general Cromwell, tried to guess where they came from and what club they supported and what they thought, but again, these were the dregs of society and didn't matter. Dragging his photos into a new folder, he made sure everything was neat and tidy before backing up and shutting down.

Removing his shoes he sat on the bed, propping himself against the pillows as he checked his messages, but there was nothing urgent or work-related so he put his phone on the bedside table and picked up the lager. In a while he would order sandwiches and coffee, have a rest before taking a shower and going out to sample the Brussels nightlife. The Nikon would stay in the hotel, but he had other smaller cameras at his disposal, plus the one in his mobile. He wondered if there would be much trouble tonight, and while he expected a few drunken skirmishes he was sure the worthwhile stuff would happen tomorrow ahead of the game. Happiness turned to contentment, and yet he would never lose his ambition. He was always at the ready.

He closed his eyes, but his mind was racing. Maybe he would eat now. Why wait? He was looking forward to getting drunk tonight, and it would be better if he lined his stomach early. He was starting to feel hungry and looked around for the menu, saw it was over on the desk, stood up and went to fetch it, returning to the bed. There was a good selection available. He would forget the sandwiches, and while tempted by the fresh lobster he fancied something more substantial and decided on the sirloin steak with French fries and béarnaise. He finished his Heineken and returned to the desk, picked up the hotel phone and called room service.

Following England keeps you sane, that's what you like to say in the days before you head off, when you're standing at the bar in your local with the other regulars, sticking to the two-drink limit you've set yourself during the week, a couple of slow pints of IPA on the way home, as you don't want to go into work in the morning with a hangover. You need to be on the ball, mentally strong, as the job can get inside your head and stir up feelings you don't want to be having, but despite your best efforts the pressure builds until you reach the point where you feel like your brain is going to overheat and burst. The positives are worth the negatives, though. It's all about the people, and the highest highs are worth the lowest lows. Work is much more than a job, and you feel bad taking the time off, that's why you joke about football keeping you sane, it's a way of making your excuses. But football did save your life. That's what you believe. Football saved you. You were ten when the accident happened, maybe eleven, ten or eleven, and while these days Brentford keeps you going from one weekend to the next, England lets you escape for a few days, gives you the chance to leave that cautious man of routine and repetition behind and become someone else. You're an explorer, a traveller, a high-plains drifter, but you still plan your trips, that's part of the fun, reading about the country and city you're visiting, finding the best prices and booking transport and accommodation, listing things to do when you're there, and while you couldn't make it to Germany, the Belgium game has come at the right time. Brussels is an easy journey on the Eurostar, and this Belgian side is reminding people of the great Dutch teams of the past with Eden Hazard and Romelu Lukaku up front and Vincent Kompany at the back, you rate him the best centre-half in the Premier League. This is a straightforward England away, but you let your guard down, didn't you, leaving the hotel early and sitting in the Grand Place soaking up the atmosphere, the great architecture, the quirks of the culture, just sitting there eating your waffles with maple syrup, drinking coffee in the morning sun after a night of beer and a feeding frenzy at Fritland, knowing this is what it's all about, feeling invincible, running through familiar faces and new friends made last night, the conversation, laughter, songs. Once you've paid for your waffles and coffee you head to the metro and take a train to Burpark, stroll like a giant through its European theme park, towering over the Acropolis and the Eiffel Tower and Big Ben, remembering the time you went to Bekonscot when you were a boy, a family day out, you and Debbie and Mum and Dad. That miniature England of Norman churches and village greens where small men play cricket and bowls, a model railway bigger than any train set you could ever have imagined. You can smell the oil and steam, see the wheels of the engines turning and the glint of the tracks, hear clicking points and clacking carriages as they pass through green fields and country stations, looping away in big circles, making the same trip over and over, and you imagine you're looking out of a carriage window counting plastic sheep like you're a replicant in a Philip K Dick novel, feel the motion and worry you're going to be sick, but you don't want to puke up in this hotel bed here in Brussels, that's the last thing you need. When you leave Burpark you go to Atomium and take the escalators between the pods, a tiny figure inside an atom looking towards the King Baudouin Stadium, knowing it used to be called Heysel, you've seen YouTube footage of the disaster in 1985, heard older men talk about the European Cup final between Liverpool and Juventus. It's impossible to imagine the crush and panic, but coming back into the centre of Brussels on the metro you're thinking of the haunted families of the dead, the trauma they've lived with since that day. Maybe it was a premonition, a warning of what was about to happen, and you should have listened, but you know how these things work, do you listen to everything or listen to nothing, travel in circles or only move forward? Is it really twenty years since the accident? Were you ten or were you eleven? You still can't remember. Does it matter? You've got your post-cards and need the right words, but it's hard to think straight when your head is hurting like this and you can't move without the pain racing through your body that is battered and bruised, bleeding under the skin and maybe deeper inside, you should have gone to the hospital, seen a doctor, but it's too late, you're too tired. It's better to concentrate and go somewhere else, away from the punches that put you on the ground, the kicks in the head and the stamping feet, something heavy hitting your skull. How can so many men hate you and want to hurt you and damage your brain and even kill you? You're a fool not feeling the same way back, but that's your nature, fucking useless, you're a useless ginger cunt, as you've been told. Football saved your life. Football and Mr Blackshaw. All you wanted was to be on your own for a few days, but not *alone*, because with England a lone ranger can travel freely, sleep on trains and linger on platforms and worry the vending machines, drink too much of the local beer and talk to strangers without being seen as a crank. Instead, you're admired for your loyalty. It's the best sort of holiday. You told Kelly at work that England is like owning a dog, that a four-legged friend lets a man walk on the common or in a park without women looking at him and seeing a rapist, gives him a reason to be there, and it's the same with football. You're going away with Brentford, crossing the country on the official coaches as a kid, eating the sandwiches Mum's made, drinking soup from a flask, changing to trains when you're older and working, shifting to beer and chips, lots of beer and lots of chips, never mind the pies, mushy peas, curry sauce. The idea of eating makes you feel sick again, but don't throw up, for God's sake. It's different at club level, vital to have friends, important to go with your mates, first with Glen from school and these days there's the four of you travelling by car, with the Satnav and your favourite routes you know the places to stop, the best motorway services and pubs, the streets where it's safe to park, and in the dangerous towns you know to keep your heads down and stay out of trouble, keep away from all that KNOCK DOWN GINGER stuff. You head into the Midlands, the North and Wales, see cities and towns that feel rundown and empty, while the fields of Wiltshire and East Anglia are flat and lonely and leave you sad and homesick. The others moan, but you like it when the traffic clogs up around the satellite junctions, it means you're nearly back in London. You love going away and you love coming home. A long day away with Brentford is enough, but the England trips are different, and it would be wrong to let this attack ruin things. It's important to stay strong. Forget the mights and maybes. As soon as you're on your way overseas the weight lifts, and there have been times when you've wished you could keep on going, or in somewhere like Portugal stay and live out the rest of your life as a stranger, and perhaps it would be nice to never understand the language, never know what is being said. Yet as soon as you're approaching London again you feel excited. It doesn't make much sense, but then you haven't worked anything out, have you? Not really. You've never been a winner, got no competitive spirit, you're a man of mixed emotions, you smile at that chestnut and wince from the pain. You'd be happy staying outside the Premier League, talk about social cleansing, keep Brentford pure. England is a treat. Fantasy football. The players earn huge sums, but whatever the snobs say they remember where they're from and they love their families, and when it comes to the national side nobody can question the loyalty of captains such as John Terry, Wayne Rooney, Harry Kane. Football is your escape, but what if you're stuck on one of those model trains and travelling in circles that are so big you forget you've been this way before, not recognising sheep you've already counted, and your mobile is vibrating and singing softly, you don't want to talk to anyone, just let it ring until it gives up and goes to voicemail.

To be honest, I can't wait to get back to England. Have a hot bath instead of a cold shower, order an Indian, wash it down with a couple of bottles of London Pride, sleep for two days then put on some clean clothes and stroll down the pub for a proper pint without a mob of nut-nuts waiting to bash my head in. I've had enough. Mind you, a couple of these Belgian lagers will liven us up. Took us three days to get here. Three fucking days. Seems more like a month. It would've been quicker walking. You hear all that bollocks about European super-firms, organised squads of sober body-builders, every town with its own paramilitary crew only interested in some ultraviolence, robots in designer clobber, but I don't see it myself. It's propaganda. Suits the Old Bill, journalists, politicians, TV, radio and all those other divs who take themselves far too seriously. I just see loonies the same as us. It's a laugh. But three days...

Getting out of Berlin was our first mistake. All we had to do was be at the station on time, meet the others and catch the train to Brussels, land early and find a hotel, have some breakfast, plot up in a bar and let the locals know the messers have arrived, the England boys who are going to mention the war and piss in their special fountain. No chance of that. Too easy. We had to have one more drink. Would have been rude not to. One more German beer. How many times have we done that in the past? Fair enough, it was me doing the ordering, saying there was no rush, I'll hold my hands up to that. We'd been treading carefully as well, dodging the Gestapo and their mates the Stasi, but we got too comfortable, kept on drinking, ended up missing the train.

Three in the morning, and we're wandering the streets in the rain with our bags. It's cold and miserable and Carter says we need to borrow this van over here. Why walk around wet all night when we can be dry and on the move? It makes sense, so he starts the engine easy enough, talking as if he knows where he's going and what he's doing, but of course he doesn't have a clue. The Germans are famous for their autobahns, dead straight roads that cut through the countryside, superhighways that don't even have a speed limit. Kraftwerk efficiency is what they're famous for. That's what they tell us. You blink and a hundred miles have passed by. But we couldn't find one of these roads. There was no high-speed travel for us. If there was a dead end or a one-way street or a road shut for repairs or a gas leak or a crashed UFO blocking our path, well, that's where we ended up.

The van's full of wood, tools, bags of nails and screws, Italian football papers, an industrial drill that looks like a rocket launcher, and this was sliding forward every time we had to stop, so we're working out where to sit to keep the heavier stuff still, five of us stuck in the back, Harris in the front with Carter. We finally reach the outskirts of Berlin and it was time to choose and Carter picked a road and followed it into the dark, out where there's no traffic, no light, no nothing. Then he fell asleep and next thing we're skidding and flipping on our side and end up in a ditch. We were lucky to survive. We've lost our wheels, which means a tropical storm starts. Maybe the van owner had put a curse on us, and who could blame him, but when you're drunk you don't think about the rights and *wrongs of things, do you? Thunder was booming and lightning crackling, and the rain was pelting down. It was getting louder and more electric and you could almost smell the grass burning.*

There I was, stuck in the middle of nowhere with six pissed-up herberts, couldn't see a thing, sitting in a stolen van, screws in my back, rain pounding on the roof, white light flashing, threatening to fry us, wondering if that pong is petrol. And I'm sitting there and I have to ask myself the question, the one we've all asked ourselves. I mean, is it worth it? Is it really fucking worth it? I could have been at home in a nice warm bed, sleeping off a gallon of drink, a blonde head on the pillow next to me, but no, and I thought about Vince Matthews sitting in the sun, dark glasses reflecting that same bird in a pink bikini, and Vince had a Foster's in his right hand and was humming along to 'Liquidator'.

You never met Vince? You've heard of him, though? That's the one. He was a handful in his day, but had enough, saw the light and went off to see the world and never came back. At least not to stay. Did it when he was young as well. Every so often a postcard arrives. Even now. He sends them to The King's Head these days. India, Vietnam, Indonesia, Thailand, Japan… Lives in Australia but spends three or four months a year on the road. Grows and sells Japanese trees. They shoot up fast and provide shade. He comes back to England every year or two, but doesn't hang about. Can't stand the rain and the cold. I couldn't help smiling when I thought of Vince sitting in the sun taking the piss like that, but the van is lit up by lightning and there I am, wide-eyed and grinning ear-to-ear and holding a screwdriver. The others thought I'd gone mad. I'm sure I heard one of the lads crying when it was dark again. Thought he was going to be murdered I suppose.

Eventually we got to sleep and didn't wake up until after twelve. It had stopped raining, and we stood by the side of the road waiting for someone to come along. After an hour we hadn't seen a single car so we started walking. There were no houses, just barren fields and trees, and it didn't feel right, it was like we were in the twilight zone, hungry and thirsty, marching on and on, and then hours later we hear the rumble of a Panzer. We stop and look back down the road and here comes Angela Merkel driving a tractor. She stops and asks if we want to climb into the hay with her. She's a big girl, not ugly, but hefty, and a bit too forward, especially out here. Even Carter took a step back, and he'll fuck anything that moves. Her English was good, it was just the 'with' bit she got wrong. Turned out Angie was offering us a lift, not a ride, so up we go into the cart she's pulling behind the tractor. And there we are, lost in Germany, seven Englishmen in a haystack, crossing the Fatherland at five miles an hour. This was only the beginning as well. Just the start.

With Pat safely back in his hotel, Matt led Stan and Darren towards the Tunis. If curry was the best English food going, then two days in Marseilles with Chelsea had shown him that couscous did the same job for the French. Given the connection to Belgium, there was a good chance the rules also applied here. A plate of harissa-heavy stew was better than all that French muck – the dead horses, snails, foie gras. Fucking horrible cunts force-feeding ducks until their livers exploded then eating the mess. You had to be a perv to think that one up. He was no vegan, but the people respon- sible deserved a bullet in the head. The French bread was okay, some of the cheeses, but he needed more than a brie-and-pickle bap to keep him going. Matt loved his spices. The hotter the better. How previous generations had survived on salt and pepper and a dollop of gravy was beyond him.

– You're fucking joking, Darren said, when they reached the Tunis and Matt suggested something to eat. I'm not going in there. We've just been fighting this lot. They gave Pat a kicking because he's English. What's the matter with you? Fuck that, let's go and have a burger.

– It's not Turkish, Matt replied. Pat found it on the internet. Five stars. Family-run. Reckons it could be the best restaurant in Brussels. Cheap as well. Come on, I'm starving.

– Not me, I wouldn't give these cunts a penny. I'll see you in O'Driscoll's. You coming, Stan?

Darren turned to the big man, who wasn't sure what to do, but he was closer to Matt and hungry, could do with some food, so he shrugged and chose the Tunis.

– Suit yourself, Darren said, not looking back as he walked off.

An elderly man was sitting at a desk tapping numbers into an old calculator when they entered. They were the only customers, and he raised his head and rang a small bell, gestured towards the tables and returned to his calculations. What had to be his son appeared. He seemed nervous, Matt smiling to show that they came in peace. Seated and handed menus in silence, they were left alone to decide. It didn't matter if you were in Belgium, France, Tunisia probably, the locals had been warned about the English. It was a shame, made things difficult, but he was more bothered about getting into the match tomorrow than being loved by the natives. None of them had tickets, and the touts were charging a fortune they couldn't pay.

– Do you think we've upset Darren? Stan asked, as he examined the menu.

– Can't get him to have a curry, so it's not a surprise. Up to him, isn't it.

Matt didn't care about Darren going off, he'd half expected it, was more surprised that Stan had come in with him as they'd both wanted to get to O'Driscoll's in case they missed anything. Matt had been thinking he could lose them for a while so he could do what needed to be done in peace.

– I had a curry with Darren last month, Stan said. The Kathmandu.

– You sure? It wasn't a Darren lookalike? His double? Fucking hell, one's enough.

– No, it was definitely him. He wiped his plate clean as well. Mind you, it's Nepalese. Everyone loves the Gurkhas. He stopped using Paki shops when he heard about the grooming gangs.

– This is Tunisian.

– Still Muslim, though.

Matt saw Darren nutting that pimp last night, after he'd slapped a skinny teenager he was trying to sell on the street, said it was the same as what was going on in places like Rotherham and Bradford, where Pakis were noncing English girls. He didn't care what anyone said, it was allowed to go on because the kids were white and the social workers and police and media didn't want to accuse the Pakis and be called racist. You couldn't say fuck all about Muslims. They all knew it was true.

– If Jimmy Savile was a Paki, you still wouldn't know he was a paedo, Darren had said, just before he ambled across the street and headbutted the pimp.

A pot of mint tea arrived, and this was poured in silence. Their orders were taken. Matt had the Couscous Royal, while Stan chose Tagine Berber, served with rice. Both had flatbread. The man serving them wasn't any more talkative, but Matt decided he was distracted rather than unfriendly, something serious on his mind. He looked like he had been crying.

– Who are you meeting then? Stan asked, once they'd had some tea.

– Friend of a friend.

– A woman?

– No, I've got to pick something up.

– What?

– I'm doing someone a favour. Don't know the details.

It wasn't that Matt didn't trust Stan, but he honestly didn't have a clue. He was on edge now he was in Brussels, thinking of the money he was carrying, the pressure to make the exchange and bring the cargo safely back to London, the contents of the bag he was meant to collect. Rules had been laid down. He'd given his word.

– What happened earlier, that's nothing to what's going to happen when we meet Anderlecht.

– There's a few scores to settle, Stan agreed.

– There'll be others... Charleroi, Antwerp, Standard Liège. Harris won't have forgotten.

Stan frowned and leaned forward, suddenly serious.

– We should've taken Pat to hospital, you know. He wasn't right. It only takes one kick. A single punch can kill you if it's in the right place. He's not well. We shouldn't have left him.

– He'll be fine, Matt replied. Just needs to sleep if off. I know he's a bit different, but he's strong.

– No, Stan insisted. We shouldn't have dumped him in his room like that.

– He goes to hospital and the doctors call the police and who knows what will happen. That could have knock-on effects at home. Lose him his job.

How could twenty-plus men attack Pat like that? How could they attack *anyone* on their own? But especially peaceful Pat. Knowing him, he'd probably tried to understand the first couple of punches, looking for the reasons why and ready to forgive and forget, holding up the hand of friendship as he was on the ground, saying a prayer for those kicking him in the head as he lost consciousness. Matt and Stan discussed their hatred of bullies at length, how paedos were extreme versions, rapists more scum using sex to belittle people. Bullies came in all shapes and sizes. Every age, sex, class, colour. Some were sneaky and wore a person down mentally over time, or broke you financially. There were plenty of inflated egos strutting around talking about respect when they meant fear. Their food arrived and they started eating.

– This is great, Matt remarked.

Stan agreed.

– Darren's probably sitting in McDonald's right now, chewing rubber.

– Bollocks, arseholes, eyelids…

They ate in silence, heard a radio come on in the back of the restaurant, picked up some familiar names, a Belgian voice talking about the game against England. Matt thought of Terry White while Stan forgot Pat and wondered if his car had passed its MOT, how much it was going to cost him when he got back to London. He should find another mechanic. Next time he would.

– The food was okay? the waiter asked, reappearing when their plates were empty.

– Very nice, Matt replied, back in the moment. You came recommended. Our mate Pat…

The man frowned.

– You are here for the football?

– That's right. Leaving the day after the game.

He handed Matt a leaflet. A boy's face looked up. Eleven, maybe twelve years old.

– This is my nephew, Sami. Will you take some and give them to your friends? He is fourteen. We can't find him.

– He's gone missing?

– There is English on the other side. Sorry.

Matt turned the leaflet over.

– He came to Belgium nine days ago. We were supposed to meet him at the airport, but there was confusion with the time. I spoke to him on his mobile phone and told him to take the train to Midi, that I would wait for him there, but he did not arrive. There is no reply when I call his phone now.

– Have you told the police?

– They are looking for him, but there is no news. Will you put some of these in the places you go? Give them to your friends? We tried the hospitals, but nothing.

The address of the Tunis was at the head of the leaflet, with phone numbers and an email address.

– Give us as many as you want, we can spread them around, can't we?

Stan nodded and a big pile arrived in a plastic bag.

– We are very worried.

They left a decent tip and walked in silence until they reached a square, continued to a bigger road, the face of the boy dissolving in the late-afternoon crowds. They passed a kneeling beggar with his head bowed and arms outstretched as if he was being crucified, and were nearly knocked down by two running rag-and-bone pensioners pushing trollies as if they were having a race. An accordion played inside a nearby shopping mall. O'Driscoll's was ahead of them in the distance. They stopped at a crossing.

– I'll see you in an hour or so, Matt said.

– I hope you're not turning into a drug smuggler.

– It's nothing to do with drugs. I'm meeting someone, that's all.

They went their separate ways, with Stan taking the bag of leaflets, and once he was alone Matt stopped to look at his phone and see where he was going before continuing and turning into a street where the windows were heaving with fancy chocolates and cakes, next up a row of souvenir shops selling Manneken Pis bottle-openers with huge corkscrews for cocks. The lanes he was heading into became tighter, closing out the light, dusty displays showing off mountains of secondhand comics, books, records, CDs, medals, tin soldiers, robots, keyboards. Kebabs took over, and he was passing a line of takeaways, each one selling the same lamb and pitta, and this was replaced by the lighter flavours of rice and chow mein, and then he was in a small square dominated by a fenced-in church, saw people gathered around a painted van eating mussels and drinking white wine.

He stopped and breathed in the fresher air of the square and checked his map again, directed into lanes where graffiti spread across breeze blocks and boarded-up shops, stencils of rats and dogs and riot police on wood and metal. The pavements were more uneven here, dotted with dog shit, the cobbles cracked, small bars busy with older, daytime drinkers. Two huge, mutant Smurfs looked down at him from an end wall.

It took Matt another ten minutes to reach the Taverne Marion-ette, and he went straight in and stood by the door waiting for Thomas to introduce himself, but nobody took any notice and he had no idea what the man looked like. Seeing as he was early, he assumed Thomas hadn't arrived yet. A woman passed with a tray, carrying three Diekirchs to a table, the froth taking up a fifth of each glass. There was a serving area rather than a proper bar, the counter so high he could only see the head and shoulders of the character working in the gloom behind it, the set-up reminding him of a Punch And Judy show. There were marionettes hanging from the ceiling near the far wall. Matt guessed he had to sit down and wait to be served.

The dark-brown wood panelling was impressive, and while most of the furniture matched it, there were three booths and a couple of tables that belonged to the 1950s or '60s with their

Formica and vinyl tops. Brass bowls were overflowing with exotics whose leaves needed dusting, while a maze of wires ran along the room's ledges. Framed photographs of young men in uniform hung from thinning string, their rifles clearer than the faded faces. The clientele here ranged from a smart couple in their eighties or nineties nursing glasses of Ricard to scruffy men and women in their thirties sipping beer as they studied newspapers. The waitress arrived and Matt ordered Hoegaarden, the cloudy-white wheat beer quickly delivered. It had started to rain outside, and he didn't mind if Thomas took his time. He liked the bar and was happy to sit here on his own and enjoy the atmosphere, but before long his mind was drifting in another direction.

The Taverne Marionette was a lot different to the busy London pub he'd been sitting in six days earlier, two pints of Guinness on the table between him and Terry White. He saw himself tucking Terry's envelope inside his jacket, and he hadn't been properly worried having so much money on him until right here, right now, sitting in the Taverne Marionette and looking over at the elderly lovers with their Ricard and spotting the pimp from last night walking past the window. It was nice to see him bandaged up, to know Darren had done some lasting damage, but the last thing he needed was to run into him when he was holding so much cash, or maybe worse, carrying the bag he was here to collect. He lowered his head a little and raised the Hoegaarden, but kept his eyes on the pimp who continued walking and was soon gone.

Matt knew he had to stay alert, couldn't relax for a second, not until the exchange had been made and the bag was stashed in the locker he'd rented at Centraal. He couldn't afford to drink too much and let his guard down. He was on a mission, replaying his orders, back with Terry White in a London pub drinking stout. There had been an amused look on that scarred, chiselled face opposite, and Matt had taken Terry's warning as a joke at first, only later fearing he was serious.

– It's valuable what you're picking up, Terry had explained, leaning over the table. Priceless really. It is important to me, and I'll be very upset if you don't bring the merchandise back, especially as

I'm paying you so well. I'm trusting you on this, so you mustn't let me down.

– I'll do my best, Matt had replied.

– You need to do better than your best, Matty boy. Mess it up and you'd better stay in Belgium.

– It'll be fine, honestly. What's in...

Terry put a finger to his lips.

– Whatever you do, you must not look in the bag. And don't ask Thomas. It's not drugs or guns or anything like that. It's nothing illegal. Nothing you have to worry about. But it *is* private. I will know if you look. And Thomas will tell me if you ask. This is personal. Remember, curiosity killed the cat. You're not a cat are you, Matt?

Terry started chuckling, but it was an odd sound, wooden and harsh.

– And don't get yourself stopped at Customs.

Terry seemed emotional suddenly and raised his pint to his lips.

– Life is all about treats, Matt. The little luxuries. Great expectations.

Terry's eyes were glistening when he put his glass down and he took a purple handkerchief from his pocket and dabbed them dry. The amused expression returned and he looked back over at Matt, and it was only later, once he was in Brussels, that Matt admitted he had been threatened, that he really could not afford to fuck this up. He'd heard stories about Terry White. The man wore pink shirts and loved the cheesiest disco ever recorded, wrote soppy poems apparently, but he had also shot a rival dead outside a pub and never been convicted. That's what Matt had been told.

He finished his Hoegaarden and waved to the waitress, picked up the beermat his glass had been resting on and inspected the fleshy face of the monk staring back. The haircut was a proper pikey mullet, but he had a Father Ted grin on his face and who could blame him? The Belgians knew what they were doing when it came to brewing, took it so seriously they'd given the job to men who were free from the usual temptations and able to concentrate full time. Women got you into trouble, the same as drink, drugs, money. Terry had to be doing something dodgy, and while the obvious was Class As, Matt wanted to believe him when he said it wasn't drugs. There again, he wouldn't have chosen an amateur, unless it was a double bluff.

His second Hoegaarden arrived, and he drank it fast and ordered another. He wouldn't have minded living like the monks, rent-free in a monastery, starting each day with a singsong and a fry-up, brewing with his mates until midday when they stopped for lunch and a couple of pints, going back and making more beer in the afternoon, finishing and going on the piss at five, polishing things off with takeaways donated by the grateful locals. He saw himself with the mullet, getting fatter and fatter, permanently pissed and only ever topping up. Stan and Darren could be part of his crew, hauling barrels while he gave the orders.

– You are English?

Matt looked up. A middle-aged man was leaning over him. He was swaying and seemed drunk.

– Thomas?

– Thomas? No, my name is not Thomas. Who is Thomas?

Matt shrugged.

– Are you okay? You looked worried.

– I was just wondering what it was like to be one of these monks.

He held up a beermat.

– Thomas is a monk?

The man sat down. His hair was long and he needed a shave, but the eyes were alert.

– It would be a good life.

Matt agreed.

– I'd miss the ladies, Matt said.

– You think those monks didn't have girls? They had them every night. Gorgeous ladies. They weren't married and didn't have to pay to feed their women once the passion was over.

– You really think they had women as well as beer?

– Of course. Praying, drinking, feasting, fucking – that was their existence. Today, maybe it is harder, not so many monks are involved, and everything is business. In the past they could do what they wanted. That is why they became monks. To serve God.

– I could live that sort of life.

– We are less free now. The motherfuckers won't even let you smoke in the bars. I take no notice and do what I want.

He turned to look for the waitress, but seemed to remember something and leaned towards Matt.

– I must go. My wife wants me at home. I am late. She will be angry. Praying, drinking, feasting, fucking... Not for me. For the monks. Only the monks.

They shook hands and Matt eased back in his chair as he watched the man hurry out of the bar, rolling the Hoegaarden around his mouth as he enjoyed the returning calm – a gentle rustle as newspaper pages were turned, the faint clink of glasses and bottles, hushed conversations in a language he didn't know, the footsteps of the lady serving the drinks.

Angie dropped us off on Frankenstrasse, right outside this undertaker's with a coffin in the window. She pointed down the street, said there was a bierkeller at the end, owned by her friend Big H. That's what she called him – Big H. The tractor rumbled off and the temperature fell. There were parked cars around, but no sign of human life. No colours. No sound. The curtains moved in the undertaker's and I swear I saw a giant watching us from behind the nets. It was a trick of the light, because I blinked and he was gone. It was the lack of sleep, not having anything to eat, but even so... The sun was sinking and these long shadows were forming, and when a church bell rang we all jumped. Everyone was feeling the same way. Those nightmares you have as a kid were coming back. Real horror-film dreams. Vampires, werewolves, man-made monsters.

We started towards the bierkeller, wanted to get inside where it was safe, and it didn't take us long to spot a fancy sign in the shape of a stein. The place would have a roof and four walls, beer and food, give us the chance to make friends with some Germans after the trouble in Berlin. There would be rooms to rent, with thick eiderdowns and comfortable mattresses on the beds, radiators and heat and, best of all, private bathrooms. We'd clean ourselves up, relax and rest, have a good drink and move on in the morning. That was the plan. We were feeling positive. You have to be positive, don't you? Can't be miserable. Things could only get better.

Big H's bierkeller was along a narrow little alleyway and down some winding stone steps. These were so tight we could only walk in single file and had to bend our heads. The door was low as well, had a wolf cut into the stained glass, and I was thinking about SS resistance groups, blood-and-soil stuff, dead stormtroopers who wanted revenge on the descendants of the English Tommies who'd wrecked their empire. Not a bunch of foetus-looking orcs who double up as aliens, but Nazi ghost soldiers. Skulls and swastikas. Anyway, we went through the door and the ceiling was higher inside, which meant we could stand up properly and look around, but fuck me, we had a surprise, because all the people inside were dwarves. The noise stopped and every face turned our way. Talk about standing tall and standing out. Didn't have a clue what to do next. Flummoxed. That's the word.

You might walk into a pub full of Scousers, say. Not your bushy-tashed joke-cracking Mickey Mousers off the telly, but those horrible hundred-to-one Stanley-knife scum-of-the-earth tinker scallies, and they'll suss you out in a second. Or you might be over in Mile End on a social, sit down for a curry in the Ali Baba and twenty West Ham stroll in just as your mobile goes off and plays 'Blue Is The Colour'. Or maybe you fancy a game of pool and wander into a Riley's where Celtic have planned a St Patrick's Day bash wearing a Blues Brothers badge and a No Surrender patch. Thing is, with all of those you know exactly what's going to happen next. This was different. One of the blokes at the bar welcomes us in English. Asks if he can buy us a beer.

Hans was a diamond and his mates were gentlemen. Turns out he's Angie's boyfriend. After five minutes it was hard to see them as dwarves. They could drink as well. Don't know where they put it, but they were caning the beer, and it was steins, two pints a go.

Hans might have been friendly, but he was no fool, had obviously done well for himself, making the money to buy the bierkeller selling computer parts he imported from China, yet he hated them for how they'd treated the Tibetans. He loved the English, though. Especially Paul Gascoigne. And Alan Shearer. He said he was worried about Gazza's health, but knew it came with the territory. Was Newcastle a great city? He wanted to go there one day. Drink in the Geordie pubs. A friendly, clever man. But there were seven sulkers sitting in the corner who didn't like us being in their boozer. You could tell they were angry, but I never worried about it, seeing as Hans was the guvnor.

We were in there for a good two hours before the place started filling up with headbangers and a heavy-metal DJ set up his decks. He was a Motörhead fan. Very proud of the umlaut. Admired Lemmy and his German medals. We were still the only tall boys in the place, and it was a great night until Rod got overexcited and started going on about dwarf-tossing. I shut him up, told him about the Midget Protection League, made him grin and calmed him down, thought it wouldn't be noticed with the difference in language and the noise and everything, but he went off and next thing 'Bomber' is playing and he's picked up a tiny rocker and is getting ready to chuck him. Rod was drunk and only mucking about, I know that, but what a wanker. This stocky geezer Alf jumps off his stool and runs forward and nuts Rod in the bollocks, did a flash sort of kung-fu kick to his head when he was on his knees, and then there were all these other Germans piling in and giving him a lesson in good manners.

I didn't want any of this, partly because they were dwarves I suppose, but more because we'd been treated so well. It was rude. Showed a lack of class. The sulkers steamed into Mark and Harry, who were laughing at Rod getting done over by the midget mob, and there was no way this could be smoothed over. Truth is, we were going to get a hiding if we weren't careful. A good fifty Germans were going mental and the birds were worse than the blokes, so I thanked Hans for his hospitality and shook his hand and said sorry about Rod. He shrugged his shoulders. Said it was *typical of the English. He expected nothing less. We meant no harm. He knew that. But what could he do?*

We had to fight our way out of the bierkeller, and it's hard with people so much shorter that you. Wouldn't think so, would you, but it's true. You can't punch them, and when you try and kick them they grab your leg and hang on and do their best to pull you down. Fucking nightmare... We were dragging the battered dwarf-tosser out by his feet, and I was angry at Rod, I can tell you. We had to carry him up the stairs and the Germans were mullering us as we went, falling over themselves to get stuck in. They chased us down the alley and into the street, stopped and stood on the pavement, chanting in German and taking the piss, and then they were singing 'Who The Fucking Hell Are You?' in English. All of them pointing at us and really enjoying themselves.

But keep it to yourselves. We don't want the world knowing we got done by the Heavy Metal Hobbits, that Frodo Baggins and his German Firm ran the English. Except they were dwarves, not hobbits. Definitely dwarves. Fair play, those Germans were game. They might be small, but they can definitely have a row.

You're walking home from school, walking with your sister, walking on the path that runs behind the warehouses next to the park, a short cut that saves you five minutes, but it's cold and dark and drizzling and the overhanging trees make it hard to see where you're going, so you focus on the streetlight at the end of the tunnel, it keeps you moving in a straight line, and when you come into the open you turn right on the pavement that follows the main road, keep walking until you reach the traffic lights, stop and wait for the colours to change, standing on the corner as the cars indicate and brake with a crunch, but it's the smell of wet hair that stays with you later, the smell that will stay with you forever, not the swipe of windscreen wipers, not the red of the bus, not the faint rustle and gasp, no, and it's the hollow thud that makes you turn and see Debbie on the ground, your sister lying there as a black puddle forms around her head. And you are running in the rain, running through red puddles, running to your car and shoving your mobile in one pocket and taking your keys from another and opening the door and climbing inside and turning on the engine and driving to Maggie's flat and as you go you have a thought and take your phone from your pocket and make a call in case the call hasn't already been made, and inside ten minutes you're parking and tapping in the code and have the key that opens the door and you find Maggie collapsed on the floor in the kitchen, unable to get up, a bundle of bone and brain, and you are trained and you are professional and you know what to do, her right arm is broken but she hasn't banged her head and she isn't bleeding, that's good, she's easy to lift being eighty-seven and skinny and fragile, you're cradling her in your arms, carrying her to the living room, and when she's comfortable you check on the ambulance, Maggie embarrassed, saying she's sorry for causing all this fuss, she keeps saying it again and again, sorry for causing all this fuss. And you're travelling in the ambulance, travelling with Debbie, travelling with Maggie, travelling to the hospital. And Debbie comes home, Maggie comes home, the doctor visits Debbie, the district nurse visits Maggie, and you see them all. And Debbie stares at the wall and she stares at the ceiling and she stares through the window as you read from the books she keeps under her bed, stories of girls in big houses and children without adults telling them what to do, stories of lions and wardrobes and magical worlds, stories of horses and giants and fairies, and you read slowly and out loud because the doctor says it could help her, and the books tell you things about your sister, her interests and dreams, there's an Atlas as well, but you can't read from that, or the marks she's made, you're trying to imagine what it must feel like to be hearing and thinking and unable to speak or move, and while you act happy and positive around Debbie you know she's brain-damaged and life will never be the same, and after a year Mum hardly speaks and Dad sleeps on the couch. And you sit with Maggie, sit in her flat, sit in an armchair drinking her tea and eating the biscuits you've brought as she tells you her stories, the things she remembers, stages of life and the changing times, the people who are born and the people who die, her ideas of sickness and of health, the material and the spiritual, her views on politics and religion, the rich and the poor, May and Corbyn, the right and the left, and she tells you about her soulmate and how his hair is just like yours, *was* just like yours, and you think of Debbie's hair, your mum in the hospital, your dad in the ground, next to your sister, and most of all Maggie talks about her daughters and grandchildren, their photos fill the room, and you have a laugh with Maggie, she has this way of speaking that lifts you up, the subject doesn't matter, and you've decided she's a natural optimist, doesn't have to fight to be positive, when you leave she tells you to have a great time and stay safe and don't forget her postcard. And you're walking alone, walking in circles, walking head down and straight into trouble and the bully Stuart Mee shouting KNOCK DOWN GINGER, Mee and his gang, younger boys than him, the same age as you, Mee pulls back his fist, he knows you're scared, the threat always makes you cower, but this time you don't care, keep on walking, and Mee's under pressure, what does he do, he punches you in the side of the head and you call him a wanker so he punches you harder, KNOCK DOWN GINGER'S SISTER, your nose is bleeding, maybe it's broken, you just stand and stare, he calls your mum mental and your sister a vegetable, another fucking carrot, and as you run at him he shouts KNOCK DOWN GINGER'S SISTER WITH A BUS, punches you again, your head snaps back and you are on the ground being kicked by Mee and his gang, and when it is over and they have walked away you stay there until an elderly couple help you up and once your head clears you are running and don't stop until you get home. And Larry forgets to close his door, Larry forgets where he puts his glasses, Larry forgets he used to be a fireman, but he never forgets to offer you a drink, a bottle of cider or a glass of rum, he rarely goes out these days, not on his own, not without you or one of the others, he says he doesn't care, he's happy in his flat with the railings and bed, he's never married, has no family, once a week you arrange your day so you see him last, bring food in your bag, and when you've had a couple of drinks you offer to make a meal, seeing as you have the food in your bag, you're not a great cook but neither is Larry, he forgets to eat, and when it's ready you sit at his kitchen table and he asks you questions, what you think, sometimes he talks of a tropical island and a place in the sun, but he's better off here, this is his home, he's glad about the cladding on his block, but what about Grenfell? And you don't want to leave your house, don't want to leave your room, don't want to leave your bed when Debbie dies and the funeral is over, Mum stops washing and Dad moves out, then two weeks later Mr Blackshaw knocks on your bedroom door, that is a shock, your teacher is in your house and Mum has answered the door and let him in, and you sit in chairs in the living room, sit in the gloom with the curtains nearly closed, you and your teacher, no drink is offered, no tea and no biscuits, he tells you a story, about life and its lessons, about using your time, either fight or give in, and do you believe in fate or free will, you don't say very much, don't know how to answer, but Mr Blackshaw is dedicated, loves his work, he's respected in the school, known as a fair man, he suddenly stands up and walks to the window and opens the curtains so sunlight floods in. And Beautiful cries when you leave, cries at the window, cries when you wave, and you're feeling like shit as you drive away, but her mum will explain things better than you can, you'll be back soon enough, she'll explain in their language, and you know something of their story, where they have come from, and you tell yourself again that you are lucky to live in this country, to live in a democracy, to live in London, this is your home, you are a long way from home, you have postcards to send, to Maggie and Larry and Beautiful, and you need to be strong, listen to your teacher, Mr Blackshaw, you have to get out of this room and use your time, because time runs out before you know it, yes, you're here for the football, you haven't got a ticket, have to find a ticket, you've come all this way, and there are postcards to write, people waiting, postcards to post, stamped and ready, a ticket to buy, you try to move, but your body is stiff, use all your strength, you stand for a second and fall back down, what's the point, your chest is tight, you're starting to panic, stuck in this room, alone in this room.

*

Matt was trying to work out what was different about the Taverne Marionette. Not its maverick flavours and not the eccentrics drinking here, but something else, something more subtle. The answer was in his head, he was sure of that, but out of reach. Stan would have known as soon as he walked in the place, saw things other people missed, always had done, right back to when they were at school together. He could have been a detective. More DCI Banks than Barnaby, although he'd probably have preferred the old-firm approach of Jack Regan. Maybe Stan was right about Pat and they should have forced him to go to hospital. He could be lying there dead in his room right now.

He would give Pat a call and make sure he was okay, go outside and do it as he couldn't use his phone in here, but there again, he couldn't exactly stand in the street either, not with that pimp in the area. His brain clicked. There were no phones in the Marionette. That was the difference. No one was talking, messaging, staring at screens. There were no iPhones or Galaxies posing on the tables. Not a single one. No tablets or laptops. It was mental. Whip out his mobile in here and it would be like standing on a chair and flashing his cock. He was a man on a mission and meant to be keeping a low profile, and maybe that explained the choice of venue. He would check on Pat later, knew he was worrying about nothing. Pat was fine. At least he hadn't been stabbed.

– Matt?

A woman was standing over him.

– I am Thomas, she said.

He was confused.

– No, my name is Natasja. I have come instead of Thomas. He says he is sorry he can't be here himself. He is sick.

Her face was round and cheerful, eyes big and blue, hair blonde and bobbed. She was beautiful. Too good to be true. Best of all was the energy in those eyes. There was a holdall in her right hand, and she put this on a chair, pushed it in tight against the side of the table, probably so it was hard to snatch, which was clever. She sat down opposite. He was staring at the bag. Nobody was going to miss this fucking thing when he left the bar. It was the brightest yellow he had ever seen. He might as well stick a flashing light on his head.

– Thomas has a very bad cold.

The waitress appeared and Natasja ordered Heineken. Matt resisted her offer of another drink, would make his third Hoegaarden last. The bag was a reminder to pace himself. He was on duty.

– As you can see, I have brought the merchandise.

– Nice bag…

– It is normal. The correct size.

There was caution in her voice as she tried to work out why Matt was grinning.

– You are a good friend of Mr White? she asked, moving on.

– Not really. He drinks in a pub I use sometimes. He heard I was coming to Brussels through a mutual friend. That's all.

– He must trust you.

Matt considered the idea seriously. It was a strange one.

– Thomas has done a lot of business with Mr White over the years, but transportation is a problem. Neither of them wants to take a chance. The risks are too great.

Sitting here with this bag holding fucks knows what, having been nicely paid to make the collection, trusted with a large sum of cash, it dawned on Matt that he was missing something a lot more important than some mobile phones.

– These are the sort of men who demand perfection, Natasja said.

She loosened her jacket, and he tried not to stare at her tits, the way they stretched the front of a white Fred Perry. The piping was royal blue. Her Heineken arrived.

– So, you have something for Thomas?

Matt had forgotten his part of the exchange. He slid the envelope over to Natasja, who put it inside her jacket and zipped an inner pocket shut. She didn't look at the contents, which was reassuring, although she was hardly going to count out the money in the middle of the Taverne Marionette. Clearly, the two sides trusted each other. Maybe not so much trusted as feared. He feared Terry White, yet wouldn't class him as a bully.

– You don't want to look inside the bag? she asked.

He shook his head.

– You can resist temptation?

– Sometimes.

– You must trust me as much as Mr White trusts you.

– I trust you more than that, Matt said, noticing the Ben Sherman logo on the plastic handbag she took off her lap and placed on the table.

– Mr White is a private man, Natasja reflected. I met him once. Here, with Thomas.

She lifted her glass and drank half the Heineken in one go. He was impressed.

– So what do you think of Brussels? she asked.

– I've been once before, but haven't seen much of it really. Not the local places anyway. You get stuck in the centre if you don't know someone who lives in a place like this. I like it, though.

– It was the same when I went to London. Belgium is not the same as England.

– I suppose not. You work for Thomas then?

– On occasion. Do you like this bar?

– It's great. Feels like the real Brussels. Where the locals drink. It's going to be hard finding my way back, though, even with a map.

– I worked here when I was eighteen. For two years. It is quiet at this time of the day. Later it becomes more busy. It is a traditional bar. Old Brussels. There are other places.

Despite himself, Matt had finished his beer. Natasja saw this and did the same.

– Do you want another drink? he asked.

One more wouldn't hurt.

– No, she said.

Blunt, but fair enough. It was a bad idea anyway. He needed to get the bag stashed.

– It is too quiet here, Natasja continued. It reminds me of work and sore feet. We can go to a better bar on the way to the centre. I have to talk to someone there. That way you won't get lost.

Matt paid for the drinks, stood and took the holdall off the chair, looping the straps under his right armpit and adjusting the angle so it was against his back, resting on his shoulder, and he noticed that the bag was padded and fitted nicely, lined with bubble wrap maybe, protecting a heroin shipment, or at least the way he'd seen it done on the TV. Fuck this, he wasn't a drug smuggler, wasn't being paid enough to end up in a Belgian prison. No, he had to get a grip and stop imagining things. He followed Natasja outside.

– This way, she said, setting off.

She led him through a series of narrow streets, telling him about the area and some of its history as they went, turning left and right and left, pausing at the end of what he at first took for a tunnel. The brick walls were straight and high, the alleyway narrow so he thought it must have a roof, but the ground was wet from rain that must have fallen while they were in the Taverne Marionette. There was a door in one of the walls with a neon advertising Corsendonk, the logo showing Mary holding the baby Jesus. When he paused Natasja tugged at his free arm and hurried him on, only slowing when they reached a cobbled path running under some arches. Matt adjusted the holdall which kept slipping, suddenly cautious as this was the sort of spot where he could come unstuck, and the thought dawned on him that Natasja was being too friendly, showing him the sights when really she was setting him up for an ambush. She had the money and was going to reclaim the bag.

There was another sign around the next corner, *Maes* blazing blue between glass blocks selling Leffe and Stella Artois, and she led the way into a bar that was long and dark with a single velvet bench running along one side. Mirrors lined the walls. Between each of these was a shaded red light, and below this a hook for hats and coats. Middle-aged men stood at the bar, faces drained of blood, eyes on their beer, several heads nodding, lips moving. The younger drinkers were talking in small groups, using the bench and the small brass stands bolted to the floor for their drinks.

The landlady was thin and stern, her husband fat and friendly.

Natasja ordered Jupiler for Matt and a bottle of framboise for herself.

– This is raspberry beer, she said, when they had stepped away from the bar. It's not very strong, but I like the taste.

She poured it into a tall, thin glass and placed the bottle on the nearest stand. Even in the half-light it looked tempting. Matt had a taste and had to admit it was refreshing. He had moved the holdall from his shoulder to his left hand, but felt stupid standing like this, could imagine people looking at him and wondering why he didn't just put it on the ground. What was he protecting?

– Why don't you leave the bag on the bench, Natasja said.

– Someone could take it when I'm not looking.

– Or hang it on one of the hooks. Nobody can remove it from there without us knowing. It will be safe on a hook. Be careful with it, though.

He lifted the holdall up with two hands and arranged it on the nearest hook. Despite its size and colour, and the fact it looked odd suspended from the wall, nobody seemed to be taking any notice. Either way, he could enjoy his drink and talk to Natasja. She was a smart, good-looking woman, but her eyes were drifting away from him already.

– Excuse me, she said. I see the person I need to talk to. I will be five minutes.

He watched her walk to the far end of the bar and approach a tall man with a ponytail. They sat down at one of two tables in an alcove, Natasja reaching into her bag and bringing out a tablet. She turned this on and propped it in a holder, and the two of them leaned forward and concentrated on the screen. Every so often she reached out and ran fingers over the surface. Matt checked his bag was still on the wall, turned on his phone and ignored the incoming messages, texted Pat. It was too noisy in the bar to call.

He had a mouthful of beer and thought about the trouble earlier, how he'd been on the receiving end of something similar to Pat in Barcelona, caught out by locals as he was coming back from a shop near his hotel. He'd been stabbed and left unconscious, and while he hadn't thought it at the time, he had been lucky. The stabbing of English supporters went right back. You heard it from those who went to football in the glory days, and it was the usual suspects then as well – the Italians, Spanish, more recently the Turks. It could happen anywhere of course. Wrong place, wrong time. Luck or fate, he didn't know. UEFA did fuck all. The British government didn't care and never had done, probably liked the idea of the plebs getting knifed. In the last five years how many Englishmen had been stabbed and slashed? How many over the last four decades? The authorities weren't interested in statistics of that sort.

He'd had his head smashed against a wall and been knocked out, the first thing he saw when he stirred and opened his eyes was Lionel Messi watching from the other side of the street. Messi was alive, a ghost, a stencil on a powder-white wall, but where was Ronaldo? He would be the firm's knifeman. Who was the leader, the best player in the world, the guvnor? It had to be Messi. His ears were humming. Zidane was being filmed across the length of a match, and Matt was sitting in front of a screen eating popcorn. The camera never left Zidane and there was no commentary, just the murmur of an unseen crowd, the sound of the ball being kicked. Zidane was nutting Materazzi in the World Cup final, defending his sister's honour, which was only right. Matt's head ached.

He'd been stabbed and was shocked by the realisation, pulling himself up on his side to look. There was a lot of blood on his clothes and on the ground, but it seemed dry and the wound was wrapped in some sort of material. A woman was crouching next to him, one hand steadying herself on the pavement, the other on his shoulder, a rougher Catalan version of Pamela Anderson. The bandage was her shirt and she was left in a white bra, said something in Spanish, urging him to stand up as he had done with Pat. Leaning on her, he'd hobbled to a battered Peugeot where she took a cardigan from the back seat and put it on before driving into a maze of backstreets, her perfume mixing in with the smell of engine oil, petrol, an ashtray of cigarette butts. Pointing past his head, she mentioned Pablo Picasso, kissed her right palm and placed it on his cheek.

A doctor stitched his leg up, and he'd spent the night in hospital, for concussion as much as the stab wound, and he had slept for ten hours before being discharged and arrested, taken to a police station and questioned by a sergeant who seemed to be going through the motions, eventually released and told to go home. He'd missed his flight and was forced to buy an expensive ticket back to London. Fucking Stansted as well, which was in the middle of nowhere for someone trying to get to West London. He'd never seen the woman again, wished he could have thanked her. She had left while he was with the doctor and he didn't know her name or anything about her, but later he wondered if she'd saved his life. He had been stabbed in the leg, not the heart, but without her he could have bled to death.

He looked at his phone, scrolled through his messages while he waited for Pat to reply. His brother was asking about Frank's food. Another text said he had found it under the sink. A third included a short clip of Frank running for his ball in the park. There was a photo of a cheeseburger from Darren. A *Peaky Blinders* meme and a couple of forwarded jokes. Stan had sent him a three-second clip of what looked like the head on a pint of Guinness. He glanced down to where Natasja was sitting and she was still concentrating on her screen. There was enough data on his phone, and he checked to see if the money from the Edwards job had come in yet. He forgot then remembered his password as more people came into the bar, moved over so he had room, finally into his account. No, they hadn't paid. That Edwards couple. Pair of cunts. It wasn't like they were poor. He was a solicitor and she was a madam. They even had a *Stop Brexit* poster in a window of their three-storey townhouse. He'd added CAT to the bill. A fair rate at ten percent.

He knew to tread carefully, wasn't going to get into an argument and threaten them, as the Old Bill were only ever going to take their side. Those sort of people always won. They had the power. Maybe they'd forgotten, had so much money they didn't realise how the rest of the population lived, that it was all about cashflow, but no, he had sent them reminders. They were making him wait, putting him in his place. It could be personal, but probably not. It had been a big job and was worth the hassle, and he knew he would get paid in the end, but these things ground him down. They also wound him up. He put his phone back in his pocket. Pat must have turned his off, or had it on charge, asleep and enjoying his dreams. The extra Matt had got from Terry White had come at a good time, giving him his spending money for the trip plus some. There was no messing about there. It was true what Natasja said, but in a roundabout way. He was trusted to deliver.

– This is a dubbel, Natasja said, reappearing with a drink in each hand.

They were marked *Trappistes Rochefort*, and Matt loved the way these Belgian beers had their own specially designed glasses. You got them in England now, but the Belgians were the masters.

– It is brewed in Trappist monasteries. It is strong.

Matt was back in grey robes, living the life, head shaved skinhead-style rather than pikey mullet, guzzling from a tankard. The Trappistes Rochefort was heavy, and he didn't like it that much, but pretended he did. The light was dimming and the bar was busier and music had been added to the equation, something he hadn't noticed until this moment, and it was hard to hear Natasja. He checked the holdall was still on the hook. Class A drugs. Tracked from Columbia or Afghanistan, undercover police were following him through Brussels. Natasja's lips were moving and he wanted to kiss them, leaning in closer to hear what she was saying.

– We can try a tripel next, if you like.

If he was starting to feel the effects, Natasja must be as well. There was space on the bench and they sat down.

– Sorry I was so long, she said. I was showing Marc the work I have done.

– What sort of work? he asked.

She put her glass on the nearby stand, reached into her bag and removed an iPad, almost dropped it but was quick enough to catch it, relieved and shaking her bob as she placed it flat on her lap, one hand keeping it steady, and she was telling him about Flanders and the country north of Brussels, the split between the Flemish-speakers and Walloons, the French and Dutch influences of each group. She was mixing English and Flemish, and because they were getting pissed together he understood without knowing the words, as if they were on their own private wavelength. She was saying something about *bandes dessineés*, repeating this three times, moving her lips slowly so he could read them and be clear. She was on a roll and they were at ease, her already cheerful features beaming as she spoke. There was a museum in Brussels she was sure he would love. If he wanted, she would be his guide. The iPad slipped, and it was his turn to stop it falling to the ground.

– This is too dangerous, she said, putting the iPad back in her bag. It is crowded and I am drunk.

She could certainly drink, and he watched her finish her Trappistes Rochefort and hold up the empty glass. Pulling him in close again she made a suggestion and he went back to the bar, asked for two Westmalles.

– Wayne Rooney...

One of the drained men was speaking to Matt after he'd ordered from the landlady. Her face may have been hard, but she was still attractive, and he thought about the woman in Barcelona, how he had imagined taking her flowers as a thank you for saving his life. It would have been a nice thing to do. Wayne Rooney? He wondered if he would turn into one of these lone drinkers one day, or if he would do something special to make the kindness of that Catalonian lady worthwhile.

– Wayne Rooney fucks old women...

Matt wasn't going to argue, didn't bother to take it as an insult if it was meant that way, knew that humour could be lost in translation. He glanced over at the holdall as he waited. The yellow seemed even brighter than before. It could be guns and explosives in there. A deadly arsenal. He could pull out a shooter and blow this man's head off if he wanted.

– So do I, he replied. The older the better.

Natasja squeezed up so there was room for him to sit next to her, taking her Westmalle and drinking a big mouthful, putting it on the stand and shifting in close, her breasts brushing his body, and he was trying to work out if this was an accident or on purpose, heard the word 'Brexit' but pretended he hadn't, wanted to keep things sweet and avoid a row. He thought she followed this up with 'thank God for the British', knew he'd got it wrong, but she put her lips to his ear and he could feel her breasts firm against his arm as she said 'thank God for the English'. She adjusted her position and kissed him on the cheek. His balls were tingling and it was a Belgian responsible. He loved Europe.

Just as things were looking up, he saw a Stone Island firm closing in. He didn't want to attract attention to the bag, in case they'd somehow missed the radioactive spaceship hovering above his head, or at least hadn't linked it to him, and Natasja was on her feet and at first he thought she was trying to protect him, which was kind and brave, but he wasn't going to hide behind her if they were looking for a fight, and then he realised she knew the big man at the front, wanted to introduce them. Matt stood up and shook hands with her cousin Jan, two of the others with him doing the same, the three remaining Belgians in the background, nodding, waiting to leave.

Jan was a lump, but had the same happy face as Natasja, and was clearly a proper football chap. This lot weren't going to go after a lone ranger. That was the problem with some of these other Europeans, they wanted to be like the English but didn't understand the rules. Like the Russians in Marseilles, but that was a military operation run by Putin. Mint tea in the woods? Training sessions in the snow? Turning up in France wearing gumshields and knuckledusters? They were hard cunts, it couldn't be denied, but where was the romance, the sense of fun? The filming they'd done had showed them up, kicking individuals almost to death so they could be internet superstars. What the fuck was all that about?

He talked with Jan for a bit, the Belgian interested to hear about the FLA marches at London Bridge and in Central London, the way the shared values of the different mobs shined through, a continuation of what you got at the England aways, but those had been special occasions and something to be proud of, and like

Natasja he asked what Matt thought about Brussels, mentioned Molenbeek and Salafists, the terrorist attacks in the city, asked about known faces from the past and present in London. Tickets for the England game were hard for the Belgians to get hold of as well, and none of this lot were going. They agreed that football had been ruined by TV and gentrification before shaking hands again, as Jan and his mates were on the move.

– I should go home soon, Natasja said, once they were back on the velvet bench. I have to put this money in my apartment before I am too drunk. It doesn't belong to me. Shall we have another drink first? It would be nice to have one more beer.

The holdall caught his eye when he raised his head. It looked different. There was a stolen painting by Picasso rolled up inside, brought from Barcelona in a battered Peugeot, pressing against the zip. Diamonds delivered by Eurostar cutting the fabric. Antiques stolen here in Brussels stretching the stitching. Matt's brain clicked. The bag was hanging at an odd angle. Someone had got into it while he was drinking and flirting and talking football. This was where things went pear-shaped for so many people who had been trusted with important missions. People like him who weren't up to the job. But there was something else going on.

He squinted and leaned forward, trying to focus on the hundreds of yellow bags disappearing into a tunnel, and below them were hundreds of shrinking Natasjas and Matts. It took him a few seconds to realise he was staring into a mirror on the opposite wall, and this was bouncing reflections back and forwards with the mirror above their heads. He looked over his shoulder and the holdall was how he'd left it. Terror turned to joy. This Belgian beer was powerful stuff. He was a lot more pissed than he'd thought. They'd have another drink and he would offer to walk Natasja back to her flat if she still wanted to get going, make sure she wasn't attacked and robbed on the way home.

Robert and Chris rendezvoused at Q, the two friends arriving in the best of moods. Robert had spent fifteen minutes chatting with former colleagues in London, explaining the behaviour of the English before detailing events to a reporter on the newsdesk. The story had strong political connotations given Brexit and the English public's reactionary attitudes towards the EU, and he had agreed to monitor the situation and supply regular updates. Robert was overjoyed. He had been a little liberal with the facts, but the ginger-haired fascist would have dished out far greater violence if he had been in the position of the locals, and it was important to send a clear message when confronting racism. If every cloud had a silver lining, then the confrontation he'd witnessed had provided the perfect opportunity to reach out to some dear friends. The timing could not have been better.

Chris was also revelling in his earlier success. Shortly after receiving the pictures he had sent, his editor was on the phone purring at the story they told and the promise of more to come, Chris having insisted the tension was increasing on the streets of Brussels. Serious disorder was a given. Several photographs had already been posted online and another would be appearing on the front page of tomorrow's print edition. He had been asked to provide the text to accompany seven further images that were going to form a spread, and he had done this quickly and cleanly, producing captions he knew would appeal to the publication's owners. Fact and fiction were easily conflated. News was entertainment, after all.

The friends greeted each other enthusiastically. Big grins were followed by bigger hugs. There was much to talk about, and they were looking forward to sharing their good news. Drinks were ordered as they settled into the VIP seats Robert had thoughtfully reserved by the bar's longest window, taking a quiet moment to savour the scene outside. In the distance flickered the faint lights of the suburbs, graffiti-sprayed neighbourhoods neither had any reason to visit, but up here, on the crest of the ridge, looking out towards the great guildhalls of Grand Place, the European Quarter at their backs, they were on top of the world.

– Fantastic view, Chris began, resisting the urge to show off and tell Rob about his photographs and the brilliant response. You've done well. Can you believe it's six months since we met up in London?

– Thanks, mate, Robert replied, matching his friend's restraint, controlling his desire to speak about his renewed contacts and developing Plan B. I love this city to bits. I never want to have to leave. It's mad I know, but it's more like eight months since London.

– Eight months? That's insane. So... how's life? You've been busy, I know. I loved those pictures on Instagram by the way.

– Apart from that one break it never stops, but things have been awkward, as you can imagine, with Farage strutting about, making his speeches in Parliament and upsetting Juncker and Tusk. They're good people here, though, understand it's a minority responsible, but it is all so fucking embarrassing. God, I hate Farage. He's worse than Hitler. Jo Brand got it right. Mind you, acid's too good for Farage.

– It's not going to happen, though, is it? Theresa May knows what she's doing. Brexit means nothing, and Brexit Means Brexit means even less. She's dragging things out nicely, and Olly will keep us connected if it gets as far as a deal, so we can press the button and instantly rejoin in a few years' time. But it will never get that far. Trust me. We still have the power. It's only a matter of time before there's a second referendum.

– I know, but it would be a mistake to take anything for granted. Who saw the referendum result coming? The political will here is rock solid, though. We've come too far to let these Little Englanders ruin everything. Michel Barnier isn't going to bend, and the EU will punish the UK, mark my words.

Chris nodded his agreement.

– The British state doesn't want Brexit and they'll stop it, don't worry. I know you're on the frontline here, but we just needed things to settle and drift, keep on at the leavers, and when the second referendum is held we'll get a good result. It's happened before. Denmark, France, Ireland. Twice in Ireland. The old people who voted for Brexit are dying off so the remain vote is becoming stronger by the day. A heavy dose of flu in the winter and we're laughing. Parliament is blocking Brexit and Bercow's playing a blinder. I really wouldn't worry too much.

Robert was listening, but clearly exasperated. A passionate, caring soul. Chris heard him out.

– Why the fuck did that wanker Cameron let pensioners have a vote in the first place? That's what I will never understand. It was a referendum on the future not the past, and there is no future outside of the EU. How could he let it be decided by some care-home fascists, narrow-minded idiots who think in analogue and will be dead soon. They've ruined the lives of the young.

– People are selfish, Chris pointed out. I've always told you that. I know what you'll say, but you're an idealist and I'm a realist. Remember, your average Brexit voter is stupid. Thick as shit. Give them a screen and stick them on Facebook and they'll believe everything they're told. I doubt most pensioners knew what they were voting for in the first place. They're uneducated. The lot of them. White trash.

– The English are racist, that's the truth of it. Let's be honest. Anyone who voted for Brexit *has* to be racist. I tell you what, I'll never listen to Morrissey again.

They disagreed when it came to immigration, but Chris didn't need to respond. He had never liked Morrissey, and on top of Brexit he was vegan, a fucking soy boy.

– Things could work out well in the long run, he mused. Think about it... Win the next referendum and the EU will insist on deeper integration. Our Parliament will happily agree and tell the public that the issue has been debated at great length and a final decision made. Democracy has prevailed. Remember, the country will have been humiliated and has to behave itself. We will join the euro and the ECJ is going to demand more powers. Guy Verhofstadt is the one to listen to on this. He is direct and honest. The EU needs to speed up its development, and Brexit could be the catalyst. This crisis will make the EU stronger and our lives easier. Believe me, Rob. Fuck Farage and fuck Corbyn and fuck that fat fucking loser Johnson.

Their drinks arrived.

– Bollocks to Brexit, Robert said, raising his glass in the air.

– Bollocks to Brexit, Chris agreed, completing the toast with a clink.

The boys sat back and sipped their One Loves, returned to the view outside.

– They know how to mix a drink here, Robert stated.

– You can say that again. They're certainly generous with the alcohol. What's in this?

Chris had earned the right to drink himself silly, reflecting on his wife Veronica's joy when she heard about the front page as Robert listed the ingredients that went into a One Love, the base white rum for an authentic taste of the Caribbean, and yet Veronica was worried about what might happen if he was identified by the men he had exposed, Rob explaining that while these VIP seats had been hard won everything was possible when you knew Kraken, which confused Chris as he was sure Kraken was a type of rum, so perhaps Rob was still talking about the One Love, and hadn't he promised Veronica he would be careful, that he was exhausted and having a quiet meal with Robert before returning to his hotel for an early night?

– Luis modelled the interior on Z in New York…

If the majority couldn't understand the importance of a free press then the hooligans had no chance, would give him a good hiding if they could, but he knew how to drift in and out of situations and remain anonymous. He was a street-wise photo-journalist who knew his trade, but where was the respect for his role in protecting democracy? The search for truth had to be conducted by all means possible, and that so-called phone-hacking scandal had highlighted society's double standards. Rules had to be broken. No harm was intended. In this clickbait, image-driven world of Big Tech he could either smash it or give up. It was survival of the fittest. He was a winner.

– Two more One Loves, please, Robert said to the waiter.

Fuck, there were times when he was more of a bullshitter than Rob, although at least he was aware of the fact. Freedom of the press? Democracy? Helping the masses? More bollocks. The same as his EU talk. Everything was about money, power, self-interest. Costs, fees, wages, profits. Circulation and advertising. Even the best people were corrupt. Rob loved the good life as much as Chris. His friend was a cunt. The same as him. The world was full of cunts and the biggest cunts were the richest cunts and the richest cunts were the biggest cunts.

– Long live the cunts, he announced too loudly, lifting his glass into the air and finishing what was left.

Robert glanced around nervously, but the VIP clientele hadn't noticed.

– Not so loud, Chris. We can't use the C-word here, mate. You shouldn't be using it anywhere.

– Cunt? Is that a swear word? he said, mimicking a favourite comedy exchange.

Robert grinned and, lowering his voice, explained that he was a Q regular and colleagues might hear and be offended. This was a classy joint, and they had to behave accordingly. Not that it was stuffy, far from it in fact, but there were certain guidelines, respect for gender difference being one of the unwritten rules.

– Bollocks to Corbyn, Chris said, compromising on sex and genitalia and lowering the volume as he touched on that Sex Pistols element driving the People's Vote rebellion.

– Bollocks to Corbyn, Robert responded.

Chris had missed Robert. He was a good guy who would one day forget this PC bullshit. At the moment he was playing the game, riding trends as he built his career, but eventually he would relax and be himself. Chris had felt intimidated by most of those he'd met at university, and yet in time he had seen that they were fools, but despite this he'd always got on with Rob. It was an odd combination, yet it worked. Together they made quite a team and were more than happy to sit here chilling. It would be a long night. Their drinks arrived.

– Bollocks to Boris.

– Bollocks to Boris.

Chris saw his photos setting off a chain reaction as journalists spotted a familiar target and a nice source of income, and this would fuel an increased demand for follow-up pictures as the media went into a feeding frenzy. The story might run for several days, and if his work really kicked on and went viral the politicians would be jumping on the bandwagon and, who knows, an MP might appear in Brussels for a spot of arse-licking. Chris imagined his images being sought out internationally, his phone vibrating non-stop as the offers poured in from New York.

– Bollocks to Benn, he toasted.

– Hilary's doing a good job.

– I meant his dad, Tony.

– Bollocks to Tony Benn.

– Bollocks to Tony Benn.

Robert was surfing the waves of goodwill crashing in from his rekindled bond with core colleagues, excited about where his new freelance gig might lead, something he was thinking to discuss with Chris later. He was still undecided, as while he loved his best mate to bits, the agency he was imagining would be more upmarket and sophisticated than the outlets with which Chris normally dealt. Robert would be tapping into his community here in Brussels, the political contacts he had made, never mind what happened with Brexit. He was European, not British. He was following his principles, and luckily that meant following the money.

– Bollocks to Leadsom.

– Bollocks to Leadsom.

– Hello, Robert, a woman said.

Chris narrowed his eyes. One fucking love… Tight black skirt, matching high heels, big tits, nice arse. The face wasn't bad either. Her accent was foreign, verging on Dutch, but maybe Danish. He wouldn't mind bending that over the back of a chair and fucking it rotten. Cunt, mouth, arse. Fill her up with diesel. These EU secretaries were pure filth.

– Jannah, Robert gushed, how are you?

Jannah glanced at Chris, but her eyes didn't linger, and he sensed her distaste, as if she was reading his thoughts. Bollocks to Jannah as well.

– I am translating for the Commission again, and arrived in

Brussels last week. I was four months in Luxembourg. I've been very busy.

– That's great. Do you want to join us?

– I can't, I'm afraid. I have work I need to finish tonight. But it would be nice to meet up.

– How's Petr?

– He is well. I am seeing him soon. Look, I have to hurry, but I will message you and we can have lunch or go for a drink one evening?

Robert stood up and they kissed each other's cheeks, Jannah nodding briefly to Chris before leaving the VIP section and making her way through the bar. Chris waited for Rob to speak.

– I worked with her last year.

– Dutch?

– She's from the Czech Republic. Speaks five languages and has a degree in economics.

– Did you?

Robert smiled and shook his head.

– You don't change, do you? Crude as ever. But to answer your question – no, I did not. She's a lovely person, I can't deny it, and who wouldn't want to make love with her, but she's married. I've met her husband. He's very different to Jannah. I do wonder why they're together sometimes. She stands by him, really seems to love him. It's odd. If she wasn't so devoted I would try my luck.

– How is he different? Chris asked.

– He's a bricklayer. They've known each other since they were teenagers. He had a problem that upset Jannah. Drink, I think. Or depression. It could have been depression. Or both. I'm not sure. What comes first, the drink or the depression? Never mind. She did tell me, but I've forgotten. That's terrible, isn't it? I'm a bad person. Her husband rarely comes to Belgium.

Chris was finishing his One Love and feeling the rush of the rum and seeing his father, a working man married to a lady who loved to dance, someone who would do anything for his wife, glimpsed himself when he was a boy, back when life was simple. He had rejected his father's views in his teens, possessed an ambition his parents lacked, and when cancer killed his dad at the age of fifty-nine Chris likened him to a horse sent to slaughter when he was lame, instantly forgotten by those he had helped to keep rich. His father retained his sense of fairness to the end, and while Chris thought he was a fool, he would always admire his decency.

– There must be something special about him to keep a woman like that, he reasoned. How many white-collar females go out with a blue-collar male, especially if he earns less? He must treat her well. Like a queen. They're soulmates who talk and dance and listen to each other. They don't fancy anyone else, but if they do, then they don't do anything about it and nobody else ever knows.

Robert was staring at Chris, who noticed and stopped talking, another round of drinks arriving to spare his blushes. He didn't remember Rob ordering. The One Loves came with a couple of kamikazes. He drank the shot and started on his Love.

– Or maybe he's got a massive dong, he continued. Makes Plastic Bertrand look like a pygmy penis.

Robert brushed this joke aside, wondered if Chris had been thinking about his father, envied him his sentimentality, even if it was a weakness that had long hobbled the masses. Robert had lived with the cold conservatism of his own parents for too many years, finally turning his back on them when he was out of university and set up, working and earning good money. It had been difficult, and when he thought of them growing old he felt sad, but he had been forced to make a stand.

– It's funny how things turn out, Chris said, sitting forward and producing his phone. If I hadn't been held up in traffic I wouldn't have got these.

Robert couldn't see the images clearly due to the size of the screen and Q's lighting having been turned down, although he knew these were important photographs, searched in vain for the ginger-haired fascist. It was brilliant news that Chris had made the front of a leading daily. They may have had some political differences, but never let these spill over into real life. He couldn't wait to tell his friend about his own interpretation of the same story.

– More One Loves and shots? Robert asked. Or do you fancy a

bottle of champagne? We need to celebrate. I've got some good news of my own, but I will tell you in a while. Where's the fucking waiter?

– We're still going to Zanzibar, though? I like the look of that place. I followed the link you sent me.

– Maybe. We've got plenty of time. But I've got something special lined up for later.

– What's that?

Robert sat forward again.

– Do you remember The Alexander? The last time I was in London?

Did Chris remember The Alexander? Of course he fucking remembered. Robert had come over on business and been lording it, cutting loose and flashing the plastic. Chris may have been envious of his spending power, but Rob was more than generous. It needed two to tango. Well, three in this case. They had pushed things to the limit, fully utilising the services of a Polish tart. The diesel had certainly flowed. Fantastic. All holes filled. So Robert was thinking along similar lines? This was interesting. Very interesting indeed.

The room had no door. There was one tiny window, and that was barred. It was freezing cold, and the air was stale and smelled of earth. The rabbi's hands were dripping with mud, and when he'd finished building his monster he told him to go to the bierkeller and kill Hans, Alf and the rest of the boys. I don't know how we got downstairs, but there were seven coffins lined up on the floor, six sealed and one open and empty. The golem was careful not to tread on these coffins as he went out into the street. He moved slowly, but took huge steps, and I was running to keep up, shouting that he'd got the wrong people. What was the point of revenge if you didn't serve up those who deserved it?

We were inside the bierkeller and he was pulling people's heads off and sticking them in an empty stein. I saw Lemmy's face looking up at me and even though he was dead he was crying.

There was another stein full of peanuts and the heads were shrinking and turning the same colour. It was hard to tell what was a nut and what was a head. They were all covered in salt. I was hungry and wanted to take a handful, but what if I fucked up and became a cannibal? I was trying to stop the golem killing my friends, jumping up and doing my best to make him hear me, but I was too small, tiny like a toy soldier, and I knew what it was like to be Hans. When I headbutted the monster in the knee he stopped, picked me up and tossed me through the air. I landed back in Berlin.

That was where things changed. In Berlin. Twenty years ago. I shouldn't have returned, because now I would never be allowed to leave. There was a magnet in my chest that only let me go so far. My phone was vibrating and Vince was on the screen and blowing up into a hologram. He was sitting by a swimming pool in Australia drinking a cold lager, telling me I was going to die in Europe. I was a clown, stuck on repeat. He asked about Hans and Lemmy, but I didn't want to tell him what had happened. I suddenly felt sorry for Vince being on the other side of the world, but not for long. The feeling faded. He was happier than me. Thing is, you tell yourself you're doing okay, working and getting somewhere, but it's a lie. Deep down you know it's not true. The same people are always in charge. Their words might be softer and maybe they mask their faces with big smiles, but they still have the power and they still get their way.

I was standing on a street corner. There were cameras lining the walls and rooftops. They could record my thoughts and translate them however they wanted. Who was going to check? It was midnight and important to get out of the spotlight before the police arrived. I saw a cemetery and a voice told me this was the safest place in town. Inside I found those seven coffins and was tempted to get into the one that was open and empty and go to sleep, but what if an undertaker nailed me in by mistake? Buried me in this same graveyard? It was safer on the ground and I was just falling asleep when two sets of hands came out of the earth and started pulling me down. Witches were whispering spells in German and for a few seconds I thought I understood what they were saying, but I didn't. I started rocking side to side, trying to shake the hands off as I couldn't move my arms. I was confused and scared. Didn't want to die. The dreams I had in that place...

Harris was kicking me awake. A train was coming. There was a station across the road from the cemetery, but it was little more than a platform and we hadn't noticed it in the dark. We legged it over and got there in time. Hungover and tired, bruised and dirty, we were relieved to be sitting on proper seats and on the move. Turns out this was the slowest train in Germany, but we didn't care. We crawled through villages and small towns, waited in the middle of fields, stopped and started, Rod suffering from last night's kicking. The other passengers were on their way to work, clean and neat and looking at us like we'd escaped from prison, and I was thinking about POW tunnels and started whistling the song from The Great Escape, but it wasn't long before I was thinking of a different sort of camp, the ones the inmates never left.

Anyway, we didn't have long to wait before our next meeting with the Boche. One of the sulkers from the bierkeller must have called down the line, seen us get on the train, because the first big town we arrive in there's thirty or more Germans waiting. This lot weren't going to be buying us a drink like Hans. They were dressed in black, wearing balaclavas, armed with baseball bats and at least one hammer. This lot were younger and fitter and didn't care that these things are meant to happen around a football match, not two days later in another part of the country at eleven in the fucking morning. Maybe they were self-employed, unemployed, unemployable. Marched out of their jobs when they heard the English were coming. Who knows? But they wanted to hurt us. It was all about the aggravation. The train stopped and the blackshirts were ready to come aboard.

They're banging their fists on the windows, kicking at the doors, know they've got the numbers and the tools and can see we're seven-handed. There was a long pause that probably only lasted a second or two, and I thought the driver was going to have mercy on us, realised what was about to happen and would keep the doors shut, but they opened up and in they came. Harris got done right off with a baseball bat, so that's him and Rod out of action, and we were in some serious trouble. But Harry had other ideas. He reaches into his bag and pulls out the rocket launcher from the van. It's battery-powered, so he doesn't have to go searching for a plug, and there's this roar and the drill is slicing through the air. Harry's a friendly chap, but he hasn't eaten and he isn't bluffing. The Germans don't fancy this at all. They don't like the cold steel. Don't like it up them. Ran straight back out of the train and the doors closed and off we go.

Harris's head was split open and he's covered in blood, so we're thinking we need to get him and Rod seen to. Half an hour later we came into a decent-sized town and made a decision and left the train. Carter stopped a cab and went off with Harris and Rod, while me, Mark, Harry and Young Ian headed across the road to a bar. It was nothing to look at, a dosshouse really, but it wasn't the sort of place where a dressed-up young ultra is going to spot us and call his pals. This was another Germany. Huge, heavy drinkers. Fucking giants. Beer only. Apart from the spirits. We got stuck into the Pilsner, and they did food so we had our first proper meal since Berlin, filling up on sausages, chips, sauerkraut, gherkins, rye bread. This was more like it, and the afternoon passed, regulars coming in and staying, giving us a quick once over and getting on with their lives.

When the rest of the lads arrived Harris was stitched up and revived, like he'd been on the ching, and he starts going on about a local derby, a non-league affair that the doctor who treated them has recommended. It's a twenty-minute walk from the bar. Rod was a lot happier, but football was the last thing on anyone's mind. Of course, we got pissed and Harris persuaded us, and the doctor was waiting with his team, except these weren't your normal healthcare professionals. Doc Savage was in a different frame of mind. This was a smart, traditional firm – white Sta-Prest and Fred Perrys, Harringtons, cherry reds. The cast of A Clockwork Orange. These droogs wanted to fight fair, without the masks and tools, and neither were they a righteous dwarf army about to muller a lonesome seven. It was a classy turnout. All about the style.

What happened? Nothing. Nish. German coppers appeared out of nowhere and stuck us in the back of a van. The officer in charge wanted to know what was wrong with us. Did we have a death wish? But instead of putting us in the cells they took us to the station. Me and Mark were escorted over to the bar to pick up our bags, which the landlord had let us leave there, and we took these back to the platform and waited. The police stood around chatting and made sure we got on the fast train to Holland. They did us a favour really. Mind you, I reckon we'd have had a good drink with the clockwork crew after. It wasn't personal. We were there... They felt obliged. But you should have seen this lot. Pure style. One of them was even wearing a bowler.

While Robert and Chris celebrated with champagne at Q, the England boys were busy draining the barrels in O'Driscoll's. The prices were higher than at home, but that was true across the eurozone. Those who'd been to Spain and Greece in the golden era enjoyed sharing their nostalgia for the peseta and drachma with the younger lot, describing a heaven on earth where the drink and hotels were dirt cheap, the food new and even cheaper, tickets easily had, and hipsters didn't exist. Few wankers travelled in those pre-Murdoch, pre-Sky days. Now you were talking silly prices for everything, and it was hard for those used to being ripped-off to believe that world ever existed.

Darren, Stan and the others filling O'Driscoll's had little time for New Fans. Decked out in team shirts and noddy hats, with painted faces and leaking inflatables, numpties had colonised the big internationals, turning them into a children's fancy-dress party minus the kids. These divs spent their time watching the big screens inside the ground, and when the corporate eye settled for more than a second they screamed and pointed and waved for the sponsors. There were two TV screens in the bar showing clips from the previous days' games, a camera zooming in on a row of middle-aged Germans wearing lederhosen and carrying big blow-up sausages. They pumped their fists and flashed their saveloys and thought they were at the Super Bowl.

– Wankers, Darren remarked.

Their Spanish equivalents preferred matador capes and plastic guitars, while the Italians opted for centurion helmets and rubber swords. The Irish came as leprechauns in green jester hats. The second screen celebrated a goal by focusing on a huge man in a toga, an SLR strapped across his chest, bulging money belt adding extra bulk to the belly, an interesting detail for the Ronaldos and Ronaldinhos of the Brazilian favelas. Those nearest him spotted themselves and became hysterical. Someone launched a Spitfire across O'Driscoll's. It was all about the fine lines. Context. Personal preferences. Everything was about something else.

– I could understand it if the Germans turned up as Hitler, Stan said. A whole end packed with the lunatic fringe and small black tashes. Germany's ace face returns. But grown men in leather shorts? It's just not right.

– The Spanish should forget the bulls and flamenco and come as Franco, Darren replied. The Italians as Mussolini. The great dictators return. Never been away.

– What about the Belgians? A stand packed with Hercule Poirots? He's up there with the great detectives. He sees the things the English police miss.

– They'd want to be Asterix, or is that the French? It would be like you turning up dressed as a morris man and standing in the middle of our crusaders.

Darren was trying to crack jokes. A rarity. But he was where he was happiest, in a pub with a good firm on someone else's turf. A drink in his hand. The fact they were overseas was even better. England away. Anything could happen.

– There's nothing wrong with morris dancers, Stan replied.

The summer before he'd taken his granddad to a cider festival in Somerset and come away impressed. They'd stayed in a pub overnight, which was a good job seeing how much they'd drunk and the strength of the cider, had even been into the orchards to see how things worked. There was folk music and morris men in the evening. People like Darren might take the piss in London, laugh at the clothes and bells, think they were too sophisticated for these rural customs, but if you were around these men you'd keep those thoughts to yourself. A lot of them worked on the land and could drink like nobody he had ever met, and he would bet on them in a fight any day of the week.

– Where the fuck is Matt? Darren asked, realising it was nearly nine o'clock.

– He's not answering. Nothing from Pat either.

O'Driscoll's had plenty of standing room, which suited the three hundred or so English inside, meant people could move around and socialise properly. Flags had been hung up and the manager was happy, seeing as he was coining it. IF IT WASN'T FOR THE ENGLISH YOU'D BE KRAUTS and TEN GERMAN BOMBERS rang out. A police van was parked across the street, but the atmosphere was good-natured. A northern mate of Harris passed, himself a friend of the legendary Jimmy Rowe. Norman was a lively character.

– You heard from Harris yet? he asked, transferring his weight from trainer to trainer.

– I think they're still in Germany, Stan said. In the countryside. Spent a night in a ditch.

– Why sleep in a ditch?

– Something about a storm.

– What are they doing in the country?

– Don't know. They've gone missing. Plus Matt and another mate of ours have vanished as well. There's something going on. I can't work it out.

– Better call Poirot, Darren said.

Norman was thinking.

– Maybe you've been cursed, he said. The devil's out hunting Cockneys. My sister had a curse put on her. She started talking in tongues, went into her bedroom and wouldn't come out. She stopped eating and drinking. We had to get a Catholic priest in. It was bad, mate. I'm not joking. Horrible things coming out of her mouth. Different voices. Men as well as women.

He continued on his way and Stan watched him go. Norman was barmy, took too much speed and couldn't have weighed more than nine stone, but he was made of steel and would live to be a hundred. He wasn't going to make something like that up, though, not about his own sister. Half of those northerners were skinny runts, but game and good lads. The world dealt in stereotypes, but theirs were more subtle than black berets and plastic onions. For the likes of Norman, London was full of foreigners, rich kids and wide boys – Arthur Daley, Del Boy Trotter, Paul Clark classic copies of the originals. He thought about the Cromwell wind-up and why it appealed to the media whores who wanted to believe. It had been going for as long as anyone could remember. A hooligan general ordering people about? Telling them what to do? Fuck off.

– Harris can't be lost, Darren decided. There must be a reason. Harris and Jimmy Rowe. England united.

Stan considered these characters, how they'd have been running up and down the street trying to punch each other when they were young. Two sides of the same coin. North and South. The FLA had tightened up something that was already there, took it on from the football and focused on shared beliefs and a common decency. The terrorist attacks in London, the murder of Lee Rigby, the Manchester bombing... England united, never defeated.

He still had the leaflets from the Tunis on a nearby ledge. Jihadis had gone on a stabbing spree at London Bridge, tried to cut Lee Rigby's head off in Woolwich, mutilated children at the Manchester Arena. Some people lit candles, others got angry. Muslims had committed these crimes, fucking scum was responsible, and maybe Darren was right and he shouldn't have gone in the Tunis after Pat and the Turks, but it wasn't the owners involved and it definitely wasn't this kid's fault. Stan had spread leaflets about when he'd come into O'Driscoll's and waited for Darren to say something, but he hadn't. Problem was, nobody in here would have seen the boy. They'd only been in Brussels a day or two. The rest of the leaflets needed to go to people who lived in Brussels. He'd find a better place.

– Have a taste of this. Flat as fuck. A Cockney pint. I'm taking it back.

Merlin was holding his glass out towards Stan.

– You've drunk half of it, he laughed. How are you?

– Fucking brilliant. I'll tell you in a minute…

– Didn't think you were coming over, Darren said. You weren't in Germany.

– It was a last-minute decision. I had a bit of business to sort out, but I got it done in time. Shame I missed Berlin, but never mind. You got tickets?

– Nobody has, Stan said. Not a sniff. Heard they were going for near enough a grand.

Merlin whistled, turned and went to the bar, spoke to a barmaid who called the manager over, and while Darren started talking with some of the Millwall lads, Stan watched that other discussion that ended with the Brummie returning with two pints, one of which he downed, putting the empty on the ledge next to the leaflets. Merlin was a scruff in a faded Levi's jacket, blond hair reaching his shoulders boot-boy style, a roll-up character who looked a lot different to the rest of the pub. He reached in his pocket and took out his phone, fiddled with it and then closed in on Stan.

– Have a look at this, he said.

It was a picture of a black barge. Merlin handed Stan the phone and was urging him to flick through and study the images. Different shots showed the barge with a deserted canal behind it in one direction, three boats moored in the other, with backgrounds that included houses and pine trees. A close-up revealed peeling paint and plastic-looking plants in terracotta pots. Merlin kept pointing things out as the photos moved inside, explaining about the cooker, the gas, the engine. He wanted to know if Stan liked the barge, and he nodded. He honestly did.

– It's mine.

– You bought a barge?

– A narrowboat.

– You bought a narrowboat?

– I've been waiting for the sale to go through. The owner had second thoughts.

Stan flicked back.

– Are you going to live on it?

– No, it's for exploring. I'll sleep on it, but not all the time. I want to travel around England. Do it properly. I'm driving up and down the country every day and the only places I see clearly are the motorway services and where I'm loading and dropping off. Most of the time I'm on the road, doing sixty or seventy, flashing through all these lives and landscapes, concentrating on the road ahead, stuck in a tunnel. You have to be alert every single second, can't let yourself get distracted, and it wears you out. Don't get me wrong, I don't mind driving, but I was watching this programme about canals and it dawned on me that if I'd been around a hundred years ago I'd be a bargeman, that I'd be ambling along and enjoying my surroundings.

– You'd have had a horse to pull the barge, Darren said, looking at the phone over Stan's shoulder. I always wanted to have a horse when I was a boy.

– It's a narrowboat. The man I bought it off was particular about that.

– You could still have a horse, Stan said.

– Those things don't happen, Darren replied. Not to me. Anyway, where would I put a horse in London?

– There's plenty of places near us. The gypsies have got horses parked up everywhere.

One of the West Ham wanted to see the narrowboat. Stan glanced at Merlin, who nodded, and he passed the mobile over.

– When I was a boy, Merlin continued. I didn't want to travel by horse, I wanted to go by car, drive across America, but I never did, and if I was going to see the US now I would do it by train. Imagine going through the backyards of Memphis with a blues soundtrack playing, or Johnny Cash singing about New Orleans. Crossing the prairies in silence. That has to be the way to see

America. It'll be the same when I'm on the canals, moving through the back of things, in the shadows, except the sun will be shining and I'll be Captain Jack Sparrow drifting along with a mug of tea in my hand. Dark satanic mills. A green and pleasant land. Everyone else on the motorways driving blind.

Merlin nodded at West Ham, who passed the phone to Arsenal and turned back to listen.

– Look at Route 66. The road Chuck Berry sang about. That was an important highway in its day, but it was sidelined by the interstates because business demanded speed. It became a drive-through museum for American kitsch. Here the A-roads were replaced by motorways, but they're not seen as romantic. A Little Chef isn't going to attract people in the same way as Twisters Soda Fountain in Arizona, say. Go back further and the canals were replaced by lorries, weren't they. Engines are faster than horses. The canals were abandoned and fell into disrepair, but they've been cleaned up and are appreciated again, and in a way they have that Route 66 romance about them. True, a canal is slower and more industrial, but it lets you into a parallel world. There's no money to be made. It's all about the local. Does that make sense?

Heads nodded. Arsenal handed the mobile to Stoke.

– When they were built, the canals were the future. Think of the engineering and hard work that created them, and they built them straight, like the Roman roads. In fact, the Romans probably put in the first canals, for irrigation. But the canals we know started out transporting coal.

Stoke passed the phone to Leeds.

– I've never driven a narrowboat before, but I'll get the hang of it, I'm sure. The bloke I bought it off is going to show me. It'll be interesting using a lock for the first time. Funny, but I'm nervous about that.

– You're used to driving a lorry, Stan said. Should be easy enough.

– Which way are you heading first, a Mackem asked. North or south?

– The Birmingham Canal Navigations. That's where I am going

to start. Thirty miles, more or less. Birmingham, Wolverhampton, the Black Country.

– The Grand Union goes to Birmingham, doesn't it? Darren asked.

– Brentford to Birmingham – a hundred and thirty-seven miles. There's one hundred and sixty-six locks on the Grand Union.

– There's six or seven at Hanwell, Stan said.

– That's the Hanwell Flight, another Chelsea lad pointed out. Seven locks.

He wanted to see the narrowboat, and Forest passed the phone over, having received it from Leeds.

– I'm only just learning about all this, Merlin said. But I want to travel everywhere. Through the Midlands and into Wales, head north and south, along the Kennett & Avon, but after the BCN I have to get some work done, and there's a yard in Uxbridge I've been told to use, so the Grand Union will probably be next. I want to go on the Leeds & Liverpool, though. Before or after the Trent & Mersey. I want to do them all.

– Is that Uxbridge yard opposite The General Eliott? Stan asked Darren, who wasn't sure. It's right on the canal. Has to be the same place.

Stan turned back to Merlin.

– Let us know if you do come down and we'll meet you and have a pint. There's some good pubs around there. The General Eliott has a little garden on the canal. We can go to George's. Best curry in London.

– He's a legend, Darren agreed.

Stan looked at him. Said nothing.

– Can you get to Mile End Lock from there? one of the West Ham asked.

– I'd have to leave the Grand Union at the Paddington Arm. That leads to Regent's Canal through West and North London and into East London, ends up at Limehouse. The network is huge. It's going to take me years to do it all, especially with work, but in twenty-five years, when I retire, if there's still places I haven't seen yet, maybe I'll live on the barge full time.

– It's a narrowboat, several people said, and Merlin slapped his forehead.

– Who's this, a Plymouth supporter asked, holding Merlin's phone up, the gathered crowd squinting to make out the person concerned.

– My goat. He's called Gary.

– You've got a goat?

– Gary Goat.

There was a commotion by the door and O'Driscoll's turned to see what was occurring. Punches were being exchanged and a gap appeared, followed by a surge as those nearby started piling outside. A Belgian firm could be seen moving back past the window, flashing the Stone Island. The fighting picked up and spilled across the street as the bar began to empty, a crush forming at the entrance as the majority snapped into action, the drink that had been mellowing them out suddenly pumping them up. Merlin called after the man with his phone, but wasn't heard in the racket, ended up standing alone with his pint.

This skirmish was quickly broken up as the police van opposite drove between the two groups with its siren and lights blaring, the officers inside out on the road and separating them further, while riot police appeared from a nearby street. They couldn't be bothered chasing the Belgians so went after the English instead, who threw a few bottles and backed off, truncheons soon cracking the nearest heads and sending everyone back inside O'Driscoll's.

There was a lull as the police handcuffed those they'd caught and put them into the back of another van, more vehicles already on the scene, lights turning the street into a rave minus the music. Two undercover officers in casual gear were peering into the bar through the main window, talking into their phones, another fight starting as the police tried to get inside. The doorway was narrow and they were driven back as the screens kept spreading their pictures, zooming in on a woman wearing a white blouse and a Viking helmet. She was waving at Merlin and he waved back.

There was another pause, nobody sure what to do, not wanting to fight the police as there was no winning against this particular firm. The door opened again and one of the plainclothes officers started spraying those nearest him, and as they held their faces and moved back he came further in backed up by riot police, who formed a wedge and cornered some of the English, spraying them again so those affected couldn't see and were easier to hit, their eyes burning as they came out of O'Driscoll's and were beaten and dragged away, made to sit on the kerb in a line, several of them puking in the gutter.

– Come with me, said the manager. Quick.

Stan and Darren went with those following the landlord, who was raging at the police, his bar sprayed for no good reason, the violence started by the Belgians on a good-humoured, big-spending bunch of Englishmen. He led them past the toilets and a kitchen to the fire escape, a back exit where they could lose themselves in the darkness. This they did, keeping their heads down, going in different directions and arranging to meet up at a sports bar five minutes away.

The Chelsea boys were in a group that included Merlin and most of the narrowboat enthusiasts, among them the Plymouth supporter, who still had the captain's phone. He handed this back, complimenting him on a handsome goat as well as a fine-looking barge – sorry, narrowboat – eager to know if Gary Goat would be joining Merlin on his journeys around the country.

Once we crossed into Holland we knew we were safe. The Germans had been on us all the way, but we'd earned our freedom. You know what the Dutch are like, half of them don't have a pulse they're so laid back, so we were looking forward to some peace and quiet. I love the Dutch, love them for Ruud Gullit and Jimmy Floyd Hasselbaink and Arjen Robben; for their beer and their puff; for Vincent van Gogh and satay sauce and the city of Amsterdam. Life was going to be a lot easier from now on. We strolled into De Cof and it was like we'd come home.

The bar belongs to one of the Bad Blue Boys from Zagreb, ex-army, fought against the Serbs in the war. Spitting image of Modrić, so everyone calls him Luka. He had tears in his eyes when he saw Harris and wouldn't let us pay for a thing. Drink, food, beds for the night. After the handshakes and introductions, a couple of cold Amstels served by two beautiful Polish barmaids, he said we must be hungry and led us across the road to the caff he owns, cooked up this Croatian food like nothing you've ever tasted and would never forget if you had. There was a full-time manager, a woman from Surinam trained as a baker, so we ended up having a three-course meal. We were stuffed. Luka loves Harris. He gave him his start in England, before he met Anneke and moved to Holland.

There's a couple of rooms Luka rents out above the caff and they were empty and he said we could stay there. We dumped our bags and had our first showers in three days. We must have reeked, but he was too much of a gentleman to say so, though when one of the barmaids appeared with seven towels and seven bars of soap she told us not to hurry, winked and held the end of her nose. We were back in business. Six phones on charge and Young Ian waiting to borrow an adaptor. Clean and fed, we marched back into De Cof like the magnificent seven. Seven dwarves? Cheeky cunt. What have you got against dwarves? You need to meet Hans and Alf.

Eight Amstels were lined up on the bar. The sun shone through the front window and hit the lager. It was a special moment. Liquid gold. There's a picture behind the counter that shows Boban kicking a copper during the riot between Dinamo Zagreb and Red Star Belgrade – Boban, the Zagreb captain. Luka explained it to us later, how the match led into the war that broke up Yugoslavia, about those who'd joined up and fought and died. There were photos of Davor Šuker and Marco van Basten, two pictures of Modrić himself – one in that mental Croatia strip with the red and white squares, another wearing a Real Madrid top – but that was it as far as the football goes. This wasn't a sports bar. Much more classy. Anyway, Luka takes an Amstel from the line and we're off.

This was a long, slow, relaxed session with a soft mattress waiting across the road. We're swapping stories with Luka and a couple of his Dutch regulars, the numbers increasing as the time passes. There's a pool table in a side room and when one of the barmaids takes a break she starts playing by herself. Carter's nose is twitching as he watches her lean over the table to take a shot, bum in the air, tight blue jeans stretched tighter, and you can hear his brain ticking. He ambles over and asks if she fancies a game. She's a lot younger than him and he's got no chance. She suggests playing for ten euros a game and he's not going to say no, but she's beating him every time. He's not going to stop, though, sees it as an investment. Harry went over and sat at a nearby table, drinking steadily, offering advice, having fun putting his friend under pressure, cramping his style.

I was looking at Carter trying to impress and Harry doing what he does, and I couldn't help seeing him sitting there with his best mate Balti – murdered he was, you wouldn't know him, that's right, he was shot – and I was thinking about Rod and Mark and how long we've known each other, Dave Harris with energy to spare, stitched up and bandaged and sitting at a table in conference with Luka. More old friends. Plus there's Young Ian who's ended up with us by chance. He's gone over and is sitting at the bar chatting up the other barmaid, who seems to like him. Ian's got youth on his side. Harry's making the other Pole laugh, and I can see Carter is getting the hump.

Yes, Luka was pleased to see us and not just because of Harris. Turns out he's been having trouble with these Serbs who've started coming into his bar over the last couple of weeks. There was a fight and the police came and threatened to shut down De Cof. The new life he's built with Anneke was being put in danger by people who were never going to like him anyway, but had spotted an easy target. They wanted the Boban picture removed. Luka was isolated, but not going to be bullied. Where would it end? So Harris volunteered us for the mission. He's suddenly planning a night raid. Total war. Blitz the Serbs in the bar they use twenty minutes away. But Luka backed off. Said it wouldn't solve any-thing. It would only escalate the problem us going there, upset the bar owner and the locals, and worse than that, the police would become involved again.

Around nine o'clock the Serbs arrived. There were six of them, and they'd ordered with stern faces and gruff voices before turning to face Luka who had walked over, and it was then they realised he had some friends visiting. They were bullies. Outnumbered bullies. Harris was standing next to Luka, eyeballing the man at the front who fancied himself as the leader. He avoided Harris's stare and tried to act friendly. Me, Mark and Rod were between them and the door. Carter strolled over with a pool cue in his hand. Harry was by his side. Young Ian turned on his stool and picked fluff off a Serb's jacket. Luka told them to finish their drinks and leave and not to come back. They were banned. They drank in silence. Quickly. We said nothing. Just stared. Then they were gone. Shows the power of a deterrent, I suppose. No violence required. Not a single punch thrown. No threats necessary. That's how it should be. Diplomacy. Consensus.

It was a long night and we had a late breakfast in Luka's caff this morning, before we got the train to Brussels. Luka's nervous now Croatia is in the EU, the big European companies are moving in and buying up land and getting into the islands where he'd hoped to live one day. Independence and those who fought for it have been sidelined, the politicians telling the people they're going to be rich. Was that what he'd fought for? He asked about Brexit. You know me, I hate the EU. Always have done. Luka's saying Croatia is a small country and won't survive, while we're a civilisation that has existed for a thousand years. We'll be fine. I told him there's a good chance they'll ignore the vote, that the enemy is within. Always has been.

But I haven't told you about the Italian, have I? Fuck me, that's a story. We were in De Cof and Mario marches in. This is after the Serbs have left. Super Mario is on his own and not happy. He's doing his nut in fact. Raging. You see, it was his van we'd taken in Berlin and he's tracked us to Holland, didn't stop at the border like the Germans, kept on going. Got no idea how he did it, but he was there and wanted to kill us with his bare hands. A scooter boy in a Klasse Kriminale shirt, he didn't care about the odds. But I'll tell you about him in a minute. It's my round. What do you want?

Have you had one of the Trappist beers yet? Brewed three times. I had it last time I was here. Trust me, it will blow your fucking head off.

Robert removed the cocaine from the envelope that contained the tickets for the Belgium–England game. The expats' favourite fixer had delivered once again, and Kraken had done him a deal on the cost of the coke. Rob arranged the envelope on a shelf, made sure it was secure under his wallet and phone, while Chris dipped inside his jacket and produced the knife he had confiscated earlier. The mechanism clicked and he carved the air in slow-motion strokes as Robert tipped the powder on the surface to the right of the sink. On cue, Chris stepped forward and used the blade to sculpt a series of lines, his moves exaggerated as he continued the humour. Both men were already buzzing from the alcohol consumed at Q, their excitement intensified further by the bright light, a huge mirror on one of the walls and the rent boy waiting in the bedroom.

– Let's get the party started, Chris said. It's Vaseline Vaz time.

Robert found this comment offensive, but refused to bite. The sting involving Keith Vaz had been deeply problematic, carrying as it did strong racist and homophobic undertones. As a Labour MP from the BAME community, Vaz deserved better. His alleged offer to purchase cocaine couldn't be condoned, but these things happened in the real world and surely proved that he was human, while the employing of sex workers was merely a transaction between consenting adults. The fact that the newspapers concerned felt it necessary to mention that they were of East European origin was also loaded with insinuation.

– Maybe it's time to give the man a break, Robert responded. Like Margaret Thatcher did.

Chris kept his counsel. The idea that Maggie would have known about and ignored the behaviour of the paedophile Jimmy Savile was a slur on one of the country's finest leaders, but typical of lefties such as Rob who had benefited hugely from her free-market policies. Without her it was unlikely that Tony Blair would ever have become prime minister, and hadn't she herself described Blair as her greatest achievement? Did Rob *really* want to live in a society run by Momentum? Of course not. His friend was rightly furious at extremists such as Corbyn and McDonnell. Would the current generation of hipsters even exist without Maggie?

– Forget Vaz, it's time for the Dildo Brothers to get stuck in, Chris countered.

Robert was a loyal Hammer and disliked the insult aimed at directors Gold and Sullivan. The abuse levelled at the two Davids and Karren Brady by a small number of Neanderthals who refused to accept that West Ham had moved on from the dark days of *Green Street* was a stain on his beloved club. The protests against the board were clearly rooted in anti-Semitism and sexism, as the move to the London Stadium had given West Ham the chance to compete in the big time and attract a better sort of supporter. The reactionaries were no longer welcome.

Since leaving Upton Park, Rob had immersed himself in the working-class traditions of the club, having fallen out of love with Manchester United post-Ferguson. Living in Brussels, it was impossible to attend West Ham matches regularly, but he had been to a number when back in London and was as genuine a fan as any of those locals who could easily walk to the ground. The young supporter buying official club merchandise in Singapore was just as valuable as the middle-aged gammon who had lived in Stratford his entire life. More so in fact. To say otherwise was probably racist.

– Time for Mr Rugger Bugger? Robert enquired, continuing the verbal joust.

Chris smiled, and while he did prefer spending an afternoon in one of Twickenham's excellent hospitality suites to a seat at the Emirates with his brother-in-law, he was no faggot. He resented the suggestion, but remained silent, tempted as he was to come back with a crack about West Ham and raving irons. Chris had always regarded Arsenal as a far more cultured club. The Gunners had been ahead of the curve with the move to Ashburton Grove, the higher prices and breaking up of cliques going a long way to marginalising those rougher Irish and West Indian elements among the local support. And while West Ham had to make do with Ray Winstone, Arsenal boasted one of Britain's top journalists in Piers Morgan.

– Chelsea rent boys, Chelsea rent boys, Chris softly sang, deciding to ease back on the banter before Rob became upset, as his friend took his football very seriously.

While they both disliked Tottenham, the two men were united in their hatred of Chelsea. What angered them more than the club's independent wealth and incredible success over nearly two decades, was the sheer confidence of John Terry. Where was the contrition? The public apology? The collapse in belief when things had gone wrong? Terry had moved into coaching now, but his legacy and reputation remained. He had gone to Aston Villa with his head held high, and that was unacceptable. The presence of Russian money at the Bridge and Putin's key role in the Brexit vote only added to Chelsea's long list of crimes, while their hard-drinking, fun-loving supporters revelled in the fury directed their way. Despite this clever bonding jibe, the football banter was starting to bore Chris. It was a dull sport played by morons.

– Look how straight these lines are, he said, moving things back to where they needed to be. The work of a master craftsman. George Osborne would be proud.

They both had a soft spot for Gorgeous George. Another fine journalist.

– There's nothing like some famous Robert Marsh hospitality, Chris continued. No expense is spared when the Marsh Man is on a roll.

Robert was pleased. He enjoyed entertaining and sharing the life he had created for himself here in Brussels. The city was his playground, and he liked to show it off. A hard-working, modest man, his socialising tended to take place in the trendier bars and restaurants, with the occasional soirée at his apartment, and while this was all very civilised things changed dramatically when his friend turned up. Robert enjoyed a cutting-edge, cosmopolitan culture that was frankly alien to his more lower-class mate, yet he had always felt relaxed in his company, and also a little special as he knew Chris admired his style. They balanced each other out. Yin met yang. The two chums worked hard and partied hard, and there was nothing wrong in that.

– You've got enough here for a week.

The coke was a risk given his work, but Robert was a free spirit and demanded the right to make his own decisions. He understood that the drug industry fuelled organised crime around the world, but its use here was private and victimless. His conscience was clear. Chris, while a firm believer in zero-tolerance policing – and especially where drugs were concerned – didn't give a fuck. He was quite capable of limiting his usage and was hardly responsible for the actions of the scum trafficking and consuming illegal substances. The usual rules did not apply.

– After you, Chris said magnanimously.

The right-winger stood aside and let the left-winger do the honours. Robert leaned forward and demolished a line with panache, stepped back and waited for his friend to follow his example. Rob had already dropped a blue bomber and was pleased that his hard-on was becoming harder. His cock was literally throbbing, and he wondered if this was partly due to the arousal he'd experienced sitting in the Charlemagne watching the Turks beat the shit out of that ginger-haired fascist earlier.

– That is good gear, he mused.

Robert watched Chris lay the open switchblade on the marble surface and take his turn, theatrically rubbing it into his gums for the mirror opposite. Rob noticed how happy they both looked, a pair of carefree Harry Potters setting off on a magical journey, which, in a way, was true. They were off on a cultural trip, a celebration of an unfairly maligned neo-liberal system that they were free to mould in whichever way they pleased.

– You're right, Chris confirmed. I can feel my heart banging.

Chris appreciated Rob's choice of venue as well as drugs. The bathroom alone was huge. These fuck hotels were used by sex-hungry EU workers for their flings and affairs, beyond the gaze of wives, husbands and partners, and this was clearly at the top end of the scale. A short walk from the European Parliament, discretion was guaranteed, although he felt Rob had taken things a little far by insisting they do the charlie in the khazi, but he was the boss on this one.

– Come on, let's get this show on the road, Chris urged after they'd done a couple more lines each, returning to the Vaz theme.

– After you, Boris, Robert replied, taking aim at the buffoon they both hated in the hope of ending the taunts.

It was time to rock n roll, and Robert unlocked the door and led the way into the bedroom where the boy sat waiting at the foot of the bed.

– We should have ordered another Pole, Chris said. Hitler coming in from the West, Stalin from the East – the red raw flesh of Poland in the middle, fucked by both sides. She loved it as well. Cunt, mouth, arse. Fucking loved it. Pure diesel.

Despite the crudity, Robert giggled, although there was no way Stalin could be compared to Hitler. Everyone knew that fascists were worse than communists. The Soviets may have killed more than the Nazis, but this had been done in the name of equality. Chris disagreed. Without the Nazis, the Soviets would have taken over the world, and Stalin had exterminated his own people over a far longer period than Hitler had killed Jews. Both agreed that totalitarianism was wrong.

– How about a Greek tart? Chris continued. Roasted by Germany and France and paying for the privilege.

Robert was more interested in the boy than the banter. The kid looked even younger than he had on his arrival, and for a moment he wavered, but Kraken had assured him that he was of legal age, eager and willing, albeit a little nervous as this was his first time. It had to be the drink and drugs clouding the issue. The boy was of North African extraction and didn't speak English, but he was in safe hands. Robert would look after him and make sure he came to no harm.

Chris was standing over the ice bucket and fondling a bottle of Moët Impérial Brut, easing the cork forward before giving it a nudge so it shot out and hit the ceiling with a bang, making the boy jump. Little champagne was lost as Chris moved fast, filling two flutes and handing one to Robert.

– Bottoms up, Chris said.

He turned towards the date.

– Bottoms up, Chelsea rent boy.

Robert ignored Chris's coarse humour, saw a young libertine from an ancient desert society, a free spirit who had escaped the conservatism of his culture – not that Rob was *criticising* that culture. He thought of the Beats and the romance of Tangier, the boundary-breaker Bill Burroughs hard at work, expressing himself in an orgy of hashish and young flesh. Rob felt as if he was part of a rebel set, living the tradition of Burroughs, Wilde, Polanski. Free-thinking intellectuals. Kindred spirits.

– Stronger together.

Chris, meanwhile, regarded the boy as a dirty little arse-bandit who deserved everything he was about to receive. These people would do anything for a few euros. The Arab who'd delivered him was a nasty bit of work, probably an older brother or cousin, part of an extended paedophile family. Fucking animals. He had no problem with gays, but had little interest in the lifestyle. His role in this evening's entertainment would be that of an observer. He was more interested in the power aspect than the sex. It was a chance to see his lefty pal Rob put the scum threatening Europe in its place without having a clue that this was what he was doing.

– Stronger together.

Merkel had been a decent enough leader, but overwhelmed by guilt for the Holocaust she had gone mad, ignoring the Fortress Europe model and inviting an army of jihadis into Germany and thereby Europe. The Muslims were a time bomb that would destroy the Continent with their allegiance to alien forces and a population that was increasing as that of the native Europeans fell. The EU had to be a lot stronger if it was to survive, and as Guy Verhofstadt rightly said, what it needed was more power, not less. This would happen. It was only a matter of time.

– Let's get those clothes off, Robert said, seeing as the boy was still dressed.

There was no reaction, and Rob realised he should be leading by example. He believed in showing solidarity at all times and started removing his clothes while Chris picked up the ice bucket and champagne and sat in the only chair in the room. He was feeling the effects as he rested in the director's chair and wondered if he should get his mobile out and film the action, at the same time wishing they had a girl in here instead, or maybe as well. They had fucked a lot of whores together over the years and he had no interest in queers. Rob had apparently become bi-curious, and while Chris doubted anyone could fake a sexual preference, there seemed to be no limits beyond which a trendy lefty would go to break down the walls of oppression.

– Come on, don't be shy, his friend said, standing naked now in front of the boy, an impressive erection a metre away from the youngster's face.

Rob was swaying and swinging his knob like it was made of rubber, and Chris was enjoying the show, this comical scene where his posh lefty mate was kidding himself that he wasn't taking advantage of poverty and doing the things he said he hated, and it was like an X-rated *Inbetweeners* remix, where a man was allowed to use the word 'cunt', with Rob as Will, or Rob had changed series and was Fleabag, although Chris would have fucked Fleabag no problem, but never his friend. They were more like brothers than mates. Rob was an idiot sometimes, yet still he loved him for his idealism, and especially the way in which he could justify anything if it suited his ends.

There were tears in the kid's eyes, but Rob didn't notice, looked like he was dancing on a stage with his face screwed tight and slurred words coming out of his mouth.

– I see Plastic Bertrand turned up, Chris said, pointing at the dildo Rob had brought along. I forgot the brothers were really triplets.

The two friends laughed, but the boy didn't even smile. He felt sick. Kidnapped by men who had offered him a car ride to his family's restaurant, they would kill him if he didn't do as he was told. The drugs he'd been given distorted this new world in which he found himself, and looking away from the naked monster in front of him he was drawn to the bright light in the bathroom.

– Chelsea rent boy, Chelsea rent boy, Chris softly chanted, and despite the homophobia Rob grinned as he massaged his cock and reached for the K-Y. He fucking hated Chelsea.

The boy ran into the bathroom and grabbed the open knife, held it towards the man who came after him ten seconds later, jolted as the blade buried itself in a plump belly. Chris Bradley rocked back and froze, saw himself in the mirror, blood spreading across his shirt. He sat down on the toilet seat and held his stomach. The boy stared at him for a few seconds before he ran back into the bedroom. Robert was sitting on the edge of the bed shaking as he tried to turn on his mobile phone, and the boy instinctively lunged at him, stabbing him in the neck, turned and walked to the furthest wall and leaned against it and slid to the floor, watching as Robert Marsh tried to stem the blood spurting from his throat, first with his hands and then with a sheet he wrapped around his neck and head, the sounds he made muffled as he fell back on the bed. He shook for a while and then he was still.

There was the sound of footsteps in the corridor outside the room, and the boy was terrified that his kidnappers had returned, but the footsteps passed the door and faded away. Maybe he had imagined them. He looked into the bathroom at the body sitting on the toilet, the eyes wide open and blank, and he stood up and went back in, took the wallet, phone and envelope. He had to leave this place quickly, while he had the chance, but the shock and the drugs in his system meant he was unsteady on his feet, and so he sat down in the chair, needed to rest for a few minutes until his head cleared and his strength returned, and then he would escape.

It was nearly three in the afternoon when a well-known England face, an old-firm Chelsea boy with a domestic and international reputation, walked into Zagaman. On the road since the night of the Germany game, Harris and the six men with him had booked into their accommodation and headed straight out to the bar. This was filling up with the English trooping in from nearby cafés, pizza and kebab takeaways, chip shops, waffle windows. Last night's hangovers were slowly fading, stomachs lined for the session to come. Harris shook hands with Jimmy Rowe, while Mark did the honours.

Tommy spotted Stan and Darren but couldn't see Matt, peeled away once he had a drink in his hand and was soon holding court – *Getting out of Berlin... seven sulkers... all about the style... no violence required...* Tommy Johnson shook his head and rolled his eyes and looked to the ceiling.

– What's going on? Harris asked Jimmy Rowe.

– Local Dibble attacked the bar we were in last night. Beat up a few people, arrested a lot of others. The Belgians had come looking for a fight, but it was over quickly, the riot police were waiting in the backstreets. The Irish landlord got us out the back. It's going to be busy today. So, you got here in the end?

The Cockneys had been meant to meet them at the station in Berlin, but hadn't shown up. Too fond of a bevvy, that was their problem. Jimmy had almost done the same, though, Norman the one who made sure they didn't miss their train. Norman with his granddad's watch on a chain. Jimmy saw Harris singing 'Any Old Iron' in Blackpool. Norman didn't mind. Harry Champion was fine in Blackpool.

– Pleasant journey?

Harris smiled, but because he was watching Norman hopping foot to foot. The man was Bez to Carter's Chas Smash. Happy Mondays meets Madness. Northern monkey and cock sparrow. The memory of Carter and Norman doing the Peter Crouch in Blackpool – robot dancing on a tiny stage as the pensioners looked on, an Alvin Stardust nut singing 'Jealous Mind' as he tapped out the tune on a rubbish synth – would stay with him forever. That and a Soul Suite night a few years later.

– You enjoyed Deutschland then, Dave?

Harris repeated Tommy's headshake and looked to the same heavens.

– We've slept in ditches, yomped halfway across Germany, met fräuleins with pigtails, travelled in haystacks, drunk and fought with dwarves, been bushwhacked by German ultras, met the cast of *A Clockwork Orange*, met up with a Blue Boy mate from Zagreb in Holland, dealt with some Serbs, been held to account by an Italian carpenter on a Lambretta.

– Dwarves? You mean like midgets?

– Small people.

– Inter City Hobbits?

– No, just dwarves. Germans.

– What happened?

– Don't ask, mate. Do not fucking ask. I can't believe we made it to Brussels.

– Come on, Norman said, closing in. Tell us the details.

Harris pointed towards Carter.

– Him over there... he borrows a van and takes us into the twilight zone.

Harris nodded at Harry.

– He's been carrying a rocket launcher across the Fatherland.

Mark brought a drink across to Harris, shook hands with Jimmy, who was fresh-shaved and well-rested and looking forward to doing the Belgians, not the sort who stood around listening to other people dragging out their stories. Norman had started pulling some strange faces, full of powder and the cheapest draught lager, his attention wandering. Mark shook his hand as well.

– Anderlecht are drinking near Midi, Jimmy said. Them and half of Belgium.

Harris perked up.

– We owe that lot.

– They're coming to De Brouckère at five. It's not far, on the main road.

– Do we fancy it?

Jimmy Rowe laughed. Was the Pope a Catholic? Did a bear shit in the woods? Was that soft shandy-drinker Carter going to empty his sac in Brussels? He thought back to one of the annual Blackpool piss-ups, how the sex machine had shagged this bird he'd taken a fancy to himself, a big old Yorkshire lass with a Leeds tattoo called Sandra. Carter had opened his mouth and given it some wide-boy chit-chat and next morning the lads were having a fry-up by the Winter Gardens and he pulls something out of his pocket and wipes ketchup off his chin with her G-string.

Even now the Sandra memory rankled, although Jimmy knew it shouldn't. He had known Dave for a long time. Carter was his mate and no harm had been intended. It wasn't a John Terry versus Wayne Bridge situation. Plus Norman had his moments. Like the time twenty of them met in Mabel's Tavern, near Euston. They'd been over to West Ham while Chelsea were on their way back from Birmingham, Norman so pissed he'd spilled a pint over Harris's brand-new mobile. The Chelsea loon had controlled himself, but by the colour of his face it was an effort. It worked both ways. Life was all about give and take.

– This Italian...

Something was bothering Harris.

– This Italian turns up in Holland. He's been following us from Berlin. We borrowed his van, you see, when we were stranded.

– Borrowed?

– We can't work out how he found us. He wouldn't say. He's working in Germany and knows the language, that's a help I suppose, but he tracked us like a hound. Turns up in the bar we're drinking in and wants to fight us all.

– What happened?

– He was going mental, could hardly get his words out he's so angry, and you can't blame him, because his tools were in the van, and it's his livelihood. A Lambretta is parked outside, we can see it gleaming under the streetlights. He doesn't care that he's on his own. I felt terrible. Guilty. It was nothing to us, but that van and his tools meant everything to him.

– What did you do?

– It's nice to be nice, Harris said, quoting a legendary White Hart doorman and Brian Connolly lookalike. What could we do? Mario was in the right and we were in the wrong. We calmed him down eventually. The drill was a present from his old man, so at least he got that back, and the insurance would pay for his van. We had a whip-round. A proper one. Serious euros.

– Could have just told him to fuck off, Norman remarked.

– No, we were in the wrong. He's a working man, trying to make a living. Once we got to know him I felt ashamed. We all did. It's funny, but times have changed. I used to hate the Eyeties. Really hated the cunts. Zola, Vialli, Roberto Di Matteo changed that. Mario's our mate now. Super Mario.

– Fucking dickheads, Norman said, placing his hands on the shoulders of Dave Harris and Jimmy Rowe. They're the Scousers of Europe.

Harris didn't want to get into an argument with Norman. They'd had a good drink with Mario, and Luka had let him sleep in the bar. He'd come for breakfast with them in the morning.

– I tell you what, we shouldn't be standing round here all day waiting for the Belgiques to come to us, Harris said as he scanned the pub.

There were men of his own age in here and plenty of youngsters, but a good core of thirty- and forty-year-olds who could have a fight. He knew most of the faces. A good range of English talent was present.

– We're off the streets in here, Jimmy said. They're at home. Mistakes have been made in the past, haven't they?

Harris reluctantly agreed, turned back to Norman. There had been a couple of times when he was on the verge of doing Norman, had really had to clench his fists in Mabel's Tavern, but he didn't mind him so much now, and time had passed. Norman used to be a lot more stroppy. They all had.

– There's been Turks picking on ones and twos, attacking shirts. There was a story going around that an English supporter was in intensive care. Then that he had died. Haven't heard anything more so it was probably just a rumour.

Matt came into Zagaman, Darren and Stan waving him over.

– Where have you been? Stan asked, annoyed but relieved.

Before he could answer, Darren was waving his phone in his face.

– Have a look at this. You're famous.

Matt's heart jumped as he focused on the image. There he was on the front page of the online edition of a British newspaper under the headline THE BEAST OF BRUSSELS – his right fist connecting with a shocked face. On one side of him was the back of Stan's head, on the other the blurred outline of Darren. The picture was all about Matt. He was the star. His features were clear as day, and it looked as if the man he was hitting was on his own, the Turkish mob behind him erased. There was no sign of Pat, no picture of him lying on the floor kicked unconscious. The strapline read *Scum Shames England*.

Matt wanted to say something, but didn't know what.

Darren was laughing.

– It's not funny, Stan said. He could end up inside.

Matt was trying to think straight. He couldn't believe it, even though every mobile had a camera and there were people who recorded everything that ever happened, a photo like that, splashed across the internet by a major newspaper – which meant it would be seen by millions of people – that was different. It would stay on the internet forever. There might be a printed version as well. He was fucked.

– At least it's an English paper, Stan said. Not many Belgians are going to read it.

– English Old Bill are here, don't you worry, Darren said. Collaborating with the Belgians. Then there's Immigration when he goes back. The whole world can see that picture. It doesn't matter about the words. It's the photo and the headline.

Matt stood very still, like one of the drinkers at the bar last night, listening to Stan and Darren as they discussed his prospects, but he couldn't hear the details of what they were saying, their voices blending into a drone, which merged with the noise filling the bar. Others had crowded around and were looking at the picture and then at Matt. He noticed Tommy Johnson.

– You know what you should do? Tommy said.

Matt shook his head.

– Get your face painted white, with a Cross of St George. Same as the doughnuts. You could keep the greasepaint on until you're back in England. Blend in with the shirts.

It wasn't a bad idea. Humiliating, true, and where did you go to get that sort of thing done, but they couldn't ID him if he was disguised as a clown. Did the fancy-dress mob bring their own make-up artists along? He didn't want to end up nicked, and definitely not here in Belgium.

– You'll have to be careful when you get home, Tommy continued. It's not like before. Your own government will deport you, no questions asked. Fucking European Arrest Warrant...

The distortion was growing louder. Stan tilted his head and Matt moved over. They drifted away from the others.

– Where have you been? Stan asked. First Pat, then you. He wasn't in his hotel this morning, I went round there early and tried to find him. He hasn't been seen. Something bad has happened. We should have taken him to the hospital. Made him see a doctor. What about you?

Matt didn't answer.

– Where did you go?

– I picked up a bag. I was told not to lose it, but I did. I got drunk and left it in a bar.

– Serious?

Matt nodded.

– I went back this morning and it was still there.

– What's in it?

– I don't know.

– You haven't looked?

Matt shook his head, knew more than ever that he had to keep his mouth shut. The terror he'd felt when he opened the zip and slipped his hand inside the bag returned. He had been sitting on a train to Centraal, the holdall on his lap, alone in a tin carriage, hungover from the drink and his earlier panic, thinking of Natasja, the night he'd spent with her and the life-size blue-suited air stewardess painted on the wall at the end of her bed. It had taken him a few seconds to know where he was when he woke up, but seeing her blonde hair on the pillow next to him had brought it all back. Life was sweet. And then he remembered Terry White's bag.

Natasja had helped him search the flat, but neither of them could remember bringing the holdall out of the bar, and he was suspicious again, despite himself. He was a mug, letting her get him drunk so he would forget the merchandise. Drugs, guns... it had been a narrow escape. But if the gear was still in the bar it would be handed to the police, and they would find him easy enough. There were plenty of witnesses, and CCTV, but worse than that, Terry White would kill him, so once Natasja was dressed and ready for work they went into the street and she told a taxi driver the name of the bar, and there he was, ten minutes later, tapping on the window, the holdall hanging on the same hook where he'd left it, handed to him by an old man who was mopping the floor.

Sitting on the train to Centraal he couldn't stand it any longer, opened the zip and found a layer of bubble-wrap, slipped his hand in and felt something soft, guessed it was powder, angry at himself for getting involved, but there were harder edges in there, and he traced his hand over small stick-like objects that moved, couldn't work it out, felt a longer block connected to something heavier, and so he pulled the bubble-wrap back and retched, pushed the bag away, was almost sick on the floor of the carriage.

– You look like you're going to puke, Stan said. We'll work something out. The police aren't going to spot you tonight.

Darren put his hand on Matt's back.

– Come on, we're going.

England were on the move. Harris and Jimmy Rowe were already outside, and everyone else was drinking up and following, the push of bodies meaning Matt was carried along with the flow, happy to lose himself in the crowd and forget about that train ride to Centraal, the way he had closed the zip again and cradled the bag on his lap, feeling as if he'd been stabbed in the chest, finally stashing it in the locker when he reached the station. Before he closed and locked the door he'd made himself face the horror, undid the bag once more and moved the bubble-wrap away, the cotton he'd felt covering a small head, the open eyes staring but seeing nothing.

– The metro's this way.

He thought of the painted face Tommy had suggested.

– The Belgians are going to get a surprise, Darren said.

The English moved through the streets, Harris and Jimmy Rowe at the front, Matt smelling chips and hungry, realising he hadn't eaten since the Tunis. Did he really need more trouble? He could duck out and order a cone, wait for the cook to fry his chips, add mayonnaise, but once he was done he would be on his own and easily spotted. It was better to stay with his mates.

They reached a main road and turned towards De Brouckère, majestic buildings rising six and seven storeys on either side of them, iron railings spilling from bulging balconies, heads and letters carved in stone. The road was long and straight, pruned trees lining the pavements, skeletons linked by knotted wire. People stood back and watched them pass, and they were straggling as they crossed over, weaving their way through buses and cars, the traffic at a standstill, modern shopfronts built into the ground floors of century-old buildings, a series of bright yellows and reds, signs for Hector and Neckermann, the crinkled face of a woman specked with powder on a bus stop, blowing at a handful of snow.

They had almost reached the metro as the first Belgians came off the escalator and into the street. This was their firm and they looked the part, had been thinking the same way as the English, just couldn't wait until five, the excitement too much as the child in all these men took over. The power of the two mobs cut through the sludge-like air. Matt forgot the holdall and its contents, the photo and the headline, Terry White and the police and Pat. The Belgians started fanning out as more and more of them came up from the station below, and the English closed in and the first punches were exchanged and the fighting began.

Pat stood at the bar nursing a Leffe. It was getting dark outside, and the lights were turning on, reflecting his brighter mood. He had woken up on the floor of his bathroom with the worst headache he'd ever had, an hour later dressed and flagging down a cab.

The hospital kept him in overnight, and he'd been give the all-clear late this morning, and while he should have been relieved he was struggling as he walked back to his hotel. Resting on a bench below the Palace of Justice, a domineering presence on the slope where Upper and Lower towns met, he saw how the clouds pressed down on the city and everything seemed hopeless. He was crushed. But the gloom passed as it always did, and after eating in the Tunis and finding tickets for the game he felt fantastic. This was what life was all about. His phone vibrated. It was Matt.

– Thank fuck. Are you okay?

– Couldn't be better.

– Where have you been? Stan thought you were dead.

– No, I'm still alive.

– Didn't you get the messages we left? You could have phoned.

He should have done, but he'd had other things on his mind.

– It wasn't charging up properly, he lied. Seems okay now.

A police van raced past the bar, tyres screeching when it reached the corner. Pat hoped it wasn't connected to the football, but knew it probably was. He told Matt about the tickets.

– How many have you got?

– Six... Four for me, you, Stan and Darren. Plus two spare. Face value as well.

– Fucking brilliant. Where are you?

Pat gave directions, finished his Leffe and ordered another. The bar was a backstreet local, empty apart from a handful of old-timers and the barman, and he went and sat at a table, placed his three postcards in a row. He put a lot of thought into these cards, both in terms of the pictures he bought and what he wrote. He couldn't help smiling. Maggie was getting the young ginger hero Tintin, pictured here with Snowy and Captain Haddock. Manneken Pis was for Larry, who liked a drink. Beautiful was getting the Atomium because it was such a beautiful building. He took out his pen and wrote his messages, would post the cards in the box at the end of this street when he left for the match.

His phone went again. It was Stan.

– We're where you said, but can't see the bar. What's it called?

Pat went and stood by the door, realised he had to go out into the street as the entrance was tucked back and there was no sign, saw Matt further up the road and waved, four figures coming out of the shadows and following him along the pavement. They started to jog and were soon ducking inside, twenty seconds later another police van speeding past, packed with robocops.

– It's gone mad out there. First the Belgians, then the Old Bill. There's police everywhere.

Pat waited for Matt, Stan, Darren, Dave Harris and another man he didn't know to catch their breath and order. Once they'd joined him and he had their attention he produced the tickets. These were taken and kissed and sniffed and tucked away, wallets opened and euros passed over. Matt was sure they'd all agree that Pat was a diamond, the Brentford Lampard, one of the very best. He could have sold the tickets on and made himself a nice profit, but he didn't think that way.

– Where did you get them? Matt eventually asked.

– Remember I told you about that restaurant?

– The Tunis, Stan said. We went in there. Great food.

Darren pulled a face and mumbled something they couldn't make out.

– I had a meal in there, Pat continued. Fantastic it was. Good price as well. Anyway, there was this boy sitting with an old man, playing around with a calculator, and they had these tickets and gave them to the waiter who brought them over and offered them to me. When I asked how much he wanted he pointed to the price on the tickets. Said he'd had some English in the day before and they'd helped him out with something.

Matt and Stan looked pleased.

– I ended up in here and let you know.

– Where have you been? Stan asked, after a pause. We were worried.

Pat was glad to be with friends. He was strong again. Invincible. His head was carved from the same stone they'd used to build the Palace of Justice. But the time was passing and they still had to get to the ground. The English would be targets. Even he knew that the European police took no prisoners. He didn't want to talk about the hospital but couldn't lie, was about to answer when the man he didn't know emptied his glass and spoke.

– Come on, it's my round. Let's have one for the road.

– Shouldn't we get going? Pat ventured.

– We've got ages yet. Plenty of time. There's still an hour and a half until the game starts. They'll probably shut the bars down near the ground. We'll have a quick drink and be there in time for kick-off.

The others agreed and so Pat relaxed. What was the point of being alive if you couldn't enjoy yourself? The bloke went to the bar. Pat glanced at the famous Dave Harris.

– Alright? Harris said, catching his eye.

For a split second Pat was concerned. He had heard stories about this man, but the feeling passed – you might be wary, but you haven't been scared of anyone since your sister died – Pat was a peaceful soul – you're not a violent man – nor was he a coward – you're not a coward – and what could be worse than what had happened to his family? Debbie, Mum, Dad... You never gave up – it was hard to keep going – you started at the bottom – he had worked his way up – you're grateful to Mr Blackshaw – Pat wanted to make a difference – you *do* make a difference – he'd only strayed once – KNOCK DOWN GINGER – you won't stray again – KNOCK DOWN GINGER'S SISTER – you can't forgive that – KNOCK DOWN GINGER'S SISTER WITH A BUS – he would never forget the words Mee had shouted in the street – about your mum as well as your sister – what sort of person behaved like that? – you remember the look on Mee's face – Pat and Glen, all grown up – you got a lift from Uncle Terry – Glen's Uncle Terry who waited in the car – you had to do it on your own – but Glen was there, the odds weren't fair – you know life isn't fair – he never raised a hand – you did it yourself – moral support – you wish life was fair – same as everyone – you're doing your best – rough justice – call it revenge – pure and simple – justice – revenge – no excuses – no regrets. Football saved your life. Pat was looking forward to the game. He couldn't wait.

– Thanks for sorting us out, Harris continued. I won't forget it. I owe you one.

Matt had his phone out and had messaged Natasja. He wasn't going home with the rest of the boys, not with his picture everywhere and THE BEAST OF BRUSSELS headline hanging over him. The Old Bill would nick him before he got out of St Pancras. He would leave it a few days, have a think what to do, plus it was an excuse to stay and try and see Natasja again. She said she wanted to, but maybe she was being polite. How could he know? And who'd have thought that of Terry White? Fuck. The marionette in the bag had a big wooden head and a body dressed in a black suit with a velvet collar, Dracula meets Ronnie Kray, and it even had black brogues on its feet. The face was that of a younger Terry White. Carved, chiselled, varnished features. It had freaked Matt out. The man was seriously mental. The puppet was tall and fucking creepy, especially the eyes, which seemed to have changed by the time he looked at it again inside the locker. He had calmed down now, but Matt was still on edge, although he had to admit it was better than carrying drugs or guns or explosives or diamonds or great works of art by Pablo Picasso or, worst of all, kiddie porn. Terry could never know he had peeked. Natasja texted back. He was on.

A tray of drinks arrived. With the beer flowing and money and tickets in their pockets, it didn't matter if you were a shirt or one of the chaps, if you had all the chat or mumbled into your lager, what the corporates did to steal your football from you, it was still the people's game. The man who had bought the drinks and delivered the tray, the one Matt called Tommy, toasted Pat, who looked embarrassed and turned red, but he drank with the rest of them and was the first to finish and put his empty glass down on the table.

LONDON BOOKS

FLYING THE FLAG FOR
FREE-THINKING LITERATURE

www.london-books.co.uk

PLEASE VISIT OUR WEBSITE FOR

- Current and forthcoming books
  - Author and title profiles
    - Events and news
  - Secure on-line bookshop
- An alternative view of London literature

London Classics

The Angel And The Cuckoo *Gerald Kersh*
Doctor Of The Lost *Simon Blumenfeld*
The Gilt Kid *James Curtis*
It Always Rains On Sunday *Arthur La Bern*
Jew Boy *Simon Blumenfeld*
May Day *John Sommerfield*
Night And The City *Gerald Kersh*
Phineas Kahn *Simon Blumenfeld*
Prelude To A Certain Midnight *Gerald Kersh*
A Start In Life *Alan Sillitoe*
There Ain't No Justice *James Curtis*
They Drive By Night *James Curtis*
Wide Boys Never Work *Robert Westerby*

NEW FICTION

SHE'S MY WITCH

STEWART HOME

Strange things happen on social media, such as the almost chance
encounter between a London born-and-bred fitness instructor and a
drug-fuelled Spanish witch. At first Maria Remedios and Martin
Cooper share their love for super-dumb, two-chord stomp in private
messages, but when they meet magic happens. Maria knows that she
and Martin have been lovers in past lives, and sets out to convince the
former skinhead that her occult beliefs are true.

The main narrative takes place in London between 2011 and 2014,
detailing riots, rock-and-roll excess, and the times of austerity leading
up to the Brexit vote in 2016. In online messages Martin and Maria
hark back to other eras – his immersion in London's 1970s punk
explosion and her tales of teenage drug-dealing and murder on
Spain's notorious Ruta Destroy party scene. As Martin gets ever
closer to Maria, she constantly surprises him by detailing different
aspects of her life – such as running a bar for a criminal motorcycle
gang in Valencia, her seven-year stint as a professional dominatrix,
and a decades-long struggle with heroin.

She's My Witch is a dark romance with an incendiary conclusion,
written to reflect today's social-media world and a
resurgent interest in the occult and kink.

London Books
£9.99 paperback
ISBN 978-0-9957217-4-6

NEW FICTION

SLAUGHTERHOUSE PRAYER

JOHN KING

When a boy realises the grown-ups are killing animals and that
he has been eating their bodies, he gives up meat. But should he
share the truth and break another child's heart? As a youth he
wants to believe in the ability of words and peaceful protest to
end the slaughter, while struggling to resist a desire for revenge.
Now a disillusioned man trying to rebuild his life, he must choose
one of two paths. Acceptance means security, but those meat-
industry adverts keep taunting him and some familiar insults
– *smelly pig, dirty cow, chick-chick-chicken* – fill his head.

Slaughterhouse Prayer deals in human invention and our treatment
of non-human animals, the manipulation of language and the
corruption of innocence. Society's pecking order is challenged as
the story moves to its margins and beyond. A book of dreams, where
visions are more real than reality and sentimentality is a strength, it
asks a series of questions. Can a person honestly kill without
emotion? Could a vegan soldier stay professional and humane?
And will we ever confront the terror that surrounds us?

London Books
£9.99 paperback
ISBN 978-0-9957217-2-2

New Fiction

DOCTOR ZIPP'S AMAZING OCTO-COM
AND OTHER LONDON STORIES

DAN CARRIER

The London Evening Press And Star is a local newspaper holding its own in a time of fast-moving, celebrity-obsessed, click-bait global news. And the unnamed narrator of this book is one of its reporters, an old-school journalist dedicated to his community and his craft. But with every news item there is a bigger, more complex tale, and drawing on his notebooks he reveals the stories behind the stories, and the journeys he has taken to discover their hearts.

Meet Eddie Roll, karaoke-barge proprietor, and find out how he keeps his business afloat on the city's canals. Hear how Batman and Robin leapt from the pages of a comic book to come to the rescue of someone in need. Discover what links Elvis Presley and meals on wheels, learn of Kermit The Hermit of Hampstead Heath, and spend time in the company of a generous Irishman from NW1. And read about the life and death of the enigmatic Doctor Zipp, a marine biologist and inter-species language expert who believed we could learn a lot from the octopus.

If a city is its people and their stories, then this is London at its warm-hearted, eccentric best.

London Books
£9.99 paperback
ISBN 978-0-9957217-0-8

New Fiction

BARRY DESMOND IS A WANKER

MARTIN KNIGHT

Barry Desmond is an only child. He's had a sheltered upbringing by ageing parents distrustful of the outside world. This leaves him ill-equipped to deal with the savagery of school, the trials of adolescence and the reality and politics of the workplace.

At school he is a figure of fun, excluded and picked on. At home he struggles with the eccentricities of his parents and is alarmed and confused as his hormones spring into life. He finds guilty pleasure in self-relief. Later, he follows his father into a career with the Empire Bank, a throwback organisation doomed to become extinct. In middle age, and following the death of his parents and redundancy, Barry ventures out into the wider world determined to live his life and strike up relationships. Unlike his parents Barry believes that people are fundamentally decent. Will he find the fulfilment and interaction he craves? Will society repay Barry's trust?

This novel from Martin Knight, author of *Battersea Girl* and *Common People*, explores and illuminates 21st-century suburban loneliness and the grim reality of having a face that doesn't fit. *Barry Desmond Is A Wanker* is a seductive and surprising book, laced with humour, shot through with poignancy and sensitivity.

London Books
£8.99 paperback
ISBN 978-0-9551851-9-9

NEW FICTION

MALAYAN SWING

PETE HAYNES

Aidan is different. He is small, awkward and often silent, an easy
man to ignore, mock or exploit, yet on the inside he is intelligent and
thoughtful. He speaks to the reader in a way he can't manage in
everyday life, reflecting on the world around him with great insight
and an almost childlike honesty. This is the internal life of an outsider.

We meet Aidan not long after he has moved into a room in a
shared flat, forced from the home in which he felt secure by a policy
labelled 'care in the community'. But the community is dismissive
and threatening. He becomes lonely and scared, his best friend
the radio he carries everywhere. An old shed offers a hideaway
during the day, while his evenings are often spent in the local pubs.

Aidan's physical and mental state starts to deteriorate, and when
he bumps into Joey from the home he comes to the notice of some
bad people. He wanders the streets and is attacked, his life quickly
spiralling out of control. The story ends in dramatic fashion, but it is
Aidan's decency and a sense of escape that remain with the reader.
Malayan Swing is a moving novel, a testament to those living on the
margins of society, and as such is a brave and important work.

London Books
£8.99 paperback
ISBN 978-0-9551851-6-8

London Classics

IT ALWAYS RAINS ON SUNDAY

ARTHUR LA BERN

Set over a single day in 1939, *It Always Rains On Sunday*
captures the East End of London shortly before the start of
the Second World War. The book is centred around the residents of
Coronet Grove, its focus the Sandigate family. People go about their
lives, heading to the local church and pub, while those looking for
excitement are drawn to the bright lights of Whitechapel. Rose
– a former barmaid in The Two Compasses – is married to George
Sandigate, twenty years her senior, the thrill of her time with villain
Tommy Swann firmly in the past. Church bells ring as small-time
crooks plot in the pub, a newspaper headline telling Rose that
Swann has escaped from Dartmoor.

It Always Rains On Sunday is the atmospheric debut novel of Arthur
La Bern and features a large, colourful cast of characters. Dreams
and reality clash as arguments rage, gangsters lurk, madness
simmers, violence is threatened. Sex and death hang heavy in the
air. Described as a predecessor to Alan Sillitoe's *Saturday Night And
Sunday Morning*, the film adaptation was a great success and *It
Always Rains On Sunday* remains a classic of British cinema. The
book and its author were likewise lauded, and La Bern would go on
to write a series of largely London-based, working-class gems.

London Books
£11.99
ISBN 978-0-9568155-5-2

London Classics

DOCTOR OF THE LOST

SIMON BLUMENFELD

When young Thomas Barnardo arrived in London in 1866, he planned to study at the London Hospital before venturing abroad to work as a missionary. The conditions he found in the East End stopped him in his tracks. Unemployment, poverty, overcrowding, alcoholism and deathly diseases were bad enough, but seeing thousands of half-starved children living on the streets broke his heart. Inside a year Dr Barnardo had opened the ragged-school Hope Place and by 1870 the first of his eponymous homes was in operation. His work continues to this day. *Doctor Of The Lost* is the fictionalised story of Tom Barnardo's early years in East London.

Author Simon Blumenfeld grew up in the same streets, his cult 1935 novel *Jew Boy* capturing the magic of the Jewish East End of the 1930s, and *Doctor Of The Lost* (1938) recreates the area in Dr Barnardo's day. Drawing on a friendship with his widow, Blumenfeld brings Barnardo vividly to life, showing the struggles he faced and the battles won. *Doctor Of The Lost* is set in a London of rampant industrialisation, when the few became rich at the expense of the many, and yet this was also a period of charity and good works, when idealists such as Thomas Barnardo were prepared to stand tall and fight back.

London Books
£11.99 hardback
ISBN 978-0-9568155-2-1

LONDON CLASSICS

PRELUDE TO A CERTAIN MIDNIGHT

GERALD KERSH

A sex killer haunts the afternoon fog of 1930s London. He is on the prowl, looking for a schoolgirl. This monster, in turn, is being hunted. Detective Inspector 'Dick' Turpin understands the psychology of his prey, but is more adept at finding habitual criminals than sex murderers. So it is up to formidable do-gooder Miss Asta Thundersley to poke her nose into the investigation. She is a habitué of the Bar Bacchus and believes one of the regulars is the killer, invites them all to a party and laces each one with alcohol to loosen their tongues.

Could the murderer be Amy Dory, a masochistic beauty whose eyes have become like 'a couple of cockroaches desperately swimming in two saucers of boiled rhubarb?' Is it Mr Pink, a demented theologian who translates the Bible into modern tough-guy slang? Is it Tom Beano, a freethinker, who once tried to overthrow the Salvation Army? Or is it one of the dozens of others who fill the Bar Bacchus?

Gerald Kersh places his story in bohemian London, peoples it with artists and criminals and dresses it in the mystery genre, but his real concern is to find the hungry beast that lurks within every person. First published in 1947, in the aftermath of the Second World War, the author is driven by his fury at the atrocities committed by Nazi Germany, reflected here in the rape and murder of a child as the conflict looms. *Prelude To A Certain Midnight* is classic Kersh, full of outrage and cutting satire, but with enough punch to leave you with a bloodied mouth.

London Books
£11.99 hardback
ISBN 978-0-9568155-4-5